Born
For
This

ALSO BY CAITLIN DEVLIN

The Real Deal

Born For This

CAITLIN DEVLIN

LAKE UNION

PUBLISHING

Text copyright © 2025 by Caitlin Devlin
All rights reserved.

Published by Lake Union Publishing, Seattle

www.apub.com

Amazon, the Amazon logo, and Lake Union Publishing are trademarks of Amazon.com, Inc., or its affiliates.

ISBN-13: 9781662522925
eISBN: 9781662518256

Cover design by The Brewster Project
Cover images: © Oleg Zaicev / plainpicture; © PremChokli / Shutterstock

Printed in the United States of America

For Paul

Prologue

RACHAEL

When people ask what I have learnt from this experience, I say, 'Probably not a lot.'

They say, 'Really? You don't think you're more guarded now? You don't think you're more careful?'

I have been more careful and more guarded since I was eighteen years old. It never did me much good. We aren't designed to be like that, as human beings. We can maintain it ninety-five per cent of the time, but that fraction, that five per cent, will always be our undoing. Every now and then, we will bare our souls. We will be vulnerable, because it feels good to be vulnerable. We will talk, because it is nice to be listened to. Every time we do this, we will think the person we are talking to is someone that we can entirely trust, and that they will entirely understand us. Many times, we will be wrong.

But we never think like this. We think the words we say will be taken in the spirit that they are meant. We don't imagine that they will be turned against us, because if that's how we were supposed to think, we would never share anything with anyone at all. And all the talk show hosts would starve.

The talk show host that I say this to thinks that this is very funny.

'So, you think that you might end up trusting the wrong people again in the future?' he asks.

'Oh,' I say, 'definitely. I think that's inevitable.'

Unnaturally, he turns towards the camera. 'Don't go anywhere, because after the break we'll hear more from Rachael Carmichael.'

The camera swings away. The host gives me a smile. He's in a jumper and jeans – he just had a baby with his wife and he looks like a dad, sitting there, friendly and non-threatening. He's been doing this a long time now. Still not as long as me. To me, he is fresh-faced and green. I smile back, indulgently.

'What do you like to do in breaks?' I ask him.

'Oh,' he says, in a cheerful New York accent, 'I usually let the audience ask some questions. Only if you're comfortable, of course. None of it will air.'

I'm comfortable. He lets me choose the audience member to call on. It's a woman who looks slightly like my mother did thirty years ago, only rounder and with more kindness in her face. She stands up, trembling a little. Even after all this time, it's still strange to me that people tremble when they get to ask me a question.

'Are you angry?' she asks.

It's a great question. I tell her as much. She beams. 'Yes,' I say, 'a little. No one likes to feel that they've been manipulated.' I shrug. 'But I can't be too cross, can I? The whole thing has very much brought me back into the public eye.'

'Oh, you never left,' says the host, to be polite.

'But,' asks the woman, before the producer manages to take the mic away from her, 'do you feel as if you were used?'

'Yes,' I say. I don't elaborate.

She's confused by my one-word answer. She nods – she can't argue – but she's frowning as she takes her seat again. The host looks a little perplexed too. A producer starts to count us down. We ready ourselves.

'So, Rachael,' says the host. 'Rumour is that you have something very interesting in the works.'

I smile. I feel the room lean closer. How wonderful, to have everyone lean forward to listen before you've even said a word. It's a feeling I'd almost forgotten. 'Yes,' I say. 'I do.'

In the car, on the way back to Kent, I wonder if I should call her.

Chapter One

HARLEY

One of life's greatest tragedies is that many people never get a chance to do what they were born to do. Take Africa, for example. All the orphans? Or not even orphans, but they're poor and their schools aren't good, right? And so maybe one of them has the cure for cancer, just like, in his brain. Or hers. Or they have, like, this incredible voice, but they can't go out and sing around the world because they don't have any money and maybe, like, their parents are sick. And what about all the people who die? There are so many people who just *die*. You know?

'You know?' repeated Carlton, sprawled on a beanbag in his dad's game room with a joint in one hand and his dad's Grammy in the other. He passed the joint to Julia, who was giggling. 'So, I just think we're doing those people a disservice if we don't *jump* on opportunities.' He made a small movement in his beanbag like he was going to jump on Julia as he said this, prompting a squeal. 'Harley, what are you doing?'

I had pulled off one of my socks and was fixing it over the smoke detector, standing on the table to do so.

'My dad's going to kill you,' said Carlton, throwing the Grammy from hand to hand. Julia's wide eyes followed it.

'I'll take it off before we leave, obviously.'

'No, for standing on his table. It's, like, a million years old or something.'

'Pretty solid for it.'

'Owned by some prime minister or other, I think.'

'They didn't have prime ministers a million years ago.'

'Get down,' he ordered. 'And I repeat, what are you doing?'

I climbed down to admire my handiwork. 'Self-explanatory, no?'

'For the smoke?'

I nodded.

'Harl-*ey*,' he said with a languid smile. 'I turned it off, obviously. No need to make it look like a crack house in here.'

'Spoken like someone with no frame of reference for a crack house,' said Julia, smoking.

'And you do?'

'Wayne took me to one once.' Her dealer ex.

Carlton squinted at her. 'I'm pretty sure that was just a student hall.'

Julia and Wayne. Talk about life's great tragedies. She loved the *Romeo & Juliet* of it all, them versus their families (Julia is a Cagnoni, as in the film studio, and Wayne's family are communists). He loved that her heart was generous and her pockets were deep. Metaphorically. Julia doesn't wear anything with pockets.

'What was I saying? Just, there's nothing wrong with taking every opportunity.' Carlton pointed the Grammy at me. 'The way I see it, you owe it to those less fortunate. If everyone worried about everything being entirely fair, then literally nobody would take any job ever and the world would go to shit.'

'I don't think the stakes are that high here,' said Julia.

He rolled his eyes. 'You guys know what I'm trying to say. Stop being so woke – it's not a competition. And if it was then I would obviously win – hello? I was literally at Pride yesterday. Where were both of you?' Then his face softened, and he reached over to pat my leg. He knew where I was.

It's a strange thing, being aware of how different you are from everyone else. It's mostly nice, but you have to remember to acknowledge it loudly, all the time, in a way that doesn't seem like you're bragging. At film school, surrounded by every postcode from East London to the back of Bumfuck Forest of Nowhere, I was constantly conscious of it. If I mentioned that my mum had once been in a book club with Emma Thompson or that my dad had hired a jet to take us all to Athens that summer, I had to follow up with: 'I'm aware of how insane that is!' And a little self-deprecating laugh.

Your family owns their own plane?

No! We just hired it. Another laugh. *I know that isn't normal either!* Another.

But the thing is, when it's what you know, it is normal. So all the caveats and the jokes and the little laughs feel like pretending, and midway through the term you realise that, because of them, no one has much idea what you're actually like. Which, yeah, poor me, I know. (I'm doing it again.)

We'll pause here, because you already hate me. Or you don't hate me exactly, but you're going, *God, she's awful, isn't she?* and kicking your feet in delight under your duvet. Right? I suppose I'll spend my life trying to convince you otherwise. Everything I say will always ring a little dissonant. I'll never be quite self-aware or self-deprecating or self-sacrificing enough. But if I insert little laughs in-between every sentence of this account then you'll hate that too, and, really, I'm not trying to change your mind. I just want the truth out there.

This is where it starts. Me, Julia and Carlton, in Carlton's parents' game room, getting high. All of us twenty-five now, Julia having had her birthday last week. The joint and the beanbags and the crisps all over the floor are part of a routine we have. It isn't a happy one.

'Ah, well,' Carlton told me. 'Fifth time's the charm?'

I put my head in my hands and groaned.

Julia wriggled in her beanbag and lay across me, her head in my lap. Blonde hair fell over my jeans. She blew smoke in my face as I looked down at her. I flicked her in the temple and she yelped, dropping the joint just shy of my foot.

'Bitch,' she said, as Carlton screeched something about the rug and dove for it. 'I liked this one, Harley. I think it's kinda sad.'

'Oh, thanks.'

'Really sad. You looked great in that uniform.'

'And it was *funny*,' said Carlton. 'That's what I don't get. They all want good comedy and then when they get it, they get rid of it.'

He handed me the joint. I took it and inhaled deeply, staring up at the ceiling.

Four failed pilots.

They'd trotted out one after the other over the last three years in a merry little sequence. First, there was the drama about hookers on Hollywood Boulevard, sort of a gritty take on *Pretty Woman*. I could feel the pilot was mediocre as we were shooting it and my mum didn't love the idea of me playing a prostitute so, fine, whatever, it didn't go anywhere. But then the hospital drama. That one really hurt. God, I *loved* playing a nurse. I got to descend on the suffering like a guardian angel, so authoritative and needed. I was genuinely heartbroken when the show didn't get picked up for a full season, so out came the beanbags and the weed in Carlton's dad's game room, until I was stoned enough to think maybe I actually just wanted to try nursing. The next day, I read one course curriculum online and came to my senses.

Then Cassandra. The Lover, I called her. A young woman in her early twenties, completely head over heels for this guy who barely looked her way. I *lived* that, in film school, with Hugh. I held Cassandra entirely in my soul. Being her was challenging and familiar all at once. We shot the pilot in three achingly glorious – if damp – days in the Edinburgh spring. I chased the ghost of Cassandra down snaking alleyways and over unpredictable cobblestones and emerged, gasping and half-dreaming, into rolling parks and bright, clear coldness. Time passed differently. When I watched it, I loved it. I knew it was good. When it wasn't picked up, I cried for a month. I couldn't believe I would never get to play her again. I saw her everywhere. The Hooker and the Nurse haunted me too, in different ways, but the Lover was different. I would keep thinking I saw her in crowds, only to realise with a jolt that no version of Cassandra existed without my face.

I stopped acting for a year after that. It hurt too much. The next spring, my agent called.

'I know you've needed some time off,' he said, 'but this one's too good not to try for, Harley.'

He sent me the script. It was a dark, campy boarding school murder mystery, sardonic in tone but with moments of real heart. I pored over it. By the time I went in to read, I'd had to print a new copy – the first was covered in notes and annotations, and lines that I'd circled over and over.

It was a fight for the role. It came down to me and two other girls, and I knew that Warren, my agent, had to convince them to put me in that final three. I could feel that they were lukewarm on me when I walked in the room. When I was done reading, though, they asked me who I thought the murderer was.

'Jasmine,' I said. The character I was reading for. She was a quippy, back-talking, sulky teenager, not at all what I'd been, but very enjoyable to play.

'How do you know?'

'I don't. But I hope it's her.'

'Why?'

'Because then she won't get killed off until the end.'

A roar of laughter. I knew I had them. And I knew that this was going to be the one. Up until yesterday, when Warren called to give me a gentle, 'I'm afraid I have bad news,' and I spent the rest of the afternoon lying in the bath until my fingers and toes wrinkled.

Every project feels different when you're shooting it. But then you look back, and they all start to blur, and you think, *What on earth did I have to be so excited about?*

'Oh, Harley,' said Julia, looking up at me from my lap as my lip wobbled. 'It's okay. It takes some people years, you know.'

'It's *been* years.'

'I know. But you've just got to keep working at it.'

'It's alright for you. Cagnoni's a family business.' She didn't argue. 'And Carlton doesn't have any ambitions.'

'Hey,' said Carlton.

'Sorry, what was it you said you wanted to be?'

'A stay-at-home son,' said Carlton. 'Give me back my weed.'

'It's done, babe. Go get another one.'

Carlton trotted off to his stash in the kitchen and Julia reached up to take my face in her hands. She kissed me on both cheeks and then on the nose, and then tapped all three spots with her finger for good measure. 'Stop being sad,' she said.

'Alright then.' She was staring very hard at my face. 'What is it?'

'You've got freckles. I didn't know you had freckles.' Her hand swatted at her own nose. 'Do *I?*'

10

'A few.'

She clutched her nose and let out a peal of laughter.

'Julia's baked,' I said. Carlton stood in the doorway, two more joints between the fingers of one hand and his phone in the other. He shrugged, tossing me a lighter. 'So, you think I should do it.'

'What?'

'Dad's film. All your talk about opportunities.'

'Oh, yes. Yes!' He sat down across from me, re-energised. 'Why wouldn't you? It's work.'

'You know what people will say.'

'Fuck people.'

'No, Carlton, not fuck people. People decide whether I get to stick around.'

'They'll say, "Ew, Jeremiah Roth cast his daughter in a film, how gross is this industry?" And then they'll say, "Wow, where did Harley Roth come from? She's *great* in that film." People are fickle. Why are you looking at me like that?'

'I wish I lived in your world.'

'Everyone does.'

I lit the joint.

'There must be something else,' said Carlton. 'There's no way your inbox is empty.'

'*Strictly Come Dancing*?'

'Oh, do *Strictly*!' sighed Julia.

'Rather not. Can't dance.'

'But you'd look hot in the costumes.'

'Got an offer for a Netflix dating show,' I said. 'Or maybe it was Roku.'

Carlton raised an eyebrow. 'Bit of a difference between those two.'

'Hardly, these days. Anyway, the gimmick was weird. They wanted us to do this whole *Bridgerton*-style set-up and wear

11

Regency dress. Ostensibly as some kind of social experiment, but I reckon it was just because they already had the sets.'

'Tacky,' said Carlton.

'That sounds *fun*,' said Julia, at the same time.

'Also Ahn called, last week. Talking about something.' I inhaled. 'But that wasn't a role, I don't think, just a favour she wants me to do for her.'

'Who's Ahn?'

'That girl from her film class,' said Julia, from my lap. 'You know. She came to that party in Shoreditch – Tim's brother's. With the huge nose.'

'She has a huge nose?'

'Tim's brother has a huge nose. And a flat, in Shoreditch, where we met Ahn.'

'You're not making any sense,' said Carlton. 'Harley, who's Ahn?'

'Some awful girl.'

'Ah, much clearer.'

'You know, the screenwriter I took some classes with. She did that Janis Joplin biopic.'

He spread his arms. 'Well, that's something. Isn't it?'

'Not really,' I said. 'She didn't want me. She wanted Rachael.'

And they went quiet, and they waited, wide-eyed, for me to carry on. Just like people always did when I talked about Rachael.

Ahn Lu was not the kind of girl who asked for favours. At film school, she and I had been natural enemies from the off – me, the trust-fund baby entering the family business, and her, the second-generation immigrant living in a flat share who bought her trainers at Primark. Once we'd established that she hated me, my family and everything I represented, we actually got along together quite well. She was a screenwriter now – she'd just done a Janis Joplin film that had gone down pretty nicely and I'd heard her name a

12

couple of times at Julia's family parties, which was usually a pretty decent barometer of success. I was happy for her. People like Ahn need wins like that. Unfortunately for people like Ahn, they also need people like me.

'Hi, Harley!' Faux warmth in her voice. 'How are you? It's been forever.'

I was in my living room in Notting Hill, sat with my feet up on the coffee table. *Real Housewives* was on. I knew one of the housewives – I'd been in a tennis club with her daughter when I was about twelve. Nice girl, pretty nonplussed about the divorce and happy that her dad had won custody. Her mum had turned up at one of the fundraisers, fresh off the plane from Bel Air with two bottles of Moët & Chandon and a signed Sofia Kenin racquet for the charity raffle. She'd been a lot quieter than she was now on *Real Housewives.* She'd had her boobs redone since then as well.

I paused *Real Housewives* and put my bagel down on the coffee table, plateless. It left a smear of cream cheese on the wood and I wiped it with a cushion cover. Carlton calls me a beautiful slob, but there really isn't any point paying a cleaner three times a week if there isn't anything for her to clean. I like my lifestyle to make financial sense.

'I'm good,' I said.

'What are you up to these days? I heard you shot *Final Form.* Lots of buzz around that, wasn't there?'

'Quite a bit.' There still had been, a week ago. I was still feeling like hot shit. I should have known as soon as I saw her name come up on my screen. Ahn always seemed to materialise in moments of deepest misfortune. Tim's brother's Shoreditch flat party had been one such moment. I'd been outrageously sick at that party, seeing Hugh walk in with some Slovakian model. I emerged from the bathroom, sweaty and close to tears with my hair stuck to my forehead and bumped straight into Ahn and her slicked-back bun.

'Amazing,' she said, and then she paused. 'So, listen. I was wondering if you could help me out.'

'What's up?' I wondered who she would want. *Is there any chance I could get your dad's email address? Is there any way you could send me your mum's number? I know you're friends with Sidonius Cagnoni's granddaughter, and I thought I'd ask if you could please, possibly—*

But Ahn went for the big one.

'Could you put me in contact with your aunt?' she asked.

This obviously wasn't the first time someone had asked me something like this about Rachael. At film school, I'd hardly been able to take a step without tripping over a freeloader. *Do you think your aunt would want to talk about this film? Do you think she'd want to read my screenplay? Do you think she'd want to be interviewed for my Twentieth-Century Horror class?* One particularly earnest writer had asked, in total sincerity, if Rachael would want to collaborate with her on her film about age-gap relationships. The easy answer, of course, was, *No, I don't think she'd want anything less.* The honest one was this: *I don't know what Rachael would want.*

The truth was that in my twenty-five years of life, I had never been in the same room as Rachael Carmichael. She didn't even hold me as a baby. She didn't come to my christening, or my first Christmas, or any of my birthday parties. As far as my mum was concerned, it was like she didn't have a sister at all.

'But that was her choice,' Mum told me, when I was about eleven and first started to ask questions. 'She doesn't want anything to do with us.'

'Why not?' I asked her.

'Oh,' she said, 'she's always been like that. She's a deeply jealous person.'

'Right. Like Rachael Carmichael has much reason to be jealous of us.'

'She's alone,' said Mum. 'And unloved, and friendless, and childless. All things that I'm not. I think I remind her too much of the life she might have had.'

If that was true, we were reflections of each other, Rachael and me. I represented some alternate past, and she was a premonition, a promise of what my future could be, if only I kept trying.

I asked Mum this same question many times over the years. The answers were always in the same vein. Rachael resented her because she wanted what Mum had; she was jealous of our nuclear family; she hated having no family to go home to and hated even more that her little sister did.

'But *why?*' I would ask. 'Why would she hate you for that?'

'It's just what she's like,' Mum would say. 'It's just who she is.'

I never quite accepted that. I bought DVDs of all Rachael's films when I was young, and watched them in secret in my room after my parents had gone to bed. *East of Eden* was her big awards winner, and *Women Who Laugh at God* is the one that will immortalise her, but I'd always liked *Here's Hoping.* She was so young in that, and so full of anger, this hockey-stick-wielding college girl just bursting at the seams with rage and disappointment, and yet she managed to be so funny with it as well. I loved how much she confused people, in that film, how she made them feel like they didn't really know who she was at all. But I felt as if I knew her. The screen shimmered away, and that was the closest we came to being in a room together. Nose to nose. Two young women just looking at each other.

'I'm sorry to ask,' said Ahn, when I made no immediate response. 'It's just – well, I don't know if you've seen the news today?'

'Not yet.'

'Right,' she said. 'Well, have a look. It's on BBC.'

'I don't think Rachael will want to be in a war film.'

'I'm not talking about any war, Harley. Just look, will you?'

I put her on speaker and went to my news app. And there it was.

Greg Foster said to be writing 'tell-all' memoir about classic thriller.

Women Who Laugh at God director Greg Foster is ready to reveal all about off-screen romance with Rachael Carmichael, claims source.

'I've done some digging,' said Ahn, as I scrolled through the article, 'and it's true.'

'Greg's writing an autobiography?'

'A memoir.'

'Right.' Same thing. Same Ahn. 'So, what, you want a quote from Rachael?'

'I'm not a journalist, Harley,' she said sharply, as if screenwriting was a far higher calling, a contribution to the arts that those vampires in journalism could never understand. 'I want to write a film,' she said.

'Okay.'

'About Rachael. And Greg. And all of the stuff that went on. All the things we don't know about yet. There's insinuations that this book is going to make waves.'

'So, you're going to option Greg's book?' *Get to the damn point, Ahn.* One of the housewives was still frozen on my TV screen, mouth open in impatient indignation.

'I take issue with this story being told by Greg Foster,' said Ahn. 'The power issues at play in their relationship were disturbing to say the least. The way in which he talked about her afterwards was, to me, abhorrent.' I love the way people like Ahn use the words 'to me'. Like it's their opinion and not one they've lifted from someone else's Instagram story. 'If people are going to be talking about this,' said Ahn, 'then I want them to be talking about Rachael's story, not Greg's. I think we owe her that.'

'We you and me?'

'We society.'

'Okay.' I still wasn't really sure what she was on about. I wanted the rest of my bagel. 'What are you after, then? Her number?'

'Could you pass on a message from me?' asked Ahn. 'Could you say that I'm very interested in telling her story the right way, before Greg gets a chance to, and if that sounds good to her then we should jump on a call.'

'That's a pretty vague message.'

'I'll put it in an email,' said Ahn tersely. 'Flesh out some details. But pass it on if you could, Harley? I think this could be really special.'

I think this could be really special is what people like Ahn say because they're too classy to say *I think this could make me a lot of money.*

She did send me an email. I still hadn't replied to it. Carlton took my phone and read it aloud.

From: ahnlu@ahnluwriter.com
To: harley.r0th@outlook.com

Hi Harley,

Good to chat earlier. Just wanted to clarify some points in writing. Would be great if you could pass the below on to Rachael and give her my contact info in case she's interested in following up.

We're coming up on thirty years since *Women Who Laugh at God* and the film remains one of the classics of its genre – and genre-defining in its own right, intersecting horror, psych-thriller, dark romance and dark comedy in a way that challenges and delights audiences. Greg Foster has certainly reaped the rewards, and his rumoured practices on set, his inappropriate relationships with his employees and his conduct in the years following have been swept under the rug – because genius outweighs all.

I am of the opinion that genius excuses nothing. I believe that this is Rachael's story to tell.

We know some of the events surrounding *Women Who Laugh at God*. We know that it was the catalyst for an offscreen romance between Greg Foster and Rachael. We know that Foster's wife Anna Bianca claimed the affair was a 'public humiliation', and that these two women split popular opinion down the middle. We know that the relationship soured after only a couple of years. But there's a lot that we don't know. A particularly pernicious rumour about a secret pregnancy has followed Rachael for years and spawned several conspiracy theories. True or (most likely) not, the rumour has served to keep public interest in the relationship fresh over the years since, as it bounces between social media platforms and captures the next generation of internet users.

Rachael gave an interview, a few months after the end of her marriage, in which she said she had suffered 'a harm that can never be undone'. With Foster set to write and shop around a memoir about his relationship with Rachael (because I highly doubt the story he really wants to tell is one about film-making) that harm looks set to be repeated.

What if we could pre-empt this attack? What if we could take the public behind the scenes of *Women Who Laugh* and show them the truth?

God Laughs would see us approach *Women Who Laugh* from a new angle, recreating some of the film's most famous moments, whilst also exploring what happened on set and behind closed doors. If Rachael were willing to attach herself to this project and co-operate with writers and producers, we would have on our hands a goliath, something never been done before. *Women Who Laugh at God* represents the intersection of art and pop culture, a *Silence of the Lambs*-level classic with a Brad-Jen-Ang circus surrounding it. *God Laughs* would marry those two worlds – and prove a victory for any woman whose voice has been silenced by an older man.

Please do convey this to Rachael and let me know her thoughts. I'm very keen to work collaboratively with her on this and make it something surprising. Please also let her know that I have pitched this idea to a few studios already, and her involvement would make this a priority for several of them.

Thanks, and take care,
Ahn
Ahn Lu
Screenwriter and freelance journalist

*One day I will find the right words, and they will
be simple – Jack Kerouac.*

'She can definitely write,' said Carlton.

We waited for Julia, who has always been a slow reader. Her eyes travelled down the screen, widening, and she looked up at me in triumph, like all my problems were over.

'*Harley*,' she said. 'You should do it.'

I met Carlton and Julia when we were all eleven. Julia had been the popular girl at her primary school – she'd swanned in, BlackBerry in hand, buoyant on a veritable cloud of good opinion. I recognised who she was immediately. I don't mean in the 'Oh shit, she's a Cagnoni' sense. I'm not sure I really had much of an idea of what that meant at eleven, despite the fact that film-making is my family industry. I mean in the sense that we were the same, her and I, that we had lived almost the same life up until that point. In our elite, six-figure-tuition private primary schools, we'd been the super-elite. The ones whose sleepovers everyone wanted to be invited to, whose playdates were handed out with all the ceremony of seats at Paris Fashion Week. Any kid who had a swimming pool in their basement in London of all places got to set the barometer of cool.

I can see you ready to interject. Again, let me save you a job. I know that primary school popularity is an illusion. I'm very aware that I wouldn't have been anywhere near as much of a hit if my father hadn't been renting limos for my birthday parties and reruns of my mother's show hadn't been playing after school almost every day. I knew it back then as well. And so when Julia swanned in with her mother's stolen Michael Kors over her arm as a schoolbag (a ridiculous look on an eleven-year-old in hindsight, but we all lapped it up), I looked at her, and she looked at me, and something clicked.

We adopted Carlton in our second term of year seven. His mother met mine at a party and said, 'Harley couldn't *possibly* look up Carlton sometime, could she? He's just having a *rotten* time.'

Carlton was at the companion boys' school to ours, about ten minutes down the road. It was a rugby school, which meant that rugby defined the social hierarchy, which meant that Carlton, who held aspirations of stay-at-home-sonhood even then, was very much on the outs. He found his feet eventually, but not before Julia and I rocked up to meet him outside the school gates one afternoon with a tray of Starbucks, a sigh and a 'Our mums say we have to be friends.'

Other friends come and go, for all of us. But Carlton, Julia and I are all the same, and through the years we found ourselves pulling tightly together. It's nice to find people you can drop the act around. Being self-aware is exhausting.

'I wish I just wanted to be a doctor,' I said, as I followed the two of them through to the kitchen. It's not Carlton's dad's actual kitchen, just the little one attached to the game room. His dad calls it Carlton's 'mess room', which is an accurate description of what it looks like when Carlton tries to cook. Julia had already dug a packet of Yorkshire puddings out of the freezer and was ripping into the packaging, dumping them on a baking tray.

'Just,' said Carlton.

'You know what I mean. Something where you follow the steps, however hard they are, and at the end you're guaranteed to end up somewhere.'

'I don't think you should let any doctors hear you say that. Julia, what are you doing?' She'd ripped into a packet of hash browns with similar force. 'You know those will cook at different speeds.'

'They'll be fine.'

'Let me call Jess.'

'I don't need your housekeeper to help me cook frozen hash browns,' said Julia.

'Or, like,' I persisted, 'a teacher. Or just in marketing, or something wholesome like that. I wish I didn't want the acting thing so bad. Everything would be so much easier.'

'I don't understand why you're not just doing Ahn's thing,' said Julia, as she slammed the oven door. Carlton winced. 'I know she's annoying, but it sounds perfect.'

'Your reading comprehension is shocking,' said Carlton.

'What do you mean?'

'She doesn't want Harley to be in the film. She's just trying to get to Rachael through Harley.'

Julia frowned. 'I thought she wanted you to play Rachael.'

'She didn't say that.'

'But she must be thinking it.' She guided me over to the mirror. 'I mean, Harley,' she said, positioning me in front of it with both hands, her long nails catching on my jumper, 'you look *exactly alike*.'

I'd heard this before. Casting directors said it to me all the time. 'Gosh, you look just like your aunt.' Then they'd sit back expectantly, waiting for her second coming. I sometimes thought that was the main thing working against me. Rachael and I had the same face – the high, arched eyebrows, the straight nose, the thin lips, the pale skin that mottled easily, that betrayed emotion by shifts in colour hard to disguise. But we didn't use it the same. I could act, I knew that, but I didn't act like Rachael. When they watched me act, it was like watching someone else wear Rachael's face.

Here is the thing about Rachael's face. Leatherface had his mask of human skin. Mike Myers had his baggy, blankly grey one.

Ghostface had the plastic monstrosity that launched a thousand low-effort Halloween costumes. Even Hannibal Lecter, for all Anthony Hopkins' terrifying, soulless staring, is best remembered wearing that jaw restrainer.

Rachael didn't have a mask in *Women Who Laugh at God*. Just her face. Her terrifying, empty, beautiful face, full of sound and fury. Betraying nothing. Signifying everything.

Her face had been the face of the UK's favourite neighbour's daughter, doodling on her bed and having arguments with her mother about skirt length. It had been the face of the women in the romantic comedy that flirts and resists and fucks and falls. The face didn't change, but suddenly, in *Women Who Laugh at God,* you were scared of it. You feared it, and more than that, you feared the fact that you still desired her. *That*, as every film journalist has ever written in every piece that I have obsessively read, is the genius of Rachael's performance in *Women Who Laugh*. She makes you wonder if that face has always been a mask; if you don't really know what Rachael Carmichael looks like at all.

Imagine having the same face as someone like that.

'Here.' Julia turned me towards her. She applied her lipstick gently to my lips, gave me a tissue to blot. 'She always had a red lip,' she said.

'Oh, she looked *great* in red,' said Carlton.

'And so does Harley.' She faced me towards the mirror again. 'If you just took a few inches off your hair,' she said, playing with it, 'and maybe plucked your eyebrows a bit thinner . . . I mean, shit, Carlton, look. She's her twin.'

'You are,' agreed Carlton.

It was an interesting idea for a film. *Especially* with Rachael attached. Extra especially if they were finally going to address the whole secret baby thing. I'd never believed it – it all seemed to hinge on one overheard comment by a chauffeur, and there's no telling what these people will make up for a payout. But it was a compelling hook. If what Ahn was saying about studio interest was true, I could understand it. And Ahn would surely be able to appreciate how much that interest would be bolstered by having Rachael played by her own flesh and blood. The estranged niece with her face. That was quite the story.

'Do you really think I could do it?' I asked.

'You totally could,' said Carlton. 'It's uncanny. And kind of perfect timing, no? Jules, your hash browns are burning.'

'Shit.' She sprang over to the oven.

'You'd be a great person for it,' said Carlton, 'because you've got the inside track.'

'Hardly.' I wasn't even confident that Rachael knew I existed. I had about as much of the inside scoop on her marriage to Greg Foster as *TMZ*, and they'd incorrectly reported her pregnancy at least three times.

He shrugged. 'It's something, isn't it? A chance. You might as well go for it. Or you can keep doing terrible pilots instead, if you like.'

'You said you liked this one.'

'I did,' he said. 'But it was obviously never going to get picked up. When it comes to goal setting, you've got to be the right combination of ambitious and realistic.' He slapped my shoulder. 'Pharrell Williams told me that once.'

◆   ◆   ◆

I called a car early in the morning from Carlton's back to my flat in Notting Hill, slept for four hours, and then woke up and rang Ahn first thing. I could see her so clearly in my head, looking down at my name on the screen, rolling her eyes, reaching deep inside herself.

'Hi, Harley!' she said, bright and squeaky as a cartoon squirrel.

'Hi, Ahn. How's things?'

'Pretty good, thanks. Did you get my email?'

'I did. I think it sounds great. I'm definitely going to pass it all on to Rachael.'

'Oh, that's fantastic,' she said, suddenly sincere. 'That's brilliant, Harley. Thank you so much.'

'I just have one thing.'

'Okay,' she said. We were back to bright and squeaky.

'I want to play her.'

A pause. 'I think that sounds really interesting, Harley,' she said. 'We could definitely bring you in for an interview.'

'Let's be real here,' I said. 'You're not going to find anyone that looks more like her than I do.'

'Well, that's true. But, of course, we'll be looking for other things as well.' Bitch. 'It's definitely an interesting idea,' she said. 'I'll definitely give it some thought.'

She liked having me on a hook, so I let her have her small victory. She could only get Rachael through me. If I told Rachael that this was my film, Ahn would have to make it so.

The main problem: telling Rachael anything at all.

Here was the situation as it pertained to my family and Rachael Carmichael: she wanted nothing to do with us. It didn't seem like this was specific to us, either. Rachael Carmichael wanted nothing to do with anyone. About twenty-five years ago, armed with an already hefty net worth and the promised few million from the superhero franchise she'd just signed on to, she'd retreated to a country estate in Kent and locked the door to the outside world. She emerged every year or so to film a few scenes about saving the universe, never with any detectable light in her eyes, and then she would fly home to her empty house. That was all I knew of her, which was about as much as anyone else.

My mum texted the family group chat. *Harley, dinner at ours tonight? I'm going to try something Asian.*

What kind of Asian? asked my dad.

I jumped in. *Don't answer that.*

Uh-oh, he fired back, *the woke police are here!*

This maybe isn't the best introduction to Jeremiah Roth. He's far more well-intentioned than he might come across here, and he's actually known as one of the nicer British directors to work with. Plus, he came out of #MeToo very well.

At seven, I turned up for dinner at my parents' Kensington house. When I was picking out my first flat, I wanted something cosy and warm, not too flashy, nothing ostentatious. It's how I landed on my cheerful little three-bed in Notting Hill. I think that's the difference between growing up with money and acquiring it later in life. When you grow up with money, making 'rich' part of your decor just feels tacky. My parents are different. My dad had a fairly comfortable childhood – privately educated, nice house, frequent holidays, and then a whole lot of money when he started acting – but my mum really came from nothing. She wants to think *I made it* every time she looks around her home. Which is how my parents ended up in a huge white townhouse by Holland Park with a grand piano in the entranceway. None of us can play, by the way.

'You look so good it's disgusting,' said Mum, when she opened the door to me. 'Truly. Who's doing your hair these days?'

'Francis,' I said, hugging her.

'Who?'

'Exactly, so why would you ask?'

'Very funny,' she said. 'Come join us in the kitchen. Does it smell good?'

'It smells like you're attempting something.'

'Well, I am! So that's not bad.'

She's not much of a cook, my mum, but she does like to try. She has this black-and-white picture hanging in her kitchen by a photographer who was supposed to become someone. *Grub's up!* it's called, which I always thought was a disgusting name for something hanging in the kitchen. It shows a family sat around a long table, a dad with eight children of various ages, all dressed in a heightened, gaudy version of 1950s garb, whilst the mother stands at the head of the table cradling a turkey the size of a small horse, brow shiny under the effort of it. My dad says that it's a satire on traditional families, but my mum has always liked the image of the mother providing for the family like that, seeing their beaming faces turned towards her as she struggles to wrap her arms around an impossibly large game bird. She says it makes her nostalgic, although I'm not sure what for. She was born in 1976.

Anyway, every now and then, when Poppy has a night off and the actual kitchen downstairs is empty, Mum walks into her nice, shiny, hardly used upstairs kitchen and gives the whole housewife thing a really good go. She's a very bad cook, but she does look cute in an apron.

My dad was observing her from a safe distance, a tea towel slung over his shoulder. He wears it there to pretend that he's involved in the cute little domestic picture when really I'm not convinced he knows how to boil an egg. He raised his eyebrows at me and I punched him lightly on the shoulder. This was our usual greeting. 'Harley,' he said.

'Dad.'

'You look well. Considering.'

'Jer,' scolded Mum.

'Tough break, kid.'

'Tough business.'

'Offer's still there.' He had something in the very early stages of development that he kept insisting I'd be perfect for.

'I know,' I said. 'I can't. Thanks, though.'

I know I'll never really understand what it's like to have no allies in this industry, to have to work your way up from nothing. But at least when you get there, no one can doubt your talent. No one can say you don't deserve your success. It's a different kind of torture to have the perfect, career-launching opportunities right there, created for you by people who love you and want only the best for you, and know that if you take them, your name is mud.

It was actually surprisingly easy to bring Rachael Carmichael up over dinner, because my dad can't get through a single meal without scrolling through the news on his phone.

'Look at that, Lis.' Dad slid his phone over the table towards Mum, who picked it up and squinted at it. Then she rolled her eyes and slid it back, no comment, not like her at all.

'What?' I asked.

'Greg Foster's writing a book.'

'Oh, I saw that.' He passed the phone to me anyway. It was a different headline. *Greg Foster's memoir 'will definitely ruffle some feathers', claims source.* There was a picture of Rachael in this one. Not Rachael in the nineties, but Rachael as she was now. Her and Mum might have had the same nose, before Mum's rhinoplasty. There was none of Mum's fullness about her, though. Rachael didn't have her curls or her pout, just this thin, precise quality to her face – not angular exactly, or harsh, but certainly defined. She was still beautiful. I'd seen images of Rachael before, of course, but this time I was looking at her and seeing me. Was this what I'd look like in thirty years?

'Do you think I look like Rachael?' I asked Mum.

She looked at me, and then she looked again. 'Yes,' she said. 'I've always said so.' She'd never once said that to me, actually. Sometimes, growing up, I would find a picture of Rachael on the internet and do my hair and make-up to match, and I would come downstairs ready for Mum to gasp over the resemblance. If she ever noticed, she never said so.

I moved my fork through the noodles. She'd stuck some kind of vegetable in there, boiled to the point of ruin. It came apart, mushy and steaming. 'Do you think I could play her?'

'Like acting?'

'Like what I do for a living, yes.'

'I'm not sure it really counts as a living yet,' said Dad.

'Jer, please.'

'She knows I'm kidding. You know I'm kidding, don't you, Harley?'

'I'm serious,' I said. 'Do you think I could?'

He put his fork down. 'What's this about?'

'Just hypothetical.'

He looked at me, slowly chewing the gluey noodles.

'I wouldn't want you to,' said Mum sharply. A crinkle appeared in her perfect nose. 'That woman's head is big enough as it is.'

In the end, I didn't ask Mum for Rachael's number. She probably didn't have it, and even if she did, I didn't want Rachael to be able to hang up on me. I decided that this would have to be an in-person attack. I would surprise her into talking to me. How often do you open your front door to see someone standing there wearing your face, after all?

One con of being Rachael Carmichael is that your address is relatively easy to find online. I saved the route in my phone when I got home that night, and then I put on *Women Who Laugh at God* and watched it alone in my flat. I examined her, twenty-two and so compulsively watchable, the exact woman that Greg Foster had first fallen in love with. The darkness she'd had in *Here's Hoping* was there, but it hadn't rotted into whatever unsettling quality she'd had in her later work. Those had been films that made you want to look away. In *Women Who Laugh at God,* even when what you were watching was frightening and sometimes horrible, you couldn't help but keep your eyes on her. She made you love how much you were afraid of her. You would have let her rip your heart out. At least, I would have.

I wanted to climb inside her mind. The Hooker, the Nurse, the Schoolgirl . . . none of them mattered to me anymore. Even the Lover had just been a first crush. The role of Rachael Carmichael was going to be the great love of my life, and I would hold up the boombox beneath her window until my arms went limp.

Her estate in Kent wasn't exactly the cosy bolthole I'd pictured. I pulled up in front of red-brick walls and huge wooden gates, nothing visible beyond. A couple of security cameras were perched atop the walls and there was a keypad next to the gate. I leant out of the car window to press the 'Call' button and waited.

Nothing.

I pressed again.

A pause, and then, 'Hello?' I recognised her voice.

'Hi, Miss Carmichael?'

'Who is this?'

'It's . . . Harley.'

'I don't know a Harley.'

'You do. I mean, you don't really, but you do.' I knew this was a gamble. It was possible she had never heard my name. 'I'm your niece,' I said. 'I'm Elisabeth's daughter.'

'Elisabeth's daughter?'

'Yes.'

'Well, anyone might say that.'

'If you just look at me,' I said, 'you'll know.'

A pause. I thought she'd simply walked away from the intercom. Then there was a click. 'Alright, Elisabeth's daughter,' she said. 'I'll look at you.' She could see me already, of course. There was a small camera winking away on top of the wall.

30

The gates opened inwards. Two curved gravel roads encircled a stone fountain, leading up to a set of enormous steps. At the top, in the centre of a huge red-brick house, was a dark wooden door with a round brass knocker in the middle. It was a little green in places, as was the brick of the house, weeds growing along the top of the walls and down the sides. I drove slowly over the gravel, pulling up beside the fountain. I was unclipping my seat belt when the front door opened. I half expected a maid or a butler, or at least a bulky security guard, but it was just her, looking very small in the huge entranceway. There was a scruffy brown thing that might have been a dog sat by her feet. Her dark hair was pulled back from her face, twisted up in a clip. In her jumper and jeans, she could have been someone's mum.

I opened my car door and got out. Then I waited, one hand on the door, the other on the roof of my car. I realised suddenly that I was afraid.

She looked at me.

'It's nice to meet you, Harley,' she said. 'Did you want to come in?'

Chapter Two

RACHAEL

3 April 1988

Writing is apparently a great way to vent your frustrations so I have picked up my pen to say this: my shoes are missing. They were in the hall yesterday, lined up neatly between my trainers and my slippers, and now they've vanished. Mais swears she hasn't seen them anywhere but they couldn't have fallen into anyone else's hands, unless Mickey has developed a new fetish. They're red, with a little ankle strap. Real leather, which Mais has always sworn off, although apparently that was all for show. Or maybe she just assumes I wouldn't be able to afford real leather. She's not wrong. They were a charity shop find.

I know why she's taken them too. The two of them are gearing up to move out. I'd say it was about time for them, if it wasn't so inconvenient for me. The wedding is only a few months away and they'll both be twenty-seven by the time it happens. They're already looking past it and thinking: *house, dog, kid.* Also: *let's make sure to steal all Rachael's really good shit before we go.* I'm not invited to the wedding, shockingly. Mais stressed that it was 'just our family and really good friends', the subtext being that they do not consider the eighteen-year-old housemate they were forced to take in for financial reasons a really good friend. That's alright. I'm not a huge fan of them either. Sometimes I wish I could just sleep in the restaurant, curled up on the kitchen floor. It wouldn't be so bad. It's a nice place, very clean, and it always smells amazing. Plus Ha-ru would be there. Maybe, if I asked him nicely enough, he'd curl up on the floor with me and we'd sleep there together, with my fingers pressed very gently into his palm.

Mais caught me going through the bottom of her wardrobe. 'What are you *doing?*' she screeched. I think her and Mickey keep the sex toys down there. I did spot a couple of suspicious-looking shoeboxes tucked away at the back. 'I told you,' she said, dragging me out by my arm, 'I haven't seen them. You've probably left them at some guy's house.' Mais says stuff like this to me all the time. I want to ask her, *Mais, when was the last time you saw me with some guy?* And the answer would be never.

The shoes are frustration number one. Number two is that the Woolworths on Tooting High Street has the perfect shirt for my BBC audition – I passed it again this morning, it's in the window – and I cannot buy it because I still owe Mais for the electric, even though I think any debt should be waived whilst she's holding my shoes hostage. Number three is beautiful Ha-ru, who I love enormously, and who will one day inevitably marry an equally beautiful Korean girl. It's a dismal state of things. I do think his parents like me, based on all the free stuff they give me. I've eaten nothing but Korean food for the last year and I've forgotten what it's like to have an appetite for anything other than kimchi and bulgogi kimbap. They've also given me lots of pamphlets about God, although I can't be sure if that's because they're generous or because I'm exhibiting behaviour that concerns them. Regardless, they wouldn't like me with Ha-ru. It's something both of us know, even though we never say it. We never say anything much. Just surface-level chat about the restaurant and Ha-ru's school and life, when we both know none of it's what we'd actually like to be talking about.

Frustration number four is that Mum and Elisabeth have called to inform me that we are due another visit.

'What do you actually want to do?' I asked Mum on the phone.

'Well,' she said, 'see London! Of course.'

'You've seen London. You saw it last time.'

'It's a big place, Rachael.'

'It's deceptively big. Most of it's just houses.' I was sitting at my desk, watching Mickey shovel snow from the path up to the door. It's a shared building, which makes this job very much not his responsibility. Which might lead you to believe that Mickey is a selfless do-gooder, when he's actually a self-important dick. Mickey is one of those little old ladies that consider themselves the backbone of their cul-de-sacs, only he's twenty-seven and male and he drives a Ford Fiesta.

'I want to see a West End show,' came Elisabeth's squeaky little voice in the background. I pulled my desk drawer out, ready to slam it.

'Your sister wants to see a West End show,' said Mum.

'I guess she's paying then.'

'Don't you know people? From the acting world?'

'No.'

'It's a bit expensive, love,' said Mum to Elisabeth. 'How about London Zoo?'

'I hate zoos,' squeaked Elisabeth.

'Is this the animal rights stuff? Get over it already. Honestly, Rachael,' said Mum, 'she's doing my head in with all that.'

'Alright.' I did slam the drawer then. 'You think about it. Looking forward to seeing you.'

'You're alright, then? Generally?'

'Generally.'

'Good.'

Mais opened the door. I've given up on asking her to knock. 'What was that noise?'

'What noise?'

'What?' said Mum.

'I've been looking for the phone,' said Mais.

'I'm using it.'

'I need to make a call.'

'Oh, a *call*? You should have said.' She glared at me. 'Mum, I have to go. I'll see you guys next week.'

'Okay then,' said Mum. 'I'll hear all about how everything's been going when we get there, then.'

'Sure.' I hate the 'how everything's been going' conversations. So does she, but she drags us both through them like it's a motherly duty. Neither of us want to talk about how badly I'm failing. 'Bye.' Barely had I hung up the phone than it was in Mais' hand. I would have thought it was a magic trick if one of her nails hadn't scratched my arm. 'You're welcome,' I said.

Another glare. She slammed my door. Maybe I should watch how I speak to her, but I know they're moving out anyway, so really there's nothing to lose. I was so skittish when I moved in here last year, so embarrassed to be teenaged and in their space. My first flat share had been with two music students, both boys, barely older than I was. We took it in turns to try to get served in off-licences and cooked terrible curries and never tidied up. They thought I was quite cool, the independent sixteen-year-old who'd come down to London to make it in acting. Mais and Mickey think I'm the biggest loser on the planet. Sometimes I agree with them.

The first agent I worked with, the one who looks like Jack Nicholson's slightly melted son and who dropped me when I started getting tits, said, 'Rachael, all actors hate themselves a little. That's why they spend so much time being other people.' Bullshit. The ones I meet don't seem to hate themselves at all. They think they're amazing. They're so sure they'll make it. I used to be like that too.

'Eighteen is a little too young to be jaded, don't you think?' said Ha-ru at the restaurant yesterday evening. Wonderful Ha-ru. He was wearing a sweatband to keep his hair out of his eyes. It made it all stand on end like he'd been shocked. 'At least give it a couple more years.'

'I feel like an old, ugly cow,' I said, my head on a pile of menus.

'Oh dear.'

'I wanted to be a young, hot star. Kick things off when I was fifteen or sixteen or so, and by the time I was eighteen I'd be established, and then everyone could talk about how young and beautiful I was. Even if I book a job now, I maybe won't be a name until I'm twenty-one.'

'Ancient,' said Ha-ru, scrubbing a pan.

'Can you stop giving me one-word answers?'

'I'll tell you how young and beautiful you are, if you like.'

'Oh, don't.' I threw a menu at him. I think he does love me, not that he'd ever be able to say it. It's all a bit *Romeo & Juliet*. I love that about us. 'I just want to be able to tell my mum something good for once. It was okay when I left home at sixteen because we both knew I was going to go be a famous actress. Now it's like, what did I really do it for? I think she's starting to wonder that.'

He carried on scrubbing the pan, not saying anything.

'Ha-ru? What is it?'

'Would this really be so bad? A life like this, and never anything else?' Some of the suds sprayed upwards and clung to the front of his apron. His grip was tight around the sponge.

'Yes,' I said.

The kitchen door swung open. The rest of the staff were starting to arrive. Ha-ru kept scrubbing, still staring at the pan. For the rest of the night we were oddly quiet around each other. When he sent me home, he said, 'Same place, same time tomorrow?' It's a joke he often makes. I laughed. 'I know you can't,' he said, 'but I wish you could work here forever.' Then he disappeared back into the kitchen, before I'd figured out how to reply.

◆ ◆ ◆

I moved to London two years ago, but we'd been talking about it for much further back. I don't remember when I first told Mum that I wanted to be an actress, or if I ever had to, but I remember being seven or eight, sat on the carpet with my Barbies, Mum on the sofa telling a friend, 'Of course, Rachael will have to be in London sooner rather than later. For the acting thing.' About six months later, eating Kung Pao chicken out of plastic tubs at the kitchen table, she said, 'You know your dad lives in London, don't you, Rachael?' She ate a forkful of chicken, chewed, and said, 'If he hasn't moved. If he's still alive.' She met him on a night out with a friend, my dad. She knew him for twelve hours in total. Didn't even get his name. Similar story with Elisabeth's dad. I went through a moralistic phase at about ten years old where I was absolutely scandalised by my roots, but I grew out of it quickly. Now I think it's sort of funny.

I asked her if she was saying I should try to find him. 'No,' she said quickly, and then more thoughtfully, 'No, no.' Her fork scraped the bottom of the plastic tub. She played it off as thoughtless – she'd thought 'London', she'd thought 'Rachael's dad', and she hadn't really thought further. I let the breadcrumb lie where she'd dropped it, because really, what did it matter? She'd made a similar comment the previous year, when we'd passed a red car parked outside a church and she'd said casually, 'I think your dad had a car like that. I don't really remember.' Remarks like this didn't feel cruel at the time, but they stayed with me. Looking back, I think these random, out-of-thin-air allusions to my dad were just a way to remind me of what a stranger he was to me. *You know your dad lives in London?* Because, of course, I didn't. Because the three of us only had each other.

Two years is a long time to live in London and audition and be lonely and not get anywhere. Two years is a long time to see your mother and sister every few months, to make minimum wage and pay your own bills and slowly realise that you've forgotten almost everything you ever learnt in school, so you probably couldn't even fall back on your education anymore. Two years is a long time to hear, over and over again, that you're too plain, or too chubby, or too wooden, or too harsh, or too just not right. Two years is a long time to not book even a single job.

But the awful part is, in the grand scheme of things, it isn't. So to give up after two years would be like giving up without really trying at all.

Two days ago, I had my very worst audition ever. It's why I sat down to write, only it's harder than you think, writing. Your mind goes in a hundred different directions and it's difficult to just come out and say what you want to. But Mais and Mickey are out now – she slammed the door behind them about five minutes ago – and the place is quiet, and I've burned a candle that smells like oranges and soap almost down to the metal ring on the bottom. Take two, as they say in the industry, not that I'd know.

Usually you get in the room and they all look like you a bit, only taller and prettier. I used to think this was a cliché, just something people said, but it's actually quite impressive how the casting office is able to pull off the same sick joke every time. This time I walked in and they were all blonde. Every single one. Brigitte

Bardot blonde, with the tits to match. I stuck out like an evil step-sister in a room full of Cinderellas.

I thought, *If it goes badly, you might as well ask them why you're here.* Had it been a mistake? The script said nothing about the part being for a blonde. It was some kids' show about a teenage detective and the script introduced her like this:

> *TILLY, 14, sits up in her bed and yawns. She's a clever-looking girl with her hair in two braids.*

I had worn my hair in two braids and done my best to look clever. Most of the girls around me had their hair down, blonde curls sitting large and loud over skinny shoulders. I definitely looked closer to fourteen than most of them. My instinct told me that in this particular case, this might not be an advantage. The one sat next to me had a beauty spot in the exact same place as Madonna and a blowout so voluminous she looked like a girl in a Looney Tunes cartoon who's seen a spider. She was beautiful, though. They're always beautiful. Sitting in those rooms, you'd think there wasn't an ugly girl in London.

The woman with the list called my name and into the room I went. It was just two men behind the table. You never know how many to expect. They're usually men, sometimes one woman between them, very rarely a woman on her own. I walked over and shook both of their hands.

'Good morning,' I said, cheerfully, breezily.

'Good morning.' One of them gripped my hand and looked me right in the eyes. The other one gave my fingers a brief squeeze and said nothing. He was over forty, greying, his stomach filling up the space between his chair and the desk. 'Rachael?' said the cheerful one, pushing glasses back up his nose.

'That's me.'

'Take it away, then, Rachael. Whenever you're ready.'

The scene involved Tilly waking up from bed, which forced me to do an awkward standing yawn before I launched into the incredibly twee dialogue between her and her high-tech, vaguely sentient alarm clock. The man with the glasses read for the alarm clock. The other man sat and stared down at my résumé the entire time, arms folded, tipping slightly back in his chair. I don't know what he was finding so interesting. It was all local theatre, no film or TV work at all apart from one advert for a chocolate selection box. I'd been fifteen and calorie-obsessed at the time, because I didn't want my tits to come in. You do better as a child actress without tits. I stopped counting calories after my agent dropped me because what was the point? I only went up to a B cup and then no further growth, so it was all much ado about nothing in the end.

We were about midway through the read and it was going well, when there was a beep from the jacket of the man in glasses. 'Shit,' he said, pulling out his pager. 'Sorry, Rachael, but I'm going to have to go make a call. Keep going with Lawrence here.' He dashed out of the room, the door swinging behind him.

The other man still didn't look up at me. I remained in character.

'Clock, do a scan of the area. Let's see if there's anyone who needs—'

'You did *The Crucible*,' he said, his eyes on my résumé.

Alright, we were done with the read. 'Yes, I did. I was Abigail.' Unpaid, naturally.

'Hm.' He finally looked up. 'I don't see Abigail.'

'It was definitely a challenge.' Being looked at wasn't much better than being ignored. He stared at me like I was a piece of furniture and he was trying to work out my dimensions. 'I was young when I did it,' I said. 'Only fifteen. It was youth theatre.'

He didn't seem to be listening. Instead he beckoned me over to the table. When I hesitated, he beckoned again, more impatiently, and made a 'hmph' sound. I walked over to him. He reached up and tugged on one of my plaits.

'These age you down a lot,' he said. It sounded like a good thing, but I wasn't sure. Before I could stop him, he had pulled the hair tie out and was undoing the plait with his fat fingers. I stood there, frozen. 'Better,' he said, and started undoing the other one.

'I thought she was supposed to have plaits?' I managed.

'Yes,' he said, 'but now you're Abigail. I can see it.' His hand lingered in my hair, came to rest on the side of my head. 'Temptress.'

There was movement in the edge of my vision. His hand had disappeared under the folds of his shirt, into his lap. I jerked backwards, but his other hand was still caught in my hair and it didn't seem like he was planning on removing it. I stared at the dull movement beneath his shirt, aware of his eyes on my face, waiting for a reaction.

The door swung open again. The man's hand slid smoothly out of my hair. His other hand slid smoothly back on to his knee.

'All good in here?' asked the man with glasses cheerfully.

'Thank you, Rochelle,' said the other man, face expressionless. 'We'll let you know.'

I decided on the Tube home that if they offered me the part, I wouldn't take it. But even as I repeated the conviction to myself, I faltered. To refuse paid acting work went against everything in me. A series lead, no less. Who knew what I'd be willing to do for that? I certainly didn't.

It didn't matter, of course. Robb, my agent, rang the next day to say that they'd gone in another direction.

'Apparently,' he said, 'they envisioned her as a blonde.'

41

5 April 1988

A call from Robb. 'Got something for you,' he said. My heart knotted. Is that the expression? That's what it felt like. These are usually exciting words from Robb, even after two years of them coming to nothing. But suddenly I never wanted to walk into an audition room again.

'What is it?' I managed.

'New sitcom. There's a really nice part for a teenager. It's by the team who did *Just Fine,* did you see that?'

'No. Heard it was good.' I very rarely get to pick what to watch on TV because Mais is always watching her makeover stuff. Occasionally she'll tune into the odd episode of *Only Fools and Horses* and I'll be permitted to watch with her, but that's about it when it comes to informing my craft. God forbid I want to rent a movie. The only one I've ever talked her into letting me choose is *Children of the Corn* because I said I'd heard that it was about a family on a farm. She didn't speak to me for a week.

'It was *very* good,' said Robb. 'This is a hot script right now. And they're keen to cast an unknown for Jill. I'm going to send you in. I'll fax the pages over later.'

'Sounds good.' Robb faxing the pages over usually involves me standing guard over the fax machine all afternoon so that Mais can't get hold of the pages and read them first and give me all her opinions. Every time I have heard Mais' opinions on a script, I have walked into the audition room and bombed. I swear that woman is some kind of witch.

After Robb hung up, I sat on the edge of my bed with the phone in my hands for a few minutes and I spoke to myself sternly, with no soft words. I was not born to try and fail. I did not move here to waste my own time. I will go to this audition. I will do my best. I will wear my hair twisted back and pinned right out of my face. I will keep going.

8 April 1988

The audition was surprisingly good in the end. For one, there was a woman behind the table, and just one other man. The woman had dark hair, like mine, pulled back in a ponytail, and very dark red lipstick on. The man was young, maybe only late twenties, and very blond. They both smiled when I came in, almost in an approving kind of way, which I've only noticed happen a few times in auditions and I think means you line up with the image of the character that they have in their heads.

'Rachael.' The woman stood up, extending her hand. 'Nice to meet you.'

'You too.'

'I'm Kara. This is Frasier.'

'Hi.' I shook both of their hands. 'Rachael. Oh, crap, you knew that.' They both laughed. This was calculated. It was exactly the kind of thing Jill, the character, might do.

'Whenever you're ready,' said Kara.

She really threw herself into the role of Jill's mother. Sometimes people behind casting desks give you nothing to go off, but she read her lines like she was the one auditioning. *This is fun!* her performance seemed to say, so I let myself think that it was fun as well. And it was. Just the two of us, acting out a great scene.

'Thank you, Rachael,' she said. 'That was terrific. We'll let you know.'

On my way out of the room, I passed a girl sat in a green plastic chair who looked a little like me, only younger and shorter, with a thinner face. She stared up at me as I passed her, like I was something she'd only seen in dreams.

12 April 1988

Picked up my pen again because I have more frustrations but also some good news, and it feels appropriate to record both. Frustrations first. Mais has taken two tops and a hairbrush. The tops aren't completely unexpected – she's been eyeing my white shirt for a while, even though I only wear it on auditions for waitresses, baristas and schoolgirls. The hairbrush is a little more surprising. I'm sure she must have one of her own. She continues to deny having ever seen any of the missing items. 'Maybe you've left them at a guy's house,' again, even though as far as she knows I could be as gay as the day is long.

Good news now, which far outweighs anything Mais could pull. I booked a job!

'An acting job?' asked Mum suspiciously when I called her.

'Yes. Obviously.'

'Does it look legitimate? Where did you meet the director? Not in a bar.'

'Obviously not.'

'Okay,' she said, still unconvinced.

'It was an actual audition. I mean, Jesus, I'm good enough to get a job outside of a bar, I think.'

'You haven't yet.'

'Cheers.'

'So what is it? The part?'

'It's *great*.' I lay down on my bed. 'It's an ensemble comedy about families living on a British cul-de-sac, called *The Avenue*. Really funny. I play this couple's daughter, Jill. They're kind of the main family, I think. She's fifteen. She's really smart. She has this great bit with this guy – he's hitting on her, and she just totally puts him in his place.'

'It's a TV show?'

'Yes.'

'So it'll be regular work,' she said, brightening up. 'Regular money. That's wonderful, Rachael.'

'Well, it's just the pilot right now.'

'Oh,' she said, crestfallen, 'of course.'

'But *hopefully* . . . I mean, *eventually*—'

'Well,' she said, 'you'll just have to keep us posted.'

Her reaction wasn't disappointing – I know better than that by now – but it definitely dampened my excitement somewhat. I downplayed the whole thing at the restaurant with Ha-ru.

'It's just a pilot. Nothing's for sure.'

He picked me up and spun me around anyway. Wonderful, wonderful Ha-ru. His mother cut his hair recently. It looks awful. It was for school photos, because Ha-ru is still in school giving himself options and expanding his horizons, unlike silly old me. One of my feet hit the work surface when he spun me and it made a metallic clang, and he dropped me quickly, in case his mum came in. So hot.

'I guess you're done with this place,' he said, suddenly sad.

'*Never*. I'll be taking shifts here even when I'm raking in the millions.'

'You better. Where else will my parents find another white girl to confuse all our customers with?'

'London is short on white girls, it's true.'

'On ones as cool as you,' he said, 'maybe.'

I let him kiss me in the storeroom, against the vegetable shelf. Just once, and probably never again. Because I'm not going to be working at the restaurant anymore. I'm going to be a TV star.

23 May 1988

God, how fast life goes. I'm tired as anything. I've been meaning to pick up this book and write but I keep reading my *Sweet Valley High* books instead. They're truly dire but I can get them for a pound fifty each in Woolworths, and Jessica and Elizabeth Wakefield's problems are so absolutely inconsequential that reading about them is a sort of meditation. I never have time to really sit and think about anything, between the restaurant and auditions and everything else. I wonder if that will change, come September, or if life will only get busier?

Where did I leave off? We filmed the pilot in Watford. There were ten of us. Me, Brenda and Chris made one family (Susan and Dave, and their teenage daughter Jill). Teri, Duke, Lili and Lola made another (Shauna, Jacques and their five-year-old twin girls). Geoff, Yvonne and Jerry were the final three (Matt, Mary and their eleven-year-old son, Ben). There would be other supporting characters if the season got picked up, we were told, maybe more regular players, but we would be the main residents of The Avenue. The core ten.

If a full season was ordered, we would get a soundstage. For now, we were filming in a real cul-de-sac, a street of eight houses that had been shut off, four that we'd rented to have the run of. Three were sets, and one was used as a green room. Most of us sat downstairs in the living room and kitchen, and the rest was quickly taken over by the three kids. They disappeared upstairs for school every couple of hours, which meant there was a constant start and stop feel to the production. We got as much work as we could get done without them, but the rest of the time I was sitting with the three adult couples behind drawn lace curtains, waiting to be called for the next scene and trying to sound older than I was.

They were kind to me. They've all been on TV before. Brenda's the most famous – she's had reoccurring stints on big shows throughout the last couple of decades, has worked with French and Saunders and John Cleese and pretty much every member of the British comedy ruling class. When I walked in for the table read she said, 'Oh, my daughter!' and hugged me so tight she really could have been embracing her long-lost child. When the conversation between the adults left me in the dust, she would come and sit beside me and ask me questions about my life. Was I in school? I'd left? I must be very brave, to come here and do this on my own. I have never liked being patronised, but for some reason I did like it when Brenda called me brave. Did I have a boyfriend? I didn't, I said, but then for some reason I ended up telling her all about Ha-ru and the restaurant.

'Oh my,' she said, with twinkling eyes. 'Forbidden love.'

'I don't love him. He's just nice.'

'Are you going back there, after this?'

'I think so,' I said. The thought was deflating. I'd loved the restaurant, but now I had something to compare it to, and I knew I would never love it the same again. Brenda saw me falter. She squeezed my hand.

'Oh, don't worry,' she said. 'I don't reckon it will be for long.'

Mum and Elisabeth came to visit two days after I wrapped the pilot. We took Elisabeth to London Zoo (she'd quickly come round on the animal rights issue). 'It's on our TV star,' said Mum, and even though I hadn't received my money for the pilot yet, I handed over my credit card.

'This was kind of you,' she said as we stood a little way behind Elisabeth, hands in our coat pockets. Elisabeth was sitting cross-legged on the ground, watching the penguins swim behind the glass. She's tall for eleven, skinny and sinewy from her swimming, and she's also young for her age. I'd known exactly who I was and what I wanted from the time that I was eight years old. Elisabeth says she wants to be in the Olympics but I don't think she'd even go to swim practice if Mum didn't make her. She's not the kind of person who wants things. She just sort of waits for them.

'It's okay,' I said. 'Hey, hopefully if they order a full season I'll be able to help out with more than just zoo tickets.'

'Oh, Rachael,' she said, and squeezed my arm. 'That would be so wonderful. I'm so proud of you. You've been so resilient. And now it's all paying off.'

A penguin dove right down in front of Elisabeth, almost as if it was trying to get a good look at her. She turned back to check that we'd seen, a delighted grin stretching across her face.

'Did you know she was scouted for county?' Mum asked.

'No. Was she?'

'They think she's got quite a future. It's those long limbs of hers. You know, I've been thinking of trying to get her into modelling.'

'Really? You think she'd like it?'

Mum shrugged. 'I don't know. Just an idea. Just trying to think of paths for you girls. Options, you know?'

Of course, it's about that time. I was eleven when Mum and I started brainstorming paths for me. Elisabeth is now in training for the day that she too can contribute to the family finances. Watching her watch the penguins, I almost felt bad for her. She's an annoying kid, but so would I be if I was left alone with Mum. And the pressure isn't fun. The worry that if I – now *we,* I suppose – don't do something about it, Mum will slowly waste away, and die never knowing how it feels to sleep on silk pillowcases and have a membership to the National Trust.

On the walk back to the Tube station, Elisabeth asked me when I was going to be on TV. 'Soon,' I said. 'Hopefully.'

'That's good,' she said. 'I need a new blazer.' She showed me a picture of her in her blazer, skinny arms jutting out of either sleeve, cuffs hitting a few good inches above her wrists. What an odd thing for her to be carrying around with her, I thought – and then again, not so odd at all.

They ordered a full season. I must have been expecting it because I didn't even get excited. Excited is something you only get when other people are around, I've noticed. When it's you alone, you just go, *Huh. How about that.*

'Sixteen episodes,' said Robb excitedly. 'Those are States numbers. The hope is that it'll rival the situational comedies they've got going over there.'

'Sixteen.' It was a dizzying number. I'd been expecting closer to six. He told me what they were planning on paying me per episode. I was freshly dizzied.

'We're moving out,' said Mais from the doorway mere hours later, with my cardigan on.

'I'm going to be a TV star,' I shot back. That stumped her.

Ha-ru spun me around again when I told him. And then I said, 'Ha-ru . . .' and he stepped backwards, and said, 'Yeah,' and that was how I handed in my notice. I delivered a handwritten note to his mother the next day, formalising it, but he wasn't in. She said he'd gone fishing. I think he'd told her to tell me that in order to make me laugh. It worked.

I wonder if I'll ever see him again. Somehow, I don't think I will. I think I'll have to exchange some beautiful things for others as I go, trade my way into the magic places. I don't have a lot of beautiful things right now, but beautiful Ha-ru is one of them. I'll leave him at the bottom if it means I can take that escalator skywards. I won't even look back.

Chapter Three

HARLEY

Rachael's dog was one of the ugliest I had ever seen. I couldn't tell what sort of breed it was meant to be, or which breeds might have combined to make it, or even what strange interspecies relationship might have led to its birth. It glared up at me out of two beady little black eyes, the glint of them just visible through layers of scraggly brown fur. When I sat down on Rachael's sofa, it curled its lips back to growl at me. Its gums were black.

'Cute dog,' I said.

The dog closed its eyes. Now it really did look like a mop. Or a very old toupee.

'His name is Raph,' said Rachael.

'Short for?'

'Short for nothing. That's just the sound he makes.'

'Raph,' said Raph, eyes still closed.

She didn't offer me a drink or ask after my parents. I still had my shoes on, because she'd strode ahead of me into the living room with so much purpose that pausing to take them off would have felt like disobedience. I'd followed. Now we were sat beside a brick fireplace, the kind so large that it extended out of the wall and had a roundness to its edges. I sat on the orange leather sofa, and Rachael took the cream armchair opposite. There were framed pieces of art along the wall behind her, part of the same series of squiggly black and beige lines. The kind of art that rich people love because it makes you feel absolutely nothing.

'Your house is lovely,' I said. Rachael was arranging the cushions behind herself, not looking at me. 'Is the fireplace real?'

'Does it work, you mean?'

'Yes.'

'Maybe. I've never tried it.'

Satisfied with her cushion placement, she turned back to me. Raph's eyes opened and his head swivelled in my direction at the same time, the two of them almost exactly in sync. It gave me goosebumps, the way they moved together like that. It made you feel as if they were one creature in two bodies.

'Right,' said Rachael. 'Let's work this out.'

Her jumper swallowed her, sat there like that. She lost her neck in it. She was all white cable knit and cream armchair. She'd always been small. Not just skinny and not just short, but small, with something wispy and delicate about her. On screen, she'd had this uncanny ability to grow, to harden her bones, to put metal behind her voice. You'd see pictures of her at the premieres for these films and think, *That can't possibly be her.* But they both were her, somehow: the fragile girl in the delicate slip dress, and that serpent-tongued, iron-cored force of destruction on screen.

You could see them both in her even now, as she reached out to scratch the top of Raph's head and asked, casually, 'Do you need money?'

'Oh my god, no. Nothing like that.'

She didn't believe me. She went on scratching Raph behind the ears. The dog gave little indication as to whether he was enjoying the action or not. 'Are you sure? I've been following your career, and I gather it's not going too well.'

Conflicting emotions. Rachael Carmichael had cared enough to follow my work, and Rachael Carmichael thought I was a failure.

'Could you not have asked your parents?' she asked. A little jolt went right through my heart and out the other side, hearing her reference my parents, but her face gave nothing away. It was like she'd never even met them.

'I don't need money. I'm – I'm supporting myself.' A lie, but what was I supposed to say? That I was living off my trust fund? Come on.

'How?'

'What?'

'How are you supporting yourself?'

'I'm a waitress.'

'Ah,' she said. There was the first hint of a smile. Raph yawned.

'Anyway, even if I did need money, I definitely wouldn't turn up on your doorstep begging for it. We've never even met before. I'm not that kind of person. I don't beg for things.'

'Well, I wouldn't make any kind of definitive statements on that front,' said Rachael. 'I've begged for things before. Don't knock it until you try it.'

She was completely stone-faced as she said this, scratching the dog's ears with the corners of her mouth turned down, but I got the impression that she was making fun of me.

'If it was just curiosity,' she said, 'then that's alright. But it's strange to me that you waited this long. How old are you? Twenty-five?'

'Yes,' I said, surprised.

'That's a long time to never get curious before.'

'I've been curious since I was a kid,' I said, leaning forwards. 'Honestly. I have all your films on DVD. I mean, I did, back in the day. I used to watch them all in secret.'

'What was your favourite?'

'*East of Eden.*'

She shook her head. 'That's no one's favourite. What was it really?'

'*Here's Hoping.*'

Then she smiled. Properly. Red lips parting to reveal teeth that had probably cost her as much if not more than my school fees. 'That was a fun one,' she said.

'I've always wanted to meet you. Honestly.'

'So, why now?'

'I don't know. I just wanted to talk to you. I didn't really think it through.'

She looked at me, face blank. People never actually mean it when they say that, but Rachael really could make her face display nothing. It was a kind of talent she had, one that had served her well in films like *Women Who Laugh at God*. She could empty her expression of anything, so that she was only features – two eyes, two eyebrows, a mouth, a jaw, each as still and quiet as if she had been restored to factory settings. People had written about it since the early years of her career. It had been an *SNL* punchline once. 'Then she hits me with that Carmichael gaze.' Cue laughter. But it wasn't a Carmichael gaze – my mother didn't have it, and neither did I. It was wholly Rachael's own.

She turned it on me for a second longer. Then she stood up. Raph jumped off the footstool.

'Do you play tennis?' she asked.

Rachael Carmichael's house had seven bathrooms. Shortly, I was in one of them, on the ground floor, round the back of the house with a view of the gardens. The main lawn was enormous, striped in different shades of green. Beyond that I could see an orchard, a swimming pool, and, in the distance, grass courts outlined in white. Rachael was already standing on the closest. She disappeared and reappeared through the hedges, practising her serve. Never actually hitting the ball, but throwing it up repeatedly, racquet pulled back like she was going in for it, and then catching deftly and trying again.

I wondered if she was a little bit mad. Maybe that was why Mum didn't want her in our lives. She'd lent me a tennis skirt and a little white polo top, like we were in an Enid Blyton boarding school together. They were draped over the side of the clawfoot bath, white trainers on the tiles underneath them. Strangely, even though I was taller than her, we were the same size in everything, right down to our size five and a half feet. What were we doing, dressing up to play tennis together with barely a proper introduction? Was she that starved for company? Maybe that was it. Raph was hardly the most charismatic of companions.

When I appeared at the gate to the courts and she walked over to let me in, she looked so young, dark hair pulled back into a ponytail just like mine was, our clothes almost identical. I wished I could see us both side by side.

'Coin toss,' she said. 'Come up to the net.'

'You can serve first, I don't mind.'

She shook her head. 'We have to make it fair.'

We met at the net, racquets tucked under our arms. We watched the coin as she flicked it upwards, as it twisted. 'Heads,' she called, and slapped her palm over it. Heads it was. She tossed the fifty pence piece to the side of the court, where it rolled for a few seconds on the thin grass and came to a stop under a bench. She took a few running steps backwards, racquet clutched in both hands. She bobbed on the balls of her feet as she waited for me to assume my position on the other side of the net. I watched her ready stance, her focused eyes. The steel in her face.

I thought, *I could be you, Rachael Carmichael.*

Her first serve whizzed past me before I'd even had time to reach for it.

'One,' called Rachael.

'What?'

'That's one for me.'

'Fifteen-love to you, you mean.'

She waved a hand. 'I don't bother with all that.'

So we kept going with her strange scoring. I could never get a serve past her, and returning hers made my shoulders burn. I was quite a good tennis player, or so I'd fancied myself. When you grow up rich in Kensington, you play tennis. Rachael hadn't grown up rich in Kensington, but she was excellent. When we finished – when Rachael decided we had played for long enough – the score was twenty-two to Rachael, thirteen to me. I can't be bothered to translate that into real tennis terms. Safe to say she won.

'You're not bad,' she said, coming up to the net. 'It's nice to play with someone. No one around here plays tennis.'

What on earth did she mean by 'around here'? There was no one around here. Just Rachael and Raph. Did she have staff, I wondered? Or neighbours, a few minutes' drive down the road?

'Just leave the clothes on the bathroom floor,' she said, taking my racquet from me. She must have had some kind of housekeeper, I thought. I couldn't envision her picking my clothes up off the bathroom floor for me. 'Have a shower if you like. Meet me in the kitchen when you're ready, and we'll have some lunch.'

I did have a shower, not because I really needed one, but because showering in Rachael Carmichael's house felt like such an outrageous thing to do that I couldn't resist. There was a small pile of light-green towels in a woven basket by the bathroom door. I wrapped myself in one and stared into the mirror, trying to imagine how Rachael looked when she stood there like that. Then I realised that she probably never used this bathroom at all.

Her kitchen was a proper farmhouse one – not, of course, the kind that you'd find in an actual farmhouse, but the kind a wealthy person might design for themselves in order to feel rustic and cosy and near to the land. I've been in a fair few of those kitchens in my time. Rachael's was one of the nicest, all dark wood and huge windows, with a red Aga against the back wall and all her copper pots and pans hanging from the ceiling. She was boiling spinach when I entered, pushing a huge pile of green leaves down into the pot with a wooden spoon.

'There you are,' she said.

'Can I help?'

'No, you just sit there.' Then she turned, pointing the spoon at me. 'Actually, you can cut the tomatoes. You can do that?'

'I think so.'

She pointed to a bowl of cherry tomatoes on the counter, knife and chopping board beside them, like she'd set them out for me deliberately. 'Off you go,' she said. 'Just into halves.' Off I went, just into halves. She started pouring tagliatelle into another pot. 'So,' she said, 'you're twenty-five now.'

'Yes.'

'And how long have you known you wanted to act?'

'My whole life.'

'That's never true,' she said.

'It wasn't true for you?'

'Of course not. I was eight when I decided.'

'That's still pretty young.'

'But it was a specific moment, that's the thing. I remember it clearly. I was in a play at school, and I remember telling my mum that being someone else on that stage was the most like myself I'd ever felt, and wasn't that funny?'

I didn't believe for a second that any eight-year-old had ever said anything like that, even Rachael. 'That's beautiful,' I said.

'What was the moment for you?'

I thought. 'I don't have one. Honestly. I can't remember a time when I didn't know it's what I was going to do.'

She looked at me, then turned back to the pasta. 'Hm.'

'Not that I've had much success with it so far.'

'No, I haven't heard of you making any kind of big splash.' I swallowed the insult graciously and nodded. 'But you've worked,' she said. 'Some would call that success. It's more than a lot of people get.'

'I've hardly worked.'

'Really? Hardly?'

'A bunch of bit parts. Guest slots on different TV shows, two lines in a film when I was twenty-three.' A twinge of pain in my chest. 'Four failed pilots.'

'I would call that quite a lot.'

'But nothing real.'

'It's all real.'

'You know what I mean. Nothing like what you did. You were one of the biggest names in British television by the time you were nineteen. You'd won a Golden Globe by the time you were my age and made pretty much all of your biggest films already.'

She turned back to me, eyes gleaming. 'Is that right?'

'Not that— I mean—' *Shit.* 'You'd wrapped up most of your mainstream stuff. Other than *Traversers*.' Her shitty superhero franchise. No one quite knew why she was still attached to it; it was so incongruous with everything else about her. 'You were doing all the cool arthouse projects.'

'Everyone's career is different. And if it's really what you want to do – I mean, if it's really what you're passionate about, then you're happy with anything. You're happy just to do it at all, even if it means no one ever really knows your name.'

'Would you have been happy with that?'

Her back to me, she placed the wooden spoon down on the kitchen counter. 'No,' she said, 'I suppose I wouldn't have.'

I was done with the tomatoes. I pushed them towards her over the island (even rustic, faux-humble rich person kitchens need an island).

'Can you dice garlic?' she asked.

'No,' I said honestly.

'Never mind then, I'll do it.' She did it at the island, where I could watch her. Her knife was deft and her movements suggested experience.

'Do you do all your own cooking?' I asked. I was still expecting a household staff to appear from somewhere. I didn't believe she managed this whole place on her own.

'Always have.'

'I'm a terrible cook.'

'Well, I suppose your mother never taught you anything. She was never much good herself, as far as I remember.' Another mention of Mum. This time I could feel that we were both aware of it. The room got a little smaller. 'Of course,' Rachael continued, tipping the garlic into a pan with a little olive oil. 'I wouldn't know. She might have improved.'

'She hasn't,' I said.

Her eyes met mine over the island, and we both smiled. She turned away, walking to the other side of the room to pull open the fridge. She took out tomato puree and a tub of cream cheese. She noticed my eyes following it.

'I hope you're not weird about food,' she said.

'I don't think you're supposed to say things like that.'

She scoffed. 'Please. I was an actor in the nineties. Everyone was weird about food. I was incredibly weird about food. Still am, to a degree. But you have to actively reject things like that.'

'I don't think it's always as simple as that.'

Rachael shrugged. 'Maybe it is, maybe it isn't. Depends on the person. I'm just saying, for your sake, I hope you're not weird about food. Besides, the industry's different now, isn't it? Skinny's not so important anymore. Body positivity, and all that.'

'I don't think any of what you're saying is politically correct. And people still want you to be skinny.'

She rolled her eyes, scooping cream cheese into the pan. 'Do they want you to be skinny enough that they could snap you like a chocolate finger? Because that's how they wanted us. They want you to have butts and boobs and thighs now.'

'And waists, and cheekbones, and toned arms.'

'Eat the damn pasta, Harley.'

'I will.'

She nodded once, shortly, like she'd won that one. The spinach had disappeared in on itself, no longer visible over the top of the pan. She stirred it once, drained it, mixed it in with the tomato and cream cheese sauce. I watched her taste the pasta, dipping a fork into the pot, wrapping one long string of tagliatelle around it and nibbling it deliberately. Then she drained that too, tossing it over the sink, and mixed it all up together in her huge, shiny pan. She divided it into two bowls, ground salt and pepper over the top. For someone so small she wasn't flighty – she was grounded, very deliberate, her face still and hardly shifting. You had to watch her closely to ever see it change.

She caught me looking. 'You're a very intense person.'

'Am I?'

'You watch like a hawk.'

'Sorry. I just didn't think I'd ever actually meet you. This is very strange.' She slid my bowl towards me. I took a stool at the island. 'You must hear that kind of thing a lot.'

'People are always amazed that I'm real. It makes me feel as if I should be amazed by it too sometimes.'

I laughed, but she looked at me very seriously, like I should have known that she wasn't joking.

'Were you a loud child?' she asked, twisting pasta around her fork. 'You seem like you would have been.'

'I could be. I was always a performer, I suppose. And I didn't always have the best-behaved friends.' Julia and I between us had not had a stellar attendance record at school and were always getting thrown out of class for talking.

'I don't like loud children. I wonder if I would have liked you. Being your aunt.'

I wasn't sure what to say to that. I took a bite of my pasta. 'This is amazing,' I said, through my food.

She didn't respond, just went on eating. She looked deep in thought. We ate in silence for a few seconds. She cleared her plate much faster than I did. She watched me finish.

'You're really not a bad tennis player,' she said.

'Thanks. I played a bit in school. When did you learn? You're amazing.'

'An old boyfriend,' she said.

This was the moment. I was trying to think of the right follow-up, chewing my pasta slowly, when she spoke again.

'If you like,' she said, 'you could come back and play tennis with me some time. I don't know many people that play near my level, and I don't like paying people to keep me sharp. I'd rather have someone who was here because they wanted to be.'

'I'd love to.'

'Brilliant.' She pulled my bowl away from me as I swallowed my last mouthful. 'You know where to find me. Do you have my number?'

'I don't think so.'

She wrote it down on the back of an envelope and slid it over to me. 'I suppose you should be going.'

This was less of a supposition and more of an order. I followed her towards the front door. Raph, appearing from seemingly nowhere, trotted after her.

'Thank you for the pasta,' I said, out on the front step. 'And for talking to me.'

She nodded once, again, and closed the enormous front door. It took her two hands to do it, Raph's stumpy little tail wagging through the gap until they both vanished from view.

◆　◆　◆

We went to the Ivy Asia that evening for Carlton's half-birthday. And let me pre-empt your eye roll, your little snort of 'Ridiculous.' Yes, it is ridiculous. We have told Carlton repeatedly that celebrating a half-birthday is ridiculous. Carlton, the king of ridiculous, has celebrated his half-birthday every year since he was twelve (and a half), because being only six months away from his teenage years was a milestone worth celebrating, especially because he'd decided thirteen would be the year that he lost his virginity and therefore a monumental one, and what we were really celebrating were the last six months of his childhood. Carlton's plans to lose his virginity at thirteen were thwarted somewhat by the fact that there was only one other gay kid in his school and he had a face that, when you looked at it side on, sort of seemed to come to a point, like a salmon. Or like Phineas, from *Phineas and Ferb*. Carlton would eventually lose his virginity at sixteen in Ibiza, which isn't stereotypical at all and which we definitely never made fun of him for.

Anyway, when Carlton was twenty-two (and a half), Julia and I finally decided that a decade of half-birthdays was more than enough and we really had to put our foot (feet?) down. So we let him book his table at Nobu, but we told him that he would have to invite some other friends, because Julia and I weren't coming, and we certainly weren't going to get him presents. And Carlton said, 'Alright, fine. Suit yourselves.' Very chilled, very unconcerned. We thought it had gone quite well actually.

But then on the evening of Carlton's half-birthday, Julia and I were sitting on the edge of my parents' pool with our feet in the water, passing a bottle of Jack Daniel's between us, when she grabbed my arm, making me drop the bottle of Jack in the pool, and she said, 'Harley. Carlton doesn't have any other friends.'

Our first thought was to go over to his dad's place, but I knew that Carlton wouldn't have cancelled the table. And he hadn't. We turned up at Nobu with towel-dried hair and a watch that we'd bought on the way, and he was just sat there at the table surrounded by gold balloons, waiting for us. Calm as you like, as if we were just five minutes late. We've never tried to cancel his half-birthday again. Carlton is a force of nature.

This year I got him a ring with a ruby in it. I found it in a vintage jewellery shop. He's very into red at the moment, and rings, and also vintage. 'Har-*ley*,' he said when he opened it, which is how you can tell that Carlton is happy.

The waiter brought us free appetizers. Julia turned to Carlton. 'Did you tell them it was your birthday?'

'Of course.'

'It's *not*.'

Carlton pointed to his appetizer. 'Explain this, then.'

'How old did you tell them you were? I bet you didn't say twenty-five-and-a-half.'

'I didn't tell them anything. They wouldn't have dreamed of asking.' He looked down at the ring on his finger. 'Didn't Greg give Rachael a ruby?'

'Which show is this?' asked Julia.

'Harley's real life, Julia.'

'Oh my god, he *did* give her a ruby.' I'd seen pictures. It was a cushion-cut ruby on a gold band – she wore it long before people realised that they were sleeping together. Some people had thought at the time that it came from Adam Feldman, her first public boyfriend. Others had guessed at the truth. 'It was a whole scandal.'

'Why?' asked Julia.

'Because he was married,' said Carlton. 'And after he had announced that he was separating from his wife, and he and Rachael made their relationship public, it became apparent that he had given her the ring. But then everyone kicked off, because that meant he had given it to her whilst he was still married. She was photographed wearing it the same day that he was photographed taking the boat out with his wife and kids.'

Julia grimaced. 'Yikes.'

'How do you know so much about this?' I asked Carlton.

'Everyone knows. The ruby thing is such a *thing*. You know?'

'I've never heard any of it,' said Julia. She was flicking through her menu. 'I want a bowl of noodles as big as my head,' she said. 'I really shouldn't. I'm going to. I thought you said people didn't know much about your aunt and Greg?'

'They don't,' I said. 'They never really spoke about each other in the press.'

'Anna Bianca spoke about them loads, though,' said Carlton. 'I was listening to a podcast about it the other day. Some of the quotes she gave were wild. Have you heard some of the things she called your aunt?'

'My favourite was "that peaky-faced harlot".'

He tipped back in his chair and laughed. 'Classic. What a line.'

'Speaking of which,' I said. 'Guess where I was today.'

His eyes widened. 'Well, fuck me,' he said. 'A family reunion. How joyous.'

Julia slapped a hand over her mouth. 'No. Really? Did she slam the door in your face? Did she shout? Did she slap you?'

'Why would she do any of that?'

'Doesn't she hate your mum?'

'That's not my fault. I wasn't even born when they fell out.'

'Does your mum know?' asked Carlton.

'Of course not. Be serious.'

'So?' pressed Julia. She was looking particularly pretty that night in white lace, curls clipped back from her face other than a couple of tendrils, which dangled dangerously close to the rim of her martini as she raised it to take a sip. 'What happened?'

'We played tennis.'

'And did you bring up the film?'

'I couldn't. I wanted to. It felt like too much. But she's asked me back.'

'When?'

'Whenever I want.'

'This is amazing,' said Julia. 'This is incredible.'

'This is the best half-birthday present ever.'

'Oh, shut *up,* Carlton.'

'Really, though,' said Carlton, laying a hand on my arm, 'this is perfect. You'll get to know her, she'll get fond of you, and then you strike. When she trusts you the most. You just go in for it.'

'You make it sound like I'm going to kill her and take her place.'

He grinned. 'Is it that different?'

◆ ◆ ◆

I waited two days before I texted Rachael. It was agony. I don't even wait that long to text men. But I didn't want to give the impression that I wanted something from her. I wanted it to seem like I'd just been living my life for two days, wandering around Notting Hill, until the thought crossed my mind that, *Huh, I sort of fancy another game of tennis.*

Hey Rachael, it's Harley, I said. Rachael seemed like someone who texted with proper grammar. I considered 'Aunt Rachael', but that felt like laying it on a bit thick. *Thanks for the game the other day. Would you want to do it again sometime soon?*

She replied with a thumbs-up emoji. I'd read that one wrong, then.

We settled on Saturday. I considered asking Julia for a game the day before, to warm me up, but Julia was worse than I was so it wouldn't have been much help. Besides, I got the impression that Rachael quite enjoyed how badly she'd beaten me. Not bad enough that it hadn't been a fight at all, but a definitive victory all the same.

That Saturday, when I pulled up to the call button, she answered immediately. 'Hello?'

'It's Harley,' I said. The gate buzzed open.

She was already waiting in the doorway when my car pulled into the driveway, dressed in her tennis whites. Raph sat at her heel. She waved to me as I drove in and said something I couldn't hear. I switched the engine off, opened the door.

'Hi,' I said brightly.

'You've got something stuck to your window,' she said.

I bite dicks off, read the sticker, pressed high at the top of the window on the driver's side. It had been a present from Julia in sixth form, after I had accidentally bitten a dick (no one you'd know, just a guy from school). She'd replaced it every time I'd changed cars. 'Oh, it's just a stupid inside joke,' I said, locking the car.

'You shouldn't stick things to your window like that,' she said. 'Might obstruct your view.'

'It's high up enough, I think.'

'Hm,' she said, in that way she did.

'I've never had an issue with it.' I hoped she couldn't read it from where she was.

She looked at it for another minute, and then shrugged. 'What would I know? I can't even drive. Do you want to come in?'

She and Raph led me straight to the door of the same bathroom I'd changed in last time, on the ground floor, near the kitchen. 'Your stuff is in there,' she said.

I looked back at her, confused. I was wearing a matching coffee-coloured Adanola set and beige Hokas. 'I'm changed.'

She looked me up and down. 'Really?'

'You thought this was just my driving outfit?'

'It doesn't look like a tennis outfit. I mean, you don't look like a tennis player.'

'It probably wouldn't fly at Wimbledon, sure, but I reckon I'll be alright for a casual practice.'

'Hm,' she said.

'Raph,' said Raph.

There was a pause. 'I can change if you want to take pictures or something,' I said.

'Only if you want to,' said Rachael, and turned away. She herself was dressed in gleaming white from head to toe. Everything looked fresh out of the box. She *must* have had someone taking care of her things, I thought. There was no way it was just her and Raph rattling around in that house. 'I'll meet you out there,' she called over her shoulder.

She didn't take pictures, but she gave me an approving nod when I stepped on to the court in all white, and served with such force that if the ball had hit me in the face there would have been a crater where my nose used to be. Raph stood at the side of the court, strange bushy little tail standing straight upright. Every time I lost a point or a ball bounced out of bounds, he would say, 'Raph,' once and quite politely, like he was umpiring the game. After a while, he lay down with his chin resting on his two front paws and watched the ball, eyes moving back and forth.

We were at fifteen-seven to her when she stopped the game. 'Are you hungry?' she asked.

'Sure.'

'That's not an answer. I don't want to cook if you're not hungry.'

'I'm hungry,' I said.

'Good.'

When I had showered, I met her in the kitchen. She was alone again, cutting the leaves off tender-stem broccoli. 'Do you like fish?' she asked.

'Sure.'

'*Sure* makes it sound like you aren't sure at all.'

'Sorry. Yes, I like fish.'

She raised her eyebrows at me and turned to the pan on the hob, in which she was cooking two salmon steaks. Today's lunch wasn't going to be made up of things she'd sourced in her pantry then; she must have got these for the occasion. I was oddly touched.

'You're very polite to me,' she said. Her hair was still pulled back into a ponytail, but she had changed into blue jeans and an oversized green cardigan that came down past her knees. She'd put on a little make-up as well. She hadn't been wearing any on the court but now I could see mascara on her eyelashes, blush on her cheeks, gloss on her lips. I'd thought I was wooing her. Was she the one trying to impress me?

67

'Of course I am.'

'Hm,' she said.

'What?'

'I don't get the sense you're always this polite.'

'What makes you say that?'

She shrugged.

'Because of who my parents are?'

She laughed. It startled me. She'd never even looked close to laughing in any of the time that I'd spent with her, but her laugh sounded easy when it came, sweet even. 'Perhaps a little.'

'I'm not a rude person. I say things how I see them, sometimes, I suppose, but not in a rude way.'

'What does that mean? To say things how you see them?'

'Calling it like it is.'

She waved a hand, poking at the salmon steaks with a wooden spoon. 'I've heard the expression, Harley. People use it in different ways, though. When you say it, does it mean that you're honest and strong-willed? Or that you're blunt and sometimes cruel?'

I watched her put the broccoli into another pan, with minced garlic. I thought about how to answer.

'I am blunt,' I said. 'I don't think I'm ever cruel.'

She nodded. 'I can be cruel. I have been. I was just wondering if we were the same.'

She salted the pan. *We are the same,* I wanted to say. She wiped her hands on her jeans and bent down to fill Raph's water bowl. He'd been napping on an armchair on the other side of the room, but he jumped down at the sound of the water and trotted over. We both watched him drinking.

'How long have you had him?' I asked.

'Ten years. He was a gift.'

Jesus. Being gifted a dog like that felt more like an insult. 'From who?' I asked.

'Someone I liked so much that now I have a dog.'

I wondered if the giver had been Greg Foster. 'He's cute.'

'He is,' she said, 'in his own way. I always loved dogs. I always wanted to do a film with a dog.'

'You never did?'

She served the fish, arranging the broccoli in a neat forest beside it. I watched her take half a lemon in each hand and squeeze, one over each plate. 'You've seen all my films, apparently. Remember any dogs in any of them?'

'No. That's a shame. Maybe you and Raph should make one together.'

'I think my movie-making days are behind me.'

'I don't believe that. You're still making *Traversers,* aren't you?'

'Oh, please. I'm not sure which of those I'm even in. They just call me up now and then and I run on down and shoot a few scenes and get compensated. Keeps this place running, but it's not exactly acting. Not as I remember it.'

'Well, why don't you do something new?'

'I don't want to,' she said. 'I mean, I'd love to act, but only if I could do it with a completely different face.'

'Why? You have an amazing face.'

'I don't need reassuring. I don't mind that I got old.'

'You're not—'

'I'm older than I was, and that's enough. It's not an enjoyable thing to know that every time anyone looks at your face, they're just thinking, *You used to be young.* Not in the way parents do when they look at their children – it's in an almost accusing way. Or sad. Like, *You used to be young, and now you're just a person, aging. Isn't that tragic?* And they feel sorry for you. For aging. It's fucked up.' She clicked her fingers. 'What does Goldie Hawn say in *The First Wives Club?*' She put on an American accent. 'There are only three ages for women in Hollywood.'

'What were they?' I asked.

'I forget. Damning, though.' I nodded sympathetically. 'Don't look like that,' she said. 'You don't know. You're twenty-five, and you're not famous.'

'But I can empathise.'

'Hm,' she said.

'Anyway, *I'd* love to see you in a movie again.'

She pushed her knife into the salmon steak, and a little of the meat fell tenderly away. 'I don't know,' she said. 'Maybe I wouldn't remember how to do it.' Her eyes were cast down at her plate, but I saw it in her then. Rachael Carmichael ached after it all just like I did. Even when you'd done it – acted in wonderful films, won awards, been adored – the ache never really went away. This is what I was opening myself up to. A life of hunger. It didn't put me off. If I got to feast for just a little while, like she had, then I'd starve for decades after, and do it happily.

For just over a month, Rachael Carmichael and I played tennis twice a week. I would come round to her house and put on her tennis whites and her shoes, pick up her racquet, stand in front of her on her court and do my very best to return her serves. We would play until she was satisfied – fourteen–twenty to her, nine–fifteen to her. Once we played sixty points, all in all, and she won thirty-five of them. As I improved, she seemed to improve exponentially, which made me wonder if maybe she'd actually been taking it easy on me before, if she was even better than she'd been letting on. After we played, she would make lunch. We had seafood, sushi, salads. As time passed, the meals became more and more elaborate. Once she made a curry that took two hours to do properly, whilst I sat at the island and chatted to her and scratched Raph behind the ears. Another time we had caviar-topped scallops. Rachael prepared everything herself. I began to notice how she would remember things I told her – she made chocolate-covered strawberries, after I said that I liked them, and she started stocking oat milk instead of cow's milk for my tea, even though she never drank it herself. She would wipe the surfaces after we ate, working around me if she was finished before I was. Once, when her driveway was muddy after a storm and my Hokas got dirty, she insisted I take them off, and then she took them over to the sink and cleaned them herself. I was in awe. Rachael Carmichael, scrubbing dirt from my shoes.

I finally asked her if she had any help. 'Help?' she asked.

'You know. A cleaner, a housekeeper, someone. This place is enormous.'

'Just me and Raph,' she said.

I thought of all the times I'd left my tennis clothes on her bathroom floor and wished that I hadn't. It was so strange to think of her cleaning everything. But after a while I noticed that the house was clean in a very surface level way. It was always tidy when I came over, and there was never anything on the floor, and the vases were always full, but the windowsills were dusty. Crumbs gathered in corners, and the hob was sticky. Her coffee table had rings on it. Her backsplash was stained and her mirrors had marks. I couldn't understand it. All the money in the world, and she couldn't pay someone to scrub the dried conditioner from the floor of her shower.

My visits stretched longer. We talked about our childhoods. She'd grown up in Devon, moved to London alone when she was sixteen. She didn't like talking so much about Devon, didn't want to describe life with my grandmother and my mum. I'd never known my maternal grandmother – she'd died when I was a year old. According to my mum, the funeral was the last time she and

Rachael had seen each other. I asked Rachael if she ever missed her mother.

'Not really,' she said.

She liked to talk about London, though. 'When you make it,' she said, 'talking about the years before you made it becomes just the most fun. It isn't always fun at the time. But then you look back on that period – living with strangers, working in restaurants, being young and scrappy and just getting by – and you think, why wasn't I just *revelling* in it?'

Eventually, we got on to her career. We talked a lot about *Here's Hoping*, about how much fun it had been to act huge college party scenes with all those extras and to pretend to beat someone's head in with a hockey stick. We talked about *East of Eden* and how difficult that role had been to get right, how gratified she'd been by the awards that followed. We skirted around *Women Who Laugh at God*. Eventually I asked her if she liked the film.

'Oh, yes,' she said. 'I love it. It's a masterpiece.' Then she changed the subject.

It always felt too dangerous to bring up Greg. I could see her looking at me sideways whenever we approached him, whenever we mentioned something in periphery to him, as if daring me to cross the line. I never did, but at home, I would brainstorm ways to make her mention him. *Rachael, one of my friends is seeing this much older guy and he's being sort of strange with her. Like, she's not allowed to go for a fucking drink anymore without his permission. What would you do?*

Well, Harley, that reminds me of this time in my own life . . .

Yeah, right.

In the end, I didn't have to mention Greg at all. It was a Saturday, and she had changed from her tennis whites into grey knitted trousers and a matching cardigan after beating me twenty-one to eighteen – not a bad showing from me. My hair was wet from the shower and smelled like her shampoo. She'd made her own tomato soup and sourdough bread, and we were sitting at the island, dipping and eating in a comfortable silence.

Out of nowhere, she said, 'Harley, what are you doing?'

I looked at her. She held the bread halfway to her mouth, regarding me as she did sometimes, like I was a mildly interesting piece of art that she wasn't sure whether or not to purchase.

'I mean, generally,' she said. 'You aren't just living off your parents, are you?'

'No, I'm an actress. You know that.'

'Yes, but are you making any money right now? Are you even auditioning? I never hear you mention any auditions.'

'I'm taking a break from auditions. My therapist thinks they aren't good for me.'

'Auditions aren't good for anyone. They're fucking torture. That's the point of them, to see who survives the torture.'

'Believe me,' I said, 'I'd love to be making my own money.' I tore the bread, dipped it in the soup. Her tomato soup wasn't her best dish. It was too thick, and a little clumpy. It didn't quite move right.

'Well,' she said, 'then you should make something happen for yourself. Go out there and do something. Don't just sit here talking to me. *Think* of something.'

This moment was critical. I drew on all my acting talents to nod, nonchalant, and push my bread through the soup like I was considering this. 'I did have one idea,' I said. 'I'd like to produce a film. I've got this friend – she's a great writer, and we thought maybe we could write it together and I could get it produced.'

'Well, that's great,' she said. 'What's the film?'

'I don't know if you'll like it.' I looked up at her then. She was sitting with her hands clasped under her chin, her food pushed to one side. Her face was open and inviting, more so than I had ever seen it. If I had ever doubted it before, I knew it then. She was rooting for me, despite her distanced manner and her slight eccentricities. She cared about me. Maybe she even loved me.

'Try me,' she said.

That evening, I texted Ahn.

Rachael Carmichael wants to meet with you.

◆ ◆ ◆

Ahn was very composed as we drove up to Rachael's gate, but she didn't fool me. We pulled into the huge driveway, surrounded on all sides by those red-brick walls. The gravel crackled underneath us like flames. Ahn turned her face to the window, staring along the length of the property.

'There's tennis courts in the back,' I said. 'And a pool.'

She could hear that I was making fun of her. 'It's a nice place,' she said.

'You must have seen a lot of nice places by now.'

I could feel her resentment permeating through the back of my head as I turned to open the car door. Ahn stood a car's width away from me on the gravel, brushing off her skirt, which was black and silky and knee-length. She'd tucked a sleeveless white blouse into it with a bow at the collar. *Poor Ahn*, I thought, not for the first time since I'd met her. Her talent could be intimidating, as could her way of speaking as if she was the last word in propriety, like she was always waiting to make you check yourself. *I think we should all practise sensitivity* had been her line in class when there were ideological differences. She never meant sensitivity towards each other, but always towards someone mentioned within the debate that she considered trodden underfoot. If we were talking about *Charlie and the Chocolate Factory*, Ahn would be the one asking us to practise sensitivity towards the Oompa Loompas.

She was pretty in a very sensible sort of way, I'd always thought. Or, to put it better, she was a very sensible level of pretty. She wasn't pretty in the sort of ridiculous, obnoxiously in your face way that Julia was, and she didn't have the kind of face that made you want to keep looking at it and figure out why it was so captivating, like Rachael did. She was just pretty enough that no one could ever call her ugly, and that her face could pass completely under the radar. God, when crafting Ahn's face, had pulled back, shrugged, and said, *This seems like a good enough place to stop.*

She would never have beauty enough to show up to what might be a business meeting in jeans and a jumper. Maybe one day she would have enough money to do so, but not yet. So here she was, fooling nobody in a pricey skirt and blouse, whilst I locked my car and started over the driveway in ripped jeans and beaten-up trainers that probably cost more than anything she was wearing. It sounds like I'm being a bitch, but if you knew Ahn, you'd understand.

I knocked. Ahn, huge black handbag slung over her arm, hovered behind me. Rachael opened the door in black slacks and a striped t-shirt. Raph slipped past her, trotting over to Ahn's ankles to sniff them.

'Raph,' he said, uncertain. He ignored me completely, as he usually did. Ahn took a small step away from him.

'Not a dog person?' I asked. Her eyes, suddenly a little frightened, looked from me to Rachael, and she gave an awkwardly professional laugh.

'He's cute,' she said.

'Raph, come here,' said Rachael. Raph retreated, and Ahn tripped forward to shake Rachael's hand. There was a second where she was holding it out in empty space, Rachael looking at it, and I knew that we could all see it trembling. Then Rachael gave it a brief squeeze, before turning and leading us towards the living room.

Eyes down, Ahn turned to close the door behind us. I heard her exhale slowly. She didn't look at me.

The truth was, when I'd told Ahn that Rachael wanted to meet with her, this had been a generous use of the word 'want'. I'd kept my description of the film vague, but when I'd said, 'We want to fill in some of the gaps,' a big Greg Foster-shaped gap had floated up to hang in the air between us.

'Hm,' Rachael had said. She'd agreed to the meeting, but she hadn't offered me any dessert.

Now she sat across from us both in her beige armchair, Raph on his cushion, and waited for one of us to talk. Ahn, once she had ascertained that me and Rachael were not about to exchange any familial pleasantries, cleared her throat.

'Miss Carmichael,' she said. 'Thanks for meeting with me.'

'Rachael,' said Rachael. 'Only my lawyers call me Miss Carmichael. And other people's lawyers.'

Ahn smiled. 'Rachael. I really appreciate it. I've been so interested in your career for such a long time. You were one of the main reasons I wanted to study film in the first place.' Was that true? I examined Ahn's smiling face from the side and couldn't work it out. 'Have you ever been approached about making a biopic before?'

'No,' said Rachael, 'but lots of different people have tried to get me to write a book.'

'You've never been tempted?'

She spread her hands. 'Who has the time?'

Probably people who do nothing but hang out with their dog, I thought, but Ahn was in full business-meeting mode and probably wouldn't have appreciated the interruption. 'When you say a book, you mean people wanted you to write an autobiography?'

'On the face of it.' Rachael shrugged. 'Really,' she said, 'I think they just wanted to know the same things that you two do.'

'What things would those be?' asked Ahn, in a manner she probably thought of as very smooth and not at all transparent.

'What my marriage was like. Why I did all those weird films. Whether there was a baby.'

A slight hesitation from Ahn, before she skipped over that last sentence. 'I think those weird films were brilliant.'

'You've seen my later stuff?' Rachael nodded towards me in a way that was deliciously familiar. 'This one claims to have watched every movie I've ever made, but I know she means everything up to *Soccer Mom* and nothing beyond.'

'I've seen some beyond,' I said.

'I've seen all of it,' said Ahn. Kiss arse. 'You seem unleashed, by that point. No reserve. You can't even see you making choices anymore – you're just this force.'

Rachael was looking back at her in that way that she did, her face perfectly still. I couldn't tell if she was flattered by this or finding it all funny. Eventually she said, 'Thank you. I appreciate it.'

Ahn leant forward. 'Rachael, we'd love to—'

'I haven't offered you any tea,' said Rachael suddenly. She stood up.

'Oh, it's okay. I don't want anything.'

'I do. I want a tea. Harley?'

'Coffee,' I said. Rachael wasn't a big fan of 'please' so I'd stopped saying it, but I could see that it shocked Ahn. Rachael nodded once and disappeared down the corridor. Raph remained on his cushion with his eyes tightly closed.

Ahn turned to me with an expression so concerned that I had to laugh.

'Stop that,' she hissed, 'she'll hear you. Do you think it's going well?'

I shrugged, because I truly didn't know, and laughed again.

Ahn slapped my arm. 'You've got skin in the game too now,' she said. 'Remember that.'

When Rachael came back into the room, I took my cup from her quietly. She sat back in her armchair. 'What's the pitch, then?' she said. 'Everything from screaming infant to playing tennis with my niece?'

'No,' said Ahn. Rachael's head tilted. 'We don't want this to be a typical biopic. We want to capture a handful of years, that's all. A snapshot of nineties cinema and its influential faces. A true behind-closed-doors drama, small in scope, almost claustrophobic in its focus on its two leads, but with this whole busy Hollywood backdrop.'

'And that handful of years? That would be my marriage?'

'The filming of *Women Who Laugh at God*, mostly, but also—' She hesitated. 'The aftermath.'

Rachael nodded. 'If that's what you want to call it.'

'Public figures are afforded very few mysteries,' said Ahn. 'If we leverage yours, this will be a hit. We'd have you on as a producer of course, and you'd have final say on the script. If we're going to tell your story, we'd want to do it right.' She paused. 'I don't know what happened between you and Greg Foster. No one does. But if my instincts are right, then it's a truth that might help others.'

For the first time since I'd met her, Rachael seemed caught off guard. There was a pause as I watched her mind work. She swallowed. When she spoke, her voice was a little raspy.

'I don't want to make him angry,' she said. 'It's all at rest now.'

'I understand that,' said Ahn. 'It's your choice, obviously.'

'But—' She paused again. Her eyes were on me now. 'Often, I've wished everyone knew. Without me telling them. I've wished I could just insert it all quietly into their minds, just so they'd know, so they'd understand and they'd see him for what he is and they'd stop all the wondering. So there would be no more questions.'

Ahn nodded. She leant forward again, hand outstretched, as if she could somehow reach across the enormous living room and touch Rachael's knee. 'I think,' she said, 'that this could be the next best thing.'

'And who would play me?' asked Rachael.

I cleared my throat. 'Well,' I said, 'we were thinking, maybe, me.'

She looked at me again. And then she smiled.

Chapter Four

RACHAEL

8 August 1988

Mum bought me a chair. I was so surprised when she turned up with it, her and Elisabeth red in the face and standing on either side of it on my doorstep, that for a moment I just stared at her. I held the door and stared, and she gripped her bag and stared, and then she said, 'Rachael, this is very heavy,' and I said, '*Oh,*' and I helped them bring it upstairs. Elisabeth whined the whole way up. She's started strength training for her swimming, Mum says, but apparently she doesn't want her arms to get too big so she makes excuses to get out of it as much as she can. I could feel that she wasn't really lifting as we were going up the stairs and I was yelling at her to actually put some effort in, and she started yelling back, and Mum was going, '*Girls!*' and I guess that just shows, really, that you can be an actress on TV, renting your own place in Clapham, and everything can still be exactly the same.

That's stupid to write. It's ungrateful, and it also isn't true. Because this isn't the same, sitting here in my flat that I'm renting entirely by myself with a view of the common, and it definitely isn't the same that Mum bought me an armchair. That's something she never would have done before. She didn't really acknowledge it, just helped me place it under the window in the living room, opposite the TV set, and looked at it with her hands on her hips. 'There,' she said. 'That looks nice.'

It *was* nice. It had a grey floral pattern and a comfortable seat, reassuringly solid. It didn't go at all with my sofa, which was a plain navy love-seat provided by the landlord, but I didn't mind. They've opened a big IKEA store near Wembley Stadium and I've been itching to go. When I get paid next week I'm going to go look for a big rug to tie the room together, as they say. Honestly, I have no eye for design, but Brenda says she's going to help. I love working with Brenda. Chris is nice enough – he says he'll help me buy a car, if I want one (I don't) – but Brenda's wonderful. She's taken me shopping a couple of times now. Occasionally when we're out together, someone will stop her and say, 'Haven't I seen you on the telly?' She'll always smile and say, 'Probably!' like it's a surprise to her as well, and then they'll laugh about it together like it's all one huge coincidence.

'Is this your daughter?' someone asked her once.

'My long-lost daughter,' she said, putting her arm around me and squeezing my shoulders. Of course, we look nothing alike. She's very beautiful and full featured, a Molly Ringwald type. She's actually met Molly Ringwald. I asked her what she was like, and she said, 'Oh, Molly's a gem. A little shy, but so very clever.' I wonder what she'll say about me one day, when people hear that she once worked with Rachael Carmichael.

Of course, no one knows who I am yet. Mum made some kind of comment that she would have thought a TV star would be able to afford a bigger place. I reminded her that 'star' is a tad generous when we're still in the process of filming our first season, and anyway, this is London. I don't mind her being passive-aggressive about my flat though, not after she bought me that chair. It must have cost her some real money. That means something.

We went for a walk on Clapham Common and then I took the three of us out for dinner. Mum asked what it's been like being on a real TV set. Elisabeth acted like she wasn't interested, but I could see her waiting for me to answer. I gave the honest answer, which is that three months is long enough to get used to anything. It's wonderful, and I'll never not be grateful for it, but it's also work. It's early starts, and long days, and weighing myself, and Lili and Lola's high-pitched voices and Jerry looking up at the sky and saying, 'Think we're in for a dreary one,' like he isn't a thirteen-year-old child.

'But you love it?' said Mum, and I said yes, I did. 'Then it isn't really work,' she said. 'I hope you'll never have to know what real work is.' Like my time at the restaurant hadn't happened. Like that whole other life, with Mais and Mickey and Ha-ru, had just been a sort of dream.

I am trying to remember to write. That's why I picked up this book again – to remind myself that Mum bought me a chair, and to remind myself that I have my first film role. I hate the script, but it is a film, and it is a lead, and I'm still pinching myself so frequently I have bruises down my arm. It's called *Kiss It Better* (barf) and I leave for Brighton to start filming two days after we wrap series one of *The Avenue*. I had a chemistry read a couple of weeks ago with my co-star, Killian, and he is maybe the most boring man I've ever met in my life, but the only thing he really needs to be in the film is there, so he'll probably manage. I have three weeks left on set, so three weeks to learn my lines and brainstorm conversation topics with a man whose main interest is craft ales.

I'm not complaining. I am imbued with a purpose I have never had. When I turn up on set, I know what I have to do, and I do it perfectly. I am hilarious, charming, sweet, sharp as a knife. When I begin my long commute home from the studio, I play the scenes we filmed in my head as if I'm watching them on a screen, and I can see exactly how wonderful I look doing them. I'd talk about craft ales for a million years to stay in this world. Hell, I'd even brew them.

25 August 1988

We had our wrap party in a bar in Monument. They rented out three rooms in the basement, which wasn't dingy at all but elegant and candle-lit, and Brenda and I drank espresso martinis and strawberry bellinis and sang 'Material Girl' in the karaoke room. I tried coke in the bathroom with Marilou, a producer in her late twenties with very short strawberry-blonde hair that she gels up to look all spiky. I didn't like it very much, which is to say that it felt amazing and that scared me. I don't trust anything that makes me feel that good.

Tomorrow I get on a train to Brighton and go shoot a film so nauseatingly sweet that it tastes like strawberry bellini coming back up the other way. Today I am nursing my hangover and lying in bed with my fluffy socks on and nothing else. I'm going to put this book away for a bit and bring *Anna Karenina* with me on the shoot instead, because I think I'd like to be the sort of person that knows a thing or two about Russian literature. When you hear from me again, I will know a thing or two about Russian literature. And probably a thing or two about craft ale.

23 October 1988

The thing about craft ale is that it really serves as a blank canvas for the brewer, allowing their creativity to triumph over any puritanical ideas about what beer should be.

I'm back! I buried Killian in fourteen parts under Brighton Pier. His tongue, his balls and his kneecap I buried separately, but his eyeballs I juiced and brewed into quite a lovely batch. Several pubs in London have already ordered a keg or two and many have commented on the interesting metallic tang. None of this is true.

Let me describe to you the plot of *Kiss It Better*. Girl meets boy. Girl falls for boy. Girl nearly loses boy. Girl turns up at special spot to find boy there, ready to make amends. Kiss. Credits. Sound familiar? You got it! It's every movie. But Brighton is lovely, and I was good, and Killian wasn't terrible. When we weren't shooting I mostly managed to avoid him by burying my nose in *Anna Karenina*, which I never finished because I couldn't keep track of who everyone was. Still, Tolstoy writes some lovely sentences.

I've actually been back about a fortnight but I haven't known what to say. It's all been very strange. I watched the first episode on my own in my grey armchair, with my feet on my rug (IKEA is wonderful, and Brenda helped me pick a nice one) and a bottle of vodka. Every time I appeared on screen, I took a swig from the bottle. The awful fact of the matter is that I hated all of my scenes. Every single one. I remember how I used to play them in my head on the Tube home, but none of them looked anything like how they had on the Tube. I wasn't charming or sweet or sharp – I was as blunt and rusty as the cleaver I used to hack Killian to pieces (still a joke). By the time the credits rolled I felt like I was knee-deep in a nightmare. *How* had no one told me how bad I was? No wonder I'd spent so long getting rejected.

I waited for someone to call and tell me. When the phone started ringing, I didn't pick it up. But when my answering machine started going off, they were all messages of congratulations. 'You were incredible!' from Brenda. 'Always knew you had it in you,' from Robb. Mum called and waxed lyrical about Chris: 'Isn't he good-looking? And you were wonderful, Rachael, of course.' I didn't call any of them back, but sat very still, listening to the messages, not sure how to feel. A few minutes passed, and then the phone rang again. I let it go to voicemail.

'Hi, Rachael,' came Ha-ru's voice. I buried my face in a cushion. 'I just wanted to ring and say that I watched you on TV. You knew I would. And you were so amazing, really. I couldn't believe it was you. I don't know how on earth you did it—'

I left the room after that. I couldn't bear it. He didn't sound at all like himself.

When the reviews came out the next morning, I thought the whole world must have gone mad. *Newcomer Rachael Carmichael showcases some impressive comedy chops,* wrote the *Telegraph.* That's the only one I'm going to write out, because obsessively writing out your own good reviews seems like something Killian would do. Maybe I was good. I still don't think so, and I haven't been able to bring myself to watch another episode since, so I suppose I'll never know if I improved. But I still don't understand it. It's like getting away with a crime in front of the whole world, even after you waved right into the security camera with a sack full of money over your shoulder.

One thing I do know: I will never watch myself act ever again.

They keep asking me about Anna Bianca. It's my own fault, really – I got my first few requests for interviews the day after the episode aired, and I don't have a manager or a publicist or anything like that yet so it's just me, replying to emails, saying yes to everything. I'll sit on the phone all day or run to seventeen coffee dates on opposite ends of London if it means this show does well. I had an audition for another film the other day, a high-school comedy, and the script is a few cuts above *Kiss It Better* but still not the calibre of work I'd like to be doing one day. I want casting directors to read a script and immediately say to each other, 'Oh, we *must* try to get Rachael Carmichael for this,' and for that to happen they have to know who I am.

So, I'm doing press. Some of it's set up by the studio and their press team, but most of it's just personal requests. I've listed my favourite songs for *Jackie* magazine, done a back page interview for *Seventeen,* spoken to journalists from a ton of different newspapers for a ton of different 'Introducing' features, and even gone on the radio. The radio is where I messed up. It was *Good Morning* on Radio 4. I was so excited when the request came in. We talked about the show and how funny it was that I'd been working in a Korean restaurant before I got cast – very, apparently – and then John Hamilton said how much UK families had responded to me as a role model. 'She's a nice girl,' he said, about Jill. 'Still a teenager, but not the kind of teenager we're starting to see crop up in other media – just a nice, old-fashioned British teenager.'

I knew that's what people would see when they looked at Jill. And I was fine with it, because I knew that if they saw me as a nice, old-fashioned British teenager then they would see me as someone respectable. I want to be respectable. I want to play respectable roles and work with respectable directors, and not give anyone reason to question my talent.

I was unwise enough to say some of this on air.

'I take my responsibility as a role model very seriously,' I told John Hamilton. 'I want teenage girls all across the UK to look up to Jill and I never want to do anything that threatens the integrity of the character. I'm sure I'll make mistakes, and Jill will too, but I know the two of us will always try to be on our best behaviour.'

Everyone in the studio laughed. 'Well, that's good to hear that we're not going to have another Anna Bianca on our hands.'

'Oh, absolutely not,' I said, in mock horror. More laughter.

'You're not a fan, then?'

'I wouldn't say so. Listen, I'm sure she's very talented. But I think when the clothes start coming off . . . it says something.'

Why did I say that? I wondered on the Tube home. Did I really believe that? I know I don't want to do nude scenes, but I'm not morally opposed to them. I'm not a Mormon. I still don't really know where it came from, only that I wanted to make sure they saw Anna and me as very different kinds of actresses. Which we are, because Anna Bianca is a child star turned bimbo most famous for partying, glamour modelling and getting naked in shit romantic comedies. Anna Bianca and I will never have anything in common.

Still, I shouldn't have said that thing about her clothes coming off. Someone asked her to comment on it on a red carpet a few days later. 'Who even is she?' asked Anna Bianca, button nose crinkling, tossing her blonde hair back. Tabloids were divided on whether this response was completely classless or totally hilarious.

The trouble was that a few days later, someone asked me if I would ever pose for *Playboy*.

'No!' I said. 'Absolutely not. How tacky.'

And, of course, who was the *Playboy* cover star that month?

Robb thinks I should hire a publicist, and I must say, I'm inclined to agree with him.

21 February 1989

Where to begin? We've been renewed for season two and start filming in a couple of weeks. Elisabeth has given up swimming and is trying modelling, which is going terribly, as far as I understand. I wonder if she feels the same anxiety around it that I did, or if it's totally different for her, now that I'm bringing money in. Maybe she doesn't feel any pressure at all. Maybe she's doing it purely for the love of the thing.

There's too much to say, really, always. Mum calls, and asks for updates, and I don't know where to start there either. I put this book down for a few months and it's like I live an entire life. I never used to have this much to say. I used to write in my diary to complain about Mais stealing my shoes. Someone could come in and take half my wardrobe away and I'm so all over the place that I probably wouldn't even notice.

I've been cast in *Girls Getting Ready* as Sandra – seems I'm destined to forever play characters with old-lady names. The shoots for the film and *The Avenue* season two overlap a lot, so I'll be running around like a headless chicken over the next several months and probably will forget to write for even longer this time. Also down to the final few for this thing called *Elsewhere,* which is a slightly sappy script about two long-distance best friends. *Yawn,* but Robb thinks it'll be a winner at the box office so fingers crossed.

We're filming *Girls Getting Ready* in London at least, so the commute should be easy. It's one of those all-in-one-night type of comedies, like *Sixteen Candles,* and it stars this Asian-British actress called Amy George who I met for the first time at the table read the other day. She's chatty – very – but not in an annoying, insipid way. She asked me about my favourite films and when I said I liked horror she went on and on about her obsession with *Christine* and *Cujo,* and we've agreed to go and watch *Pet Sematary* together. Adam Feldman was standing a little way off and he looked quite shocked. Maybe American girls aren't so into Stephen King.

'Want to come?' I asked him.

He jumped a little, like he was embarrassed to be caught eavesdropping. 'Sorry?' He's very polite for an American boy, Adam. Maybe he's putting it on because he feels a bit conspicuous with his accent.

'Do you want to come to the cinema with us in November?'

'Oh,' he said. 'Horror isn't my thing. I went to see *A Nightmare on Elm Street* when it came out and ended up running out of the movie theatre in front of all my friends. Pretty embarrassing for a sixteen-year-old boy.'

'Very embarrassing,' I said, and Amy laughed and swatted my arm. She's very pretty, and Adam's very pretty, so she's probably got her eye on him. I think he's interesting. Imagine you're a twenty-one-year-old boy and you've just been in your first big blockbuster and the entire world wants to sleep with you, and you can't stand there and look someone in the eye for more than a second or two without blushing.

19 April 1989

Adam Feldman has been famous for a year longer than I have. Actually famous too, not just British TV famous. He's an international star, cheesy as it sounds. *Dragonborn* was one of the biggest films of last year. When we go out together in London – me, him and Amy – people take our picture. They run up and ask for autographs. Girls are so forward with him. He apologises to Amy and me, but we find it quite funny. She's quite known as well, of course, after the *Bye Bye Birdie* remake. People will notice Adam first, and then Amy, and then they'll turn to me and say, 'You're Jill!' Adam does quite a good impression of the way they slowly realise.

Of course, the three of us becoming friends has been the best thing for the film, because we get photographed so much together that people are becoming quite curious about what's going on. Mum even called me the other day to tell me that she saw my picture in the *Daily Mail*. It was the three of us coming out of the Wag in the early hours of the morning, arm in arm. Apparently the *Daily Mail* had speculated that we were in some kind of 'bisexual group', which my shiny new publicist Gemma had shut down immediately

('Amy, Adam and Rachael are three single friends enjoying the London nightlife').

We all had a lot of fun with that article on set the next day. 'Do you think they're implying that we're *all* bisexual?' asked Adam. 'Or just you girls?'

'Bisexual men?' I said. 'I think that's a bit beyond the *Daily Mail.*'

He laughed. It's very easy to make Adam laugh. You just have to say something that has the cadence of a joke and he'll laugh. I suppose American girls aren't that funny.

When I was in Amy's trailer later that day, she said, 'You know, Rachael, you can ask if you want me to give the two of you some space.'

I looked at her. She was doing her lipliner in the mirror, even though Make-up has told her a thousand times not to bother. It just gets wiped off and redone. She caught my eye. 'What do you mean?' I asked, but she wouldn't say anything else about it.

24 April 1989

In an incredibly juvenile turn of events, it turns out that Adam has told Amy that he *likes* me, but has asked her not to tell me. You know, like we're nine. She's all aflutter about it. I'm trying hard to focus on making a good film, or at least a middling one, and would rather not acknowledge the situation. Our nights out have been put on hold for now.

On the set of *The Avenue* today, Brenda asked if I'm tired, running between projects like this. I ended up telling her everything. That's what happens with Brenda – she asks you one innocuous question and suddenly you're spilling your guts.

'Well,' she said, 'Rachael, do you like him?' And before I had a chance to reply, she said, 'Because I do think it would be lovely if you found someone you liked.'

'I'm too busy,' I said.

'Yes,' she said, 'that will always be true. But don't let it stop you.'

5 May 1989

Last week, we took Adam to see Christine. It's a plan we floated a while ago – Amy's friend runs a horror film club at this fancy screening room in Soho and Adam had confessed that he'd never seen or read any Stephen King. Amy knocked on the door of my trailer and said, 'You know, Rachael, we did say we would.' And there was Adam, standing a little way off, grinning sheepishly with his hands in his pockets. So I couldn't exactly say no.

Amy's pager beeped as our taxi pulled up. She looked at it and gave a little squeak – she's up for this big action film and she'd been waiting for news for ages.

'Shit, I don't have any change,' she said, rifling through her wallet. Adam gave her his and she ran off down the street to find a phone, leaving Adam and I stood on the side of the road, not looking at each other. He was in a thick jumper and a jacket, even though it's not cold. He's used to LA weather, he says. He couldn't look more LA, either. Tall, blond, tan. It's sickening.

'I thought you didn't want to come,' I said. He looked confused. 'I thought it was too scary for you.'

'Oh, it definitely will be.'

'Are you going to run out of the cinema again?'

He grinned. 'Maybe. I guess we'll find out.'

He's just so nice, Adam. That's the thing about him. You say something funny, and he laughs, even if it's not that funny. You say you're not feeling well, and he looks at you, all concerned, and asks if he can get you something. You say you're cold and he stands in front of you and rubs his hands up and down your arms, vigorously,

91

until you can't help but smile. He's so nice that you can't ignore it. And he shouldn't be that nice. No one who's rich and good-looking and a movie star from LA should be that nice.

'If you get scared,' I said, 'then you can hold my hand.'

It's embarrassing to even write it out. But I said it. He laughed, and then he looked at me, and then he said, 'Okay.'

Amy ran back up the street towards us. 'They want me to read *again*.' It'll be her ninth time going in. 'This'll be going on for years at this rate,' she said gloomily.

I put my arm around her and said, 'You'll get it. You can out-act anyone.' She can, which is the depressing thing. But there's not many parts going for girls who look like Amy, and the few good ones that exist are incredibly competitive. We all know it's not all about the talent, but Amy knows it more than Adam and I do.

She perked up when we got to the cinema. It was just the three of us in this lavish room, with red velvet chairs and little tables and small green lamps glowing very dimly. I sat between Adam and Amy, holding a carton of popcorn between my knees. I offered some to Amy but she said she couldn't, which suddenly made me feel as if I shouldn't be eating salted popcorn. When your appearance makes you money, eating certain foods feels like spending that money, sometimes more of it than you can afford. I put it down on the floor.

When I sat up, my hands in my lap, I felt Adam reach over and take one. The feeling of his skin on mine was so unexpected that I felt my spine go stiff for a moment, like it had turned into a broom handle. I let him slide his fingers in-between mine. I turned towards him, curiously. He felt me looking. 'What?' he whispered.

'The lights haven't even gone down.'

'I'm scared.'

I snorted.

'What?' asked Amy, on my other side.

'Adam's ridiculous.'

She couldn't see our hands, intertwined on the other side of my leg, but she laughed quietly. 'You're both ridiculous,' she said. 'Ridiculous kids.'

That's what it felt like we were being, holding hands in the cinema before the trailers started. Ridiculous kids. I hadn't got to be a ridiculous kid in a very long time.

3 August 1989

Malibu is just like all the films and books tell you it will be. Houses on the coast with waves that spray against your windows and girls in bikinis playing beach volleyball and sipping Diet Coke. It feels like being in an advert. Their accents are so loud and nasal, and they talk like they don't care who might overhear them. You'll walk along the beach past a group of girls lying on towels and they'll be going – 'Oh my god, and his *thing* was bent to one side! Like, leaning right over! I was, like, where is that going to *fit?*' Loud as you like. My Anna Bianca misstep has led many to believe that I'm a prude, but I love when girls talk like this. Especially when they do it loudly.

Adam found this book in my suitcase and took it out.

'What's this?' he asked.

'My diary.'

He flicked through the pages, not really reading but with this grin on his face like he was expecting me to lean over and snatch the book out of his hands. I just watched him.

'I don't really write in it much,' I said.

'Why not?'

'Too much to say, too little time.'

'Am I in here?'

'I honestly don't remember,' I said, but then he started reading for real and I did reach across to take it from him. He grabbed me around the waist and flipped me over so that I was lying under him. He kissed my cheek, my nose, my forehead.

'I probably don't want to know your first impressions of me,' he said. 'You can be pretty blunt.' He kissed my mouth. 'I guess it doesn't even matter now.'

My first impression of Adam: sweet, a little shy, obnoxiously good-looking, talented but not quite as talented as his legions of fans would have you believe.

Here is Adam as I know him now. He always sleeps with his arms around something. When he naps on set, it's a coat or a cushion, or once a hairdresser's dummy that we planted in his arms. He woke up pretty quickly, but not before he'd curled himself around it for a few seconds and buried his face in the hair. Amy and I nearly pissed ourselves. In London, he is always cold, always in multiple layers, but in Malibu he never sweats. When we run along the beach I am always dripping from my forehead and top lip, but he is cool as anything, turning his head and running backwards for a while to laugh at me. He tans as easily as he laughs. He has a little sister, like I do, only his is an angel and he'd do anything to bring her the world on a plate. He is twenty-one years old and perfect. I don't say that with any kind of bias. Scientifically, Adam is perfect.

He told me he loved me during his last week in London, as we lay curled up together in my bedroom in Clapham. We were about to wrap *Girls Getting Ready*. I still had a week left, but the next day I knew we were going to hear, 'That's a wrap on Adam Feldman!' It's something I have never felt before, that aching desperation to hold on to someone. To keep them in that bed with you, breathing in tune, and never be anywhere else. I have always wanted to keep moving forward. To be everywhere else. This, and everything that accompanies it, scares me. And it scared me when I heard myself say, 'Wait for me, and I'll come with you.'

'To Malibu?' he asked.

'Why not? I've got three months before I have to be back in the UK. And you don't start the next *Dragonborn* until September.'

I called Mum. I felt as if I had to tell her, especially because I'm still sending cheques home in the post to her and Elisabeth, and she would probably have noticed if they started arriving from America.

'Hm,' she said.

'What?'

'I'm just not sure.' I could tell she was doing her lipstick from the way she said the words.

'Going out, are we?'

'Jesus, Rachael,' she said. 'Are you my maiden aunt?'

'I just asked.'

'Yes, I'm going out. I have a date.' She waited. When I didn't respond, she sighed. 'Things are really turning around for us at the moment and I don't see why you have such a hard job being happy for us.'

'Who's us? You and Elisabeth?'

'You forget,' she said. 'You forget the years I put in supporting your dreams, driving you to and from auditions, letting you move out when you were sixteen . . .'

I could have said, *Oh, you let me, did you?* Instead, I said, 'I want a break. I think I deserve one.'

'I just don't think it's the right time. You've got so much going for you right now. And people forget about you like *that* in your business.'

'I'll still be on TV. People will still take my picture and ask me to talk on the radio. None of it's going anywhere if I take a few months off.'

'Hm,' she said. 'Well, I'm sure you know best.'

'I do.'

'We've worked so hard for this. I guess I'm just cautious. But I trust you, of course.'

'Listen. If I'm with Adam Feldman, my profile will only go up.'

'That's true,' she said. She sounded instantly brighter.

Anyway, it wasn't three months in the end. It was two. The *Elsewhere* shoot got moved up, and I have a meeting for something called *Always, April,* where I'll yet again be playing a schoolgirl. I did think I'd be getting better films by this stage, but I'll keep taking what I can get and hope that people keep thinking of me. I already know that *Elsewhere* is going to be a painful shoot. Not just because it's the film taking me away from Adam, but because the whole thing is about being far away, and we've been so deliciously close for three months.

There's not that much to say about complete happiness. It's so boring to write about. You're just in a kitchen baking cookies with someone's sister, and someone comes up behind you to kiss you on the neck, and you go wash your hands and change for dinner, and you and someone go and eat in a restaurant on the beach and talk about the future and how quick it's all moving, and how nauseatingly happy you both are. And I love him, so much, more than I ever thought I could love anyone, which is what everyone says and you never think they mean it until you feel it too. But I miss being scrappy and alone. Strange, isn't it? I do, though. I miss fighting my corner. I miss being interesting.

I cried at the airport, when he hugged me goodbye. I boarded the plane in dark sunglasses, like movie stars do, which did make me feel quite interesting. But the further we flew away from Malibu, on and on through a starless night, the more I felt as if I'd left a different version of myself behind, crying in Adam's arms. She wasn't Rachael Carmichael, the actress. Rachael Carmichael didn't enter herself in surf and bikini contests as a joke and sit at the kitchen table helping her boyfriend's sister with her English homework. That was Adam's Rach. I worried then that she and I would never be the same person.

But I am in love. It's something that I cannot deny or outrun. And if I can get a job that brings me back to LA, I will take it, whether it's a smart decision or not. I will run back into his arms. Just watch me. Just try to stand in my way.

1 September 1989

Kiss It Better premiered three days ago to a collective response of 'Huh. Alright.' Which is honestly better than I was expecting. I saw Killian at the premiere. He was wearing a very nice, very ordinary suit and he has grown his hair out a little so he no longer looks like he just left the military.

He said, 'How have you been?'

I said, 'Good, thanks, and you?'

He said, 'I'm good. You?'

'I'm good, yeah. Been up to much?'

'Bits and bobs.'

We somehow managed to sustain that conversation for five minutes before we were whisked away to take photos and then ushered into the theatre. The whole premiere was pretty anticlimactic. Sitting through the film surrounded by all those people was agony. I don't know how other actors stand it. Afterwards I got very drunk at the posh hotel reception with two of the marketing girls and threw up in the seat pocket of my taxi. Do you know how humiliating it is to have to call your publicist and tell her that she might want to get ahead of a story about you throwing up in someone's seat pocket? Because I do.

Cried on Brenda today. We had a cast dinner in the West End to celebrate season two ending and she asked how *Elsewhere* was going.

'I hate it,' I said.

'Why?'

'Just do.'

'She misses her boyfriend,' said Jerry. He's fourteen now and covered in spots but he thinks he's a young Marlon Brando. I've run into him in clubs before, always with a much older girl on his arm. Once I told the bouncer to kick him out and he got a red card on set the next day because he didn't want to do any scenes with me. His mother is a nightmare, so it isn't entirely his fault. She's always too dopey to know how to handle him. Still, Jerry's a hard person to feel sorry for.

'Well,' said Brenda, as I shot Jerry a glare, 'that's understandable. He's a lovely boy. I'm sure he must miss her a lot too.'

I just burst into tears. She hugged me to her without a word, the reassuring leanness of her pressing me in on myself, making me small and breathless. Jerry must have been shocked because he didn't say anything, only stood there with horror on his spotty face.

I called Adam and told him that I'd cried in front of all my colleagues.

'That's really embarrassing,' he said, and laughed.

'Don't be mean.'

'Don't worry, Rach. I've done it too.' He's filming the next *Dragonborn* right now. 'We're doing the kiss tomorrow,' he said. It's going to be a big moment between his character and that of co-star Holly Joel. 'I know it's work,' he said, 'but I don't like the idea of kissing someone who isn't you.'

'That's the job,' I said.

He was quiet for a second. 'Don't you wish sometimes that we were just – I don't know. Bankers? Cashiers? Running a cat charity together?'

I thought of the restaurant. Ha-ru. The way he cooked without even focusing on what he was doing, laughing at something I said. The way he looked at me when he knew I was leaving.

'No,' I said. 'I'll never wish for that.'

9 October 1989

Went for lunch at Le Caprice today with Robb and my manager, Eloise. This is how I know that I'm starting to be one of Robb's more important clients – even a year ago, the chances of his agency paying the bill at Le Caprice for me would have been as small as the chances of him giving me a kidney. Today he ordered the salmon fishcakes for both of us without batting an eyelid.

'How's *Elsewhere* going?' he asked, tucking in.

'Alright.'

'You wrap on Sunday? And then three weeks off before *Always, April,* right?'

'Right.'

'There's lots of buzz around you and Adam Feldman,' said Eloise. '*Girls Getting Ready* looks set to do very well.'

I shrugged. 'It wasn't planned.'

'I know. A cheerful coincidence.' She cleared her throat. 'Rachael, we know you've been keen to get back to LA.'

'I'm not thinking of pulling out of *Always, April,*' I said. 'I'd never do that.'

'We know. You're a consummate professional, Rachael – no one could ever claim otherwise.' Robb winked at me, mouth full. 'Actually, we were looking beyond that. We've had some very strong interest in you for Frank Yachty's new film. How's your American accent?'

My heart skipped a beat. 'Not bad.'

'Well, they'd get you an accent coach. It's this coming-of-age piece about a girl who falls in love with her best friend's boyfriend.'

I pulled a face.

'I know, but it shoots in LA, and they're very keen on you.' He looked to Eloise for help.

'You could be a real icon in this space, Rachael,' said Eloise. 'You could be the British Molly Ringwald.'

'I'd rather be the British Sigourney Weaver.'

Robb laughed. 'Well, that's a tall order. I reckon we start with what's in front of us and work from there.'

I tore off a very small piece of bread from the basket in the centre of the table and put it in my mouth. 'Sarah Griffin's casting something,' I said, around the bread.

Eloise looked quickly over at Robb, who was still focused on his fishcake. 'Where did you hear that?' she asked.

'From Amy George.' Amy's making a movie with Bruce Willis right now. His daughter and Sarah's are in pre-school together. 'Amy's already read for it. She says the script is amazing.'

'I don't know,' said Robb. 'I mean, Sarah's very talented, but is it the sort of stuff that you do?'

'Not right now,' I said. 'But it could be.'

I like Sarah Griffin's stuff. She made this film about a woman who catches her husband cheating and, instead of telling him, sets out to sleep with every other available man on their cul-de-sac. People hated it, but I think it's genius.

'And it's a college film,' I said. 'Not high school.'

'Is it that different?'

'It's a step in the right direction.'

They could both see I wasn't going to let it go, so they agreed to get me the script. I still had to ring Robb a few times before it actually happened. It's sat on my bedside table now. *Here's Hoping.* The title couldn't be more apt. I'll let you know when I'm done.

◆ ◆ ◆

I'm done. And HOLY SHIT.

Here's Hoping is everything I've been waiting for. Dark, very sharp, strangely funny. A revenge drama with hockey sticks, frat boys and bitchy teenage girls. It's a strange script, and I can see that

100

people might hate it. But I can also see that they'll be interested in it. Especially with me in the lead role.

They get *The Avenue* in the US now. Out there, I epitomise the English teenager. Well-spoken, well-behaved, clever and funny and not afraid to stand my ground, but never too outrageous. This would surprise them all. *Watch Jill from* The Avenue *murder a collegiate athlete.* They could sell the film on that alone.

It was late, but I called Robb. 'I want it.'

'Okay,' he said. 'Let's make it happen.'

14 November 1989

Robb told me they were planning to start production for *Here's Hoping* in September next year. 'It'll be a tricky negotiation with *The Avenue* but since season three hasn't officially been confirmed, we reckon you'll have some sway if you ask for a longer hiatus. It'll be a short shoot – Sarah hasn't got a ton of funding.' He paused. 'You're sure about this?'

'I'm sure.'

'I won't lie to you. You'll be a hard sell. This isn't how people see you. It's not what they think of you for.'

'I know,' I said. 'That's why they'll cast me.'

I went into the audition with that attitude exactly. I walked into the room and looked them in the eyes, two tired men sat behind a table, and I thought, *You're about to be so surprised by me that you'll have to cast me. You won't see this coming, and neither will anyone else.*

The first read went well. Robb rang to say that they wanted me in again. The second time I read for four people, then six. Then Robb called to say that Sarah was flying in to see me read.

'That's a good sign, right?' I asked.

'A very good sign,' he said. 'Whatever you're doing, it's working.'

Sarah Griffin is a very tall woman with straight features, long limbs, red hair tightly pulled back. Even sat down, she towered over everyone else at the table. She stood up to shake my hand and I felt like a small child.

'Hi, Rachael,' she said. 'It's great to meet you.' I still haven't got used to being greeted like that in the audition room. They never used to say things like that to me.

'Good to meet you too. I'm a huge fan of your work. And I'm not just saying that in an ass-kissing way – I genuinely am.'

She looked a little taken aback by that, but she laughed. 'That's good to know.'

I stood in the centre of the room. There were eight people at the table this time, all of them eager. You can often tell, when you get a few rounds into an audition process, whether the people have been told you're one to watch. 'Whenever you're ready,' one of them said.

Sarah read with me, holding the pages just under eye level so I couldn't see her face much. When I was done, she put her pages down on the table and rested her chin on the back of her hands. 'You have a very interesting face,' she said.

I wasn't quite sure if that was an insult, so I cocked my head to the side and said, 'Tha-anks.' Everyone behind the table laughed, including Sarah.

'I mean it,' she said. 'You almost don't have to do a lot with it. Your face is just very interesting to watch. Am I the only one?' she asked the rest of the table, and apparently no, she wasn't. 'You did great,' she said, standing up again to shake my hand. 'Can we have you in for a chemistry read?'

Robb rang me that same afternoon. 'They want you in for the read on Thursday,' he said. 'You have it, by the way.'

I had to sit down. 'What?'

'You've got it. Sarah loved you. I don't know what you did in there, but you seduced them all.'

'Then why am I going in to read again?'

'They're testing actresses against you. You're the one they're certain that they want.'

'Me?'

'You,' he laughed. 'You could sound less surprised.'

I wasn't surprised, really. I knew how good I'd been.

We'd be rehearsing from August in LA – five months in total for rehearsals and the shoot. *So much time.* I couldn't get off the phone with Robb fast enough. I dialled Adam's number with shaking fingers.

'Rach!' he said, when he picked up. He said it like a call from me was the best surprise he could have ever got.

Being in love is not always convenient, but it is frequently wonderful.

'I have some good news,' I said.

Chapter Five

HARLEY

Our first interview with Rachael didn't go very well.

'Alright,' said Ahn, clearing her throat. She was bent over her phone on the coffee table, opening the voice recorder. 'Alright, okay, testing . . .' She played it back. Her voice somehow sounded even more awkward and stilted coming out of the phone. She deleted the test quickly, as if embarrassed, and started a new recording. 'Alright,' she said again, sitting back. She tugged the sleeves of her jumper over her wrists. It was a black V-neck, the kind Julia and I had worn as part of our uniform for seven years, and she'd paired it with a pair of black trousers that had a pleat running down the middle of each leg, ironed so sharply as to be almost threatening. Rachael and I were both in jeans. 'We've started recording,' said Ahn.

'I can see that,' said Rachael. Raph sat at her feet, on a small green cushion, and glowered.

'So, could we start at the beginning? When did you first hear about *Women Who Laugh at God?*'

'Through my agent.'

'Did you read the script?'

'It would have been a challenging shoot if I hadn't.'

'I *meant*,' said Ahn, colouring, 'did your agent give you the script?'

'No. He mentioned the project in passing and I thought nothing of it. Then Greg came to visit me on set.'

'What set was this?'

'*Here's Hoping.*'

'Oh, I *loved* that film,' I said, before I could stop myself. Rachael smiled.

Ahn cut across. 'Were you enjoying the shoot?'

Rachael raised an eyebrow. 'It was fine.'

And so we continued. Poor Ahn tugging desperately on every thread that came to mind and coming up empty. Rachael just sat there, looking at her. Slowly, we established the facts of the situation. Greg had visited the set of *Here's Hoping* because his wife was a part of the cast, but he had been impressed with Rachael's performance and scouted her for his new film. This she told us very coolly, careful to add no details that might colour the scene at all. We had gone in hoping for an insight into the real Rachael Carmichael and had come away with a paragraph of her Wikipedia page.

On the way out, she touched my arm. 'Harley,' she said. 'Do your parents know you're doing this?' Her voice was hushed, like they were in the next room.

'Not yet,' I said. I hadn't figured out how to bring it up with my mum. The last time I'd been over, she'd asked if I'd found new work and I'd just said, 'Oh, there's interesting things in the timeline.' It's fortunate for me that I have parents who aren't too concerned whether or not I have employment at any given time.

'Do you promise?'

She said it eagerly, rather than anxiously. It had the effect of making her sound younger than she was. 'I promise.'

'Keep it that way,' she said. 'Please.'

'Okay,' I said, swallowing back the curiosity. The effort of doing so was immense. There was hardly a thing I wanted more in the world than to grab her by the wrist and shake it and say, *What happened? Why do you hate her so much?* But what we were doing here was so delicate. I was afraid to push her too far. She looked at me, and she saw the question anyway, written all over my face.

'I'm just not ready,' she said.

'For them to know?'

'For everything,' she said. 'The whole can of worms.'

This was brutally intriguing, but she let it hang, and showed us out without another word.

We drove home in relative silence, until Ahn said, 'Is she always like that?'

She was facing the window. I wondered if she was hiding her face.

'She can be,' I said. 'Sometimes she's very standoffish. But I've known her to be very chatty before too.'

'Well, what makes her open up?'

'I don't know, really. It depends on the day.' It had all felt so clinical, us sitting there rigidly in her living room, Raph watching us like a jealous boyfriend. 'You know,' I said, 'she likes to chat whilst she cooks.'

'Okay.' Ahn looked across at me. 'That's something. Can we get her cooking? Is it strange if we just invite ourselves for lunch?'

I considered it for a second. Then, at a red light, I took my phone out, ignoring Ahn's protests.

Thanks for today. Any chance we could come round on Thursday? I really want to learn to make that cauliflower curry.

'Are you trying to kill us?' asked Ahn, over honks from behind us.

I hit the accelerator. 'I'm *trying* to make a film.'

My phone pinged. One hand on the wheel, I picked it up. Ahn snatched it out of my hands. 'I'll read it. Could you just drive, please?' She looked at the screen. 'She's a very fast responder.'

'She always is. I think she's lonely. What did she say?'

'*Alright sure,*' read Ahn. 'To the point.'

'She's always that as well.'

'Maybe we're barking up the wrong tree here. Maybe she just doesn't really have much to say.'

I thought about those afternoons I'd spent in Rachael's kitchen, the dance it felt like we were doing around the letters in Greg's name.

'She does,' I said. 'I know she does. She's just waiting for some-one to listen.'

When we arrived on Thursday, she greeted us like she hadn't remembered we were coming. But she had all the ingredients laid out on the kitchen island, ready and waiting. The chickpeas were already out of their tin and rinsed, sitting shiny and clean in a little silver colander. The cauliflower was laid triumphantly on a small blue plate. There were fresh daisies in the vase on the table. I caught Ahn's eye.

'Are you both helping me cook?' asked Rachael.

'Just me. Ahn's going to record.'

'Alright.'

'We don't have to start yet, though,' I said, as Ahn took a seat at the counter. 'Shall I wash my hands?'

'Always a good idea.'

'And then what do we do first?'

She talked me through chopping the garlic, keeping it all pressed together between my thumb and forefinger as I diced it finely. I asked her when she'd got so good at cooking. 'I've lived alone since I was sixteen,' she said. 'There's only so long you can survive on shit food.'

'But you were making good money by your early twenties. Didn't you go out to eat?'

'Oh, yes. I went to lots of nice restaurants. But after a while, silly as it sounds, a nice meal at home becomes a novelty.' She shook her head. 'I sound seventy-five.'

'No, I get it.'

'You don't,' she said. 'No one who hasn't been as famous as I have really understands.' I stepped away from the garlic and she examined the chopping board. 'That's good. You've got a knack for it. Some people can't get the hang of garlic.'

'Was Greg a good cook?'

She didn't reply. I looked up from the garlic to find her shaking her head at me. 'Don't think I don't know what you're doing,' she said.

'I'm just asking a question.'

'You're thinking you'll catch me off guard.'

'Is it working?'

I swear I saw her smile. 'Greg never cooked a day in his life,' she said. 'And I only cooked for him once. He had a chef. I bet your parents have a chef, Harley, don't they?' I nodded, even though technically she's a housekeeper. 'Yours?' Rachael asked Ahn.

Ahn shook her head. 'My parents are teachers,' she said.

'Can you cook?'

'Mostly quite basic stuff, but yes.'

'What's your heritage? Korean?'

'My parents are Chinese,' said Ahn carefully.

'I only ask because I love Korean food,' said Rachael. 'I wondered if you knew how to make any. I worked in a Korean restaurant when I first lived in London. Fell head over heels with the owners' son.' She clicked her fingers at me. 'Slice the onion. You can do that?'

'I can do that. What was the son's name?'

She shook her head. 'I forget. He was beautiful, though. I've got some diaries somewhere. I'm sure I wrote about him – I must drag them out. I'm sure there's so much I've forgotten.'

Ahn was watching Rachael with a gleam in her eyes. She was probably imagining the kind of place in Fitzrovia that this chatter might buy her. She reached out and placed her phone on the table. 'I'm going to start recording,' she said, 'if that's okay.'

Rachael looked at the phone. 'Alright,' she said. 'Harley, are you done with the onion?'

'Almost.'

'Had you been in love many times before Greg?' asked Ahn.

'Once or twice.'

'Do you remember what kind of things you would have written about those men – or women – or whoever – in your diaries?'

Rachael shook her head, her back to Ahn. 'Not sure I even still have them. Maybe I'm getting mixed up. Harley, pass me the chopping board.' I did, and she tipped the onions into the pan. 'Come stir,' she said.

I stood at the stove and moved the wooden spoon through the onions as Ahn tried again. 'Is there someone you remember as the love of your life?'

'Not particularly,' said Rachael. 'Harley, come chop this ginger.'

It was hopeless. All the chat had gone out of her. On our way home, Ahn wondered whether she was the problem. 'Maybe she just doesn't like talking to me,' she said. 'You try.'

* * *

The next week, we made paella, and I got Rachael talking about how she'd been campaigning for more interesting roles, how she pursued *Here's Hoping* even though her team weren't really sure. She ranted about how tired you start to feel of playing teenagers when you're becoming an adult, how you know you should be grateful for any work you get because you could never work again and at the same time you're aware that people say you should be smart about your career, you should be selective, you should have a plan.

'What was your plan?' I asked. Ahn set the phone on the table. 'Also, we're going to start recording now, if that's okay.'

'Oh,' she said. 'I just wanted to make films I liked. Harley, come cut this chorizo.'

'What kind of films did you like?'

'Horror, mostly.'

'Was that why you wanted to work with Greg Foster?'

'Part of it. Can you stir this?'

'It's no use,' I said to Ahn in the car. 'It's the phone. The minute you get it out, she clams up.'

'But she knows this is for a script,' said Ahn. 'I mean, she knows we aren't just talking. Why would she agree to it if she doesn't want to be recorded?'

'Maybe it's involuntary. Maybe this is why she never does interviews.' I realised Ahn was staring at me. 'What?'

'Green light.'

'Shit.' I bolted forward.

Ahn clutched her seat belt with both hands. 'You're a terrible driver,' she said. 'How did you get your licence?'

'I took the test at my aunt's place in the Highlands. Super easy to pass up there.'

'Of course.'

'Can you write shorthand?'

She scrunched up her nose. 'A bit. I'd have to practise.'

'I'd get practising, then.'

She groaned. 'You really think there's no other way?'

'I think if we're going to do this at all, it's going to be on her terms. And she has to feel like she can just talk and talk and it won't all live forever.' I turned a corner, hands crossing over on the wheel. 'I get it,' I said. 'Someone like Rachael, you'd never know who might sell your words and where they might go. It would make you paranoid.'

'I'm worried we'll miss stuff,' said Ahn, 'if we have to write it down by hand.'

'We'll get enough.' Besides, I thought, we almost didn't need to record her. I never forgot a word Rachael said to me.

Twice a week for three months, Ahn and I went to Rachael's house. She got the Tube to my place in Notting Hill in the morning, and we would drive an hour and half to her place on the edge of Aylesford. In the mornings, we rarely spoke. We took it in turns to choose the music (me) or the podcast (Ahn), occasionally pausing to talk through our plan for the day. Ahn would sit there and flex her fingers, like she was warming up for an Olympic sport. It drove me nuts. I couldn't say anything, though, because if I did, she would ask, 'Do you want to do the writing, then?' And I obviously didn't.

We started with her and Greg's first meeting, on the *Here's Hoping* set. We talked about her relationship with Anna Bianca, her audition for *Women Who Laugh at God,* the first time she'd realised that Greg's interest in her might extend beyond the professional. We talked about her first boyfriend, Adam Feldman, their very quiet break-up, and the first rumours that began to circulate around her and Greg. Most of what we discussed was, at first, surface level, but Rachael brought it all to life, gave us details we didn't have: about the way Greg spoke to her in that audition room, the way he was with his first wife, the things she felt about it all. It was like watching a film you'd seen many times before, shot from an entirely new perspective.

Heading back to London, Ahn and I would talk almost the entire way. She would read through her notes aloud and we would decide which topics we wanted to return to. Rachael was much freer in her speech now that we weren't recording her, but there was still a sense that she didn't entirely trust us. She could be suddenly dismissive, breezy in a way that felt unnatural, occasionally annoyed without warning. She was testing the waters, as were we, both parties feeling out how much the other was willing to give, and how much they wanted to take.

'I'm going to start pushing her,' said Ahn, on our sixth drive to Rachael's. We had the beginning of her and Greg's story pretty well fleshed out, but we still hadn't really been able to get too far into what the marriage itself was like. 'I need you to help me. We need an answer to that baby question. Was there one? What happened to it? If it all comes to nothing then it comes to nothing, but if not—'

'I don't want to spook her.'

'For god's sake, Harley, she's not a horse. She's a grown woman and she's been in this industry for a long time. She's done a lot of press. We might piss her off, but we aren't going to spook her. She's not fragile.'

'We don't know that,' I said. 'We still don't really know what it is that she's been through.'

'What she's been through might turn out to be a fairly ordinary celebrity divorce.'

'I don't know.'

'We need to know early on if that's the case. If we're wasting our time here.'

'I think there was a baby.'

'Well,' she said, 'I guess I hope there was.' Quite the admission from Ahn, with all her principles. 'It would make a better film,' she said, as I grinned at her.

'I think there must have been one. I think that's why she's so strange. I mean, she practically treats that dog like a person.'

'I don't know,' said Ahn again.

'We can get her to talk. I can get her to talk.'

When we got to the house, Rachael didn't reply to our knock, but the door was open. I pushed on it. Ahn grabbed my arm. 'Don't.'

I shook her off and walked in, closing the door quietly behind us. 'Rachael?' I called.

'In the kitchen,' came the response.

She was putting candles on a cake. I stood in the doorway, dumbfounded. It was a big two-layered chocolate cake with a thin layer of icing and raspberries arranged in a circle around the top. Ahn hovered behind me as Rachael struck a match and lit the candles – four of them – shaking it out when she was done.

'It's your birthday this weekend,' she said, 'isn't it?'

'How do you know that?'

'Well, I remember when my sister had you.'

Had she kept it in her calendar all these years? What had come over her that she'd felt the urge to bake me a cake? Ahn gave me a small poke between my shoulder blades and I walked forward into the kitchen. Rachael watched me. I wasn't sure if I should hug her. 'Thank you,' I said. 'That's so thoughtful.'

'You're turning twenty-six,' she said.

'Yes, I am.'

'A bit older than I was,' she said, studying me, 'when the film's set, but you look young. You'll be twenty-seven by the time we film, which I guess is pushing it a little more, but I still think you'll be fine.'

'I don't know what to say.'

'Blow out your candles,' she said, 'and then say, "Can I have some cake?"'

Laughing, I blew out the candles. 'Can I have some cake?'

'You can. Ahn?'

'Yes, please,' said Ahn, taking a stool at the island.

She cut us both a slice. 'Now,' she said, 'what did you want to talk about today?'

Ahn looked over at me, urging me to begin so that she wouldn't have to. Rachael caught it.

'You girls have been very patient. This isn't easy for me. I'm grateful.'

Ahn cleared her throat. 'I'd like to talk about the audition. If we can.'

Rachael frowned, digging a fork into her slice of cake. 'We've been over that.'

'Yes,' said Ahn, 'we have, and we can move on if you feel there's nothing more to say. But I think there is.' Her cake lay untouched in front of her. 'You've told us that you went in, that Greg had you read for him, that he was intimidating, that he obviously took his work very seriously.'

'Yes,' said Rachael. 'That's all true.'

Ahn was flipping back through her notes. 'You said, *He made me feel young.*' She looked up. Rachael sat there, eating cake. 'What did you mean by that?' she said. 'I've been wondering about it. Because when people say that it can be something good or it can be something bad. Which was it for you?'

Rachael closed her eyes. 'It wasn't really either. He just awed me. It was a little scary, and it made me feel a little childish, but I could see how young I was to him. How right at the beginning I was, how full of promise.'

'Did you need someone to make you feel young? At twenty-two?'

She smiled. 'In this industry, you spend your life trying to be the most grown-up version of yourself. But from the moment you age past nineteen, you need people to make you feel young. Greg saw how young I was, in every way. It was both a positive and a negative for me.'

'Did you feel sexualised by Greg?'

'By that point I couldn't remember the last time I'd stepped into an audition room and not felt sexualised.'

'Really?' I asked. 'What kind of things did they say to you?'

She waved her fork. 'Oh, it wasn't so much what they said. Although they did say things, and not infrequently. But even when they were completely professional, I still felt it.' She rolled a raspberry off the top of her cake. 'There's a way men behind a table have of looking at a young woman. You walk in the room, and you know those are the first two things they've seen about you. That you're young, and you're a woman. Even if they're incredibly enlightened, even if they immediately catch that thought in their own minds and punish it, they've still noticed those two things. Of course, you could say that that's true of any one person looking at another person. We always notice those things we tell ourselves we're too enlightened to notice: sex, age, race, beauty, body. But when a young woman stands in front of a panel of men, they know there are things that they could do to her, and they know they could do those things because she's young and she's a woman. There are ways they could portray her, speak to her, control her behaviour, criticisms they could make of her – and yes, violence they could enact against her, even if they never would. She knows it too. That knowledge doesn't hang in the air in the same way when the person in front of the table is a man, or even a woman of a certain age. When it's a young woman, there is an othering that happens.' She

115

looked at Ahn, scribbling away. 'I wouldn't worry much about getting that all down,' she said. 'Others have said it better than I have.'

I took a bite of my cake. Ahn was still scribbling. We were quiet for a second, waiting for her to catch up. Then I asked, 'Do you think Greg knew that you felt sexualised?'

Rachael smirked.

Ahn had looked up from her notebook by that point and caught it too. She met my eyes for a second, cautiously curious, as Rachael dug her fork back into her cake. 'What is it?' I asked.

'I shouldn't smile. It isn't funny.'

'It's alright.' Ahn was poised with her pen against the page, her back very straight. 'He knew, then?'

'He knew,' said Rachael. She hesitated, and then she said, 'He took photographs of me.'

'Oh.' I didn't want to jump to conclusions. 'Were you—'

'Naked,' she said. She popped a raspberry into her mouth. 'Completely.'

Ahn's pen was very loud. I tried to ignore it. 'Wow.'

Rachael nodded, chewing the raspberry.

'Did you— Was that— I mean, did you know? Beforehand?'

'That he would want to photograph me naked?'

I nodded.

'Of course not,' she said. 'I had never done nudity. I was still on *The Avenue*. *Here's Hoping* was the edgiest thing I had ever done. Of course I didn't know. I would never have walked into the room.'

'So, how did you react? I mean, what happened?'

'He said that Abi was quite a sexual part, and they were playing with the idea of a nude scene. He said it in this very abstract way, as if the scene wouldn't even involve me, so I responded in a very abstract way, said that it sounded interesting. He said, *Of course, if we go down that route, we will need to know what we're working with before Abi is cast*. And I still didn't quite think he was getting at

116

exactly what he was getting at, so I just agreed. Before I knew it, he was asking, did I mind? And getting the camera out. And gesturing to me to take off my top.'

Ahn drew a breath.

'I'm sorry,' I said.

'I don't want to hear you say you're sorry,' said Rachael curtly. 'Not at any point in this process. It's just annoying.'

'Okay. Fair enough.'

'What happened to the photographs?' asked Ahn.

'He kept them.'

'Did he hold them over you?'

'Not in any especially obvious way. But there was an understanding.'

'Jesus,' said Ahn, shaking her head.

Rachael paused. Then she pushed her plate away from her and stood up. She took a plastic cover from a cupboard below the island and placed it over the remains of the cake. 'The thing is,' she said, as she carried the cake over to the fridge, 'in doing this, I want to be very sure that it's all accurately conveyed. I don't want melodrama. I don't want to villainise. The photographs, for example – I'm happy for that to go in the script, but only as it happened. I don't want a scene where Greg walks up to me on set and goes, *Remember, if you don't do what I say then the whole world will see those pictures of you,* because that simply wasn't how those things happened.'

'I hear you completely,' said Ahn. 'It's of the utmost importance to us that your truth gets told in the most authentic way we can manage.'

Rachael looked at me, as if asking me to translate.

'We'll listen to you,' I said.

◆　◆　◆

'I feel like we're doing a wonderful thing,' I said to Julia and Carlton at my birthday drinks, three margaritas deep. I'd told Mum that I didn't want a party this year – disappointing for her, as it deprived her of a month of bullying a party planner, which is one of her favourite things to do. I didn't have time to think about myself. Rachael was my entire world.

'It's looking promising, then?' said Julia.

'It's not just that. We're letting this woman tell her story. We're not allowing some powerful man to take away her voice. It really feels like we're doing something good for the world.'

'Well,' said Carlton, 'always nice when charity pays.'

The photographs were just the tip of the iceberg. The next time we visited, she told us about a time on set when she wasn't making the exact face Greg wanted her to, and how he'd physically intimidated her. Another time he called her a *lifeless, sexless product of suburbia.* ('I'm still not entirely sure what he meant by that,' shrugged Rachael.) So much about how she was treated on set made my skin tingle. I could practically feel Ahn's stomach turning. 'I have never been someone who cries easily,' said Rachael, and I believed her.

'And even after all that,' I said, 'you still fell in love with him?'

'When people who you consider to be geniuses are terrifying,' she said, 'you start to see it as part of their mystique. If they weren't so terrifying, they wouldn't be quite so genius. You realise that you would miss being afraid of them.'

'Did you miss that?' asked Ahn. 'After you were married?'

'No,' she said. 'I never stopped being afraid of Greg.'

'Never?'

'Never.'

'Are you afraid of him now?'

Rachael's hands, shredding lettuce, slowed.

She told us about the first time they slept together, when Greg called her, full of longing, and told her that he had to have her. 'I'd never felt desired like that,' she said. Then the months of gifts and secrets and arguments that followed, whilst Greg deliberated over his divorce. He would tell her he was definitely going to do it, and soon, and then the next day she'd have a new piece of jewellery and Greg would tell her that it would be a while yet, because his wife's aunt was ill, or they'd just paid to redo the downstairs bathroom, or their kid had been cast in a play. 'I never met his kids, by the way,' she said. 'Still haven't.'

'They weren't at the wedding?' asked Ahn.

'Please. No one was at our wedding. We went to Vegas and came home and that was the whole romantic affair. What a fairytale.'

We heard stories about Greg cheating, about the things he threw at the walls, about the times he struck her across the face, the one dark night when he kicked her in the ribs as she lay curled up on the carpet. 'Because I'd spoken to an old boyfriend,' she said. 'We were just friends. Greg was out every night with a different girl. But god forbid I wasn't entirely his.'

It was hard not to say that we were sorry. It was hard not to ask if she was okay. When she told us these stories, the clock wound back, and she was younger than we were and in a relationship with a man two decades older than her, a man who was her superior in every way that mattered. As sorry as I felt for her, the stories also made me frustrated. For so much of my life I'd held on to this idea of who Rachael Carmichael was. She was strong, and independent, and totally dedicated to her craft and her career. She'd made missteps in love but she'd come out of them stronger. She was intimidating. She didn't suffer fools.

'I can't understand it,' I said to Ahn on the way home.

'People stay in abusive relationships all the time,' said Ahn sagely. 'We can't judge.'

'I'm not *judging*, before you and your high horse break into a canter. I'm just saying, she wasn't stupid. Surely you know, at twenty-three, that dating your very influential, much older, *married* boss is probably not going to work out well for you? Especially when he treats everyone on set like they're mud under his shoe.'

'I guess maybe that's it,' said Ahn. 'Maybe you want to think you might be the one person that gets treated differently.'

On Rachael went. Every visit gave us another piece of Greg Foster. He drank too much, but it was kept quiet on set. He liked to take his leading ladies out for private drinks, to bring the right kind of 'energy' out of them. He wouldn't let Rachael and his first wife be in the same room. Once, their paths had crossed innocently at a party, just after the wedding. They didn't even speak, but Greg saw them at the bar at the same time. He'd pulled Rachael to the side and slapped her across the face in front of a roomful of people.

'How did that never get reported on?' asked Ahn.

'You'd be surprised what happens at these parties that never makes it into the press,' said Rachael.

I always watched her very closely as she told us these stories, to see how she felt about them. She was cold. She liked the act of storytelling, but she kept herself separate from the subject material, relating it all like it had happened to someone else. I mentioned it to Ahn. She'd noticed it too.

'I understand it,' she said, 'but I wish she'd let us peek behind the curtain just once. It would help me so much in the writing of the thing.'

Ahn had begun work on the script by that point. It was just a scene here and there, just dialogue that came to her, most of which she insisted she would scrap. But the few pages she did give me to read electrified me. Ahn was irritating, but she was undeniably talented. She was writing me a part that would sink its incisors into me and never let me go. I barely even thought about my old roles anymore. Even the Lover left me alone, slinking back into crowded café backdrops, fading away like the end of a song. I was over her. I had a new great romantic obsession.

'How do you think that went today?' Rachael asked me one Wednesday. I was helping her stack the dishwasher and Ahn was in the toilet. She passed me a plate to rinse, rings clinking against the back of it. Her voice was level, but she gave the question weight.

'You're doing great,' I said.

'I don't mean it like that. Is she happy with the story?'

'We're very happy with it.'

'You're not the writer, Harley,' she said, taking the plate back from me.

'It's a great story.'

'Sometimes I feel like she's still waiting for me to get to the good stuff. I'm not sure exactly what I should be giving her. I've made a lot of films, but I've never written one.'

She bent down to put the plate in the dishwasher. I watched her, unable to see her face. This project meant a lot to her. It was a nice realisation. And it made sense – the idea of a man like Greg Foster getting his story out in the world first must have been a daunting one. He was the kind of man who would be believed. Rachael, past her physical prime and coming off a string of unhinged indie horrors, did not have the same credibility in the public court.

'I think you should talk about the baby,' I said.

A long, awful pause. She was still squatting beside the dishwasher. She stood up, passed me a glass to rinse without looking at me. 'The baby,' she said. 'Of course.'

'I think if we really want this project to succeed, you need to talk about it.'

'There's nothing to all that,' she said. 'Just a stupid rumour.'

'Well, maybe we could dig into where it came from.'

She stood still, not looking at me, clutching a dirty fork.

'I understand it's probably a difficult thing to talk about,' I said gently.

'Not at all,' she said, coming to life again. 'There just really isn't anything to say.'

That night, Rachael called me. She never did that. It was the early hours of the morning, as dark outside as London ever gets. I half expected her to be having some kind of breakdown when I picked up the phone. Instead, her voice was very low and calm.

'Harley?' she said.

'Hello.'

'Did I wake you? You sound tired.'

'It's okay. Is everything alright?'

A pause. 'Could you come over?' she asked. 'Bring Ahn.'

'Right now?' She was silent. 'Is there something wrong? Rachael?'

'There's something I want to talk about,' she said. 'I'm ready now. But I'm worried I might change my mind.'

My heartbeat sped up. 'Okay,' I said. 'Sure. We'll be there. Can you wait a couple of hours? It's not the quickest drive. But we'll be there.'

'I'll see you soon, then.' She hung up. I prayed to God this wasn't a passing mood, and that she wouldn't fall asleep before we made it to Aylesford. I called Ahn.

'Harley? What's happened?'

'Rachael called.' I was pulling my jeans on. 'She wants to talk about something.'

Ahn groaned. 'Right now?'

'I think we should go. I— I don't know. She sounded weird.'

'What kind of weird?'

'I just think we should go. Maybe I'm wrong, but I think this is something we need to hear.'

A moment's hesitation, and then Ahn groaned again. 'Alright. I'll be with you soon.'

She'd still found time to change into a shirt and slacks when she showed up, but she wasn't wearing make-up and her hair was down. She slept for part of drive. I played one of her podcasts about the paths we take to success (I was actually starting to get into it).

'We often don't know what success looks like for us until it happens,' said the host. *How true*, I thought. I never would have guessed that success begun with me and Ahn Lu driving to Kent in my Audi TTS at two in the morning.

Ahn woke up as we came off the M2 and blinked at me, aggrieved, like it was my fault she wasn't in bed.

'What's the plan?' she asked, as we turned into Rachael's road.

'I'll talk,' I said. 'You just get it all down.'

She rolled her eyes.

'What?'

'You're practically bouncing in your seat.'

'I'm excited. Aren't you excited?'

'I'm tired,' said Ahn. She looked it. She hadn't taken yesterday's mascara off properly – there were traces of it under her eyes, and her eyelids hung low.

'This could be the thing that makes the film. We want to shock people, don't we? This could be our shock factor.'

'I never said I wanted to shock people.'

'No, I'm sure you said "provoke" or something along those lines.'

'I don't sell films on shock factor,' said Ahn primly.

'Oh, *please*.'

'What?'

'You write biopics. About famous people. Famous dead people, mostly. You just made a Janis Joplin film. You don't want to shock people?'

'I choose my subjects based on my personal connection to them,' said Ahn.

'Right, and yet to my knowledge you've never written a screenplay about your grandma.'

'My grandma's dead.'

'Ah, so she only ticks one box.'

'You know what, *Harley*—' hissed Ahn, but I leant out of the car window and drowned her out with the buzz of Rachael's intercom.

She was waiting for us in the doorway, Raph at her heels. Her hair was twisted back into a clip and her face was bare. She was in a set of striped pyjamas which were slightly too long for her, draping over her wrists and ankles. She looked very small in the doorway as she waited for us, the hall dimly lit behind her. The driveway was quiet and dark. I kept my headlights on as I pulled up. When the light washed over her, she didn't blink. She went pure white. Like a waxwork. There was absolutely nothing in her face.

We got out of the car in silence. As we approached the doorway, Rachael turned and led us down the hall, too far ahead for us to speak to her without raising our voices. A single lamp was on in the hallway, stood on a small table of dark wood. In the living room there were no lights switched on at all, but about eight or nine candles, a few very large, all plain white. They were dotted around the room on mantelpieces and side tables and windowsills. One very big one stood on the floor by the foot of Rachael's armchair.

'Sit down,' said Rachael, letting us move past her into the room. 'I'm going to get a drink.'

'What the fuck,' breathed Ahn. I shushed her. 'Is her electricity out? Or did she light all these candles just to set the mood?'

'She's dramatic,' I whispered. 'She's an actress.'

'Sure, but come on, Harley. This is bizarre.'

'You were the one saying we shouldn't judge.'

She blinked. 'Yeah. I did.' But she wouldn't stop staring around her as she sat down, brow furrowed, like she was trying to solve a puzzle.

Rachael appeared with a glass of wine. She didn't offer Ahn or I anything. Her hand was shaking slightly as she raised it to her mouth to take a sip. We watched her cross the room and seat herself in her armchair, right on the edge of the seat, back rigid. Raph settled himself on the footstool.

'Sorry to drag you both out here,' she said.

'It's fine.' Next to me, I felt Ahn slide her notebook slowly out of her bag.

'There's something we haven't spoken about.' Rachael took another sip of wine. 'I didn't think I would bring it up. But the more we've talked . . .' She leant forward. Suddenly it was like her expression had cracked open, and I could see everything she was feeling. I felt myself leaning towards her too, like we were two magnets. 'This has been healing for me,' said Rachael. 'I've almost forgotten this is a story that people are going to see. It's been healing just to talk about it all. And I thought, maybe I'll just tell you this last part of the story, and we can all decide together whether or not it goes in the film.' She waited, searching our faces.

'Okay,' I said. 'We can do that.'

She nodded, looking down at the glass in her hands. She nodded again.

'It's your story,' I said.

She smiled, raising the glass to her lips. 'If I haven't said it before,' she said, 'then let me say it now. I'm so glad you knocked on my door.'

This is what she told us.

Less than a year into Rachael's marriage with Greg, she was told that she couldn't have children. They'd been trying for a while by that point, not having any success. She knew that Greg wanted another child. 'But I couldn't give him one,' she said. 'I just wasn't able. And he resented me for that.'

'He told you that?' I asked.

'Yes, he did.'

'What did he say?'

'Oh, lots of things. How he'd thrown his life away for a fresh start and now he couldn't get it. How he wished he'd known this before tying himself to me. I reminded him that he clearly didn't consider the ties of marriage too strictly binding and we had a huge fight. That's one of the times I was most scared of him.'

'Shit,' I said. Ahn was hunched over her notepad, trying to make herself small, trying to make her pen quiet.

Rachael cleared her throat. Raph looked up at her. She reached down to scratch his head, with so much tenderness that my throat constricted. When she straightened up, she seemed to be thinking. She said the next few sentences very clearly and slowly, like they were a thesis statement.

'Greg Foster left me because I couldn't have children. That's the man he is. That's what I want the world to know.'

We went through it all – every conversation, every fight, every step that Greg took towards the door. What she described was stunningly, cinematically devastating, but her voice was clear, as she said it. Her hands were still. We sat in reverent silence, dumbed by the sight of her in candlelight, telling us a story. At the end of it, Ahn looked through her pages of notes and let out a long breath.

'And you're sure you want everyone to know about this?'

Rachael nodded. 'Yes. I'm ready.'

'Well,' said Ahn, 'I can't tell you how much I appreciate you trusting us with your story, Rachael. Truly. It's an honour.'

She paused, and I guessed that she was waiting for me to pile on the praise. I was mute. There had been a part of me that had become truly convinced that Rachael Carmichael had given up a child. I had at least expected that she'd terminated a pregnancy. The secret had added to the fog that surrounded her, the mysticism. Infertility hadn't even crossed my mind, and it felt so tragic and unexpectedly real that I couldn't quite bring myself to look at her.

But I knew that she was looking at me. 'You still haven't told your parents anything?'

I shook my head.

'Good,' she said. 'Thank you.'

'They'll find out I'm doing this eventually, you know. Probably before we start filming.'

'I know,' she said. 'But I want to keep Elisabeth out of this.'

'Why?' There didn't seem like there could have been a better time to ask the question, open as she was in that flickering light.

She was quiet for a moment. 'There's history there,' she said. 'I'm sure your mother will tell you all about it one day.'

Jealousy, Mum had always said. A resentment for all that she had that Rachael didn't – a husband who stayed, and a child. It made more sense than ever. 'I'm not sure that she will,' I said.

Rachael shrugged. 'Maybe not. Maybe some things are better left in the past.'

As we drove home, Ahn read back over her notes. She made a strange sound in her throat, and I looked at her and saw that she was wiping away a tear. She caught my eye and turned her face quickly away.

We did three more interviews with Rachael. We settled back into our usual dynamic – Rachael in her kitchen, keeping herself busy, me coaxing stories out of her, Ahn scribbling away. She didn't speak much more about what she'd told us that night, and we didn't push it. 'I can try,' I said to Ahn, 'if you need more,' but she said that she didn't. There were specific gaps she wanted to fill, by that point, just a few final pieces she wanted to slot into place. When we left that third interview, no one said it, but there was a sense that we were at the end.

Ahn called me later that evening. 'It's done,' she said.

I'd been trying to read. I was grateful for an excuse to stop. 'Just like that?'

'I just sat down to write a bit more and it all sort of poured out of me.' I was too excited to roll my eyes at this. 'Harley,' she said, and then she paused. 'It's really *good.*'

I was fizzing all over. 'Send it to me.'

'I'll email it to you now.'

An agonising few minutes before the *ping*. When it came, I grabbed my laptop and jumped over boots and coats to get to my printer. It was one hundred and seventy pages long. *Jesus, Ahn,* I thought. We would have to make cuts. The printer managed to produce about two thirds of it before the paper in the paper tray ran out and I was scouring my flat for more sheets of A4. But when I had it in my hands, the weight of it was exhilarating.

I sat in bed with the screenplay and a red pen. After a while, I put the pen down. She was right. It was excellent. A little meta, in the way that it explored the film-making process, but not so much as to be obnoxious. Certain scenes from *Women Who Laugh at God* were recreated entirely, but that worked as well. Rachael playing Abi, summoning power on the days she didn't feel like she had any, summoning rage lingering just below the surface, summoning a lust and obsession that was in the early stages of ruining her life. It was wonderful. I called Ahn and woke her up.

'Sorry,' I said. 'I just had to tell you. You're incredible.'

'Thank you, Harley,' she said, and she sounded like she wanted to cry.

Chapter Six

Rachael

6 October 1990

Dear Diary,

Today I found you in that little compartment in the top of my suitcase that unzips so that you can put stuff in there and then immediately forget about it.

Adam said, 'Oh, it's your *diary*,' and held it up, grinning, like the two of you were long-lost friends. I let him read all the bits about him. He kept laughing out loud, which I thought was a tad disrespectful. 'Why do you never start with "Dear Diary?"' he asked.

'Because I'm not eleven.'

'You should. It's not a diary if you don't.' He gave it back to me. 'You haven't written anything in ages,' he said.

I explained that we have an unspoken agreement, you and me. I may not, with everything I have going on all of the time, always remember to write in my diary. Sometimes I might leave you with nothing for months on end. But I'll check back in eventually and you'll be pleased to see me. There are no expectations in our relationship.

So, hello. This is me, checking in. I'm in LA filming *Here's Hoping.* We're mostly shooting in the Warner Bros lot but we've been doing some stuff on the UCLA campus. Adam's making a revenge flick with Scott Bailey right now – he's doing a lot of his own stunts, which he loves – and we're both working long days, sometimes meeting for lunch when we can, often eating Chinese in bed at 10 p.m. and debriefing quickly before we set the alarm for 6 a.m. and get ready to do it all over again. Both our shoots have been fun so far, at least. He's mostly running around and shouting generic action phrases, and I've been soaking in every minute that I get to spend around Sarah Griffin. I'm convinced she's a genius.

Adam came to see me on set, on one of his rare days off. Sarah let him sit and watch for a while. On our drive home, he told me that this was going to be the film that made my career. 'I mean, properly,' he said.

'People are going to hate Florence.'

'Oh, they'll *hate* her,' he agreed. 'That's what's so fantastic about it. But people will love her too. I love her.' I'd had fake blood on my forehead today. There was still some left in my eyebrow – he reached across at a red light and gently scraped it off. 'You're so angry,' he said. 'Like, terrifying, viscerally angry. Where does that come from? Who are you so angry at?'

'I don't know. It's not me. It's just the character.'

'It's the bomb,' he said. It always makes me laugh when he goes super-American like that. 'You're gonna astonish them all.' Then he grinned. 'I know someone you're angry at.'

The one thorn in my side on the *Here's Hoping* set is Anna Bianca. We found out she'd been cast as Liddy about a month after Robb had called to say that Florence was mine. I was immediately nervous. Anna had made it quite clear in the media that she was not my biggest fan. I also couldn't understand it, because – as I said to Robb – I really didn't think that she could act.

'She plays the kind of roles you play when you have big tits and people can point to the screen and go, oh, that's Anna Bianca.'

'Give her a chance,' said Robb. 'This might end up being a great opportunity for a reconciliation.' (Hah.)

In hindsight, I should have had more faith in the great Sarah Griffin. Anna is not a wonderful actress, but she is perfect for this role, for exactly the reasons that I whinged down the phone to Robb. She is the woman who will always be asking for it, in everybody's eyes. Having her play the victim of an attempted sexual assault, one who is dismissed by everyone until Florence takes justice into her own hands, was a clever move. And it was also a clever move to play us against each other. People are going to have a lot to say about the choice.

I still can't stand her. I even tried to extend the olive branch. Her first day on set, I knocked on the door of her trailer. She opened it and didn't say anything, didn't invite me in. She just stood there with her arms folded over her cropped purple cardigan, enormous tits rising and falling in her tank top. 'Hey,' I said. 'Sorry to bother you. I know we've had a bit of a weird introduction to each other, but I'm sorry about all the stuff I said. I was just being mouthy.' I held out a hand.

She looked at my hand. Then she rolled her eyes, wordlessly shook it, stepped back inside her trailer and closed the door.

I rattled off the whole interaction to Adam in bed that night. 'I mean . . .' he said, and let it hang.

'What?'

'The stuff you said about her was pretty uncalled for. I know,' he added, pre-empting my interruption, 'she said some shitty stuff about you as well. But from her perspective, this pretty young newcomer taking shots at her, unprompted, and then rocking up on a film with her and trying to act like it's all water under the bridge . . .'

'I don't know what else I'm supposed to do.'

'Just give her time,' he said. 'Bake her some cookies or something.' I don't bake. I brought her chocolates, though. She took them, and she said thank you, but she didn't smile. She continued to ice me. We had our first scene together, and she wasn't as bad as I'd thought she was going to be, but when I tried to compliment her, she acted like she hadn't heard.

Then, about a fortnight into her time on set, a piece came out in *People*. She'd done a phone interview with them after casting was announced, and of course they'd asked about whether she was excited to work with me.

'Not really,' she said. 'We've not met in person, but I know people that have worked with her before, and apparently she's pretty unreasonable on set. I don't know, you star in a sitcom back home and I guess you think you're a hot commodity. But coming to LA from England . . . it's kinda like she just fell off the back of the hay cart. This is Hollywood. I'll be interested to see what happens when she starts throwing her weight around.'

My publicist called and explained that we were going to decline to comment. ('It's classier.') Someone from the studio rocked up to my trailer to tell me that they would be doing damage control in the media. ('Rachael Carmichael is a consummate professional and a delight to have on set.') Nothing they say will matter. When word starts to get around that you're difficult, that shit sticks to you. Anna swanned on to set that morning with a vanilla latte and a smug grin. From that moment on, unless we were forced to interact, we ignored each other entirely.

It was her husband that made things worse again. He came to pick her up for lunch one day and stopped in to say hello to Sarah. They're old friends. When they hugged hello, they did that swaying side to side a little, hand on the back thing that old friends in Hollywood do. He took off his sunglasses. He was a good-looking man, mid-forties, at least a decade older than Anna. They've been together since she was about my age. Two kids. I know because

Lana in Make-up told me afterwards. He put his hands on Sarah's shoulders.

'Can I stay and watch?' he asked in his Californian accent.

'You want to see Rachael threaten Thomas?' She grinned. We were filming a scene early on in the film when Florence tells one of the frat boys what she's going to do to him and he treats it as a joke. My co-star Thomas is nice enough and a pretty-decent actor, but he has a habit of doing press-ups between takes. He snapped to attention when Anna's husband walked in, though, hovering close to him and Sarah like he was waiting to be introduced. I stayed seated in my chair, flicking through my script. Any friend of Anna's was an enemy of mine.

But I watched. In my periphery I saw him look me up and down.

'Absolutely I do,' he said, with a laugh.

It's not a difficult scene, that one, but it is intense. A really well-written scene can be one of two things, I'm discovering. Either it puts pressure on the actor to rise to the level of the material – *Here's Hoping* definitely has a few of those – or it essentially does the work for the actor. It gives the actor all the tools they need to look talented without them needing to actually exercise much talent. Anna's husband is a director and a screenwriter, so I wasn't expecting him to be taken in. I tried to forget he was there.

I focused on my character, Florence. Florence is fun. She's a spoilt college student used to having things her way. If someone goes against her personal code, she believes they deserve punishment, and she believes she has the right to dole out that punishment. She thinks of herself as invincible, and incredibly clever. She has a meanness to her at odds with a desire to protect those who she sees as needing protection. She likes to get very close to you, her eye staring into your eye, and tell you in an even, measured voice, exactly what violence she would enact against you if given the opportunity. She is small, and pretty, and she has a Valley accent, so you will probably think she is joking. She is not.

We did three takes, and then Sarah came over to talk to us. I was aware of Anna's husband watching. Anna herself was mostly just hanging in the background of the scene, not much to do other than to look lost, which to be fair to her she's fairly good at. We went again. After that fourth take – a good one; I felt it – he said something quietly in Sarah's ear, and she made a 'go ahead' gesture.

'Quick break, everyone,' she said.

Anna's husband walked towards us. By the time I realised that he wasn't walking over to Anna, but to me, it was too late to hide my surprise. He stood looking down at me, chin bristly, hair greying, not smiling but looking at me like he was trying to work out where he'd seen me before.

'Rachael, was it?' he said.

He hadn't even looked at Anna. I could *feel* her annoyance, and it was delicious. 'That's me,' I said.

'I forgot, you're a Brit. Your accent's good. Have you got a coach?'

'The studio set me up with one. But American's easy.'

'That was a great scene,' he said.

'Just good writing.'

'Hm,' he said. 'I'm not so sure.' He seemed to be waiting for me to argue. After a beat, he said, 'It's a great script, for sure. I love Sarah's stuff. It's always so unique.'

'I agree.'

'She finds unique actors. Isn't that right, baby?' Finally he acknowledged Anna. She gave him a tight smile. He turned back to me. 'You're still on that sitcom, right?' he asked.

'That's my day job.'

He laughed. It was the loud laugh of a man who thought he was doing you a favour when he laughed at something you said. 'Right. What else have you done? A romcom, right?'

'A couple. I was in *Girls Getting Ready*.' I don't know if I've written about how *Girls* did. The short answer: pretty well. It's been out

134

about six months and people liked it. I got some nice write-ups. It was easier for me to sit through than *Kiss It Better,* partly because I liked watching Adam.

'Right. That British comedy. But this is your first Hollywood movie?'

'First one, yeah.'

'You're good,' he said. 'You've got a really interesting quality. Has anyone ever told you that before?'

'Sarah did.'

'Of course,' he said. 'Smart lady. She's a real gem. She finds real gems.' He gave me another considering look. He was beginning to grate on me, but I would let him keep standing there complimenting me as long as it annoyed Anna. 'Have you ever done horror?' he asked.

He directs that arty kind of horror that's always trying to do things with imagery and make you consider that *maybe we were the real monsters all along.* I've never seen any of his films – he's not released anything since I've had money for the cinema, and it's not the kind of soapy horror I enjoy renting alone in my flat. 'No,' I said. 'I like it, though.'

'I think it would be a good genre for you. You're a little unsettling. That's a compliment.' Was it? He reached into his jacket pocket and handed me a business card. 'Listen,' he said, 'I'm making something. It's gonna be great. You should come read for me. I'd like to try you out.' He spoke with the confidence of someone who had already got their yes. Which was fair, because of course I was going to say yes. Anna was practically radiating fury. I put the card in my pocket. 'Give me a call,' he said. 'We'll set something up.'

Later that day, Anna pushed into me on our way off set. My hand went protectively to the card in my pocket. I wouldn't have put it past her to steal it.

I gave it to Adam that evening. 'Greg Foster,' he said, turning it over. 'He's quite a big deal, isn't he?'

'You don't watch that stuff.'

'No, but lots of people do. And you always say you want to do different stuff. I feel like you'd love doing horror.'

'But you'd have to come to the premiere. And then you'd get nightmares forever.' He flicked the card into my face. 'Anna will be so pissed if her husband casts me in a film,' I said gleefully.

'Maybe don't base every career decision on whether or not it'll piss Anna off,' said Adam.

He's asleep now, next to me. He doesn't mind that I often keep my lamp on to read after he's fallen asleep, because Adam could sleep through anything. He could sleep through a rave. His mouth is open and one of his hands is holding the curve of my hip. I don't know how someone grows up that beautiful in an industry like this one and remains so unspoilt.

I'm making it all sound perfect, which it isn't. We have fights. Sometimes I yell at him. Sometimes he goes out for long walks to get some space from me. But I never really remember what those fights are about after they're over. They're just two people figuring out how to fit into one life and making a lot of noise whilst doing so. I'm not always brave enough to say everything I want to say to him. If I was, I would wake him up and I would say, *I want to be here making a lot of noise with you forever*. But I've got forever to say it in. So it's okay.

30 October 1990

It's Halloween tomorrow. We're taking Adam's sister Sydney trick or treating, which makes me laugh when I think about doing it. I'm quite famous now. There's no non-embarrassing way to write that. Adam's more famous than I am. I imagine someone's mum opening her door to see the two of us on her doorstep, a smiling ten-year-old girl between us, and trying to work out where she knows us from.

Of course, that isn't really what I wanted to write about. I suppose I don't know how to begin. Which is a strange place to be in, when you're only talking to yourself, and you already know what happened, and you still feel the mad urge to lay it all out in order.

I've never taken my top off on set. The studio tried to contest my nudity clause, in *Always, April,* but I said no and it stayed. It's not that I'd never do it, but I definitely wasn't going to do it for some mid-tier romance. If I get my tits out, I'll have a good reason, and that applies to all areas of my life. I've never taken my top off in an audition room either, but that's partly because no one's asked me before. So when Greg Foster sat back in his chair and said, 'Great read. Genuinely. I loved how you did that. Alright, here comes the awkward part,' I honestly didn't know what he was about to say next. And then I realised, a fraction of a second before he said, 'I need to know what we're working with, if that's alright, Rachael.'

'Oh,' I said.

'Apologies if I've caught you off guard,' he said, but he didn't say anything else. I waited for the explanation, for persuasion, but it didn't come. He just tipped back in his chair slightly and looked at me. He was in a blue button-up shirt and grey slacks. He didn't look lecherous. His expression was clinical and removed.

'I'm—' I hesitated. I felt as if I was being played. 'My agent didn't say anything about— anything.' I was beginning to stumble over my words, which I knew would ruin his image of me. The trouble was that it wasn't just about pissing off Anna anymore – now I really wanted this part. The sides he'd given me were fantastic. It's a modern retelling of *The Crucible,* as yet untitled. I told him I'd played Abigail before. She's just Abi, in this script, and she's deliciously dangerous. I wanted him to think that I could be dangerous. I didn't want him to look at me and see a nervous little girl.

'Oh, shit,' said Greg. He still sounded completely calm. 'Crossed wires. Sorry about that.' He pushed my résumé to one side. 'So, we're playing with the idea of nudity. There's going to be a sex scene with Abi and John – a warning for you, if that's not your thing – and I think it would be really interesting to have us actually see her naked. I don't think it makes sense to dance around the fact that Abi has a body. God knows that she wouldn't be coy about it. You read the original play. You get what I'm saying.' I nodded, because I did. 'We just need to check that whoever we cast has the right look for Abi,' he said, 'and that she can hold herself confidently in a nude scene. Nudity is a skill. Sounds ridiculous to say, but some women can't do it. They just radiate self-consciousness. You can feel them hating their bodies. We can't have any of that with Abi.'

'I understand that,' I said, and I realised then that I'd already made up my mind to do it. He didn't say anything else. I took hold of the hem of my top. 'Should I just . . .'

He made a gesture for me to continue. His expression was still neutral as I pulled my top over my head. I tried to do it quickly, but not too quickly, like I wasn't hesitating but I also wasn't tearing my clothes off. Abi would be in control. I needed to be in control. My reflex was to double-check that he wanted me to take my bra off as well. I fought it and unclipped the back like it was nothing. When I stood in front of him, bare-chested, I realised that I could no longer remember how to stand like I wasn't conscious of myself.

'Great,' he said, like I'd given him the time. He reached into his bag and pulled out a Polaroid camera. He walked around the front of the table and raised it. I wondered if I would stop him. The flash went. The picture printed. He walked a few steps around me and took another. I didn't pose, but I followed the camera with my eyes. He took three more. He laid them all upside down on the table.

'Great,' he said again, putting the camera away. 'That's great, Rachael, thanks. You can get dressed.'

Stomach fluttering, I put my clothes back on. My eyes fell on the row of photos. He turned the first one over. 'You look great,' he said. The first indication that my body was something he might have enjoyed looking at. He held the photo out to me and I took it. I did look good. Defiant, and very pale, dark hair loose over bare shoulders. I tried to give him the photo back, but he held up both hands. 'Yours,' he said. 'You can keep them all.'

I frowned. 'Okay.'

'Don't take that the wrong way. I just don't need them. I was watching you as I took the photos. I saw Abi there. The pictures themselves don't matter. I'm sure it would make you more comfortable if you held on to them.'

He handed me the rest. 'Thank you,' I said, and felt foolish. He nodded. 'There's something really special about you,' he said. 'I feel like this is an audition I'm going to look back on in years to come.'

'Me too,' I said.

'Why do you say that?'

'Because I got my tits out.'

Greg Foster tipped his head back and laughed.

I've put the pictures at the bottom of my sock drawer, which is a movie cliché but I honestly couldn't think of a better place for them. I might burn them. I keep taking them out to look at them. They're good photographs. I like my face in them. But then I look at them again, and I see a hunch in my shoulders, a scowl on my lips, and I find myself disgusting.

When I got home from the meeting with Greg, Adam was ordering from the Greek place we like. He pressed the phone into his shoulder. 'How was it?' he whispered.

I shrugged.

'Two secs,' he whispered, raising the phone again. I watched him talk to the restaurant, smiling politely as if they could see his face. He put the phone down. 'Rach?' he asked.

'Hm?'

'What's wrong? Did it not go well?'

'It was good.'

He tilted my chin towards him. 'You sure?'

'I think so. Always hard to tell.'

'Rather not jinx it?'

I hesitated, then nodded.

'Alright. I'll drop it. You're not upset about anything?'

'No,' I said. I felt as if the weight of the envelope in my coat pocket was tipping me sideways. 'I'm okay.'

'I got you moussaka.'

'Thank you.' I kissed his cheek and went into the bedroom to hide the photographs.

This is the problem. If I'd done a kissing scene, I would tell him immediately. Even if I'd been on a set and they'd suddenly asked me to get my tits out, and I'd done it for whatever reason, I would tell him. But this wasn't on a set. This was in an audition room. This was just me and Greg Foster, him circling me with a Polaroid camera, me standing very still for him. I didn't have to do it. No one had forced me. I don't know what Adam will say when I explain that to him. And I am going to, of course I am. But Mum and Elisabeth are coming to visit in five days. I need everything to be simple, right now. I need everything to be okay.

Because I'm going to stay. I've made up my mind. When it comes time to renew my contract for *The Avenue* next month, I'm going to say no. I'm going to stay here with Adam, and work in LA, and never move back to London. I don't care what they offer. Mum will just have to understand.

8 November 1990

The number is bigger than I thought it would be.

'It's very generous,' said my manager Eloise, on the phone. 'I think they've sensed that you might be a flight risk.'

'It's not more than I could make out here,' I said. 'If I do the right kind of films.'

'No, it's not, necessarily. But I don't think the Greg Foster project will offer you as much. You haven't had a smash yet.'

'*Here's Hoping* isn't out yet.'

'*Here's Hoping* won't be a smash,' she said. 'Sorry, Rachael – I know you love it. And I think it'll be a great project. But it won't be a smash. Man-bashing is not a recipe for box office success.'

'It's not man-bashing.' But she's right – that's how people will see it.

'Just think about it,' she said. 'We're behind you either way, obviously.'

I walked back into the living room, a little dazed. They were all waiting for me, turning towards me when I entered like they'd been talking about me, which of course they had. They all knew that I'd been expecting this call. Adam gave me a questioning thumbs-up. He looked impossibly beautiful in a navy cable knit jumper. I looked at him helplessly.

'Are they lowballing you?'

'I almost wish they were,' I said.

Mum and Elisabeth were waiting on our sofa, two expectant blondes wearing the same shade of lipstick. It's eerie how much they've started to look like a Before and After. 'Well?' prompted Mum.

I picked up my bag. 'Let's go to dinner. We can talk whilst we're there.'

We called a car. Adam sat up front and talked to the driver. He likes to do that. They all know who he is, of course, and it's interesting to see which ones acknowledge it and which play it cool. This one was very excited. He took a selfie with Adam to show his daughter. 'She's in love with you,' he laughed, and Adam turned around and winked at me.

Elisabeth slid into the middle seat beside me. She's very tall, and very skinny, almost to the point that it would concern me if I hadn't watched her wolf down every meal set in front of her since she's been here. She's just of that age and type where none of it shows. She'll have to get used to restricting herself if she's serious about modelling – metabolisms like that don't last forever. I've been hungry since 1985.

'Alright?' I asked her, as she squeezed her long legs into the footwell.

She nodded, spreading her skirt over her thighs. 'I thought you'd take limos everywhere,' she said.

'Limos are pretty expensive.'

'I thought you were a millionaire.'

'I do okay,' I said, my eyes on the driver. But of course, he knows what Adam gets paid. The salary negotiations for the second *Dragonborn* got pretty public. I'm not a millionaire, not yet, but another season of *The Avenue* would have put me in a pretty comfortable position. Not that it matters now. A few more films in LA and I'll be able to buy a nice place. Of course, it doesn't help that I'm still supporting Mum and Elisabeth. I'm paying the rent on quite a nice three-bed house for them in Chiswick. It's needed furnishing, so of course I've done that, and Elisabeth grows at a rate of knots so I send quite a lot home for clothes. Lately I've also been paying for her headshots. She's in that awkward stage right now but I think she'll grow up pretty. She's very blonde and very leggy, my complete opposite. Clothes don't fit her well right now because she's so flat and bony, but give her another couple of years and she'll wear them wonderfully. I wonder if I'll resent her, when that happens.

Adam thinks I shouldn't be giving Mum and Elisabeth so much money.

'It's very generous,' he said, when I first explained to him the situation, 'but doesn't your mom have any of her own income?'

'She used to work, but it didn't suit her.'

'Didn't suit her how?'

'It's hard to explain. She gets restless, and tired. She can't make herself sit through a workday. It's impossible for her to hold on to a job.' Adam looked gently sceptical. 'I know,' I said. 'Believe me. Fair or not, it's just true.'

'So how did you survive, growing up?'

'Well, her mum died and we sold her house, which gave us a bit of a cushion. We were on benefits for a while.' I always feel a little embarrassed telling people this. 'She does sewing work for people now and then, mostly friends and neighbours, and that brings in a bit. And we've both just been focused on this acting thing, for a long time. Getting me to where I need to be. The idea was always that I would move to London as early as I could and start booking parts.'

'But it's very strange,' he said, 'for you to be the sole breadwinner. You've left home. You have your own life.'

The older I get, the more I think it's strange too. I don't ever tell anyone this, though. I don't even say it to Adam. It feels like a betrayal, somehow, like how when we were really struggling for money I couldn't tell anyone at school because it felt like I was airing our dirty laundry. It felt disloyal to talk about it. It isn't that I feel particularly close to Mum or Elisabeth – I'm not sure if I would even call what we share love, especially after what I've known with Adam. But if family isn't closeness, it is still obligation, and I couldn't turn my back on them. Mum is all the things that she is, but she was also the only person who believed, for so many years, that I would make it. And Elisabeth is only fourteen. She might still grow up to be someone I genuinely love, out of more than familial obligation. I would hate to look back later in life and know that anyone I loved felt let down by me.

We've never had much in common – I had a drive, always, a hunger, and I've never seen that in her. And being seven years apart in age, we haven't had many shared experiences either. But we're both our mother's daughters, and we've both grown up knowing that our presence in the world had a tax attached. In a way it relieves me that she doesn't seem to feel that weight anymore, and in another way, I hate her a little. When she turned to me in the taxi and said, *I thought you were a millionaire,* in the dress my work had bought, on the way to the dinner my work was paying for, I seethed, just a little. I thought, *What on earth would you know about money?* When I was fourteen, I thought about money all the time – how to earn it, how to save it, what would happen if we ran out of it. I'd imagined that Elisabeth would be the same by now, but all she has to worry about is what neat little luxury my money will buy her next. It isn't her fault, but it's hard to see her as innocent when I know how much her dress is worth.

We pulled up outside the restaurant. Adam held the car door open for us, which Mum liked. Elisabeth checked her lipstick in the small mirror she carries around in her purse, which she clearly feels is a very sophisticated thing for a girl to do. The restaurant we were going to has a reputation for being very discreet and considerate of its high-profile clientele, but even so, when Mum walked in and said very loudly, 'Yes, good evening, the booking should be under Rachael Carmichael,' heads turned.

The waiter led us to our table. We were sat in a booth with a curved blue velvet seat, three blue candles of varying heights in the centre of the table. Elisabeth complained about the menu – she had never seen a tasting menu before and couldn't understand why we couldn't just all have one thing. Adam said, 'I'm sure they could rustle up a cheeseburger or something for you,' but that seemed to make her realise she was acting like a child, so she coloured and shook her head.

'Incredible,' Mum kept saying as they laid down the next course. 'Incredible, the life you live out here, Rachael.'

'We do takeout most nights, Mum. This isn't standard.'

'I'm sure. She's always been frugal, our Rachael.' She addressed this to Adam. 'Very sensible with her money.' I looked down at my plate. 'We're always grateful for what she can send.' Mum cut into her food. It was a duck course, a small piece of expertly charred breast with a light orange sauce. 'You are doing fantastically these days,' she said. 'And now season three of *The Avenue*. We'll have you back in London for a bit.'

'That's the thing—'

'How much did they offer?' she asked, chewing.

I gave her the number. Her chewing slowed. Elizabeth gaped at me over her untouched food. Adam gave me a gentle slap on the back. 'Alright, Rach! You're not getting lowballed for once.' It's not as much as the big TV shows would probably pay in the US, but I appreciated his excitement.

'I don't think I'm going to take it,' I said.

Mum's face didn't change. She went on chewing her duck, really working it, until it became a little gross. Then she swallowed. She picked up her knife and fork. She nodded. She put another piece in her mouth.

'It's good money, I know, but not better than I might make out here.'

'That's true,' said Adam. 'She's up for Greg Foster's new project – did you know?'

'I don't know who that is,' said Mum.

'Very acclaimed horror director. He's made several arthouse pieces that people just loved.' I wished Adam would stop. Mum would hear 'horror' and 'arthouse' and draw her own conclusions. 'He scouted Rach on the *Here's Hoping* set. There's lots of buzz around her.'

'I see,' said Mum. 'Well, that's all very exciting.' She was still cutting her duck into bitesize pieces. She wasn't eating any of them.

'I know it would be weird not to have me in London anymore,' I said.

'The thing is, Rachael, I've been thinking about sending your sister to Grifford's.'

I looked at Elisabeth, blonde and tall, on the verge of being graceful, trying to be a model, picking at her expensive food. *Of course* she wanted to go to private school.

'What's wrong with the school she's at now?'

'Oh, it's fine, but the academic reputation of Grifford's is just so much better.'

'Sure, fine, but since when did you care about that?'

She looked at me, coldly. 'I just figured it was about time someone in this family went to university.'

'What's that supposed to mean?'

She shrugged, looking back down at her plate.

'I couldn't have gone to university. I've been working since I was fourteen.'

'Oh, please.'

'I have!'

'*Technically.* Let's not pretend you were down in the mines.'

Elisabeth snorted.

I looked at her. She was still looking down at her plate, prodding her duck with her knife. She was scraping off all of the orange sauce. Did she have any concept of how much that sauce cost? How much time had gone into preparing that food for her? How much thought, how many years of training? She had a spot next to her nose. She'd piled concealer on to it, but you could still see it. Her eyeliner was wonky. This spotty, gawky kid was living off my work, in a house I paid for. She thought she could thrust her hand into the air and say, 'Mummy, I want to go to private school, *please*,' and the money would just fall into her lap.

'I'm staying in LA,' I said. Under the table, Adam took my hand. 'Adam and I are going to buy a place.'

'Buy? In LA?' She looked up, diagonally, like she was making mental calculations. 'Can we afford that?'

'I can.'

'This food is shit,' said Elisabeth, pushing her plate away from her. 'I want to go home.'

'Elisabeth should go to university,' I said. She looked at me, surprised. 'Might as well give her some options. God knows she won't make it in modelling.'

'You shouldn't have said that,' said Adam later, in bed. My head was on his chest. I'd cried on him, which is embarrassing to admit but nonetheless true. It was the frustration. It had to come out somehow. 'I was completely on your side until then.'

'All I meant was that she didn't have the work ethic.'

'You knew how it sounded,' he said.

'I can't help it. They make me crazy, both of them.' He rested a hand on my hair and I fought to keep my voice steady. 'I thought it would be better once I'd made it. When I was living in London, before *The Avenue,* I spent my life feeling like I was letting them down. They were waiting for me to break through and I couldn't seem to do it. I thought when – *if* – it finally happened, I'd be able to breathe.' He put an arm around my shoulders, and I rolled over, head in the crook of his elbow, looking up at the ceiling. 'I don't know if this is worse, but it doesn't feel like easy breathing.'

'I know,' said Adam, fingertips stroking my hip.

'You're so lucky that your family is normal.'

'No one's family is normal.'

'Right, but there's not normal and then there's mine.'

'True,' he said. It's validating, when he acknowledges how messed up my family is, but it also makes me sad. 'Rach,' he said, 'at the end of the day, it isn't anyone's decision except yours.'

I rolled over to look at him. 'I know. I need to remember that. I can do whatever I want. It's my life. It's my money.'

'Exactly,' he said. 'Your life. Your money.'

'I want to spend it here, with you.'

He grinned. 'Your life, or your money?'

'Both,' I said. 'Is that okay?'

He reached over and cupped my face with his hand. 'Huh,' he said, with a grin. 'I could see that working out.'

He's sleeping right now. I'm sat writing with my small lamp turned on. It still amazes me how it doesn't bother him when someone turns on a lamp or starts scribbling away. I could probably turn on the big light and start dancing a rhumba and he wouldn't wake up.

Adam. Somehow, I will always end up here with you. It's a promise that I'm making to myself. I will not let myself be led down any other path. We're going to find a house in Hidden Hills with a bathtub big enough to swim in and a fireplace we can fuck in front of. We'll raise children who hate pretending to be other people and want to learn to play instruments and fly planes instead and we'll take them on trips to distant islands and let them choose their own names. We will make all this happiness, and we will hold it between ourselves in our four hands, pressed up small and tight and safe like a marble, and we will never share it with anyone. Not even one tiny piece. We will have it all to ourselves, forever.

5 March 1991

Today, Jill got a car. It was her seventeenth birthday, and she ran outside into the street to find a brand-new Ford Fiesta waiting for her in the driveway, a huge purple bow on its hood. She shrieked and threw her arms around her parents, Susan and Dave, and beamed, and said, *Thank you thank you thank you* over and over, until the director called, 'Cut!'

Then Jill died. She does this often. When she hears that word, she knows her time is up and she returns to the grave, fading away like a ghost, trodden all over by Rachael Carmichael as she stalks on to set. Rachael Carmichael is not excited about the car. She thinks the decision to put a big purple shiny bow on a red car is a crime against the eyes and she thinks that Jill is an annoying little twerp who deserves to have her skull split with a meat cleaver. This is a complicated feeling, as she and Jill happen to share a skull.

When we broke for lunch, Brenda and I sat and played Spit until they called us back. We didn't speak, except to say, 'Spit'. Sometimes I would think I was about to catch her looking at me over the cards, but whenever I glanced up she was calmly shuffling, eyes down.

Jill came back to life. She did her same grating routine over again – the shriek from her bedroom window, the run down the stairs, the hug, the *thankyouthankyouthankyou*. This time she cried. They were happy tears, until 'Cut', until Jill slipped away again, until it was just me, crying, Brenda's arms around me going, 'It's okay. It's okay. Can we give her a minute? I think she needs a minute.'

She sat me down in her trailer. We still didn't speak. She gave me a tissue, and one of the pear sweets that she likes and always has a jar of. I cried. Then I stopped. She said, 'Ready?' I said, 'Yeah.' We went back and did the scene again. Jill lived and died, and lived and died. In the shiny red bonnet of the car I saw her distorted face, ecstatic, and then mine, empty.

Two more months of this. I hate everyone. But I hate Jill most of all, because Jill makes me betray myself. She makes me jump up and down and hug people and dance around and pull my cheeks back into a smile. I wish she could die for real and stay dead and then I would never have to act happy again.

London is grey. Groundbreaking, I know. I may be the first one to ever notice.

My flat in Clapham is all wrong. The walls are too white. The windows are too small. I have to move. 'Where do you want to go?' asked the estate agent. Away, obviously. She doesn't understand what I'm looking for. 'Would you like to be more central?' No. Obviously not.

Mum calls. 'How's the series going?'

I mumble one-word responses until she lets me go with a sigh. It would be easier to never pick up the phone to her but for some reason I can't do that. I still worry about her and Elisabeth. That fact makes me hate myself.

Broke and called Adam. No response.

It was the fucking photographs, of course. I know you're waiting for me to tell you, and you're going, *Oh, the Polaroids, of course. I knew it would be.* Well, you're very clever, Diary. Hats off to you.

I was always going to tell him. That's the aggravating thing about it. If I'd just been a little quicker, I would have told him, and I think he would have understood. We might have argued, but it would have been okay. It wouldn't have been this.

It was the last day of Mum and Elisabeth's visit. They were sat in the living room watching *Friends* and I was in the kitchen tidying up. He walked into the kitchen with the pictures in his hand and said, 'Rach, what are these?'

I had a blue glass bowl in my hand. I said, 'What?'

'These pictures. What are they?'

My brain froze. I couldn't force it back into functioning. The only thing I could think of to say was, 'Why were you going through my stuff?' Which was obviously a stupid thing to ask.

He said, 'I wasn't. They were out on my pillow.'

'What?'

'Rach, what are they? Who took them?'

'Greg Foster,' I said.

He looked at me. I put the glass bowl down on the side, because I had a horrible feeling I was about to drop it. 'Greg Foster?' he repeated.

'It was part of the audition. He—'

'What did he do to you?'

'Nothing. He asked if he could take photographs of me and I said that he could.'

'But—' He wasn't even angry, yet. Just confused. That hurts to remember. 'Is that in the script? I mean . . .' He looked at the pictures in his hand. 'Even if it is . . . this feels strange. This doesn't feel like how these things are done.'

'It's not in the script. Yet. They're thinking of adding it in.'

'Did he make you do this? Did your agent say you had to do this?'

'I didn't know until I got there.'

'Did he frighten you?'

'No one made me,' I said. I couldn't lie to him. Suddenly I felt myself move towards him, trying to grab hold of his hands. 'I'm sorry. I was going to tell you, I was, but I wanted to wait until Mum and Elisabeth were gone—'

'Why?' He was still clutching the pictures, his hands raised out of reach as I tried to take them. He was bleary, like he'd just woken up. The way he looked at me was desperate. 'Did you sleep with him?'

I took a step back. He saw my expression and opened his mouth in a way that made me think he was about to apologise.

When he didn't, shame turned to rage. I would never have thought that he considered me capable of that. 'How the fuck can you ask me that?'

'Rach—'

'No!' I didn't want to be shouting at him, but the fury descended on me like panic and I wasn't in control of my volume anymore, or the words I said. 'How the *fuck*—'

'God, Rachael, you're the one that hid these!'

'I was waiting for the right moment!'

'The right moment is *as soon as it fucking happens!* Understand?'

'Don't speak to me like that.'

'There is no fucking high horse for you to get on here, Rach. Okay? You don't get to cheat on me and then act like I can't have some fucking *feelings* about that.'

'I didn't cheat!'

'This is cheating!' he said, waving the pictures at me. 'Do you get that? *This* is cheating. When you lie, when you don't tell me, when you hide them, that's cheating. You've broken a trust here.' The sound of his voice was awful. All thick and wobbly. 'Do you understand that? Do you, honestly?'

I saw that he really believed it. I remembered how Adam felt about cheating. 'Oh, god,' I heard myself say.

We stared at each other. I heard the front door open and close. Mum and Elisabeth had gone. They'd heard us yelling. They had a flight to catch. They'd decided not to bother with goodbye.

We shouted, and then talked, and then shouted, and then talked. We both cried. I don't remember most of what was said. I don't remember how it ended with Adam, sat on the floor with his head in his hands. 'I think you should go back to London,' he said.

'No.' I came to sit by him. I tried to lift his hands from his face.

'You should,' he said, not letting me. 'You should take the offer for *The Avenue,* and you should go back to London.'

'I don't want to. I want to say here, with you.'

'I don't want you here,' he said.

'You don't mean that.'

He shook his head, still with his face hidden.

'I'm sorry.' I hate the way I sound when I'm crying. I thought it vaguely, somewhere in the back of my mind, how disgusting my voice sounded. 'I'm sorry, I'm sorry. I didn't mean to lie. I love you.'

'I love you too,' he said, and in spite of it all, my heart still gave a little leap. 'But you're not the same to me now,' he said. 'It's awful. You're just not.'

That was it, really. When someone you love says that to you, there isn't really any way to come back from it.

Amy George was in LA doing a sci-fi film. I went to stay with her. Adam packed up my things and she drove over to our place – his place, now – to pick them up. She was wonderful to me. She made us do all the break-up things they do in American films, like eating tubes of cookie dough and crying during karaoke. But I couldn't stay with her long. We'd been a trio, her and Adam and me. Being around her was being too close to him. I had to get far away.

I came back to London. I landed in mid-November, in the drizzle. I wore dark sunglasses. The novelty has worn off. I was photographed outside the airport, but when the pictures came out, no one seemed to guess that I'd been crying. They still don't know about the break-up. Everyone thinks it's a perfectly innocent long-distance situation, whilst he works in LA and I work here. He hasn't corrected the record so I won't either, not yet.

It was only after I'd been back here a few days that the fog in my brain cleared enough that I was able to ask the obvious question. *Who had put those photographs on Adam's pillow?*

I called Mum to tell her that we'd broken up and that I was back in London.

'Oh, I'm sorry, Rachael,' she said. 'First heartbreaks are always hard. But I think this is probably the best thing for everyone involved.'

'Did you do it?' I said.

There was a second of silence. I hung up. I don't know how she found them. Maybe in her desperation she went rifling for something to use and hit the jackpot. It almost doesn't matter now. Elisabeth has apparently been on a mission to get herself expelled from her school. *She's so unhappy there,* Mum pleaded on the answerphone. *She's just been acting out awfully.* She's vague about what Elisabeth has been doing, but a lot of it seems to involve smoking in PE class and saying derogatory things to her teachers. *She just can't keep it together in that environment, poor girl,* Mum said. She pretended to sob.

In the end I couldn't listen to one more weepy message about my sister acting out like an Enid Blyton bad girl. I just sent the cheque. It isn't in my make-up to do anything else, and I don't have the energy right now to pretend to have more of a backbone than I do. So, Elisabeth is going to Grifford's. I hope she does well in her exams and gets a boring degree and a boring job and makes just enough money to decide that, on balance, it's all worth it, even though she looks at my life every day and hates herself for being so ordinary. I hope living off my money makes them both hate themselves. The worst part is, I know it never will.

7 March 1991

He doesn't pick up my calls. I've left him messages, but he probably deletes them without listening to them. I can't shake the idea that this is still all just some horrible mistake and that eventually it will get straightened out and we'll be right back where we were. I need to be lobotomised, probably.

10 March 1991

Something very strange has happened. Greg Foster called. I'd honestly never expected to hear from him again. There hasn't been a peep since the audition, but today he called the flat as I was home watching *Cujo* and started leaving a message. 'This is Greg Foster for Rachael Carmichael—'

I flew to the phone. 'Hello?'

'Rachael!' His accent reminded me of Adam's. 'Glad I caught you,' he said. 'I heard from Robb you're back in London.'

'I am, yes.'

'Next season of *The Avenue*, I hear. You're a wholesome teenager again.'

'Very much so. I just turned seventeen.'

'Happy birthday! Assuming you got a car?'

'Of course. With a giant bow on it.'

He laughed uproariously. Suddenly it did seem pretty funny. 'Must be a palate cleanser after *Here's Hoping*. Anna loved the shoot. Said you're going to be fantastic, by the way.'

I would stake my left tit on the fact that Anna said no such thing. 'She did great as well.' He laughs, as if he can tell what I'm thinking. 'I wasn't expecting to hear from you,' I said.

'I know. I left you hanging a while. I'll level with you – your audition was great, but I've gone back and forward. I've seen a lot of girls for Abi.' I wondered if he'd circled them all with that Polaroid camera. 'Some great actresses,' he said. 'Still couldn't get you out of my head.'

I tried to keep the smile out of my voice. 'Right.'

'You've got the talent,' he said. 'I wasn't sure if you were able to be fearsome enough. That's all that's been holding me back. I need you to be scary. You can be unsettling, I think, but can you horrify? I guess I won't really know until we get you on that set.' I was quiet, afraid to celebrate too soon. 'Could you fly out?' he asked. 'I'd like you to meet everyone. Our producers and such. I know it was a bit of a strange audition, no one else there, and even though a lot of them have seen your tape I still think someone other than me should meet you in person.' He paused. 'I like you for this, though. It's gonna be yours, I think.'

It was such a strange way of offering me the role – almost like he was talking to himself and had forgotten I was there – that I didn't know what to say.

'Hello?' he said. 'Did I lose you?'

'I'm here.' I gripped the phone. 'You're saying I have it?'

'I'm ninety per cent. I'll say that.' I put a balled fist against my forehead and squeezed my eyes shut. It was the only thing I could think of to do. I wasn't quite able to be happy, but I was *something*, spilling over with some emotion I couldn't name. 'You still want the part, I assume?' he asked.

'Of course I do.'

'Then we'll fly you out in a couple months, when you're done shooting. Obviously if the meeting doesn't go well, then that's that on that—'

'I think it will go well.'

He chuckled. 'I think it'll go well too. See you soon, kid. Looking forward to it.' The line went dead.

How do you celebrate when happy feels wrong and good news goes unshared? Here's how: you run yourself a bath. You put fancy salts in the water and light a candle on your bathroom counter. You take off your clothes. You look at yourself in the mirror and feel very strange. You get into the bath. You run it a little too hot. You slip under the water, and you close your eyes, and – just for a second – you feel completely still.

Chapter Seven

HARLEY

It turned out that Ahn had been exaggerating slightly. When she started to shop the screenplay around, I expected it to be snatched up immediately. Actually, from her talk about serious studio interest, I expected a bidding war. There was mostly silence.

'I thought you had contacts,' I said to her, when she rang to update me.

'I do.' She sounded frustrated. 'They're debating internally,' she said.

'Over what?'

'Over whether to wait for Greg's book and option it.'

'Why would they want to do that? I thought everyone wanted to be a feminist these days. This is obviously the more feminist option.'

'I know, Harley,' she said. 'This is just how these things go. It'll happen. We just have to be patient.'

About a month after Ahn finished the screenplay, Julia, Carlton and I went to dinner in Primrose Hill. We talked about the film the entire time. They'd both read it by that point and loved it almost as much as I had. Carlton called his car service to pick us up and we all popped an edible on the way home, which did a little to relieve the stress, although not much. Talking about the film was better than not talking about it, but it made me anxious to think about the possibility that we might have done all this work for nothing.

'I mean, we spent hours with her,' I said, as we drove towards Carlton's dad's house. 'I got good at tennis. I did all this research. And it all might go to shit.'

'It's only been a month,' said Carlton.

'A month is ages.'

'I don't think it is. Is it? I don't think a month is that long. Julia?'

'How would I know?'

'Well, your folks are film people.'

'Oh my god,' said Julia. 'Harley. I should give it to my grandfather.'

'Would it be his kind of thing?' Sidonius Cagnoni likes epics – war films, artsy action, big awards-bait blockbusters. They don't tend to win Best Picture but they pick up accolades in the design, VFX and sound categories fairly often. Of course, Cagnoni Studios makes everything, but Julia's grandfather is very particular with the kind of projects he throws his weight behind.

'He'd love it,' she said. 'He loves a good screenplay. And he loves something he knows people will turn out to see. And they'll turn out to see this.'

Back in Carlton's dad's house, we decided to go swimming. Carlton and I floated on our backs, staring up at the green-tiled ceiling as Julia sat on the side of the pool and called her grandfather.

'Hi, Pop,' she said, in her little-girl voice. 'How are you? How's your film going?' A giggle. 'Is Bradley Cooper behaving?' Another giggle. 'Oh, he's very funny. I met him at one of Stephanie's things.' I trod water to watch her. She was sitting with one knee pressed to her chin, in a tiny silver bikini, curly hair slick from the water. She used to never wear her hair natural but it always looks beautiful now, although I think the combined cost of the products she uses on it is well over four figures. 'How are you doing?' she asked. 'Are you getting enough sleep?'

Whatever he replied, it made her giggle again. Carlton flicked pool water into my face to get my attention and rolled his eyes at the giggle.

'Oh, not much,' I heard her say. 'My friend is working on this project. You remember Harley.'

He knew me well. I was always Julia's plus one to his dinners. Sidonius Cagnoni threw these big elaborate dinners every few months for all his most famous and beautiful friends (this list changed party to party and a lot of the women got booted off it after they hit a certain age). He always had a musical guest, like on *SNL*. At his last one I had met Adele and she had told me my voice wasn't bad at all. I'd never bonded with Sidonius Cagnoni himself much, though. He's an intimidating man. He's part of that generation of rich men who like to go on and on about their work ethic and being self-made, even though I don't really believe anyone is ever self-made, not really. Life would be much easier if we all stopped being so hung up on who is and isn't, and just accepted that everyone has advantages of some nature.

'I think they've called it *God Laughs*,' Julia was saying. 'Has it come across your desk?' She turned and gave me a thumbs-up. 'I only ask because I've read it, and I thought of you *immediately*. I think it's so original. There's so much in there. And I know there are people out there who are just *dying* to hear this story.' A pause. 'You must be so busy. Do you think you have a minute to read it, though? Just for me. And if you hate it then I'll never bring it up to you again.' Another pause, and then a grin broke out over her face. Carlton did a somersault in the water. 'You're the *best*,' she said.

'Harley will be so happy! I'm still coming for dinner this Friday, aren't I? Shall I bring a cake? I'm getting very good at baking.'

'There we go,' said Carlton, swimming over to me. 'Problem solved with a little nepotism.'

'It doesn't mean he'll want it. If nepotism was that effective I'd already be famous.'

'Nepotism *is* that effective, because you're literally about to become famous by playing your aunt in a film.'

'That's different,' I said.

'Not really.' He splashed me. 'God, you're so negative. You're rich and beautiful and your parents are also rich and beautiful. And you act like it's a curse.'

'At least I don't use my daddy's name to get free stuff I don't need.'

'You should,' he said. 'That's the point. You've literally won the lottery in life and you don't let yourself enjoy it. Or if someone suggests that you are enjoying it, you get all scared and you think they're making a moral judgement.'

'Jesus, Carlton, back off.'

'You piss me off with that stuff,' he said. It didn't sound like a joke. 'Sorry,' he said, after a minute. Julia's giggle echoed over to us from the other end of the pool. 'I guess I just don't get why you think you're better than the people who accept help.'

I ignored him. When Julia jumped back in the pool I hugged her, my legs wrapping around her torso under the water. She told me to stop hitting on her. 'I won't,' I said. 'I love you. You're so sexy. I owe you so big.'

She smiled, her pupils large and black. 'Happy to help,' she said. 'I'll always do what I can.'

Cagnoni Studios bought *God Laughs.* Julia baked her grandfather a lopsided cake to celebrate and then decided against it and ordered him a cupcake tower and a very nice bottle of whiskey instead. We ate the cake in her kitchen with three forks and felt sick afterwards. Ahn took me out for a glass of champagne, which was uncharacteristically nice of her.

'They want us to go in next week,' she said.

'Rachael too?'

'If we can get her,' said Ahn. 'I don't think she will.'

She didn't. I called her up to try to convince her, but she was adamant. 'I don't want to get involved with that side of things,' she said. 'I've given you my story. I'm trusting you to tell it. The rest is in your hands now.'

'We thought you might want a producer role. Just to keep an eye on things, let us know if we're doing it all how you envisioned.'

'I'm not envisioning anything. Just do it however you think is best.'

I was touched by her faith in me. After we hung up, I texted her. *Fancy a game of tennis next week?* She sent me a thumbs-up. I knew her well enough now to read the enthusiasm behind it.

The meeting at Cagnoni Studios was unlike anything I'd ever been involved with in the entertainment industry. Twenty execs sat down with Ahn and me and my agent, Warren, and Ahn's agent, Germaine, at a long boardroom table. Sidonius walked in last and came straight over to clasp my hand.

'Harley,' he said. 'So you've caught the film-making bug from your father, have you?' His eyes scanned my face. 'Those are some strong genes you've got. On both sides.'

We talked through the entire script. Ahn did most of the speaking on that part. We discussed the schedule, and I nodded along. I started listening more closely when we moved on to casting, which the people from Cagnoni said they were keen to get started on as soon as possible.

'We're thinking of someone like Elias Jones for Greg,' said one of the Cagnoni people. 'Someone with a lot of influence and power in the industry already, like Greg had. Classically good-looking, charismatic, but with the acting chops to pull off the darker stuff.'

'I love that,' I said.

Ahn and her agent were both nodding. 'A great choice,' said Ahn.

'And for Rachael . . .' A Cagnoni woman glanced over at a Cagnoni man, who turned the corners of his mouth down quickly, as if to say, *You're on your own.* 'How set are we on Harley?' asked the Cagnoni woman tentatively. 'Because we're thinking it might be interesting to mirror where Greg and Rachael both were in their careers. If we go with Elias for Greg then really we'd want a big up-and-comer for Rachael.'

'Well, Harley's a big up-and-comer,' said Warren. 'She's already worked with some exciting directors. She did a pilot recently with Stacey Koff.'

'Right,' said the Cagnoni woman. 'We're just exploring options here. It might be useful to float some other names.'

I could feel the conversation turning in the wrong direction. I placed a hand on the table and looked the Cagnoni woman right in the eye. Her foundation was cakey. 'My aunt was very clear,' I said. 'She's entrusting me with her portrayal. She only agreed to help us write this script on the condition that I play her.'

I kicked Ahn under the table. She nodded, with only the smallest hint of reluctance. 'Yes,' she said, 'Rachael did say that. It's Harley, or no one.'

◆ ◆ ◆

It had been a while since Rachael and I had played tennis. Raph dozed on the bathroom mat whilst I changed, occasionally raising his head to yawn with his eyes closed and then lowering it back on to his paws. I looked at myself in the mirror, in my tennis whites that were really Rachael's, in this bathroom she probably never used but I always did. Our lives were intersecting now past the point of return. I would never lift cleanly out of hers from this point on and she would always be wound up in mine. Sometimes when I stared at my own face, it felt to me as if we were the same person at two different points on a timeline, a past and future version of the same girl serving tennis balls to herself over a net.

I came out of the kitchen door with Raph at my heels and crossed the lawn, heading down towards the tennis court. When Raph caught sight of her he said, 'Raph,' very brightly, and ran ahead of me down the lawn. She looked over, and we smiled at each other, this little mop of brown halfway between us. He reached her leg and she bent down to rub his head.

'How was the meeting?' she asked, bouncing the ball a couple of times down by her heel. Raph hopped up on to the bench by the side of the court and arranged himself.

'It was great. They're really enthusiastic about the project.' We walked up to the net for the coin toss. 'They're thinking Elias Jones for Greg.'

She nodded. 'I can see that.' The coin spun. 'Heads,' she said. It was. I ran backwards to the baseline – lightly, as I'd learnt to do by imitating her. She sent it spinning towards me, but I was used to her serves by now and threw myself across the court to return it. We volleyed a little, and then I dropped it softly over the net whilst she was still near the back of the court. Point to me.

'Good,' she said, a little out of breath. 'I thought you'd be rusty.'

'So did I.'

She threw the ball up to serve, then pulled back and caught it. 'I didn't think you'd come back,' she said.

It softened me, the way she said it. It made me hope I would never be that lonely.

We made lunch together. During one of our interviews she'd taught me how to make this buttery pumpkin pasta, and this time she let me take charge and boss her around. We sat and ate it at the island together, and she didn't praise it, but she did nod slowly with her eyes closed as she took a bite.

'Are you happy to be done working with Ahn?' she said.

'What do you mean?'

'It was quite obvious that you don't like her.'

'She's not so bad,' I said. 'Anyway, we're still working together.'

'She's a bright girl,' said Rachael. 'Clearly ambitious.'

'Well, so are a lot of us.'

'Of course. So, you think it'll be good?'

'I think so,' I said. 'The script is great. Ahn wanted to know if you want to read it but I thought that it maybe might be difficult for you.'

She looked at me. 'Hm.'

Shit. 'I mean, you obviously can if you want.'

'I'm sure you know best.' She carried on eating. I wasn't quite sure if I'd put my foot in it or not. 'So, it was Sidonius who pushed the deal through? I didn't think it was his kind of film.'

'Well, he thought the script was very compelling,' I said. 'And I've known his granddaughter forever.'

'Ah,' said Rachael. 'Of course you have.'

'I wanted to run something by you.'

Mouth full of pasta, she gestured for me to continue.

'What do you think about me going by Harley Carmichael?'

Rachael swallowed. 'You're changing your name?'

'Not formally. Just for acting. Lots of people have a stage name. I've always used Harley Roth. I thought about using Carmichael-Roth but I thought it might be a bit alienating.'

'I see.'

'But a Carmichael playing a Carmichael . . . I mean, that just sounds right. Doesn't it? And exciting. And intriguing.' I studied her face. 'So?'

'You don't need my permission,' she said. 'It's your name.'

'But you think it's a good idea?'

She'd taken another bite. I waited for her to finish chewing.

'Harley Carmichael,' she said, when she had. 'Sounds pretty good.'

You know that saying they have on sets, *Hurry up and wait*? Turns out that applies to all parts of movie-making. Now that we had an executive producer attached and studio backing, I expected things to rattle along. I received updates through Ahn's agent, Germaine – we'd got this-and-this funding, so-and-so was taking care of sound. We didn't even have a director yet. I suggested to Ahn that I could give it a go. She wasn't sure if I was joking.

Everyone seemed pretty adamant that we should get a female director, but it transpired that the list of female directors that Sidonius and co. considered trustworthy was about four names long and they were all busy. In the end they settled on José Park, who's gay, and therefore considered the next best thing. At that time he was best known for making this historical drama about two brothers in the Civil War. It's supposed to be amazing. I wouldn't know, because I refuse to sit through a three-hour film.

Now that José Park was attached, chatter was starting. A meeting was held to discuss what we revealed about the project. I passed on Rachael's wish that the whole thing remain private for as long as possible, and it was thought that this was wise. The biggest dilemma we were facing was whether to keep Ahn's decision to recreate original scenes from *Women Who Laugh at God,* because it would require us to licence the rights to the film from its creators – and that, of course, included Greg Foster. He was unlikely to hand over the rights without wanting to read the script and Cagnoni were afraid that he would attempt to get the project shut down if this happened, or that he would option his memoir out to a rival studio.

Eventually it was decided that a pivot was necessary. *God Laughs* would no longer include any recreations of the original film, but would instead become *Carmichael & Foster,* a look at Rachael and Greg's relationship and the fallout therefrom, with some action taking place on the set of *Women Who Laugh at God* but none of the film itself shown.

It was a blow for us all – I'd been looking forward to trying my hand at those scenes – but no one took it harder than Ahn.

'This was supposed to be something *different,*' she ranted after the meeting. 'Something experimental, something not done before. Not just another biopic.' Nonetheless she went away to do rewrites. She sent me the new script. Both of us knew it was not quite as good as it had been before. Neither of us said it.

Whilst all of this was taking place, I occupied myself with getting on people's radar. I began to accompany Mum to some of her charity functions and her friends' product launches – not my kind of thing traditionally, but it landed us some tabloid features and a charming poll on an Instagram gossip page about which of us was hotter. Mum was delighted that I was now using her maiden name and hardly questioned it. ('Carmichael just *sounds* so much classier,' she said.) Julia and I called paparazzi on ourselves as we were leaving Cirque Le Soir and managed to get into *Tatler.* The studio were consistently not thrilled with my efforts to publicise myself – 'We want to really *unveil* you as Rachael Carmichael's niece when the right moment comes,' said one harried PR woman – but I knew that this project needed notoriety, and I was happy to help with that in any way I could.

Eventually it got out that Cagnoni was working on a Rachael Carmichael film. They stayed tight-lipped on casting and released a statement saying that the film would focus on Carmichael's 'rise to prominence', no mention of Greg yet. He tweeted about it nonetheless.

Interesting timing from Cagnoni Studios.

This was followed up two hours later with an announcement.

Delighted to finally be able to speak about the fact that @ georgeandgraybooks will be publishing my untitled memoir next summer.

My parents and I went out for dinner a few nights later. Mum cut her steak into thirty small cuboid pieces and then put her cutlery down on her napkin and said, 'Harley, have you spoken to your aunt?'

I nearly choked on my gin and tonic. 'What?'

'Bettie told me that Cagnoni consulted with a family member on the script for this Rachael film.'

'There's a Rachael film?'

That was the wrong play – she knew I wouldn't have missed news like that. Her eyes narrowed over creamed greens and thirty delicate pieces of steak. 'Really? Julia hasn't mentioned it to you?'

'It's probably Rachael herself,' said Dad. 'She's probably posing as a family member to stay behind the scenes.'

'Well,' said Mum, finally picking her fork back up, 'I can't think who else it *would* be. There's no one left on our side of the family since Mum died.' She gave me another quick, searching look. 'I hope you haven't spoken to that woman,' she said. 'You're young and good-looking and you have talent, and those are all the things that Rachael Carmichael hates most in a person.'

I burned to tell her how wrong she was. I craved the sadistic thrill of telling her just how much Rachael liked *me,* even if she'd decided to hate all the rest of her relatives. But I wasn't deluded enough to think that Rachael's trust in me was entirely robust. One *stay-away-from-my-daughter!* phone call and it might all come crashing down. 'You're crazy,' I said. 'I haven't spoken to her.'

About a month after this, I was asked to come in and read with Elias Jones. Ahn had gone to one of his previous reads and said that he was very enthusiastic about the project. 'He's a genius casting,' she said. The prospect of having him as Greg seemed to be alleviating some of her frustration at having to alter the screenplay. 'He's got that warmth,' she said, 'of course, and that charisma, but in his audition he turned on this coldness that I'd never seen from him before. I really think he'll be fantastic. He's going to really surprise people.'

Elias was about forty-five, just a couple of years younger than Greg when he and Rachael started dating. He looked uncannily like the Greg Foster of the early nineties: tall, broad-shouldered, with salt-and-pepper stubble and cheeks that creased neatly when he smiled. Greg didn't look like that anymore of course. At sixty-seven, his face had the stretched, stiff signs of Botox. His eyes were too wide, and he stood like he had back problems. He wasn't quite so buff anymore. Most of the tabloid reports about his deal with Simon & Schuster used the same picture of him at an M. Night Shyamalan premiere back in August. He was smiling very wide in the picture, showing his veneers and his creepy unlined eyes. He looked like he was about to jump out of the screen and get you. But in the early nineties, he had been almost hot enough to make me understand why Rachael had stayed.

I was glad Ahn was so happy with Elias for Greg, because she'd been pretty negative about the casting process as a whole. Names were being floated for Anna Bianca, for Adam Feldman, for my mother and grandmother – the last two felt a little eerie – when Ahn put her pen down and said, 'This whole film is feeling very white.'

Everyone in the room exchanged glances. 'Well,' I said, 'Hollywood in the nineties was very white. We can't really change history.'

'I suppose not,' she said.

'This is about telling an authentic story.'

'We hear you,' said one of the execs. 'We try to cast diversely wherever we can. Rest assured, the extras will be a veritable rainbow.' He seemed immediately unsure as to whether that was something he could say. To go by Ahn's face, it wasn't.

But when conversation turned to Elias Jones, Ahn was all smiles. I wondered if she had a crush. She came with me to my chemistry read and kept a very professional face on as she shook his hand, but I had spent a lot of time around her now and I knew what it meant when she pumped his wrist up and down three times instead of two. I winked at her. She looked immediately horrified.

'Hey,' said Elias. He'd flown in from LA four days prior – his first few reads had all been over Zoom but now that it was getting serious he'd arrived, in the flesh, to dazzle us. 'Nice to meet you. Harley, isn't it?'

'Nice to meet you too.' We shook hands. He whistled.

'Amazing,' he said. 'You look exactly like her. We met at a party once, around 1995, I think it was. She didn't stay long – she never

169

did, as I understand it – but I had a brief conversation with her. Fascinating woman. Gorgeous.'

'Thank you,' I said.

We read the scene where Rachael and Greg meet on the set of *Here's Hoping*. I could see what Ahn had been raving about. Elias was right up there with Clooney and Pitt as one of America's favourite hot dads, but he brought a level of threat to his portrayal of Greg that was surprising. When I looked over at the table, I could see that everyone behind it was smiling.

'Great,' said one of the producers. 'Thanks, Elias.'

I walked him to his car. He seemed surprised when I offered to do this, and then amused. I wanted to get him alone, away from the table of producers, and see whether he could really be my Greg.

'Thanks for coming in,' I said. 'I like you for this.'

He laughed. 'I like me for this as well.'

'I think you have it.'

'I think I have it too.' He put his sunglasses on. 'You're funny,' he said. 'This movie's important to you, huh?'

'I mean, of course. It's about my aunt.'

'You guys are close?'

'Very,' I said. I loved that I didn't have to lie now when I said that. 'I was the one who brought this project to her. She said she wouldn't have trusted anyone else with it.'

'This is all your brainchild, huh?'

I smiled.

'Impressive,' he said. 'I look forward to working with you.'

'You haven't been cast yet.'

He just smiled, like I'd made a joke, and climbed into his car.

'See you in a year,' he said.

Chapter Eight

RACHAEL

31 October 1991

It's witching hour. The lights are very low. I have a big red candle on top of my dresser which is dripping wax on to the wood. It's going to be a bitch to clean tomorrow but right now I like it. It runs over the top of the dresser and off the handles on to the carpet. It smells like forests and smoke. I don't remember where I got it. I used to be able to account for everything I owned. Now I just accumulate stuff. I just open drawers, and there are things there that I don't remember ever putting away. Maybe my house is haunted.

My house. I bought it in the summer. My home in Hidden Hills, with cherrywood furniture and a firepit by the pool. I love it sometimes, and other times I loathe it and wish I had never sunk all of my money into it, especially whilst I'm still sinking all my money into Mum and Elisabeth as well. At least my house loves me back.

I don't know my neighbours. Actually, I know one of them – a pop star who just released her very cheery sophomore album and throws big parties every weekend that I'm always invited to but have never attended. The others are a mystery. I hear their voices, sometimes, beyond all the foliage, or the engines of their cars. We are all ghosts to each other. We are all of us alone, up here.

Maybe one of them is Adam. I wonder if I'll ever find out.

This time last year, he and I were walking his sister Sydney house to house between us, filling her little pumpkin basket up with sweets. It feels like a dream. Or it feels like I've been dead since then, and now I'm reincarnated, living as a new version of myself with only the occasional flash of who I used to be.

If any one thing brought me back to life, it's *Women Who Laugh at God.* That's the title they're going with, and I love it. That's exactly what I am. The whole thing is about being dark and twisted and wicked and unhappy, which is a palate cleanser after the relentless cheeriness of *The Avenue.* I never have to smile the whole day. The rage that Adam saw in me in *Here's Hoping,* the rage he was so surprised by, spills out of me now, uncontained. On my very first day on set I got to get right up in Greg's face and scream and swear and spit, jabbing my finger towards his eye, dangerously close to it. I imagined that my finger was a knife. He looked genuinely afraid of me. Maybe he's just a very good actor.

Greg Foster is not just my director – he's also my co-star. I have always been suspicious of directors who cast themselves, but I have to admit that it was a great decision. He is a very precise director – he knows exactly how he wants everything done, down to the micro-inflection – and this just gives him one less actor to wrestle with. And god knows he wrestles with us. I don't mind it, but it rubs some of the men up the wrong way, to always be told they're doing it wrong. I don't think any of them have been on a set like this before. I love how angry he makes them. He rarely raises his voice to them, but he'll cut them off mid-scene and say, 'No. Again,' over and over, until they look like they want to cry.

We're shooting some of the preliminary stuff in LA this week, before we all head to Iceland for six weeks to film in our village.

Then we come back to LA for another six weeks to finish off. Greg says that he wants the film to have a backdrop that feels barren and brutal, and right now that sounds like my perfect kind of holiday. I told him that, actually, and he laughed in that way he does where his head tips right back and the sound fills the entire room.

'You're a strange, cold person,' he told me the other day. It sounds like an insult, but he was smiling as he said it. He's a strange, changeable one. He'll be warm and cheery one second and spit flames the next. He made that comment to me whilst we were between takes, when he asked me if the kiss had been good for me.

'No,' I said.

The kiss is in the script. I feel as if I should clarify that. It's a moment where Abi comes at John and kisses him like a punishment whilst he squirms. It's horrible. I haven't seen the footage back but Greg says the scene made him feel violated, and then said, 'Don't worry, that's a good thing,' like I'd been about to apologise.

On the fourth take he put his hand on my waist and I yielded to him a little, and the kiss stopped being punishing, just for a second. Then he pulled away and said, 'No, shouldn't,' and slapped himself on the wrist. We both laughed. I don't know why we did that.

On the next take, I came at him with such force that he stumbled backwards, and then I kept pushing him backwards, relentless, until he smacked his head against the wall. I didn't stop. He pushed me off and called 'Cut', and a medic came over to check his head. It wasn't bleeding, but he had a bump the size of a robin's egg. He turned around and made me feel it. He didn't say anything whilst he did this. He just turned, and then guided my hand to the back of his head, so I could feel the skin swollen and hard beneath my fingers. Then he turned back and looked at me, and I couldn't tell what he wanted me to say.

I like the way this film makes me feel. Strange and cold, and witchy. Like I have any man's pain at my fingertips.

18 November 1991

Very cold today. At lunch I walked down to the beachfront and stood on the dark sand, the sea grey in front of me, and I let myself get cold enough that my toes ached and my breathing was short. When I came back to set, I was shaking. Greg looked at me. 'Stop shivering,' he said, and I did.

We filmed the scene where Abi comes out of her cottage, following behind her mother with a basket of linens. She looks over at John and there is something in her gaze that both allures and terrifies him. It's a hard line to walk, to be desirable and frightening all at once. I've realised, though, that it's best just to focus on the frightening. It's better to walk down to the shore and let myself become hard and icy and angry, to show coldness in every part of me. They will still want to sleep with me. That part takes care of itself.

I came out of the cottage with the basket in my arms and I stared at him, and I felt nothing. I thought that was correct. Then Greg came out of character and called 'Cut'. It's still strange to me, to watch him go from being John to being the person in charge of John and of everyone else. He stalked over to me.

'Where's the lust?' he asked.

I set the basket down. 'You tell me.'

'No, I don't have to tell you. I'm actually fucking acting.' He nodded at the basket. 'Pick that up.'

'Why?'

'Because your arms should be aching. You don't look tired, right now. You look like a spoilt movie star carrying a basket of laundry.' I picked it up. 'Okay,' he said. 'All I'm getting from you

174

right now is the iciness, and we get that, Rachael – you're a fucking ice queen; we get you can do icy. I'm asking you where the lust is.'

'Abi doesn't lust after John.'

'What the fuck does that mean?'

'She doesn't. He wants her, but she doesn't care.'

'We've talked about this. She pursues him sexually. She is aggressive about it.'

'Yes, but not because she lusts after him.'

He looked at me. Then he told everyone to take five. He led me into one of the production trailers and gestured for me to take a seat. I did so. I tried not to look apprehensive. A sit-down with Greg, I've learnt, can take hours, and he will make you cry if he wants to.

'I'm beginning to regret casting you,' he said. I must have looked shocked, because he put both hands up. 'I know, how on earth could anyone ever regret having *you* in their film? You need to start taking yourself off your own pedestal.'

This was grossly unfair, but I knew better than to say it. 'I'm just trying to play her honestly.'

'I know you are. I don't think it's even your fault.' He leant towards me. 'This is the problem, Rachael. You see Abi as power-ful, as in control, as perpetually threatening to the men around her. Yes?'

'Yes.'

He nodded. 'So why does this mean she has to be above sex?'

'She isn't—' The conversation wasn't going how I'd expected. 'She's not above it. She has it.'

'Right, but you have all these reasons in your head as to why she might have it, and none of them are as simple as, *because she wants to.*' He tilted his head. 'Why do you think desire makes a person weak?'

I flushed. I hated myself for it. 'I don't think that.'

'You do. You can't see Abi as having sexual desires and giving in to them without it destroying your image of her. You can't have her be powerful and lustful at the same time. The men are lustful, and Abi is not, and you think that's what gives her power. You've got it wrong. If you can't understand why you've got it wrong then you're going to ruin this film.'

I was ready to argue with him, but as his words sunk in, all the fight went out of me. I had a horrible feeling that he was right.

'When was the last time you really desired someone?' he asked. 'You don't need to tell me. But I want you to think about it.' He stood up. 'I'll give you a little time,' he said. 'Reflect, explore. Hell, masturbate, if that's what you need.' I felt myself going red again. 'Give me something,' he said. 'I'm not afraid to replace you. I'm not afraid to lose money and time to get this film right. I think you know that. So, give me what I need, or you're on a plane back to LA.'

When I returned to set, I could feel that everybody was look-ing at me. My heart was racing. I was still freezing, but there was a heat pressing against the back of my head, a clamminess to my hands. Greg called 'Action', and I rounded the corner of the cot-tage with my basket in my hands. I looked at him, in his power, in his knowledge, wearing the face of someone who wanted to rip the clothes off my body. I hated him and how he spoke down to me and how he never let me be comfortable in any scene, in any choice, and as I stood there, looking at him, hating him, my toes in their boots curled.

He called cut. 'Good,' he said. 'Let's go again.'

◆ ◆ ◆

We're filming in Vik, in Iceland. The settlement doesn't have a hotel big enough to house all of us so we're booked across three, and some of the crew members are being hosted in the homes of locals. We've significantly increased the population of the town. It is beautiful here – I'm sure in the summer it's that warm, breathtaking kind of beautiful, but right now it's that bleak, cold kind of beautiful that Greg wanted. We've taken over a nearby village, filming in a collection of small houses and buildings near to the coast. My house, or Abi's, is the smallest and the most remote, standing a little apart from the others. There are herbs drying over the stove and a coarse rug on the floor. Greg made me stay in that house alone for two nights.

'To immerse yourself in Abi's world,' he said. 'To let you feel her anger.'

It was freezing. I didn't notice it so much in the day, when we were filming, but at night when everyone left and I was sleeping in Abi's small house on my own, trying to keep a fire alive, the cold crept into my bones. I was terrified of being alone as well, in that pitch blackness, no lock on the front door. I learnt afterwards that there had been crew nearby, keeping watch over me, but at the time the fear was brutal. Still, I did it, and I didn't complain. That fear and that resignation is in me now. I am carrying them both through this shoot. I am understanding what makes Abi a monster. This is the dilemma, with Greg. He's not a good person. But he makes you great.

29 November 1991

There is a face that Abi has to make at John, through an opening between two houses. It has to be totally still, and lifeless, and it has to chill him. I am almost convinced that such a face doesn't exist. But Greg knows that it does, or so he says. He can see me making it. He knows that I can do it, if only I try.

Today we did thirteen takes and each time he said, 'No. Again.' On the fourteenth he didn't call a break, but he grabbed my arm and dragged me into Abi's cottage. He sat down on the stone floor. I sat in front of him. He said, 'Do the face.'

I tried. I was scared. It didn't work.

'No,' he said. 'Again.'

I tried again.

'Now smile,' he said. 'Huge smile.' I did. 'Now the face again.' I did my best. 'No. Terrible. Smile again.' I pushed my cheeks up until my eyes watered. 'Face,' he said. I dropped the smile and found the face again, more easily this time. 'Rachael!' His voice was very loud suddenly. I flinched. 'Act,' he said. 'Is it that hard? Can you fucking act?' I nodded. His expression wasn't furious – I'd seen him look angrier – but there was something very hard and frightening in the way he stared me down. It made me feel as if I could have dropped dead on the spot, gone into some kind of seizure, and he would have just kept looking at me the same way. 'Go again.'

In my fear, I was mesmerised. I went through the motions, trying to be Abi, trying to find her face, but it was harder because I was so distracted by him, by his focus. He was blinding. His gaze was so sharp. I wanted to cry, because I was disappointing him, but at the same time I wanted him to keep looking at me. I hated myself for all of it.

We did faces for half an hour, and then he sent everyone back to their hotels. 'We'll try again tomorrow,' he said. He walked past me like I didn't exist.

I've been sat in front of the mirror in my hotel room for well over an hour, practising that face. Every time I think I have it, it slides away, and all I can see is Rachael, sweating, trying desperately to transform herself into someone else. I try to get angry and keep it all behind my eyes. I try to look at myself in a way that frightens me, that shocks me enough to stop the heart, just for a second. I don't know what my face is supposed to look like anymore. I have been squeezing my fists so hard that now I have plasters on both of my palms, where my nails have punctured skin. I took out this book because I can't sleep. All I can do is lie looking up at the ceiling with an awareness of every muscle in my cheeks and forehead, making terrifying faces at the dark.

30 November 1991

Tried the scene again. I don't what I did, but after the fourth take he came out of character and nodded. 'Good,' he said. 'Finally. We can move on.'

Then he looked at me, and unexpectedly, he smiled. It was a holy feeling.

5 December 1991

We kept my no nudity clause, in the end. I couldn't think about lifting my top over my head without thinking of those Polaroids in Adam's hand, and when Robb asked, 'Are you feeling ready to scratch it out?' I just told him no, I couldn't. I expected more resistance from the studio, and from Greg in particular, but it seemed to pass surprisingly under the radar. At the table read, Greg made a small reference to the fact that the sex scene between Abi and John wouldn't be explicit – 'All implied, nothing shown,' he said, and I sank down a few millimetres into my chair, relieved.

My character Abi never wears a bra. I don't mind this – I've never had tons going on in that department, and it makes sense for her to have these subtle ways of resisting her town's typically conservative style of dress. Of course, it's completely freezing so my nipples are perpetually hard and pointy as screws. Still, I mostly have more than a couple of layers on in the Icelandic winter so they aren't quite as scene-stealing as they could be.

Today, we were filming Abi's first seduction of John. There's a tone throughout the film that she's very sexually aggressive, she's hunting him down, she's pushing him to places he maybe wouldn't volunteer to go – all behaviours that would set alarm bells ringing if they were performed by a man and levelled against a woman, but Abi is small and feminine and attractive and so the men around her are reluctant to see her as a threat. It was one of my favourite aspects of the screenplay when I first read it, the fact that she manages to be both beautiful and dangerous and yet somehow never becomes your typical femme fatale. She is mistaken for alluring, but she isn't really. She's brutal and strange and forceful. There is only one moment in the film where a man tries to enact sexual violence against her – she slashes his stomach open and gouges his eyes out as he's bleeding to death. I told Greg that I thought it would be really interesting for her to eat one of the eyes, and he said, 'You are terrifying.' Then he thought, and said, 'Would it? No. That's just shock value.' Well, I like shock value. Shocking people is fun.

In the scene we filmed today, Abi doesn't even take her clothes off. She walks towards John and pushes him down on to the bed. She ties him up. She runs a knife along his lips. She asks him if he thinks she's beautiful. He says yes, he does. She trails the knife down his stomach. She asks if he's afraid of her. He says no. She asks him why. He says he knows she'd never hurt him, that she's got a good heart. How does he know that? she asks. Well, he says, she's a nice girl. A little strange, but good to her mother, and hardworking, and beautiful. She pushes the point of the knife into his thigh. He cries out a little. He tells her not to play games. She stands up. She says, 'Alright. I won't.' She walks out and leaves him, tied up. Later, although we aren't filming this until next week, he manages to get free from his ropes and he will see her and other girls from the village dancing around a fire on the beach, naked, blurry shapes through the flames. We'll have nude underwear on, in reality, but still. Dancing around in my underwear in this weather is not an exciting prospect.

They dressed me in a white blouse and long brown skirt. My hair was loose. Greg let the AD lead the scene, wanting to stay present, something he does on particularly important days. His chest was solid, but he fell easily when I pushed him. I tied his wrists and he shivered. As I crawled up the bed towards him with my knife, my knees and elbows pressing into his soft skin, he made a gentle sound in his throat. I traced his lips with my knife. He looked up at me, hands twitching in the rope, reaching for me but unable to touch me.

'Are you afraid of me?' I asked.

'No,' he said. Not a soul in the room believed him.

When I pretended to push the point of the knife into his leg, he cried out, and even though it wasn't real, I felt a rush. The feeling of having him under me, frightened, squirming, was intoxicating. Just for a few minutes, he was at my mercy.

The AD called cut. Greg tugged at the rope. 'Shit,' he said. 'You really tied me.'

'Let me help.' I set the knife down and helped him undo the knots. When his wrists were free, he rubbed them, grinning at me, and I fancied that he still looked a little afraid. He went over to review the footage. 'Okay,' he said, 'great stuff.' He sounded as if he really meant it. It was rare that Greg had anything positive to say about my first take of anything. 'Let's go again,' he said.

The second take wasn't quite as good. The novelty had worn off, slightly, but I was still having fun with it, still enjoying the threat of the knife and the way his breath quickened. We did four takes – a record low number for Greg – and then he said, 'Okay, that's great, Rachael. We'll just do some close-ups now.'

He was harsher here, micro-analysing my expressions again, speaking sharply if he felt I wasn't picking something up fast enough. When he finally decided we were done, he walked back over to the monitor, and I followed him, standing at his shoulder.

'What the fuck?' The words slipped out before I could stop them. Greg turned towards me a little clumsily, bumping the monitor with his shoulder. He hadn't realised I was watching the footage with him.

The shirt was see-through. How had I not realised? With the orange light on it, my breasts were fully visible. I might as well have been topless.

He reached towards me. 'Rachael, come watch the scene. See how well it works.' I took a step backwards. 'Don't throw a tantrum,' he said.

'Send me back to Wardrobe, and then we reshoot.'

'We won't be reshooting,' he said. 'This is gold. You won't be able to make this happen again, not after this conversation.'

'Then you'll be hearing from my attorney.'

'Rachael.' He caught my wrist, but gently. His thumb made circles on it. I looked down in surprise. 'I'm sorry,' he said. 'I didn't realise until I came and looked at what we'd shot. I didn't mean to mislead you.' The AD and other crew members were looking off into the distance, embarrassed for me. I wrenched my hand away. 'Would you just watch it?' he asked. I wasn't used to him speaking to me so softly, especially when I was being aggressive with him. 'Watch it,' he said, 'and then we can talk. And I'll hear your concerns out.' I imagine my face was sceptical. 'I promise.'

He positioned me beside him. My arms were crossed protectively over my chest. I watched the scene, hoping to find something about it that didn't work, a criticism that he would have to listen to, anything that might induce him to shoot it again. I couldn't find any. We were brilliant together. I watched myself talking to him in that low, sweetly threatening way, my face quiet, occasionally flickering into a wolfish grin before settling again, and I knew then, painfully and for absolute certain, that this was the best I had ever acted.

And dammit, fuck it all to hell, what he'd said to me in the audition room was right. Abi was exposed and unembarrassed, completely playing him, completely in possession of him and his senses. As her, I carried myself like I wasn't even aware that my body was on display – because I hadn't been. But it read as a total lack of consciousness in myself, a proof that Abi was missing something – a coyness, a bashfulness, a sense of prudence, whatever – that other people had. It just worked. There wasn't anything else I could say.

'You get it,' said Greg. I nodded. 'You are a marvel,' he said, and he bent down and kissed me on the cheek. 'You are helping me make the best film of my career. Thank you.'

I was so astonished that I couldn't think of anything at all to say in response.

16 December 1991

Filmed my monologue today. I expected him to pick it apart, which he did, a little, the first few takes. I had to stand very still and let the camera slowly come towards me. Those first few takes, he had lots of notes, but after a while, when I got to the end, he would just nod and say, 'Reset.'

Every time I thought we were done, we did another one. I hated him for it, as I always did when he made me do things over and over when I knew I'd done them well the first time. The camera drank it in. Eventually he looked at me and said, 'Rachael? What do you think?'

I was astonished. 'It was good,' I said.

'It was more than that,' he said. 'It was far more than good.'

23 December 1991

I've complained about LA heat many times, especially close to Christmas, but there's nothing like a dose of Icelandic winter to make you grateful for the ability to walk around in a t-shirt. I have something of a Christmas holiday now, before we finish making *Women Who Laugh at God*, but then it's back to work on the 27th and after that I return to London to shoot season four of *The Avenue*. Still, for the next seven days I don't have to worry about Abi, or her face, or Greg's opinions on it, or the fact that one of these days I might forget to pull my punches, so to speak, and whack him around the head with a hammer for real.

He was very against us having Christmas off. He thought we might 'lose the momentum of the piece'. He was forced to back down, but now I'm worrying that he might have been right. I'm sat curled up on my sofa with the French windows open, a small box of Raffaello beside me, and I couldn't feel further away from Iceland and that small, claustrophobic community, and Abi's rage. For the first time in a while, I don't feel angry at all.

He called me this afternoon and asked me to go for drinks. 'Why?' I asked, like an idiot, and I heard him laugh.

'Because I think it would be good for us to check in,' he said. 'Stay connected, stay in one space, be aware of where the other one is at. Abi and John's chemistry is what the whole film hangs on, and it's something that we've worked hard to build.'

'I'm not even your wife.'

'Pardon?'

'I mean—' I rested my head on the doorframe. 'John has a wife. Why aren't you taking Francesca out for drinks?' Francesca Chevrony plays John's wife, Elisa. She's a pretty, blonde actress in her late thirties, once in lots of quirky, arty romance films but now

184

the mother in awards-bait dramas. Greg goes pretty easy on her compared to everyone else.

'Fran and I get coffee,' he said. 'We're old friends. We have that easy chemistry that comes with an old friendship. It doesn't need as much maintenance as the intensity between Abi and John.'

'I see.'

'You're a sceptical woman,' he said. 'One drink. I just want to touch base. And then we'll go our separate ways and have very merry Christmases. The merriest.'

I looked at myself in the hallway mirror. I was still in my pyjamas and I hadn't washed my hair since getting back from Iceland or taken my make-up off the night before. I'd actively climbed out of Abi's head. It was going to take some work to turn back into the version of myself that Greg would expect to meet in dim lighting and raise an Old Fashioned to. On the other end of the phone, he waited. I wondered if Anna was listening. I pictured her sitting at the other end of the breakfast table, chest heaving in anger. 'Okay,' I said. 'One drink.'

'Atta girl,' he said. 'I'll see you at Century Plaza at nine. Want me to send a car?'

'I can get there on my own.'

He chuckled. 'Of course you can.'

I looked at myself in the mirror for a while. I thought about how I would look coming towards him in the bar, and what he would see. I thought, *Black. All over.* A velvet skirt. A top that showed a little shoulder. Heels, but small ones, like I'd just slipped them on. A big black coat. A red lip. I would not let myself shave, because this wasn't a seduction, at least not in the sexual sense. But I wanted Greg Foster to be infatuated with me. I wanted him to see me as something not quite human at all. I wanted him to imagine me waking up in my red lip and delicate heels, ready to slink on to his film set and make magic. There had been moments, in Iceland, where he had looked at me and he hadn't seen the girl whose performance hadn't quite been cutting it. He'd seen this muse-worthy, art-inspiring *thing*. The feeling that gave me was indescribable. I liked transcending my form. I wanted him to look at me that way again.

When I stepped out of the car at Century Plaza, I was twenty minutes late. It was a little later than I'd planned to be, but better than being too early. One pap lurked nearby, standing up to snap a series of pictures as I headed inside. Generously, I waved.

In the delicate light particular to hotel bars – never so low as to be seedy but always forgivingly dim – I looked for Greg. He was sitting at a table near the back of the room, a flickering flame in front of him. He saw me, and he stood, silently, his chair making no sound as he pushed it back. I couldn't read his face. He kissed my hand, which I had never seen him do, to anyone. The gesture felt far too European for him, totally incongruous with his loud-mouthed Americanisms. I was learning that Greg Foster was about four different men wearing the body of one. It was one of the things that made him so exciting to work with.

'Good to see you,' he said. He didn't comment on the time. He'd expected me to keep him waiting. 'What are you drinking?'

'Scotch.' It isn't my favourite drink, but men like Greg like to order you a Scotch. 'On the rocks.'

He waved a waiter over, not in the cheery way that Adam used to, but with a very slight motion of his hand, with the quiet confidence that he would be noticed. Immediately there was a waiter at his side. He ordered the same drink as me – a coincidence, or a flattering imitation? I wasn't sure.

'Enjoying the break?' he asked me.

'Enjoying the warmth.'

He laughed. 'Bleak, wasn't it?'

'And brutally cold. But beautiful. Exactly as you said.'

He leant back in his chair, regarding me. He was in a black shirt, grey suit jacket hanging on the back of his chair. He always has stubble along his jaw. I used to hate it when Adam didn't shave, but I like the way it looks on Greg. There's something dignified about stubble when it's greying. His sleeves were rolled up. I'd stopped noticing that he was attractive, on set, but I saw him to advantage now in this fancy bar, away from the impossible standards and the belligerent cold of *Women Who Laugh at God*. I could imagine a version of Anna and him that made sense in my head, back when she had still been very young, buoyant in her beauty and her blondeness, and he had been in his early thirties and learning how to get his suits properly tailored. I could see her on his arm. These days, he far surpasses her. He belongs to a whole other world entirely – one that eclipses the world of movie-making and is closer to art. To great work. Anna will never know great work like Greg and I do.

'Have you struggled?' he asked.

I wondered if this was a general question. 'On set?'

'Yes. I'm sure this can't be like any shoot you've been on before. It certainly can't be anything like *The Avenue*.' We both laughed. 'Have you struggled?' he repeated.

I felt strangely as if it might be a blow to his pride to deny it, so I nodded and said, 'A little, perhaps.'

'You've done very well,' he said. 'I wanted to warn you, though.' Our drinks arrived, and the waiter set them down. I smiled, heart thumping as I anticipated what the warning might be. 'It'll be hard,' he said, 'going back.'

'I know – we'll all be out of sync.'

'That isn't what I mean.' He raised his glass, took a sip. 'You trust me, don't you?' he asked. 'As a creative ally?' He caught my smirk. 'Okay, I know. You think I'm full of myself when I use phrases like that. Well, phrases like that are important. We have to be able to talk about what we do like it's important.' He set his drink down, index finger pointing at me. 'I know what you're like with other people. I can tell. *Oh, I'm just an actor. I just make movies. It's silly.* We don't do that here. We don't put caveats on what we do. Sure, we're not soldiers, we're not doctors, but what we do has an importance that you cannot undermine. Because the minute you give other people permission not to take it seriously, you give yourself permission to treat it as if it's something not worth their respect. And then, you become a bad actor.'

I enjoyed watching him get animated when it wasn't in anger. 'I don't think I need to be pretentious to take it seriously.'

'Maybe not,' he said, 'but you can't be sardonic. You can't be cynical.' I smiled down at my drink. I heard him laugh. 'I know. Look who I'm talking to. Miss Wednesday Addams over here.' The comparison surprised me. Another piece of the puzzle – another clue as to how he saw me. 'I know you take your work seriously,' he said. 'I'm not trying to suggest that you don't. All I'm saying is that you don't have to keep up the performance around me. You don't have to act as if film-making isn't the very highest calling in the world.'

'You really think it is?'

'Not objectively,' he said. 'But subjectively. As do you.'

I realised that I wasn't sure how to talk to him. He rattled off these speeches so easily and seemed so confident that we were always on the same page – it made me nervous to open my mouth for fear of shattering the illusion.

'You've been noticed,' he said.

It took a minute for the words to sink in. Greg smiled his white smile and raised his glass, his finger extended against the side of it, pointing over my left shoulder. I turned.

There he was. Sat with a friend – male, thankfully for my heart – with a bourbon in front of him. He jumped a little, when I looked at him, like his first response was to lower his head, but then he gave a small smile and raised his hand.

It had been over a year since I'd seen him last. He was even more luminous. Photos in magazines and TV interviews didn't do him justice. You only really understood how beautiful he was when you saw him in person, and he was right in front of you, smiling.

'Old boyfriend?' asked Greg, sipping his drink. He knew, of course. Everyone had known about Adam and me. Many people thought that we were still together, even though it had been a year since we were photographed. Lots of tabloids had spoken on it, of course, and sources had come forward to explain that we were done, but plenty refused to believe it without hard proof – and that was something that neither Adam nor I were too bothered about supplying.

I turned back to Greg. 'Yes. How strange.'

'Go catch up, if you like.'

I shook my head, with a smile, like it was a silly thought. 'Later.' I knew enough about Greg Foster to know that he needed to be the priority. He rewarded me with a smile of his own, leaning back to look at me in that interested way that he did. I wondered who I was in his head right then. Wednesday Addams, still? His Abi? Someone else entirely?

He kept me half an hour more. When at last he stood up, I asked why he was going so soon, and he said, 'Well, we said one drink, didn't we? And I promised Anna I'd get back.' I wondered what he'd wanted to get out of this drink and whether he felt as if he'd got it. I told him I was going to stay and finish my drink. I'd been nursing my Scotch. I waited until he was out of the door before I turned back around to Adam's table. He was still there. His friend was talking, and he was nodding along, but as soon as I turned around I watched his eyes slide into mine. We just sat for a second, looking at each other. He was still nodding.

I had been comfortable in my vampy red lip and my black velvet skirt and Abi's assurance, feeling alluring, feeling magnetic. Now he looked at me and it was like he was seeing me in costume. If I'd known I was going to be seeing him I would have dressed as his Rach, but it was too late. He put a hand on his friend's arm. He stood up. His friend turned around to look at me, and I saw that it was Shema Muhire, his *Dragonborn* co-star. We had never met, but Shema nodded at me, a polite smile on his face and I nodded back. I was aware of Adam crossing the room, standing over my table.

'Rach,' he said.

I stood up to hug him. I didn't do the overzealous, over-cheerful thing you're supposed to do with your ex – I'd always thought that's how I would play it, but I just hugged him. He put his hand on my back between my shoulder blades for a second and then let me go. 'Hey, stranger,' I said, and wanted to die.

'Hey.' He nodded at the empty chair. 'Sorry. Did I chase your date out?'

And then I realised that he had seen me and Greg together, in a fancy bar, laughing and talking. 'Oh, god,' I blurted out, before I could stop myself. 'No. This was a work thing. He's my boss. I'm doing his film. It was just a meeting—'

'Rach, it's okay.' He pointed at the chair. 'Can I sit?'

'Please.'

He sat opposite me. I felt two years younger. He hadn't changed a bit since I'd last seen him, apart from the fact that when he adjusted his watch strap I caught sight of a small smiley face tattoo on the inside of his wrist. He caught me looking. 'Got them with the cast,' he said.

'Right.' *What a stupid thing to pick*, I thought. 'Cute.'

'How are you? How's the film?'

'It's great. We just got done filming in Iceland. A few more weeks shooting here, and then that's it.'

'Has it been everything you wanted it to be?'

'More,' I said honestly. 'Too much, at times.' Even more honest. Unnecessarily so. Adam gave me a questioning look. 'Greg's intense. But a genius.'

'Of course,' said Adam.

'Are you shooting *Dragonborn* again already?'

'In the new year, yeah. We've got a cast mixer in a couple of days, though.'

'Hasn't that cast mixed enough? Everyone's dating.' That made him laugh, properly. Hearing it gave me quite the feeling. It wasn't something I'd imagined was still in my power to do.

'Well, it's an excuse for everyone to get drunk together, I guess. Initiate the new kids.'

'Let them scope out their targets.'

'Oh, of course.'

'Still liking it?'

'I mean, the scripts are steadily getting more ridiculous,' he said. 'But the people are amazing.'

He seemed happy, completely at ease. Like he'd been expecting to run into me in this bar. I felt that he looked at me with approval, like he was pleased to see that I was doing well and doing good work, and it warmed me. 'You look just the same.' I didn't mean to say it.

He smiled, but something was missing from it now. He looked down. 'Is that a good thing?'

'You know it is. A woman in Arizona turned her garden shed into a shrine to you.' He looked alarmed. 'Adam, don't you read the news?'

'What kind of news are you reading, Rach?'

I laughed, but I thought I might be blushing as I did it. Of course I look out for news about him. He must be doing the same, whatever he says.

'I'm keeping you from your friend,' I said.

'He's gone home.'

I looked behind me. Shema had indeed left, and their table was empty. 'Oh.'

'He had an event to get to,' said Adam. 'He was supposed to leave a little while ago, but he said he'd wait with me.'

'For what?'

'For you.'

I picked up my Scotch and drank, for something to do. I was worried that he could see my hand trembling. Maybe he did, because when I put my glass down he was looking solemn.

'I need to tell you something,' he said.

I knew what it would be. 'Okay.'

'I'm seeing someone.'

It still hurt. 'Well, that's great.'

'Yeah.' He didn't sound convinced.

'How long?'

'Six months.'

'Of course,' I said. He looked nervous. 'An appropriate amount of time after the break-up, but still significant.'

'What does that mean?'

'Well, you're not the sort to move on too quickly, but you wouldn't be approaching me all friendly if you didn't feel completely over it.'

'Don't say that,' he said gently.

'Aren't you completely over it?'

He looked at me, helplessly. In his face I saw the awkward boy I'd met on the set of *Girls Getting Ready*. 'Are you going to marry her?' I asked.

'What sort of question is that?'

I shrugged.

He paused, dropping his gaze. 'Maybe. If she wants me to.'

'Really? I was joking.'

'It's not a crazy idea, that you might marry someone you love.' He hadn't meant to say that last word. I could tell by the way his eyes went quickly back to my face, looking for a reaction. 'She wants me to,' he said.

'She asked you? Very progressive.'

'Rach.' He sighed. 'She's traditional,' he said. 'She thinks about this stuff.'

'What does she do?'

'She's a waitress,' he said.

'A *waitress?*'

'Shh.'

'Where on earth did you meet a *waitress?*'

'Well,' he said, 'at a restaurant.'

'You just picked her up in a restaurant?'

'I wrote down my number on a napkin.'

We stared at each other. I don't know why. I don't know what we were each waiting for.

'Shit,' I said. 'She must think she's in a movie.'

If I could go back and do that conversation with Greg again, in that bar tonight, I'd tell him how excited I was to go back to work. That nothing could keep me away. That all I wanted in the world was to prise open Abi's mind, and crawl back in, and pick up an axe, and turn men into firewood.

I asked Adam if we could be friends. 'I don't know,' he said. 'I don't think it's a good idea.'

'Okay,' I said. 'Walk away from my fucking table, then.'

8 January 1992

I'm a week late, but my New Year's resolutions are as follows:

I will fall in love only for academic purposes. If I act in a romance – if I ever do again – and the screenplay is good enough to warrant it, then I will fall in love just to recall and absorb the feelings and mimic the behaviour. Then I will fall straight back out.

I will get back into cooking. I will do things for myself, with my hands. More than just the one main thing that I do for myself with my hands.

I will never, not for love nor money, work with Greg Foster again.

He is a vampire. He is a kind of insidious fungus. He will pretend to treat you as a creative equal, a partner in the crazy ride of movie-making. He will wax lyrical about the importance of the craft and the role you both play in it. And then he will suck the life out of you and take you over completely. He doesn't care what's left of me at the end of this process, just so long as he gets his Abi on film.

I'm sat in my trailer currently. I'm shaking. The man *spat* at me. At my feet. Thirty takes of Abi's fit, of the screaming, shaking, contorting monster she has to turn herself into, something subhuman, something beyond the bounds of what a normal person can achieve. So described Greg. And I said, 'Greg, if it's beyond the bounds of what a normal person can achieve, how can I achieve it?' And he said, 'You will.'

Thirty times he made me do it. Thirty times, and now I can't breathe properly out of my left side, and I've bruised my elbow and twisted my ankle from dropping to the ground like a stone and writhing. Thirty times, and my eyes are red from straining them out of their sockets and there's a ringing in my ears from the hyperventilating I've been forcing. Thirty times, and eventually I stood up, unsteady, sure that we had it. Empty.

And he said, 'Go again.'

I looked at him.

He said, 'Go again.'

I said, 'No.'

'What?'

'You have it. I know you have it. I won't go again.' I was panting. I might have been crying. 'I can't do it again.'

'We don't have it.'

'I've done it thirty times.'

'And we don't have it. So is it my direction, or your acting, Rachael? Which is it?'

'It's your fucking direction, I think, Greg.'

Silence. I heard one of the runners gasp. *Get a grip*, I thought, but then the next thing I knew he was striding over the set towards me. He raised himself up, and I thought he was going to scream in my face, as he's done before, but instead he made this sucking sound and then he spat. It landed at my feet, just a centimetre from my bare toe. A round, white globule. I looked down at it, and then up at him. I was incandescent.

For a second, he looked like he regretted it.

I stormed past him. I was aware of someone calling my name, then of Greg saying, 'Let her go.'

They've come in since I've been writing this and tried to call me back to set, but I keep telling them I need time and I scribble on. It's the most unprofessional I've ever been but right now I can't bring myself to care.

Greg himself. His voice at the door.

'Rachael?'

I have to go.

◆ ◆ ◆

I went back to set. I did it one more time. With all of the pain and the anger and the frustration left in me, I screamed. I writhed. I cursed. I spat. Just like he had done. Spat right out in his direction. I wonder if he'll leave it in.

'Cut,' he said. He didn't make me do it again. 'You can go,' he said, not looking at me.

I stalked back to my trailer. Someone knocked, offering me ice for my ankle. I sent them away. Then came Greg's voice again.

'Rachael?'

It was softer than the first time he'd called for me.

'Can I come in?'

I didn't say anything. He pushed the door open anyway. He saw me with my foot elevated on the bed – we've done a lot of shooting at night so a bed has been essential. He tutted, like I'd hurt myself in some unrelated injury.

'Is it bad?'

I shrugged.

'You're furious with me,' he said. 'I know.' He sat on the chair opposite me. 'Just wait until you see the footage,' he said. 'It will help.'

'It was good, in the end?'

'Incredible,' he said. 'Astonishing.'

Gone was the tyrant. He looked smaller in my trailer, almost apologetic, or at least as apologetic as Greg ever was. He went to my freezer. There was a bag of frozen kale in the bottom drawer – he took it out and held it in his hands, unsure for a second, looking for something to wrap it in. I tossed him my cardigan. He brought it over to me and laid it on my ankle, carefully, almost tenderly.

'I didn't mean for you to injure yourself,' he said.

'You didn't care when it happened.'

'I was in the moment. I was in that room with Abi. I didn't have time to worry about Rachael.' I scoffed. 'You think it's a cop-out, when I say things like that, but I'm being completely honest with you.'

'Do you think the ends always justify the means?' I asked.

'My means? For my ends? Yes.' He watched me roll my eyes again. 'So will you,' he said, 'when you see the film.'

I'm not sure. I think I'll remember the pain and the humiliation, the way that sometimes being on set with him takes all the pleasure out of acting. But the way he was looking at me just then, eyes shining, was something else. He loves me. As a performer, as his Abi. As the centre of his art. He adores me like Da Vinci must have adored his Lisa. And I know he doesn't do any of this to me because he doesn't think I'm enough. He isn't trying to push me to my limit. He does it all because he doesn't think I have a limit. That if he keeps pushing, and pushing, and pushing, he'll push me up amongst the stars.

11 January 1992

I'll be going back to London next month. I'm beginning to be homesick for it, for bus wheels on rainy tarmac and walking to dinner, for coats and pubs and the shadows of buildings on narrow streets. But it feels as if every time I have to go back, something comes out of nowhere and ties me to LA. Something inescapable, and always, eventually, destructive.

I double-checked my wardrobe for the sex scene yesterday. I said, 'No nipples,' very sternly to Greg on set, which made him laugh loudly and then repeat it back to me. I made my dresser shine a very bright torch on my chest area and then my bum, just to check they weren't trying to pull anything again.

'I don't understand what you're so concerned about,' said Greg. 'You've done it once.'

'It wouldn't be right, for this bit,' I said, and he thought about it, and then agreed no, it wouldn't.

This had to be just about the act. There had to be no aestheticism to it, no pleasing slip of the blouse to reveal a pink nipple, no erotic close-ups of hands tracing skin and suggestive silhouettes. It had to be animalistic, fast, urgent, the two of them pressed up against the wall of the barn, not bothering to tear at each other's clothes but tearing at each other's necks instead with their teeth, focused solely on the sensation, on the power of it, on the immediacy. My tits aren't coming out for this one.

John finally snaps. He pushes Abi against the wall. She kicks him in the shin, he howls, his head drops forward; she seizes her moment, pins him down with her entire body. Grabs his chin and forces him to look up at her. No telling who goes in first. His hands scrabble at her skirt, pull it up. She slides him into her (not really, of course, but my hand moves under my skirt at about the height of his belt as I pretend). It happens so quickly that he cries out and she puts a hand over his mouth, and she's smiling, the first time we see her smile, but it's terrifying. She presses harder and his eyes go wide. He bites down on her fingers. She cries out. He twists her under him, her back pressed against him now, hand at her throat, squeezing just a little. Fire in her eyes at this suggestion of violence, and such a *predictable* kind for a man to enact against a woman. She thought higher of him. She reaches back and rakes her nails down the side of his shirt until rivets of blood appear, and he staggers backwards. They look at each other. And then he comes towards her again, and this time he lets her lead.

I think this is all in the script, but honestly, I'm not sure I even remember.

We did it for two hours, over and over, until we could feel that the surprise had gone out of the movements and Greg called time. But he was happy – we'd got it. There had been a few takes in the middle that were pure fury and blood and heat. I was sweating a little and trying to disguise it.

I had the *Here's Hoping* premiere across town that evening and I had to go to a nearby hotel to be made beautiful. Production were calling me a car, but Greg came towards me. He'd just showered. He raked a hand through dark grey hair, newly wet. 'I'll drive her,' he said. 'I'm done here for the day.'

We got in his car. The radio came on automatically and he turned it off. We pulled out of the studio lot and he showed his ID at the gate. 'So,' he said, as he turned on to the freeway. 'Good day.'

'I think so.'

'You were excellent.' Praise like this means more from him when it isn't meant as an apology. I smiled. 'I've felt your inhibitions dropping away on this shoot,' he said. 'It's been a joy to witness.'

'I've felt it too. I wish I could go back and shoot some of the early stuff over.'

'I know,' he said. 'I don't think you need to worry, though. I think you're going to be very pleased with this.'

'I won't watch it.'

He looked at me sideways. 'No?'

'I never watch myself.'

'You're one of those.'

'I always hate it. It makes me nauseous.'

'Aren't we on our way to a premiere?' I explained that I always slip out before the film starts playing. 'You have to watch yourself,' he said. 'Like athletes do. Analyse your game. Besides,' he added, 'I know you don't always hate it.'

'No?'

'No. You didn't hate it when I showed you that scene in Iceland. The one where you had me tied to the bed.' Our eyes met, briefly. He looked away. 'You liked watching yourself there,' he said.

At the premiere, I watched him on the carpet with Anna. She looked admittedly amazing, in something tight and clean white, smiling with her hair blown back from her face. I'd imagined walking this carpet with Adam. It was hard to stand on it alone. It was harder, because when I looked a little way down the carpet and saw Greg and Anna posing, her hands clutching his arm, I knew that they were all wrong together. As we were ushered towards the foyer, he moved through the crowd to touch my arm.

'No sneaking off,' he said.

He looked good in a suit. Not dazzling, like Adam, but tall and in charge. I shook my head, and he smiled. Anna found him. She said, 'Hi, Rachael,' with a fake smile, and then pulled him away. I watched them go. I took comfort in the fact that she will never understand my relationship with Greg. Theirs is a marriage, simple and ordinary, but he has never been her director. She has never felt that white, blinding hate that infuses the work you're doing together with a furious energy, that comes in waves and transforms, sometimes, into something else. Something low and humming, something all passion and impossible to categorise. When I took my seat and the lights went down, I knew that he couldn't see me. But I imagined that he was watching me, in the darkness, happy that I stayed.

At the drinks reception afterwards – a part that I never usually make it to – he approached me with two glasses of champagne and a broad smile.

'What did you think?' he asked.

Sarah Griffin, who had tried and failed to get me to an early screening, had already embraced me and poured so much praise on me that I'd wanted to cry. Approving words from Greg would probably tip me over the edge, I thought, but I still wanted to hear them.

'I think I was good,' I said.

He handed me a glass and raised his to me. 'I think you were exceptional.'

The relief was enormous. I'd known it had been a good performance but hearing him say it made it real. 'Thank you.' I looked over his shoulder. 'Where's Anna?'

'Gone home. She doesn't like to be out too late with the kids.'

I stared at him.

'What?'

'I forgot you had children,' I said.

'Two boys. Three and five.' He took a sip of champagne. 'She fell pregnant very early in our relationship. It's why we got married so quickly.' He wasn't talking quietly. He either didn't care if anyone in the room heard us or he assumed they already knew. 'I know what you think,' he said. 'You think we're a strange couple.'

'You are a strange couple.'

He laughed at that.

'It's okay, though. Lots of couples are strange. If it works, it works.'

'We're separating.'

'Oh,' I said, stumped.

He raised his eyebrows at me over the champagne glass.

I was whisked away by Sarah to meet people. My publicist, Gemma, never far away, whispered their biographies to me. I'm very good these days at making small talk on autopilot and letting my mind wander away. I got particularly good at it just after Adam and I broke up. Now my thoughts were of Greg, and why he'd told me what he'd told me, and why he'd looked at me the way he had.

I was aware of the way he moved through the room separate from me, stepping into conversations after I had left them, walking parallel to me amongst the crowd, like a choreographed dance. Eventually he took my hand and said, 'Rachael, are you coming to Barfly?' I didn't really want to go to a club, but I just nodded.

Cars were called. Greg and I got in one alone. He looked at me, and then he reached out and moved my chin towards him. It surprised me again, how gentle he could be. How he could rein in that force that he was and become soft for me, in the right moments. He said, 'You're exhausted.'

'Yes.'

'Tired of being told how wonderful you are.'

I laughed. 'Yes.'

'Do you want to go home? We're both working tomorrow.'

'I'm not going home with you,' I said carefully.

He smiled. 'Of course you're not. What made you think of it?'

'I don't know.' He was still holding my face. 'I don't know,' I said again, and then – the strangest thing – he leant in and kissed me. It was very light, and very brief, and I couldn't even say whether it was romantic until he pulled away and looked at me, and I saw that it was.

I had never imagined that he had fallen in love with me. But there was no mistaking it. He cleared his throat. 'I'm sorry,' he said. 'I couldn't help it.'

I sat back, stunned.

'What's your address?' he asked. He saw my face. 'I'm not presuming. I'm just going to give it to the car so that it gets you home, okay?'

'Where are you going?'

'Home as well. You're setting a good example. I like to be there when my boys wake up.'

There was something very domestic in the way he said *my boys*. It was a side of him I hadn't seen before. I gave him my address. He leant forward and related it to the driver.

We drove in silence for a while. Eventually, he said, 'Rachael. I am getting a divorce.'

I nodded. I didn't know what to say. The best thing would have been to tell him outright that I didn't love him, but then he would have asked what it was that I did feel, and I suddenly didn't know.

'You're still married right now.'

'Yes,' he said. 'We're going to separate. But yes.'

'Then we shouldn't talk about this anymore.'

He nodded. 'I respect that.' We drove on. 'I hope I haven't made things strange,' he said.

'No, of course not,' I said, even though he obviously had.

The car pulled up outside my gate. I turned to open my car door, and he put his hand on mine.

'You are the biggest curveball life has ever thrown me,' he said. His hand lifted.

When I was outside and the car was pulling away, I looked back, and caught a glimpse of him through the window. He was lighting a cigarette, with a smile.

Chapter Nine

HARLEY

Elias' prediction had been a little off. It wasn't a year until we next saw each other – it was seven months. I spent three of them in Vietnam and Laos with Julia and Carlton, resort-hopping and getting excited emails from Ahn about minor updates to our production schedule. We were very happy in Asia – it was like being eighteen and backpacking with not a care in the world. Julia slept with a cabana boy (she loves a princess/stable boy type of romance) and Carlton read an entire book. I lay out by the pool and dreamt about Rachael. Not my aunt Rachael – that would have been weird – but my Rachael. Young Rachael, falling into the grip of Greg Foster, not able to tell whether she was enamoured with the job or with the man until it was too late. I carried her with me everywhere.

About two months into our trip, I got a text from Rachael (my aunt, this time, of course). *Hvnt seen u in a while . . . film going well?* I sent her a photo of me on a curtained sunbed with Julia and said, *Starting soon!* She didn't reply.

Eventually we were getting ready to start shooting and I moved back home for a month of prep before I relocated to LA, where we'd be filming the majority of the project. We'd be doing three weeks in

Iceland at the end to shoot some of the *Women Who Laugh at God* stuff. I typed 'Iceland aesthetic' into Pinterest and found a waterfall you could stand behind. Julia agreed to come visit for a weekend so we could take pictures.

I packed up. Julia and Carlton, both perpetually supportive and perpetually unemployed, had offered to fly out with me for the beginning of the shoot to help me get settled. I went to Rachael's house for a final game of tennis. I thought she might let me win, sentimentally, but she didn't.

'How are you feeling?' she asked, over halloumi burgers and kale chips.

'Very excited.'

'Nervous?'

'Of course.' I was trying to take small bites of my burger – I had reminded her multiple times over the last few months that I was on a diet pre-shoot and she ignored me every time. 'Any advice? On how to be you?'

'I didn't feel much, during that time,' she said shortly. 'It shouldn't be hard.'

I put my hand on her arm. She looked down at it. I withdrew it.

'I have a place in LA,' she said.

'It's alright – Production already found me somewhere cute.'

'No, I mean, I think I'll be using it.'

I put down my burger. 'You'll be in LA?'

'The next *Traversers* starts in a couple of months,' she said, 'so the shoots overlap anyway. I was thinking I might fly out early, get situated. So I'll be there to keep an eye on things – on you – if you need a sounding board for any reason, or you want to run any choices by me.'

I was incredibly moved. 'Rachael,' I said, 'you don't need to do that. Honestly.'

'I want to,' she said. 'Finish your burger.'

I picked it up, reluctantly.

'I see you picking at it,' she said.

'It's your fault. You were tiny in the nineties.'

'Well, I was always hungry. You shouldn't be always hungry.'

'That's part of being an actress. Staying hungry.' I swallowed. 'Metaphorically and literally.'

She rolled her eyes. She didn't like when people were pretentious about acting.

'I didn't know you still had a house out there,' I said.

'Well, it was the first place I ever bought for myself. It's special to me. And it's nice to have somewhere that feels familiar, when I fly out to do *Traversers*. Why are your eyes so wide? Are you choking?'

'I just had the best idea,' I spluttered, around my burger. 'You should fly out with us!'

'Us?'

'Me, Carlton and Julia. We're taking Carlton's dad's jet. You should totally join – there's tons of room.'

She looked far from sure. 'Who's Carlton's dad?'

'Jono. The producer?'

'No last name?'

'I mean, he has one, but he doesn't use it. He's pretty successful. And his plane is really nice. The toilets are gold.' I pushed my plate away from me, even though I hadn't even eaten half of the burger, and she pushed it back. 'Please?' I said. 'They're dying to meet you.'

'Fine,' she said. 'As long as there's plenty to drink.'

On Carlton's dad's plane? She could not have made an easier request.

'So, here are the whiskeys,' said Carlton, waving his hand at one set of cabinet doors. 'The champagne fridge is below and the wine fridge is on the left of that, and then we've got vodkas and gins on the other side. Over there we've got all the weird liquors he doesn't like enough to keep in the house, and *here*—' He reached behind the bar and pulled out a green bottle. 'Absinthe,' he said.

'Absinthe?'

'That one's mine,' said Carlton. 'Put it there before we took this thing to Vegas. Never doing that again. Vegas on absinthe is a house of horrors. But it's there if you want it.'

Rachael blinked at him, small in her oversized sweats.

'Help yourself,' said Carlton. 'Anything's yours. My dad was very clear. Rachael Carmichael on his plane? He said you could take the pilot home if you wanted.'

'I'm alright,' said Rachael.

'Suit yourself. James isn't bad in bed, or so he tells me.'

'So,' I said brightly. Rachael was giving Carlton a look like he'd just come up to her in the street with a clipboard and asked for a few minutes of her time. 'Which seat do you want?'

She chose one at the far end of the cabin and took out a book. Julia twisted round in her chair to stare at her. I smacked her arm.

'Would you stop? You're acting like Ed Sheeran didn't play at your birthday party last year.'

'Sorry,' she said. 'It's just that we've talked about her so much. And the two of you really do look so alike.'

I chose a wine I knew she liked and poured her a glass, along with one for myself. She put her book down as I approached. 'Thank you, Harley.' I sat down opposite her, setting both glasses on the side table. 'You must have told your parents something by now,' she said.

I had. It had all reached a point where I hadn't really been able to avoid it. I'd told them most of the truth – that the rumours about Cagnoni's Rachael Carmichael biopic were true, and I'd been cast as Rachael. But I said that she'd signed away her life rights from a distance, with no involvement, and the two of us hadn't been in the same room.

'That doesn't sound like Rachael,' said Mum. 'She's a complete control freak.'

'*Why* do you hate her so much?'

'I don't hate her. She's just not a good person. You should know that, if you're going to play her.' Dad had disappeared into the kitchen for champagne at the mention of a film role, but Mum sat on the sofa and looked at me, a crease in her forehead. I always think she started applying SPF far too late in life. 'You should have told me sooner. This is a very bad idea.'

'There were NDAs—'

'Oh, fuck NDAs. NDAs don't apply to mothers and daughters.'

'I mean, legally they do.'

'God, Harley.' She put a hand to her forehead. 'You're going to give me an aneurism. This is worse than anything you and Julia got up to in your school years.'

'It's a big role, Mum. Jesus, you could at least try to be happy for me.'

She shook her head. 'I don't think you should do it.'

'This is my big break. I can't not.'

'Big break,' she said. 'I'm about to have a big break*down*. How about that?'

Dad returned with the champagne, and she pressed her lips together tightly and received a glass. The crease in her forehead had deepened. I touched my own unconsciously, although I don't think she noticed.

'To Harley,' said Dad, and Mum rolled her eyes and lifted her glass a couple of centimetres into the air.

I told Rachael all of this, or at least a slightly cleaner version. 'Okay,' she said evenly. 'I think you handled that well.'

'She was worried, though. She thinks this film is going to upset you. Wouldn't it be easier just to set her mind at rest?'

She picked up her wine glass. 'Harley,' she said, 'one thing you need to understand. The idea of me and you working together will never be a restful one for your mother.'

'Why not?'

'She doesn't think I'm a good person.'

'Is that why you didn't want her to know? Because you think she'll convince me to hate you?'

She didn't say anything.

'I couldn't hate you,' I said. 'We're the same, me and you.'

She smiled. She raised her glass to me.

'So, Rachael,' said Carlton, sitting down across the aisle from her. 'Excited to get back to *Traversers?*'

'I just love those films,' said Julia, who had crept closer whilst my attention had been diverted. 'Everyone's saying that Jacob Elordi's going to be in the next one. Is that true?'

'Maybe,' said Rachael. 'It's a big cast. I don't remember everyone's names.'

'Metal as shit,' said Carlton. Rachael looked at me, not sure how to interpret this. 'You must be excited to watch Harley's film. I'd love to watch a film about my life.'

'Please,' I said. 'No one wants to spend two hours watching you do ket and go to the spa.'

'That's not all I do.'

'Right – I was leaving out all the sex.'

'Okay,' said Carlton, a little sharply, 'so my life hasn't been quite as interesting as Rachael's.' He turned back to her. 'Aren't you just dying to see it?'

'I probably won't watch it,' said Rachael. We must have looked shocked, because she added, with a smile, 'I've never liked watching myself.' Then she went back to her book.

She kept to herself for most of the flight. I went to sit with Julia and Carlton, who chatted their usual shit and shrieked over several bad romantic comedies. I found myself trying to mitigate the conversation, glancing over my shoulder to check if Rachael found us irritating. She didn't seem to be paying us any attention. She finished her book and, as the light in the cabin dimmed and the twinkly ceiling switched on, she fell asleep, head resting gently on the back of her seat.

'Look at her,' said Julia quietly. 'No one should look that good sleeping on a plane. She hasn't even put her seat back.'

After a while, we lowered our seats into beds and curled up with blankets and pillows. I glanced over at Rachael, eyes closed, lips slightly parted, still in her upright chair. She didn't look like she was really sleeping. She looked like someone sleeping in a film.

When we woke with a bump the next morning, touching down on the tarmac in LA, she was already awake and dressed in a fresh outfit, sunglasses on the top of her head. I pushed myself up on my elbows. She was staring out of the window, watching the landscape drift past as we parked up.

'Back I go,' she said. I thought she was talking to herself until she turned and looked at me. 'When I'm far away from this place,' she said, 'and I picture it in my mind, I know I hate it. But then I get here, and it feels like coming home.'

I smiled at her. I looked out of the window on my side of the plane, up at the hills. The Hollywood sign gleaming down at us. *Home.*

I had four days to unpack and get settled in the flat that Production had found for me. Julia and Carlton had booked a hotel suite nearby. They explored LA whilst I sat at home learning my lines and preparing for rehearsals, and every evening we met up for dinner to share our days. They showed me photos of the hikes they'd gone on and the boutiques they'd visited, and I talked about the scenes I'd been digging into and the hours I'd spent in front of the mirror, holding my laptop up beside my face, trying to get her expressions correct. We always invited Rachael on these dinners. She always declined. I was still hoping to be invited to her LA house, but no invitation had arrived so far.

Our table read had happened over Zoom, so the first time I saw Elias again was on the first day of rehearsals. We were starting off just the two of us. He turned up in a black t-shirt and black jogging bottoms, a big grin on his face as he embraced me. Despite the fact that he was two decades older than me, there was a boyishness and a joviality to his manner that made the age gap all but disappear.

José, our director, had a similar warmth and cheeriness. He was relatively young, in his mid-thirties still, considered something of a wunderkind when he first entered the industry. He was a good-looking man, slightly built, about my height. Not intimidating, but the kind of person who reads as smart from the moment you meet them. You wanted José to see you as someone on his level.

We started with Rachael and Greg's happier moments. Actually, we started with the ruby. 'Play it like two kids in love,' said José, as Elias practised presenting me with it. I beamed and threw my arms around his neck. 'Right,' said José. 'It's that, but it's more. This isn't a simple love. Even in its sweetest moments, it isn't simple.'

He had a very clear idea of who he wanted our Greg and Rachael to be. It was clear that Elias and I had chemistry, and he liked that, but he often referenced some other element, a dimension to the relationship that we were missing.

On the fourth day of rehearsal, José said, 'Okay, I'm going to get you guys to kiss.'

Elias grinned, charmingly taken aback. 'Right now?'

'Right now.' José was a very impulsive director. He had ideas and things he wanted to try, and we just did them, with him bobbing in the background like an overexcited meerkat. 'Let's just break down that barrier,' he said, 'and then we can get into the harder stuff. There's that real heat between Greg and Rachael. I'm seeing a lot of friendship between you guys so far, I'm seeing the flirting, I'm believing that you like each other and that you work – but I'm not seeing heat. I'm not seeing fury.'

We kissed. I could tell it wasn't right by the look on José's face. Elias scratched his jaw. 'No?'

'We'll work on it,' said José. 'It's a jumping-off point. That connection will build as we get further into the project.'

Some of the supporting cast were coming in the week after, and I was suddenly terrified of embarrassing myself in front of them. I could access Rachael in front of my mirror, alone – I could be her when it was just me running my lines to no one. But I realised that here, with an attractive co-star and an amenable director in the room, I defaulted to Harley. I found it harder to bring Rachael's darkness and pain out in front of other people. She'd begun to feel like my imaginary friend. I worried that she wouldn't hold up in the light of day.

I texted Rachael. *Can I come over? I need your help.*

Rachael had owned her Hidden Hills home since the early nineties. You could tell she hadn't really updated the furnishings since then. Her dark wood side tables and terracotta cushions were still cute in a vintage sort of way, but the gold frames around her mirrors were gaudy, and she had a *People* from 1994 in her bathroom with a photo of Don Johnson and Melanie Griffith on the cover.

We sat outside on her patio, the swimming pool sparkling a little way off. She brought out olives and breadsticks and two mimosas. I asked if she was missing Raph.

'A little,' she said.

'Where is he?'

'He's with a friend.'

'You didn't want to bring him out with you?'

'He doesn't like LA,' she said. 'He's far too English for it.'

It was hard to explain my problem to her – that the version of her I held inside of me was too precious to bring out in front of other people, which felt like an incredibly strange thing to say to someone. I faltered a few times before I got the words out. Strangely, she seemed to understand, and she didn't reproach me for being pretentious. 'It's hard,' she said, 'to create a character before you've played them, because they'll never come out exactly as you want them to.'

'Yes. That's exactly it.'

'What are you concerned about in particular?'

'José says that we need the heat that you and Greg had. That we have chemistry, but it isn't the right sort, not yet.'

'I see,' she said. 'Yes, I see that.'

'So how do I find that? I mean, where did it come from, with Greg and you?'

She rolled an olive between her finger and thumb. 'You like him?' she said. 'Elias?'

'Yeah, he's a great guy. We're friends.'

'That's the problem,' she said. 'You can't be friends. Greg and I were never friends. Even from the beginning he wanted to sleep with me, and I think I wanted to sleep with him too, although I was too afraid of the feeling – and of him – to admit it to myself. And I hated him. It all sort of—' She waved a hand. 'Crackled. It just crackled. Something was always going to give.'

The next day, after rehearsal, I pulled Elias aside.

'I think we should have sex,' I said.

◆ ◆ ◆

Elias Jones got his big break at twenty-one, when he starred in a drama about a family-owned boxing club alongside Tyrese Gibson and Cate Blanchett. He was scrappy, boyish, charming, but with some real acting chops. Moviegoers and critics alike raved. The next year he appeared alongside Winona Ryder in a retelling of *As You Like It* and the deal was sealed. He's been *People*'s Sexiest Man Alive twice, once in his twenties and once at forty, just after the birth of his third child. There's a famous photo of him reading his edition of the magazine at a café, with one hand on his baby daughter's pram. Her small feet are just visible, kicking in socks in the early morning sunlight.

He dated several high-profile women in the early noughties, had a fling with Gwyneth Paltrow, was a rumoured rebound of Jennifer Aniston's, who has only ever had nice things to say about him. In 2005, at the age of twenty-seven, he married singer Lucille King in a luscious New York ceremony. The couple were together for thirteen years and had three children, two boys and a girl, all three of whom have their own official fan pages on Instagram. In 2018, Elias and Lucille called it quits (difficult mutual decision, much love and respect, committed to the co-parenting of their three beautiful children, the usual spiel). She's moved on with an NFL player who carries their daughter around on his shoulders on family holidays, and Elias has thrown himself into his work, with no public relationships other than some rumours about him and British model Clöe van Matre (I know her – it happened).

By the time we met he was forty-five and living full-time in LA, where every other weekend he picked the kids up from their various elite private schools and spent two days giving them everything they asked for, before handing them back over on Sunday evenings.

This is what he told me as we sat, feet dangling in his pool, each of us holding a vodka tonic.

'It's hard,' he said, 'because I miss all the parent stuff. I feel more like a fun uncle. And I know Lucille resents me for that, but really, how else am I supposed to do it? When you see them so little you just want to make them happy.'

'I get it,' I said.

He laughed. 'No, you don't. You're how old? Twenty-six?'

'About to be twenty-seven.' I regretted correcting him. It made me sound like a child.

'You're sweet to pretend though,' he said.

He set his drink down on the poolside and leant back on his hands. He was still in a t-shirt, trousers rolled up, but even covered up you could tell he was ripped. I hadn't had sex in a while, and it had been even longer since I'd had sex with someone I knew I was going to see again the next morning. Of course, Elias hadn't exactly agreed to it yet, but I knew he would.

'So, what about you?' he asked.

'No kids.'

'Yeah, I figured. Any big heartbreaks in your life?'

I raised my eyebrows at him and took a sip of my vodka tonic.

'What?' he asked. 'This is what we're supposed to be doing, right? Getting vulnerable with each other?'

'I've never been heartbroken.'

'Oh, come on.'

'There was one guy in film school. He's the only guy I've ever liked who didn't like me back. But it wasn't heartbreak, really.' I stretched. 'It was more just annoying.'

'What was his name?' asked Elias.

'Hugh.'

'And what was wrong with Hugh? Why didn't he like you back?'

I could still see him, standing in the corridor outside our World Cinema lecture. Hands in his pockets, a rueful smile on his face.

'I think he did, for a while,' I said. 'We were friends. But—'

The incident with Hugh and I had happened early in our second year of film school. Hugh and I had quickly established a friendship in the first year of our course – his parents were vague acquaintances of mine, both entertainment lawyers. Hugh's childhood hadn't been quite as unusual as mine but he'd grown up in a certain level of comfort, and that gave us an affinity – we could chat together about our family holidays and our sixteenth-birthday parties without incurring any amazed looks. I fell for him fast, and hard. He had that artsy clothes, floppy hair thing going for him and he was genuinely nice too. Everybody liked Hugh.

Gilly Cole liked him a little too much. She was a relatively pretty, slightly horsey girl from Derbyshire, one of those who talked about her path to film school like she'd clawed her way there through thick mud and hail. Hugh was completely taken in by her working-class-hero act, though, and the two were soon spotted walking across campus together, sitting side by side in lectures, meeting up for coffees after class.

Gilly was a giggler, one of those girls with no presence who cannot hold her alcohol and doesn't make an effort to be funny in conversations but instead giggles along. We were at a pre-drink at my flat, which I shared with Julia at the time, back when she was in fashion school, before she dropped out due to exhaustion. Everyone always came to my flat because it was objectively nicer than pre-ing in the uni accommodation. I hadn't invited Gilly, but she arrived on Hugh's arm, giggling away. I could see that she'd already had a few drinks – her cheeks were flushed, her smile vacant. I caught her eye and beckoned her over. The flush in her cheeks darkened. She wasn't used to being noticed by me.

'Hey!' I gave her a hug. 'We're going to play a drinking game. Want to join? It's called See-ya.'

'See-ya?'

'It's French,' said Julia, at my elbow. 'Wanna play?'

I could see Hugh turning, looking for Gilly. I waved, and he smiled, pleased for Gilly that she'd managed to get in good with Julia and me.

We'd invented See-ya in school as a method of getting rid of the sorts of girls who would turn up to parties and be a drag on the proceedings. Those sorts of girls were always lightweights. The game worked like this – Julia would deal four cards in front of each of us. We would turn them over one at a time. If one of them was a face card, we drank. If four of them were face cards, we drank four times. We went until the deck was empty. We'd invented this game because Julia was very good at cheating at it.

By the time the deck was done, Gilly was looking more than a little unwell. She staggered back to Hugh, who caught her and looked over at Julia and me. We gave him grimaces that implied it hadn't been our fault, that Gilly was out of control. He led her into the bathroom. When they came out twenty minutes later, she was searching for her keys, mumbling that she had to go home. Julia, very concerned and overly effusive, offered to call her an Uber.

'I should go with her,' said Hugh.

'Oh, don't do that,' said Julia. 'She'll be mortified if she thinks she's ruined your night. Don't embarrass her like that. It's awkward enough getting super-drunk around your boyfriend's friends.'

'I'm not her boyfriend,' said Hugh quickly.

'Oh,' said Julia. 'My mistake.'

We smoked out of the open window and watched the car drive off.

'See ya,' giggled Julia, curls tickling my ear.

Hugh never accused us of anything, but he was strange for the rest of the night, and for some time after that. When I eventually did ask him out, a month or so later, I knew he wouldn't say yes. I only did it because I had to get the words out, eventually, one way or another. I wasn't expecting him to say what he did.

Sorry, Harley. I just don't think you're a good person.

'It wasn't the right fit,' I said to Elias.

The sun was going down over his pool. He stood up, water rippling tangerine towards him, and pulled his shirt over his head. Behind him, the sky was blush and slipping earthwards. 'Do you want to swim?' he asked.

'I don't have any swimming things.'

He turned back to grin at me, and I saw that he was unbuttoning his trousers. He dove into the water in black underwear – I watched him ripple through it, strong arms and torso splintering and piecing back together as he went. He emerged on the other side of the pool and shook his hair like a dog.

'Coming?' he asked.

I slipped out of my dress. Thank god I'd had the foresight to wear matching underwear. It was a new set that Julia had bought on Hollywood Boulevard the day before. I would have to make it up to her. The water was warm. I submerged myself up to my shoulders, dark hair floating on the surface around me. Elias approached, not eagerly, still friendly and open. I could see approval in his eyes when he looked at me, attraction even, but that passion was still lacking. I swam over to him and put my arms around his neck, and when he didn't resist I hooked my legs around him and let his hands creep down to support me.

'Kiss me,' I said.

He obliged. It was a good kiss, but nothing spectacular. I disentangled myself from him and moved a few inches back, regarding him. He smiled. A movie-star smile. 'What?' he asked.

'You know the problem with you?'

'Always the question you want a girl to ask after you kiss her.'

'You're spoilt,' I said.

Something crossed his face – the first sign that he wasn't permanently affable, that he had an ego to bruise. 'Alright. How'd you figure that?'

'I've heard about you. I know you're this charming bachelor to the public, but I'm not the public. I know you've been around. You've dated models and actresses and pop stars and dancers.' He wasn't offended anymore. He looked pretty pleased with himself, actually. 'It's spoilt you,' I said. 'You're too used to it.'

'Just say what you really want to say,' he said.

'I am.'

'You're not. What you really want to say is, "Do you know what some guys would give to be kissing me in a swimming pool?"' He swam towards me and took me in his arms again. 'And you're right.'

'No,' I said, pushing him off. 'Jesus. You're awful at this.'

He frowned. 'I've often been told the opposite.'

'You have to not be this practised bachelor. You have to be Greg, stuck in this marriage, and Rachael's like water in a desert.' It was a romanticised version of events – I was pretty sure Greg had cheated on Anna plenty of times before Rachael – but Elias nodded.

'You're pretty serious about this film,' he said, and leant in to kiss my neck.

I smiled over his shoulder. 'Does that surprise you?'

'A little. Nepo baby like you.'

I pulled away. He was still grinning at me, like we were playing a game. I wasn't amused. '*What* did you just call me?'

'What?' he asked, grin faltering.

'I'm not just some nepo baby. My parents don't even know I'm doing this.'

'Right, okay, but it's still nepotism, Harley. I mean, we both know you wouldn't have got this gig if you weren't Rachael's niece.'

I crossed my arms over my chest.

He sighed. 'I was complimenting you. Most people in your position don't have a work ethic like yours – that's all I'm saying.'

'No, you were reducing me to my background. Which no one is supposed to do to anyone, except when it's done to someone like me and then it's completely acceptable.'

'For fuck's sake,' said Elias. He swam over to the side of the pool and picked up his vodka tonic. I stayed motionless in the orange centre, resting on the tips of my toes, arms still folded. 'For the record,' he said, 'people are always going to call you a nepo baby, and you'd do yourself a lot more favours if you didn't throw a tantrum the second someone brings it up.'

He shrugged, arms spread, a little vodka tonic splashing into the pool. I looked at him, and then I turned and headed for the steps, pushing my hair back with both hands as I walked up and out of the pool.

'Where are you going?' he called.

'Let's have sex.'

Behind me, the sound of him setting his glass down. '*What?*'

'I hate you right now. Let's have sex.'

'You've really gotta work on your bedroom talk.'

At the glass doors, I turned back, and looked at him.

He sighed, and then he pushed himself up and out of the pool. 'Alright. I see what you're going for. But you gotta shower and dry off before you're getting in my bed.'

'I'm not getting in your bed,' I said. I stalked into the house, dripping on to the tile floor. 'Let's just do it in the kitchen.'

'Where?' he asked, following me in with squelchy footsteps. It was a fair question. The kitchen was pretty bare – no table, just a couple of black and chrome barstools stood at a large marble island. There was nothing on the walls, and nothing on the sides either, other than a block of knives. He did have a large, spiky potted plant beside the window, which suggested to me that someone at some point had told him to brighten the place up.

'Jeez,' I said. 'How do you live like this?'

'It's hardly a dump.'

'It's the opposite. It's sterile.' I hopped on to the island. 'This will have to do.' It was cold, but at least it was the right sort of height. He stood over me, water droplets sliding slowly over his shoulders.

'Are you sure about this?' he asked.

'Yes.' I shook my wet hair back. He didn't move to unclip my bra, much less rip my underwear from my body like I imagined Greg would have done. 'What's wrong?'

He cleared his throat. 'It all feels quite clinical.'

'Yes, that's the problem. I think we should just fuck once and get it over with.'

'See, that sort of talk isn't really helping.'

'Act,' I said.

He looked at me blankly.

'You're an actor.'

'Not that sort of actor.'

'Elias,' I said, 'work with me here. You're Greg. I'm Rachael. We hate each other. We desperately want to fuck each other. Those are the two pinnacles on which our relationship is built.'

'Do you really think that's how it was between them?'

'That's how it is in our script. That's all we need to worry about. Can we just—' I made a 'hurry it up' gesture. He looked at me for a second. Then he grabbed my thighs and pulled me towards him. My elbows hit the island. '*Ow.*'

'Shut up,' he growled. He was wiggling my underwear down my legs and over my feet. I could see that he was performing now. 'If we're doing this,' he said, 'properly, like you want to, then we're going to make it useful.'

'Okay,' I said, rubbing my elbow.

'So you're going to follow my lead.'

'Was he good?' asked Carlton, over martinis at Bar Marmont later that night.

By way of response, I whistled.

I'd taken a car home as soon as we were done. Hair full of chlorine, wet underwear wrapped in a hand towel in my purse, I'd turned to him in his doorway and said, 'We should do that again.'

'We should,' he'd said. When we kissed goodbye, finally, I'd felt it. A surge of something. A chemistry that we could use.

'That good?' asked Carlton.

I leant forward for another olive. 'Let's just say, if it was like that with Rachael and Greg, maybe I understand it.'

Julia was sitting with her glass lifted, nose crinkled.

'I think Her Highness has something to say.'

'It's a little slutty.'

'That's slut shaming,' said Carlton.

'It's not. I didn't shame. It's just an observation.'

'About my sluttiness,' I said.

'Yes.'

'I prefer to think of it as method acting.'

'I mean,' she said, 'if it works, it works. Who am I to judge? I'm not an actor. I just don't think most actors do this.'

'More than you'd think.'

Her eyes widened. 'Really? Who?'

'Oh,' I said airily, 'you'd be surprised.'

I was happy with my choices. Rehearsals were so much better after that. By the time we began principal photography, Elias and I had slept together eight times and we'd only got better at it. We would trade insults. We fought for dominance. Once, I let him slap me across the face. I never let him do it again – I thought he'd do it playfully, but it hurt. He apologised afterwards and we didn't finish, because he was too 'thrown off', he said. He asked me to go home early. When I next saw him, he didn't bring it up. I was glad he'd done it though. It was a memory I held of him now, the second when he was looking down at me with his flat palm coming towards me. It would be a useful one.

After multiple discussions with our director, our producers, Ahn, and a variety of intimacy coordinators (what a con *that* gig is) I had opted to be topless in the audition scene, no body double. I was in good shape, and I knew if I wanted to be remembered in this role I had to do some things that everyone would keep talking about long after they had all forgotten who Rachael and Greg even were. We had a skeleton crew for that scene, just José, a sound guy, two camera operators, one intimacy coordinator, Elias, and myself.

They set the shot up completely and then they called me to set. I moved towards them in a black blouse and low-cut jeans, hair pulled back, made up in Rachael's minimalist nineties style. I could see people glancing at me and doing a double take, and I did feel like her ghost, moving towards the lights in her clothes, and her make-up, into one of her memories. With her face.

I stood in front of Elias. 'Ready?' he asked. We'd had sex on one of his sun loungers that morning. He'd forgotten the pool cleaner was coming and I'd rolled under it to avoid being seen. He'd told the man to come back on Thursday and then I'd rolled back out and we'd carried on. I grinned at him, shaking out my arms.

José came up to us. 'We'll start with the intro,' he said, 'get that down, and then we'll move on to the section when you get undressed, if you're feeling comfortable, Harley.'

I gave him a thumbs-up.

'In the zone?' he asked.

I nodded.

'Okay!' he said, clapping his hands together. 'Let's go, everyone.'

Elias went to sit behind the table. He could switch into Greg so easily by this point, take on his timbre and his posture, and the slight instability that lurked behind every sentence. He began by reading through my résumé. We talked about the fact that Rachael had played Abigail in *The Crucible* as a teenager. 'A born temptress,' he smiled.

We couldn't use too much of the actual script from *Women Who Laugh at God*, so our script had Greg stopping Rachael halfway through her read and getting the camera out.

'It's good,' said Elias, as Greg. 'It's fine.' He leant forward, laced his fingers. 'I'm just not feeling seduced,' he said.

As Rachael, I balked. 'Oh?'

'Mm,' he said. He walked out from behind the table.

'Do you want me to start it over?' I asked.

'Can we try it another way?'

I nodded.

He gave me the speech about how they'd been playing with the idea of using nudity, how they'd decided it was essential to Abi's character for her to use her body. I, as Rachael, listened with a fluttering heart. I weakly protested that my agent hadn't warned me. Elias, as Greg, batted my protests away. He raised the camera expectantly.

'Cut.' José jogged into the shot. 'Okay,' he said, 'good stuff, both. Harley.' He turned to me and I could see that he was figuring out how to phrase something. 'Do you think she's scared?' he asked.

'A little, yes.'

'That's not how I read her, in the script,' said José. 'I mean, she's intimidated, sure, but she's got this kind of steely focus and she's always looking to prove herself as a professional. She feels strange about this, she feels conflicted, maybe even a little gross – and that's good, you're doing that, we need to show that – but I don't think she's this scared girl.'

I swallowed a hard crust of anger and nodded.

'Okay,' he said brightly. 'We'll do it again, just up to that same point.'

Elias got back behind the table. We spoke the first few lines of dialogue. I had reached, 'Do you want me to start it over?' when José called 'Cut.'

I kept my expression neutral as he approached. 'Are you nervous?' he asked.

'No, I'm fine.'

'Understandable if you are. But it's reading on camera.'

'I'm not nervous,' I said, a little shortly.

'You've watched your aunt's films, I assume?'

'Obviously.'

'So you know that quality she has, that . . .' He waved his hands. He had a way of doing this that made him look like he was batting away interrupting thoughts. 'Truly a *je ne sais quoi*. The definition of it. It's not an easy thing to reproduce.' He smiled at me. 'Half the battle is won – you have her face. But now we need to really see her.'

'But I don't understand what it is that I'm not doing.'

He nodded, hands clasped under his chin, and thought, his head to one side and his eyes very narrow. 'It's a coldness,' he said, 'that might burn you. It's something that makes you feel like you could never hurt her. To certain men, that reads as a challenge.' He was looking at me eagerly. 'You don't need to show us that she's nervous here,' he said. 'Show us that she's confused, but she's reaching down to that steel in herself and moving forward. It's later, when there are consequences, that she questions. It's only years in the future that she realises she might have been played.'

225

He didn't get it. That wasn't Rachael. That was the version the world thought they knew, but it wasn't my aunt. 'I disagree,' I said. He nodded slowly, his face blank, and stretched out his hands to indicate that I should continue. 'We're showing her behind closed doors here. And I've *seen* her behind closed doors.'

'I know,' he said. 'That's a huge advantage. That's going to help you – and us – enormously. But I still think you're playing this wrong.'

'I just think this is something a man will never understand.'

'Maybe,' said José. 'Why do you say that?'

'Well, she was a victim here. I'm going to play her as one.'

He gave me another slow nod. 'I understand the reasoning,' he said. 'But I think you'll be doing her a disservice.'

We took a break. When we came back, it took a while to find a version of the scene that José and I were willing to compromise on. Eventually he let us move on, but his buoyant energy was somewhat dampened and he sat in his chair looking troubled and contemplative. I hoped he wouldn't make us do reshoots.

The intimacy coordinator came on to talk us through what was about to happen next, for the umpteenth time, and I said, 'Yes, got it, I'll just whip my tits out then.' She looked a little offended, but there was laughter from the rest of the crew.

Elias picked up the camera and circled me. In the version of the story Rachael had told me, she was fully naked in front of Greg – here, I was keeping a pair of nude shorts on and we were only shooting me from the waist up, but the reality of the situation was implied. I avoided the lens, staring straight ahead of me, like I imagined she would have done. Elias took the pictures from the camera and laid them on the table. When they were developed he put them in an envelope and tucked them into the drawer of the desk. Then he nodded at the door.

'You may go,' he said.

José was much happier with that section, and I only had to get undressed a few more times before he decided that we were done for the day. Elias gave me a fist bump, which wasn't particularly Greg of him, but then he leant in and whispered, 'Coming by later?'

'Of course.'

'We haven't fucked on my pool table yet.'

'Perfect,' I said, with a perfunctory nod. We'd agreed that sex in a bed was off-limits but pretty soon we would be running out of furniture to do it on. The main feature of Elias' house was empty space.

I went to Rachael's house for a late dinner and told her how the scene had gone. I explained the clash that José and I had over how to play her, in that audition room. 'Show me how you did it,' she said.

I stood up. I gave her some of the lines. She nodded.

'Was I right?' I asked. 'Or was he?'

'Oh,' she said. 'You, of course. You know me better than anyone else.'

I can't explain how it felt, to have her say this, other than to say that no orgasm Elias gave me would ever be quite that satisfying. Rachael Carmichael, eternal mystery. Known only to me.

Earlier that evening, Elias had laid me down on the pool table and licked from my chest to my belly button, down, down. 'Too soft,' I said.

'Can't I ever be soft with you?'

'Do you think Greg was ever soft with Rachael?'

'Sometimes. They were in love.'

'They weren't,' I said. 'Not really.'

He stood up over me, and I pushed myself upright, a red pool ball hitting my elbow and rolling away.

'You're not going to play this role correctly if you never let them be in love,' he said. 'I'm not sure you even understand the love part. You're all hate.'

'You don't know her,' I said. 'She isn't the being in love type.'

'I think you're projecting there,' he said.

'Projecting how?'

'You're just a kid,' he said, stood over my naked body.

'A strange thing to say to the person you're sleeping with.'

'We're not sleeping together.'

'What are we doing, then?'

'Rehearsing,' he said. I rolled my eyes. He pushed a few more of the pool balls into their pockets around me, with no urgency. 'What I mean is,' he continued, 'you've never had it good, in love, so you don't think anyone's ever had it good. You can't imagine that people might have had experiences outside of yours. That they might have lived lives totally different from the life you've lived.'

This again. Elias loved to talk down to me about privilege, because apparently his poor childhood trumped the multiple million-dollar homes he owned.

'You don't love someone who treats you like he treated her.'

He looked down at me with something like pity. 'Why else do you stay?'

◆ ◆ ◆

'Why did you stay?' I asked Rachael, out on her patio in Hidden Hills.

She squashed a bug with her finger. 'It's like gambling,' she said. 'You keep thinking, after every hand – just five more minutes. And then maybe your cards will come up.'

Chapter Ten

RACHAEL

20 February 1992

We wrapped *Women Who Laugh at God* last week. The very final thing we shot was me, standing over Anthony, who plays one of the other men in the village, wiping blood from my mouth and forehead.

'Cut,' called Greg. 'That's a wrap.'

There were cheers – of relief, most likely. I could see someone moving through the crowd towards me with a flannel but I turned my shoulder on them and caught Greg's eye. I walked over to him, fake blood still smeared across my face. He put his hands on my waist.

'My Abigail,' he said, and kissed me.

It was the first time he'd touched me since the kiss in the car a month earlier, at least out of character. Since that brief conversation, he'd been just the same with me on set, oscillating between terror and a tender sort of praise. The week previous to this one he'd screamed 'Are you fucking stupid?' at me – in front of everyone, as was his way – because he'd tried to slap me in a scene, off-script, and I'd dodged and kicked him. He explained afterwards that he hadn't really been going to hit me – he'd wanted me, as Abigail, to respond to his choice and prevent him, forcefully. I told him that I wasn't 'a fucking mind reader' and we had quite the screaming match, the two of us, in front of a cast and crew who by now were used to it. But it wasn't how it once had been, at least in my mind. There was something performative in it now, and at one point, when he looked my way, I saw this gleam in his eyes, and I suspected that he was quite enjoying himself.

I understand him better these days, and I know that this is just his way. What he says to you in those quiet moments, the things he whispers about what a *phenomenon* you are, what a *force*, what a *star* – those things are the real Greg. Those are the things he really means. The rage and the fight and the things he does seemingly to grind you down are just part of his act. He means to terrify a good performance out of you, or to provoke you to the point where you have to show him up. It's horrendous when he's doing it, but afterwards, you're strangely grateful. This is the first film that I'm excited to watch myself in. Because I know I'll be good.

I was good in *Here's Hoping,* in the end, although you wouldn't know it if you read some of the reviews. 'An awful, violent, ugly picture,' was one writer's opinion. Another – 'Sarah Griffin's feminist utopia is one in which women can punish men's missteps, misunderstandings or misjudgements in any way that they deem fit – even if the punishment far outweighs the crime.' There was a general outcry at the sight of Rachael Carmichael – sweet, cheerful Jill from *The Avenue* whose worst crime to date was kicking a kid at school for snapping her bra strap – enacting such violence against those all-American boys. But they'd all gone to the theatres, and I'd been included in several up-and-comers lists in the US on the back of the film, including one cheerfully titled *The British Are Coming!* Amy George also made that list. We went out for pints to celebrate and got mobbed at the bar. It's probably time we start seeking out those horrendous celebrity hotspots known for being exclusive and discreet.

I don't know how people will feel about *Women Who Laugh at God*. I don't know what they'll make of me committing worse violence against men they identify with less, hiding behind an Arthur Miller/Greg Foster safety curtain of male genius. But I know what they would make of me if they knew what I did last week. That's why I'm guarding this secret close to my chest until the right moment. If it gets out, it will ruin Abi. No one will be frightened of her or attempt to calculate if there is anything about her worth trying to understand. She will just be a whore.

I slept with Greg.

He called me, late at night, in a voice like I had never heard before. Not quietly commanding, not angry, not falsely impartial. Pleading, almost whining. Almost enough to make me put down the phone.

'I can't do this,' he said. 'This is killing me.'

'Are you drunk?'

'Totally sober. But completely messed up.'

I almost thought it wasn't him. That it was some strange kind of prank call. 'Where are you? Are you safe?'

'I'm at the Beverly Wilshire,' he said. 'Do you understand what I'm saying to you?'

'Not really.'

'I love you,' he said. 'You have completely bewitched me. You have ruined my life.'

It was awful to hear those words, but some part of me liked the idea that I might have bewitched someone, that I had exercised this power I had never been aware I had. 'I wasn't trying to,' I said.

'That's the worst part,' he said. 'That's the worst part, Rachael. I know you weren't. I can't even blame you. It's just how you are.'

There was a pause. I gripped the phone with both hands and pushed it hard against my cheek, listening to the way he breathed.

'Can I see you?' he asked.

'I don't think that's a good idea.'

'Why not? Because of my wife?'

He said it so offhand. Like he was saying, *Because of the traffic? Because of the weather? Because of your horoscope?* Almost as if I were being silly even bringing it up.

'Yes,' I snapped. 'Obviously.'

'We're separated.'

'Does she know that?'

'It's tricky,' he said. 'She's in a difficult place, right now – I have to call my lawyer first, get a few things in motion, and then it's a conversation I'll be able to broach with her . . .' He trailed off.

'So she doesn't,' I said.

'It's Anna. You know her. You know she's tricky. I mean, shit, the things she's said about *you* to the press. Can you imagine what she'd say about me? Can you imagine what she *does* say to me, in our home? In front of our children?'

I could.

'I know what you must think of me,' he said. 'Some guy, calling you, trying to cheat on his wife, promising he'll leave her. I've seen that movie. Hell, I've made that movie.'

I was still quiet.

'I don't know what else to do,' he said. 'I just don't know what else to do. I love you. I don't know when it happened. I don't know how. But I can't escape it. I thought I could leave it behind on that set, but I couldn't. I thought if I yelled at you, if I got mad, if I made you hate me, it would go away. But it hasn't. You kept raising your chin in the air, you kept yelling back, you kept getting *better*, and I just kept loving you more. It's like a sickness. I've never known anything like it before. I don't understand how you've done it. I just want you—' He broke off to breathe. 'Here,' he said. 'Now.'

In the mirror, I saw an image of myself that didn't quite look like me. This girl, dark hair tied up, eyes wide and black. Smiling just a little into the phone with her white hands curled around it. She looked like a siren. Like some evil spirit. Part of me wanted to laugh, but the other part felt desperately, horribly sorry that I had done this to him, however unconsciously. What had I reduced him to?

Did I love him? Whatever it was, I felt something. It wasn't like what I had felt with Adam – it wasn't this sunny radiance, this ridiculous, cheerful childishness. It was older. It was darker. It was a pull, a need, suddenly, to be at his side, to be there with his head in my lap, telling him it was all going to be okay. To be under his hands, under his body, pressed against him like we'd been on set, only this time real. Greg and Rachael. Nothing pretend about it. It didn't feel like any love that I had known before – but then, as I understand it, love never does.

'Please,' he said, and I said, 'Okay.'

He sent a car for me. They buzzed the gate and said, 'Car for you?'

I said, 'Yes, one second,' with my feet halfway in my small black heels. The walk down the driveway to the gate didn't feel like real life. I was in a trench coat. It felt like the uniform.

When we pulled up outside the hotel, the driver asked, 'Here?' It felt as if he was asking, *Are you sure? Are you really sure that you're going to go in there?*

'Yes,' I said. 'Thank you.'

I had brought a black hat, a woollen one, to put over my head, and sunglasses to wear, just for the walk up to the hotel and into the lobby. Greg had phoned ahead and told them to send me up, and I knew the staff would be quick and discreet, but I was still afraid of being noticed by anyone else. But it was night, and the street wasn't busy, and I looked more conspicuous in my hat and sunglasses than I would have done otherwise.

In the lobby, there was a concierge waiting for me. 'Right this way, ma'am,' he said, and shepherded me into a lift – or an elevator, as they say here. He pressed the button, gave me the room number. I nodded. It felt wrong, somehow, to say thank you. The doors closed. In the mirror I looked giddy, sick, young. I smoothed my hair down and took a breath.

The doors parted. Greg's room was just two paces down the corridor. I was in front of his room, ready to knock. Still not sure if I would.

But he opened it. They must have called to announce I'd arrived. Was this how affairs were conducted? Did the staff know? Of course they did – rumours were already flying about Greg and me. It's uncanny, the way these things get out. The concierge must have got Greg's call and sent a whisper through the staff: *Okay, everyone. Activate celebrity affair protocol.*

I was in a celebrity affair. Was that something I was supposed to be thinking about? Wasn't I supposed to be carried away by my feelings, so absorbed in the romance and the lust that I couldn't even be expected to pause to think about the infidelity of it all? As Greg opened the door and looked at me, in just his dressing gown, holding a glass of whiskey, I thought, *Is this the kind of man you are? Is this the kind of woman I am?*

No, of course. Not really. It's all circumstance. But then I suppose that is what everyone thinks.

'Hey,' he said.

I swallowed. 'Hey.'

He held the door open for me. His face was so full of hope, as he looked at me, like sunlight breaking through the storm. Like the long, dark night was coming to an end. I walked in. He'd poured me a whiskey already. Of course. What else do you drink when you're having an affair? *Stop it, Rachael,* I thought. *You're spoiling it.*

He pulled me in for a hug. It didn't feel like an affair, then, in the way he gripped me, in the way his hand stroked the back of my head. He hugged me like he was trying to absorb me into him. I hugged him back, tightly, and I couldn't believe how good he felt in my arms, how right. How incredible it was to support the frightening, intimidating, genius force of him against me.

He took my coat off me. I turned to pick up my drink, and when I turned back he was taking off his robe, completely naked. His body surprised me – he didn't look young. His stomach wasn't taut like Adam's had been and the hair on his chest was grey. He walked over to me and took the drink out of my hand. My heart thudded against my ribs. He set it down, then tipped my chin up towards him and kissed me. I was vaguely aware of him peeling my dress off me, helping me raise my arms above my head. He worked my underwear down my thighs and then let me slip out of them, stepping over them in my heels.

He didn't say anything. He didn't step back to admire me. He didn't ask if I was sure, or if I loved him like he loved me. I don't know what I would have said if he had. But I don't think I would have stopped him laying me down on the bed, gently, running his hand down the length of my body, sliding himself inside me before the fog in my mind had even cleared. He was calm and yet so eager all at once, and I felt again how much he needed me, how desperate he was over me, and I held him as he shuddered and finished.

When he rolled off, he said, 'We should have used protection.'

'Yes.' *Shit.* Why had I not told him to go put a condom on? It had all happened so fast.

'I couldn't stop myself.' He ran his finger down the side of my face, along the length of my jaw. 'God,' he said. 'You're like a painting. I can't count the number of times I watched you on set and wondered how on earth you were real.'

I wriggled under the arm he put around me. I didn't quite know how I'd ended up where I was. 'I can't believe we just did that.'

'I can,' he said. 'God, I can.'

'What happens now?'

'I want to be with you,' he said. He rolled me towards him, so that he could look in my face.

'I don't want to be with someone who's married,' I said.

'So much integrity.'

It felt suddenly like he was mocking me. I sat up, pulling the duvet around me. He sat up too, quickly.

'What's wrong?' he asked.

'I—' I put my hand to my head. I couldn't find the words. 'What did we *do*?' There were tears suddenly, and I blinked them back. I had never cried in front of him, despite all he had put me through on set. His face fell. He leant forward to wipe my eyes.

'Don't cry.'

'You're not going to leave her.' I put my face in my hands. 'Oh, god.'

'Do you really think so little of me?'

'She doesn't even know you want to leave. God, if she found out about this, she would *ruin* me.'

'I'd be ruined too.'

I raised my head to look at him. The black and grey in his hair, the stubble on his chin. The clever face. 'No, you wouldn't.'

'I'll call my lawyer in the morning,' he said. 'Alright?' He could see I didn't believe him. 'I promise,' he said. 'First thing. As soon as we wake up.'

I stared at him. 'You want me to stay?'

'Of *course*.' He sounded hurt that I'd even had to ask. 'How do I make you believe it?' he asked. 'You're not some one-night stand to me. You're not just some actress. I adore you. I am completely at your mercy.'

I lay awake for hours and listened to him breathe. I considered the sound. I considered the feel of his arm around me. I considered the way he'd felt inside of me. I considered my cheek against his chest.

I thought, *I could love him too.*

When I woke up, the sun beginning to slip in under the curtains, I found that he'd rolled me off him at some point. He was sitting up, talking. I held the duvet to my face and peeked over it, up at him. He had the white hotel phone to his ear.

'Yes, I'll hold,' he said. He looked down at me and smiled, brushing a strand of hair from my face. His hand cupped my cheek. I closed my eyes. 'Turner?' I heard him say into the phone. 'I'm looking for some advice. I need a good divorce lawyer.'

8 April 1992

Last week was April Fool's Day, so not an unreasonable day to expect a joke. But according to Greg, I have vastly misunderstood the situation. 'I never joke about my work,' he said in that serious way he does, and I had to lean forward and kiss the frown off his face. It's something I'm very good at.

'I just don't know,' I said.

'You don't like it? I've already written half of it.'

'You have? When?'

'Over the weekend. We went to Anna's mother's, so plenty of help with the kids. I was able to retreat upstairs and just churn it out.' I'll never stop marvelling at how his brain works. 'What's the issue?' he asked.

The issue was that *Unbeliever* just didn't sound very good. It still doesn't, even now I've read his first draft. He pitched it as horror meets romance, a man becoming obsessed with a beautiful young woman and deciding to worship her like a god, going to extreme lengths to get her attention and harming himself in increasingly gruesome and disturbing ways to predict what she might want from him.

'I don't know,' I said. 'It doesn't really sound like much of a plot.'

'It's got more plot than most of that European psychological crap.'

'Let me read it,' I said, and then I did, and I didn't know how to tell him that I hated it. I really do hate it, though. The female lead isn't much of a part for me – she has a lot of screentime, sure, but she isn't really there, by which I mean that she isn't really a character. She's the siren I saw in the lift mirror the night I came to Greg's hotel; she's an idea of a woman, a vague temptation with no clear motivations or desires. She has none of Abi's earthiness, her terrifying presence.

'Thoughts?' he asked as I turned a page, kissing the top of my head.

'What are you trying to do with it?'

'Show how dark and dangerous love can be. Show where it can take us.' He kissed my head again. 'Make another movie with you.'

That's why I agreed to it, in the end. I believe in him. And I want to make another movie with him too.

He said he could accelerate it all. Early screenings and studio previews of *Women Who Laugh at God* have everyone pretty excited, and of course the two lead actors for *Unbeliever* are already cast, so time saved there. He's thrown himself into it, heart and soul, and it's a good excuse for him not to be at home much, a good cover for his meetings with his lawyer and his meetings with me.

He's trying to be smart about custody. He loves his boys and he wants to be sure that he gets at least shared custody, so he and his lawyer are formulating a game plan, before he tells Anna that he wants the divorce. It's a lot of waiting but waiting isn't so bad when you understand why you're doing it. Besides, once everyone knows, I'll have to share what we have with the world. Right now I quite like keeping it all to myself.

Or, I suppose, as much to myself as I can manage in this world we live in. People talk, always, and loudly, even when they don't know what they're talking about. Rumours have begun to appear in the tabloids, sources coming forward to claim that there's something going on between Greg and me. Most of them are claiming that we were sleeping together throughout *Women Who Laugh at God*, which of course isn't true. Greg says that these people don't actually know anything, and the fact they've accidentally landed on a half-truth is just testament to our chemistry. I like the way he talks about other people. Like they're all idiots, and we are the only two people who truly see things the way that they are. I know it's nonsense, but it's sweet nonsense.

'What do you tell Anna?' I asked him last night, as we lay in my bed. He tensed beneath me – he doesn't like when I bring up Anna, but I don't see any point in dancing around the subject of her. She's there, and she isn't going away, not even when he divorces her.

'I tell her that they're wrong,' he said. 'And mostly they are, so it's easy. And mostly she doesn't ask.'

She knows. Of course she does. It's one thing that makes me feel better, because at least she won't be blindsided. I loathe Anna, but sometimes I still think about her and feel guilty.

He stood up, rolling me back on to my own side of the bed. 'I have something for you,' he said. He went to his jacket, hanging on the back of the chair at my dresser. I pushed myself up on my elbows and watched him, naked, rifling in his jacket pocket. He pulled out a small, square jewellery box and turned back to find me gaping at him. 'It's not an engagement ring,' he said, chuckling. 'Don't look so scared.'

He climbed back into bed and handed it to me. I opened it cautiously, a millimetre at a time. A gleam of red greeted me. It was a ruby, set in a gold band. I turned the box this way and that, looking at it under the light. He watched me, amused. 'It looks like an engagement ring,' I said.

'It's a ring. Can't a ring just be a ring?'

'A ring is always for something.'

'I wanted to get you something before you go back to London,' he said. 'To say I'll miss you, and to remind you of me. I wasn't sure if any guy had ever bought you jewellery before.'

They hadn't. It hadn't been Adam's type of gift. I took the ring out and tried not to marvel at it, because gawping at sparkly things is never a good look. It was beautiful, though. It was red as blood and glittered wherever the light of my bedside lamp hit it.

'Can I?' asked Greg. I held out my hand and he slid it on to my finger – *not* the auspicious one, but the ring still looked very serious on my hand. 'What do you think?' he asked.

'It's beautiful.'

'You really think so?'

'I really do.' I looked up at him. His smile was softly adoring. 'Why a ruby?'

'Well, what other jewel would I get you? A black diamond, maybe? But this is prettier, I thought. It reminds me of all that red on your face when I kissed you on set, when we wrapped. How your face was covered in blood, and I still couldn't help myself – all I wanted to do was kiss you, blood and all. I remember thinking, *I'm really in trouble here.* And I really was.'

I kissed him, my hand on his face. The gold band pushed into his cheek. 'Thank you,' I said.

'Wear it,' he said, 'and think of me. And come back to me.'

The statement surprised me like it always does when he says things like this. Did he really think I wouldn't? 'I will,' I said. 'I'll come back.'

5 June 1992

They photographed me with the ring when I got off the plane. They were all waiting for me outside Heathrow – it scares me, sometimes, how they seem to know these things. The driver came to Arrivals to help me quickly into the car, but they still got several shots of my hand. Of course, everyone realised straight away that it wasn't an engagement ring, but people guessed that it was a gift. It certainly doesn't look like something I would buy for myself.

No one could quite agree on who it was from. They've all clocked on to the fact that Adam and I aren't together by now, although some thought the ring might indicate a reunion. Some did speculate that it was from Greg, but the same day that the pictures of me wearing the ring came out, there he was, in several different tabloids, taking the boat out in Maine with Anna and the boys for a day of fun in the sun. It hurt to see those pictures – the way he smiled down at her as she sunbathed on the deck, the way she laughed at him, wrangling a small boy under each arm. But I know that he's a performer, and I know that he's clever. He won't let the public get the jump on him. I'm not afraid that he'll forget that he loves me, whilst I'm gone, or that some love for her will reawaken. I'm not even sure if he ever really loved her in the first place.

Five seasons of *The Avenue*. Jill turned nineteen. She's still living at home, because she has to be, because she can't be on the show if she doesn't, but it feels a little unfair to her. She's a bright girl, hard-working and good. She deserves to move out of her childhood bedroom.

I don't wear my ruby to set, of course, but Brenda and I went out for dinner and I wore it then. She picked up my hand and turned it over. 'Where did you get this?'

'A friend.'

'What kind of friend?'

I took my hand back and grinned. Brenda, her hair elegantly done up and her thin eyebrows lowered, always the most beautiful in her concern for me, shook her head. Wisps of her hair tickled her cheeks.

'Rachael,' she said, 'I'm worried about you.'

'Why?'

'You're not yourself.'

She forgets that she's not actually my mother. When I was nineteen it was charming. I turned twenty-three last month. I'm about to start work on an incredibly buzzy dark comedy with Winona Ryder and I'm seeing a man who has two young boys of his own. I don't need to be mothered anymore.

'Do you have a boyfriend?' she asked, cutting her salmon. 'It would be lovely to see you with someone.'

I don't think of Greg as a boyfriend, because the word seems too juvenile and uncomplicated. So I said no.

Jerry asked me the same question on set. He's seventeen and his skin has cleared up nicely, and he grew a foot taller over the break, so he's feeling pretty much invincible these days. 'Do you have a boyfriend?' He put a cigarette in his mouth after he asked me and lit it, to give the impression that he didn't really care about the answer.

'Yes,' I said. 'He's forty-three. And he doesn't smoke.' Then I took the cigarette out of his mouth and stamped on it.

10 October 1992

I don't know what to do anymore.

They tell you, *He's never going to leave her.* And you say, *I know. I know that's what you have to say. I can see why you would think that. But you're wrong.* They aren't wrong.

Oscar, his oldest, turned six in August. *Just until after the birthday party.* Then Frasier turned four in September. *I just want to let him have one more family birthday as well.* Then, lo and behold, Anna had already started Christmas prep. *One more Christmas, as a family.* Anna's sister just got engaged. She got a spread about it in *People.* Anna is maid of honour and has launched herself into the planning. I already know how it's going to go. *Just until all this wedding stuff is over.* There will always be something, because children grow, and seasons change, and we are never really, ever, in a period of rest. There is no point believing in some magic time when everything is soft and quiet, and all horizons are empty, and he can slip easily out of the family portrait and into my bed without any noise at all.

I was so stupid to start it. I went back and read my entries about starting it, and I wanted to reach into the page and shake myself. There was hope of return then. There was a shot at a different path. It's too late now. I love him. He worships me. It made us sick to be apart, when I was in London. Even whilst I've been shooting *Wickedly*, the only thing that has marred what has largely been quite a fun and easy shoot is the time spent away from him, how infrequently we see each other between work and his family life. Once a fortnight is about all it is now. And even when we're there, tangled up together, I spend the whole time knowing it's about to be over. And he leaves, and I'm here. Writing in my diary, like a teenage girl. Too in love to have any choices.

The other day, I saw him across the street. I was on my way back from the gym, about to step into my car, and I saw Greg coming out of some brunch spot with his family, all of them moving quickly with their heads down like they always do. It's strange seeing how his boys do it naturally, clinging to adult hands, imitating the stealthy way their parents move. But they looked happy. Him and his blonde wife and their two golden-haired boys. I was so sure that she knew. Does she?

He didn't see me. They disappeared off down the street. I got in my car and drove, and suddenly there was a *Dragonborn* billboard, looming over me as I sat at a red light, Adam Feldman and Holly Joel staring down at me with their arms around each other. It turns out they're together, or so Amy George says. He and the waitress are over. Guys as famous as Adam never hold on to girls as ordinary as that, no matter how much they love each other. He'll probably marry Holly. They'll probably have lots of famous, beautiful babies.

I looked at them, all intertwined like that with their hair blowing backwards, young and free and making movies together, and I wished that they would die.

24 January 1993

My favourite headline following the *Women Who Laugh at God* release was this one.

Rachael Carmichael: teen dream and scream queen!

There's been a lot of praise for my 'range' – which, as I said to Greg, translates to: 'She can play a woman we want to fuck *and* a woman we don't?!'

'I still want to fuck you as Abi,' he said, pushing me down on to the bed.

'That's because you're not right,' I said, and he smiled, and pulled my legs up over his shoulders.

244

I was right, about him not leaving her. It's Anna's sister's wedding now, just like I predicted. 'Sorry,' Greg said, whilst I sat far away from him on the other end of the bed and pulled my knees up to my chest. 'I just can't do it to her right now.' When he says things like that, it makes me think he still loves her, even though he denies it. I'm so sure that she knows about us, still. She must be getting a small kick out of knowing that I'm waiting pathetically like this and never getting chosen.

But *Unbeliever* is happening – we start shooting in March – and even though I still don't think much of the script, at least it means I will have him almost entirely to myself for three wonderful months. He will be consumed by me, like he was on *Women Who Laugh at God.* I will be his muse again. Which is good, because as soon as I finish on *Unbeliever* I'm going straight to the Salinas Valley to shoot *East of Eden,* and Greg isn't thrilled about that. He doesn't think it's a good move for me. Too dry, he says, too by the numbers. People have got used to me ducking and weaving. Taking unusual parts. He doesn't think I should do some long drama based on a classic novel, especially because, in his estimation, it's unlikely to touch the James Dean version. 'It's not your brand,' he says.

I don't care. I can't turn down Cathy. I'm drawn to monsters. Real monsters, strangely human monsters, who might be born from circumstance but also might just be created wicked, and it unsettles you how you can never really be sure. I argued with Greg until he backed off. Robb argued with *The Avenue* until they agreed to push back the start date for series six. I promised both Greg and Robb that I wouldn't let them dye me blonde. My Cathy is going to be an angelically terrifying brunette and everyone will just have to lump it.

'You're really sure?' asked Greg, after a particularly loud fight, after we'd made up and I was lying in his arms.

'I am,' I said. He knew I meant it. He didn't fight with me about it again after that. Never come between a girl and her monstrous obsessions.

A week after I accepted the role in *East of Eden,* Robb called me.

'Rachael,' he said.

I knew, just by the way he said it. When I got off the phone with him, I tried to think of how I would get hold of Greg. We could only call at agreed times, to agreed places. I was meeting him in two days but two days was far too long away. I sat on the end of my bed, chewing my nail. I had to leave for work in two hours.

He called me. I should have guessed that he would hear. 'Hey,' he said.

'Where are you?'

'Pre-production meeting. I've just stepped out to use their phone.' He paused. 'How do you feel?'

'You heard, then.'

'You sound so calm.' Then his tone changed. 'Oh, Rachael, do you think I'm disappointed?'

'You so deserved to be nominated.'

'The film is nominated,' he said. 'You are nominated. How on earth could I be disappointed?' I smiled into the receiver. '*You* are nominated,' he repeated. 'Rachael. I'm so proud of you. My beautiful girl.'

When I hung up with Greg, I ordered champagne and cake to the house and watched *Dangerous Liaisons.* A few people left congratulatory messages on my answering machine – my manager, my publicist – just the people who knew. I wondered who to tell – Amy, maybe? – and realised that I didn't actually have any friends. Then I realised, with a jolt, that I should probably call my mum.

We hadn't spoken properly in ages. We called on Christmas, and on my birthday, and on hers, and on Elisabeth's. She left an answering machine message on Easter Sunday with an unexpectedly religious undertone – I had never been to church and I'd never seen her set foot in one either. Each time we communicated, it was like we were going through the motions of a mother-daughter relationship, painting it in broad strokes, like reading from the script of some generic sitcom.

I wasn't sure if I loved her. I wasn't sure I would recognise the feeling if it appeared. But I knew that I should call her.

'Hello?' she said. Her voice was bright and not quite natural.

'It's me.'

'Rachael?' The register of her voice dropped. 'What's happened? Is something wrong?'

'Nothing's wrong,' I said.

'Is it—?' She hesitated. I could almost hear her flipping through her calendar in her head. No one's birthday, no major holiday. 'What's going on?' she asked.

'I have some news.'

'I hope you're not pregnant.'

'No.' I took a breath. 'I've been nominated for an Oscar.'

I wasn't sure what was happening on the other end of the phone for a minute, and then I realised. She had started to cry.

3 September 1993

I'd apologise for how sporadic these entries are becoming, but the truth is that I don't much want to keep a diary anymore. It feels childish and ultimately futile, since I'll never be able to get down everything that happens to me. It will only ever be a very vague sketch of my life. I leave it too long, and I become and kill off entire versions of myself. I shed skin after skin. How to describe those cycles once they're over? You can only say: *I was this person. This happened to me.* It never really gives a complete picture.

We shot *Unbeliever* partly in Hollywood and partly in Beverly Hills. They rented a gorgeous mansion for Helen, my character (I begged Greg not to call her Helen – it's far too 'of Troy' – but no luck). The source of Helen's income is never mentioned in the screenplay, so I asked Greg how she was supposed to have paid for the house. He said, 'She's not quite of our world. She only exists to torment. We can't really apply our logic to her.' He said this kind of thing every time I attempted to ascertain anything concrete about Helen, so eventually I gave up. I played her as he wrote her: some mythological being who enjoys toying with human feelings but does not entirely know why she is compelled to do so. I found her very dull.

The shoot was very different from *Women Who Laugh at God.* There wasn't this hushed, reverent feeling, this sense that we were making something great. It wasn't that everyone thought we were making a bad film, but everyone apart from Greg seemed to see the project for what it was: forced. He was still Greg about everything, still yelling at his actors, still making us repeat things over and over and hardly ever confirming that what we had done was usable. But it was different, when he yelled at me. It didn't fill me with rage; it didn't spur me on. It felt like foreplay. He would be in my face, screaming at me, spit flying, and I would think, *We're going to have sex later.* And we always did.

People won't like the film. I won't either. But at least it will force Greg's hand. There is no way people will watch *Unbeliever* and not know that Greg and I are sleeping together, because there is quite literally no other explanation for his having made the film.

It was like I slept through the shoot. In my head, the whole time, I was thinking – *Cathy.* My part in *East of Eden.* The pure psychopath, the wife who can never be a wife, the mother who can never be a mother. I love her truly. I swanned past glass windows holding knives as Helen, ripped open prosthetic stomachs to pull

248

out fake guts, and in my mind I was dreaming of the Salinas Valley, the beckoning mountains that Steinbeck writes about, the darkness I would find there and splash around in like a dog in mud.

And it has been beautiful. We've been here two months and I'm revelling in the thing. It's the first time I've been on a project with this high a budget – everything looks astonishingly good, all the time, but it also results in some slightly ridiculous emergencies. When things break, or fall, or spill, or catch fire, no one races to solve the problem because there's always someone on set who has been hired specifically for that purpose. One of the earliest scenes I shot involved Cathy borderline torturing a man with some old-timey sex toys. I pulled out a flogger with brown leather tassels, and our director, David Kotzias, said, 'Hang on, are we *sure* that's period? That looks out of time to me.' And then we had to call the *sex toys historian* to set for her to confirm that yes, that particular flogger would have been in use in the beginning of the twentieth century. The whole time she was explaining I was watching her, thinking, *There's money for this? There's money for* you?

Pretty much everyone on the shoot is famous, from famous child stars (they're awful – I'm so glad I wasn't famous before eighteen) to famous Shakespearian actors doing their best Californian drawl. A lot of them aren't in the scenes that I'm in and so I don't get to watch much of their work, but a few of them have come to watch me, sometimes even when they're meant to be heading home. I've never had other actors give up any of their time off to watch me work before.

I didn't win the Oscar. Emma Thompson did. And Clint Eastwood's *Unforgiven* beat us for Best Picture. But everyone knows me now. And there's that wonderful feeling going around that everyone's excited about me – everyone wants to know what I'll do next. If I keep playing my cards right, hopefully, throughout the years, no one will ever be able to guess.

It's a wonderful part, and a wonderful film, but I miss Greg. I don't like to – it feels childish, and he tells me that this is something I can be, sometimes – but I do, when I roll over in the night and he's not there, and I know that he isn't just a short car ride away, that I can't ring him and ask him to meet me at a hotel. It's Oscar's birthday again next month – how has it already been almost a year since he last used that excuse? And now it's coming round again. He's about to have a seven-year-old, and I'm still waiting in the wings of his life. I'm a fool. I hate knowing that about myself. I hate not knowing where my limit is. When does it hurt enough that I walk away? The answer is, always, not quite yet.

24 September 1993

Every time I say I've outgrown keeping a diary I find myself needing it again. I suppose when I'm happy and busy I forget what it's really for. It's only in moments like these that I know: it's a way to speak to someone and not sound crazy or worry about where my words will end up. God knows I need that sometimes.

Greg has called less and less often. When he does call, he says it's been such a busy time, that he can't always get to a phone without Anna knowing, that he's in talks to do a new *Halloween* film and there's a lot of important rooms that he has to be in, all the time. 'You don't like those films,' I said, and he told me that I needed to be less idealistic. Adults need to make money, he said, like he didn't just buy himself a penthouse flat in New York that I bet he'll never use.

He phoned tonight. I hadn't spoken to him in over a week. When he said my name his voice was low and quiet, and it shook a little. I thought it was because he was so eager, because he'd missed me as much as I'd missed him. But then I played the way he'd said it back in my head, and I realised that his tone hadn't been eager, but urgent, and suddenly I wanted to drop the phone and run.

'How was your day?' he asked.

'It was good. I shot Kenneth Branagh.'

He laughed. It was forced. 'How did he take it?'

'Very well. He was a trooper.'

'You're still enjoying it all, then?'

'Very much so. It's my favourite film I've done that hasn't been one of yours.' I wished he would just come out with it, so that we could skip the preamble. 'How are you?' I asked, to prompt him.

'Not so good,' he said.

'Why not?'

'It's been very strange, without you,' he said. 'I've made some bad choices.'

'With – with Anna? Because I understand,' I said quickly. I knew he would sleep with her again at some point. I'd steeled myself against it.

'No, not with Anna.'

That, I hadn't steeled myself against. It was a blow that took the joy clean out of me. I put a hand to my forehead, resting my elbow on the side table. I wondered whether or not I'd be able to get any cigarettes nearby.

'Not?'

'Not,' he said.

I swallowed. It was dry, and it hurt. 'How . . . ? Who?'

'This actress . . .' he said. I felt the two words like getting my ears pierced – two short stabs. 'Well,' he said, 'you wouldn't know her. She isn't famous. Or very pretty.'

I wanted to ask, *Then why?* It was almost worse, that she was just someone ordinary. It made it seem as if he would have slept with anyone.

'We just met at this party, and I went back to see her place,' he said. 'I was missing you, I guess. But god, I wish I hadn't done it. It felt so wrong, being with someone who wasn't you.'

Then he waited. I envisioned him and this ordinary woman disappearing up the stairs to her small, boring place. She would dine out on the time she had sex with Greg Foster forever. I couldn't even blame her – he would have told her that he and his wife were separating, that he didn't even love her anymore, and that was true. It wasn't her fault that he was still keeping me a secret.

My voice, when it finally came, sounded scratchy. 'Oh.' I tried to clear my throat silently, so he wouldn't hear. 'Oh,' I said again. I couldn't think of anything else.

'I wanted to tell you straight away,' he said. 'I wanted you to hear it from me.'

'Who else would I hear it from?'

'No one,' he said quickly. 'No one else knows. The press won't know.' That would have been the one silver lining, if someone had got a photograph and it had made the papers. 'It made me realise how much I want you,' he said. 'I wish you hadn't done this film.'

'How much you *want* me?'

He heard the dangerous note enter my voice. 'Rachael—'

We'd fought, in the time we'd been together. Sometimes passionately. We didn't have many opportunities to – we didn't have many opportunities to be together at all. But we'd managed to fight. In the heat of things he would always say that he hated how I was acting, that it was an ugly colour on me. But afterwards he would gather me in his arms and say how beautiful I was when I was angry. *Like lightning. I pity the man who marries you.* Smiling, like it was a private joke between us two, even though he'd never said outright that he wanted to marry me.

'You don't want me,' I said.

'You know I do.'

'Then leave her. Then keep your *dick*—' My voice wobbled dangerously, and I turned it into a hiss. '—out of other women!'

'I can't.'

'You *can't?*'

'I mean, I can't leave her. You know I can't, Rachael. Not yet, at least.'

'It's always not yet.'

'Come home,' he said, pleadingly. 'We'll talk about all of it.'

'I wrap in three weeks.'

'That's too long. Come home now.'

'I can't walk out on a fucking *job*, Greg.'

'Don't pretend you're all professional now,' he snapped. 'Too professional to take a break but not too professional to fuck your boss, huh?'

I slammed the phone down. The room filled with silence.

The cruelty of it is that he knows that I can't just leave. He knows how these contracts work. And he knows that I'm enjoying *East of Eden* more than I enjoyed *Unbeliever*. In his mind, he feels like he's being cheated on. It almost makes me want to laugh.

But as I've been sat here, writing, I've begun to calm down, and I know that the reality of the situation is this: I've been away for three months. I'm not with a patient, loyal Adam. This is the man I chose. This force, this fast-moving mind, this endless appetite. If I have truly made up my mind to accept what I can have of him – and that seems to be what I've done – then I have to stand by that.

Three months.

Has it really been—

Sorry. Put my pen down and called the concierge. Asked, 'Could you get me a pregnancy test?' very quietly into the phone. Will just have to trust that they'll be discreet. I'll see if I can get my lawyer to send an NDA over tomorrow morning.

They've just knocked and handed it to me. Is there a shop nearby that I don't know about, or do they just keep a supply of them?

Peed on the stick. Waiting. Will have to call Greg back, if it's what I think it is. How did I not notice I'd missed *three months?* Is that how immersed I've been? Can I really call him back after hanging up on him like that and deliver this news? It will seem like a lie. Or a trap, somehow. A way to force his hand.

Two minutes.

Fuck.

15 October 1993

I left Cathy behind in the shade of the Salinas Valley. Her death had been a drawn-out thing, in our film, but I like to imagine that the poison worked quickly, that she found some peace in the end. They were still shooting when I left the set but we all had drinks in town to celebrate. It was quite the scene, the whole lot of us walking through Salinas. Some people had disposable cameras – they took photographs. I imagined the people who would eventually develop the film squinting, looking at me walking down that dusty street, thinking, *Is that Rachael Carmichael?*

Greg left just two voicemails over the last few weeks, before he stopped calling entirely. The last one ended, 'I suppose there's probably nothing left to say.' I suppose there probably isn't. Certainly not this: *Before you cheated on me, you got me pregnant. What should we both do about that?*

I took a car to San Francisco Airport. It was a drive of an hour and a half through California and then a two-hour flight – not the worst commute home. I read for most of it – *The Turn of the Screw,* by Henry James, because Paramount are optioning it and I think I'd like to play the governess. I'd like to try being the one getting scared for once, rather than the one doing the scaring. Of course, everything is more complicated now. Who knows how big I'll be by the time they cast, or whether I'll be dragging a baby around with me on set. I can't imagine myself as a mother. There's not a single picture of that in my head that makes sense.

When I landed and walked out into Arrivals, it was swarming with cameras. I usually anticipate a few, in airports, but this was far beyond anything I had ever experienced. Members of the public meeting friends and relatives off the plane looked quite frightened by it. When they saw me, the place exploded – shouts and shutters and flashes – and for a second my mind went numb. I couldn't understand it. Even when you've been famous for a few years, there are still moments where you forget, and you ask yourself, *All of this, for me?*

Then he stepped through the crowd. Tall and smiling, in a navy suit. He carried a bouquet of roses.

'Hey,' he said. He raised a hand.

Dazed, I wondered if there had been some press release about his divorce that I'd missed during my flight, rushed out in those two hours. I moved towards him, and he moved towards me. The cameras had us fenced in, but it was like he didn't see them, so I chose not to, either. Beyond them, people leant on their suitcases to watch. Couples stood with their arms around each other. Mothers held their children's hands and gawked.

'Good flight?' he asked. Someone took my suitcase from my hand. I turned, but Greg said, 'It's okay, that's our driver. He'll put it in the car for you.' I watched my suitcase being wheeled away through the airport. 'Rachael, look at me,' he said. He was still clutching the bouquet of roses. It was enormous, blooming across his entire chest. He held them out to me. 'I missed you.'

'What's happening?' I lowered my voice to a whisper. 'What are you doing?'

'I'm meeting you at the airport.'

'Why?'

He looked at me seriously, over the roses. I took them. I wanted to be only half-aware of the cameras and the staring, to be enamoured by his sudden appearance and deaf to the rest of them. I was wholly, uncomfortably aware. I felt naked. But I was also there, with him, blinded by him, nose full of roses.

'I love you,' he said. The way he said it made me want to throw myself into his arms and cry. I stayed where I was. 'You're extraordinary,' he said. 'The most incredible woman I've ever met. Being apart from you is hell. I never want to be apart from you again.'

When he reached into his pocket, my mind went to the obvious place. I thought, *No, he's going for some gum.* Then I thought, *Don't be stupid. Why would he pop gum right now?* Then I thought, *That's not gum.*

It was a small box of blue velvet, dark as midnight. He lowered himself to one knee. A gasp ran round the terminal. At the time, I couldn't be sure that it wasn't in my own head. I forgot that anyone was watching. I just stared at the lid slowly lifting on that small blue box, revealing the glint of something silver. A diamond. You can't mistake the intentions of a diamond.

'Marry me?' he said.

I grinned. I couldn't help it. It broke across my face like a fault line. I thought of the small life growing inside me. He didn't even know yet. He wasn't marrying me because he had to. He had no idea how much of a family we already were. 'Yes,' I said. 'I will.'

I don't know where the roses went. I only know that the next second I was in his arms, and he was kissing me in front of everyone, one hand cupping the back of my head, the other on my lower back. The click of camera shutters was deafening. He pulled away, holding both of my hands in his, and I saw that there were tears in his eyes. 'Rachael,' he said. 'My Rachael.'

I couldn't very well say 'My Greg,' but I smiled.

He led me through the airport, ignoring shouted questions and loud applause, somehow carving a clear path through the paps. Our car pulled up, and he helped me in. The door closed, and we pulled off, the sound of the chaos we'd left in our wake dimming until it was just the two of us and the hum of the engine. We looked at each other, and we started to laugh, disbelieving. Both of us at a loss. I don't think that had ever happened before.

'Where are we going?' I managed.

'Your place. And we aren't leaving it for a week. And neither of us is going to wear a single item of clothing the entire time we're there.'

We were still laughing. There was little else we could have done. There were too many questions – the idea of asking them all and getting answers felt ridiculous. And then there was the baby, which was currently the size of a small fruit but had the potential to rip through us both like a bullet. I had no idea where to start, so all I asked was, 'How?'

'How what?'

'*How* did you just do that? What did you tell your team?'

'Nothing.'

'Anna? Your family?'

'Nothing,' he said. 'I told them nothing.' He took my hand, turning it over so that we were both blinded by the flash of the ring. 'I've been in hell, Rachael,' he said. 'It's been utter, absolute misery without you. Without you here, without your voice on the phone. I looked at my life and I decided that none of it was worth it if I didn't get to spend it with you.'

'So— I mean—' I sat back. He was still holding my hand. 'Nothing? No one? You just . . . bought a ring and asked?'

'I just bought a ring and asked,' he grinned.

'Everyone will know by tomorrow. Won't they? Do you have a plan?'

'I told you the plan,' he said, kissing my hand.

'But— Anna.'

'Fuck Anna,' he said. I stared at him. 'For fuck's sakes, Rachael, you don't even like Anna.'

'She's your *wife*. You didn't— I mean, you have a lawyer now, right? The divorce has . . . It's all started.'

'We can arrange all that,' he said.

I wrenched my hand back. 'Oh my god.'

'Rachael, I'm leaving her. I can't very well not, after that, can I?'

'But why would you do it like *this*?' I put my head in my hands.

'I thought you'd be happy,' I heard him say.

I shook my head.

'I mean—' His voice rose a few levels. 'This is what you wanted. Isn't it? For me to break it off, for us to be together. This is what you've been begging for.'

'I never begged,' I said.

He made a noise in his throat like he disagreed. It enraged me.

'This is not how you break off a marriage, Greg. I mean, what if I marry you and then you change your mind? Would you humiliate me like this?'

'You're not Anna. You've never been Anna.'

I shook my head again.

'Will you look at me?' he asked. 'Just look at me.'

I raised my head. I expected to find him contrite, but he looked angry.

'I want to marry you,' he said. 'That's my only crime here. Just that.'

'I suppose I expected that when the man I loved proposed to me, he would at least have separated from his wife first.'

We were outside my gate. The driver leant forward to put in the code, but Greg stopped him. 'Get out,' he said.

I stared at him. He wasn't looking at me.

'Do you want to come in and talk about it?' I asked.

He was still gazing out of his window, not saying anything.

'Fine,' I said, and I unclipped my seat belt and slammed the door.

As I said it, and as I did this, I saw him move slightly, like he'd already been planning on it, like he'd only meant to freeze me out for a few seconds. But it was too late. We'd both made our choices. He looked back out the opposite window. I turned to my gate to input the code. The driver pressed the pedal, and as the car started to pull off, I turned and screamed at him with all the air in my lungs.

'I'M PREGNANT, ASSHOLE.'

How very *EastEnders,* Mum would have said. I realised, half in horror and half in amusement, that it was also exactly the kind of thing she might have done. The car disappeared. The gate slid open, and I saw there was a strange bead of light dancing across it. I looked down at my hand. I was still wearing the diamond. I suppose I was really supposed to hurl it at his head, but it hadn't crossed my mind to do so. Oh, well. It could live next to my ruby at the bottom of my suitcase. Pretty, empty jewels. Festering together.

Chapter Eleven

HARLEY

He was leaning over me, grabbing at my hand, trying to tug the ring from my finger.

'Give that fucking diamond back!'

I had my hand on the car door. 'Touch me, and I'll jump out of this fucking car!'

'Daniel, lock the fucking doors,' he told the driver.

'Unlock the doors, Daniel!'

'You are not jumping out on to the fucking highway.'

'How am I meant to stay in this car with you?' I turned, eyes flashing, or so I liked to think. 'Do you know what you've made me into? Do you know what they'll say about me, after that little stunt? What am I good for now? Just Greg Foster's piece on the side.' I buried my face in my hands and gave a sob.

'Cut,' called José.

Elias and I straightened up. José had been sat in his chair, watching us on his tablet as we wrestled inside the car – now he came over to us and opened the door.

'Climb out for a second,' he said. 'Elias, you can take a few minutes. Everyone can take a few minutes.'

Inwardly, I groaned. I was still waiting for the day when I was allowed to take a few minutes, and Elias had to sift through all of José's many opinions about his performance and pick a few that were actually constructive.

We had three months left shooting in LA before we headed to Iceland. I was without Carlton and Julia now – they had both flown home to do whatever it is they do when the three of us aren't together – and Rachael was starting *Traversers* next month and would be far less contactable. I had been trying to keep my head down, to focus on the part in front of me, but I was slowly starting to panic. José really just didn't seem to like me very much. In the first few weeks I would have worried that I would be fired if I wasn't essentially un-fireable. Now we were a month in and he was still obsessing over every choice I made, never quite happy with how I was working in every scene. He was always polite about it, but it was affecting the atmosphere on set – everyone was frustrated with his constant interruptions, and I was worried that it was starting to reflect badly on me. I couldn't seem to make him understand how deeply I knew Rachael Carmichael, that I mirrored her to a level that neither he nor anyone else on that set could appreciate.

He took me aside as Elias and the actor playing the driver leant against the side of the car to chat. Elias was gracious with all of the supporting cast, condescendingly interested in them in a way that made me nauseous. He was rarely that nice to me these days. I felt his eyes on José and me as we stepped away.

'First of all,' José said as I folded my arms, 'don't look frustrated. You're doing your job and I'm doing mine.' He'd used this line on me before. 'I just have some notes.'

'Okay.'

He hesitated. 'I need to feel as if you're ready to receive them.'

'I am.'

He looked doubtful, but he cleared his throat. 'It's coming across a little comical.'

'*Comical?*'

I hadn't meant to be quite that loud. Elias and the driver looked over to us, breaking off their conversation. A few of the crew averted their eyes. José looked alarmed. He made a motion as if he was about to put a hand on my arm, and then thought better of it.

'Come on,' he said, instead. 'I think we should go for a chat.'

We walked across the lot to his office. I was conscious of everyone's eyes on us, and José seemed to sense this – he kept our chat light and friendly, asking after my mother, who he'd met before at some event, and my father, who he'd worked with in the past. He asked if Rachael seemed happy with the updates I'd been giving her, like that was the real purpose of the conversation, and I nodded along. When we reached his office, he closed the door and offered me coffee. I accepted. He called his assistant to put the order in, and when he put the phone down he said, 'Harley, I'm really not trying to upset you.'

He said it very sincerely. I did believe him, even though I was still annoyed. José is definitely one of the nicest people I've met in the industry, although he is so particular.

'I think you're talented,' he said. 'I honestly do.'

'Thank you.'

'But I'm going to be completely real with you,' he said. 'I don't think you're ready for this role. If it were up to me, I wouldn't have cast you.'

Jesus.

He saw my face. 'I'm sorry if that's hard to hear. I'm speaking my mind – you can speak yours.'

I swallowed back the response I really wanted to give and opted for the professional one. 'Rachael wouldn't have trusted me personally if she didn't think I could do it.'

'I'm sure that's true,' he said. 'Your aunt is a very smart woman, and I'm sure she has good reasons for trusting this role to you. But I worry that Elias is going to show you up, in this project, and that people are going to notice. That could have a negative impact on your career, and neither of us want that.'

His face was so understanding and faux sympathetic. I wanted to slap him. 'So what can I do? I can't just suddenly be the actor you want me to be.'

'You're right,' he said. 'The frustrating thing is that I do think you're a perfect cast, in so many ways. The family tie is incredibly intriguing and you obviously look perfect for it. There are moments when I really see her in you. In an ideal world you would be able to go away and get more experience and come back to this role, but by then you'd be too old and we would have missed the boat on this project, timing-wise.'

His assistant knocked on the door with the coffees. José thanked her – a smiling, blonde, twenty-year-old thing – and she dimpled at him prettily and closed the door behind her. Lucky girl, to have a job so simple that she couldn't help but do it well.

'You're going to have to work with me,' said José, as I sipped my coffee. 'That's all I'm trying to say. You put up a lot of resistance to my notes, like they're criticisms of you, when really this relationship should be two people working hard to build something together.'

'It feels personal sometimes,' I said.

He shook his head, a little frustrated now. 'Okay, Harley, but it *isn't*. That's what I'm trying to say to you.' He leant forward. 'I really believe that this part is in you. I think you have the capability, somewhere. But I'm asking you to trust me. I'm asking you not to get defensive when you need more guidance than an actor twice your age, with five times your experience. Take the notes, apply them, learn, grow, and you'll play this part better than you ever thought you could.'

The anger was dissipating. I still felt fiercely protective of my version of Rachael, but this was what being an actor was. Creation was collaboration. Rachael herself had been questioned and challenged on her sets. She'd gone through it all with Greg and it had pushed her to new heights. 'Alright,' I said. 'I— I'm sorry, if I seemed defensive.'

'And I'm sorry if I seemed harsh,' he said. 'Now, when we go back and shoot this scene, here's what I want you to think about. You're playing her very hysterical right now, very distraught. Find that ice in her. Find that fury. Look at him and think, *I hope you burn,* in only the way that someone who feels that passionately about someone else *can* feel. But also, remember, there's a naivety in that fury. She's young, she's impulsive. And she's trying to kid herself into thinking that she's this ice queen. That she isn't, underneath it all, desperately tired.'

When we went back to set, and I sat beside Elias in the car again, he didn't look at me. He was sometimes like that, trying to get into the part, pretending I wasn't there until José called 'Action' and he looked over and saw Rachael. Now he had his eyes closed, drumming on the car door to some irregular rhythm. I shook my hair back, closed my own eyes. I thought about everything José had said to me. And I thought about Rachael, staying, waiting for her cards to come up. It wasn't a kind of love I had ever really believed in. But it was a kind of love all the same.

'Action,' came the cue.

We were pulling away from the airport in the car. We looked over at each other and laughed. Disbelieving, overwhelmed and so in love. Until Elias' Greg told my Rachael that this was how the world was finding out he wanted to leave his wife. I pushed him on this.

'Is this how Anna's finding out?'

'Yes.' He didn't see a problem. He was kissing my fingers around the diamond, smiling. I wrenched my hand back. 'What?' he asked.

'I didn't want that,' I said. 'I never wanted that.'

'You never wanted that?' His voice changed. 'Are you kidding?'

'Why would you think I wanted that?'

'Why?' Now he was yelling. 'You've been fucking *begging* for this diamond—'

'I have never begged you for anything. Don't misidentify me.'

And then we were into the section of the scene we'd been doing before José called cut. I let it escalate, but I wasn't getting upset so much as white hot. I looked at Elias – Greg – and thought, *I hope you burn.* Then I thought, *I will burn you.* Then I thought, *You make me burn.* I held all three of the thoughts in my head as I stared at him.

'Do you know what you've made me into? Do you know what they'll say about me, after that little stunt? What am I good for now? Just Greg Foster's piece on the side.'

'You've got a *ring*,' said Elias. He turned his head. 'Crazy bitch,' he muttered.

I stared at his head, still facing the window. 'What did you call me?'

'I said you're a crazy bitch, Rachael. Who acts like this after a proposal? You switch up so fast. One minute you want to marry me, the next you're acting like you hate me.'

'I do hate you,' I said. 'Right now, I hate you.' I practically spat the words.

He slapped me. I'd told him to do it for real. I'd thought it would be pretty easy, to say you wanted to get slapped for real and for it to just happen, but I'd had to speak to a couple of different people about it – 'For safeguarding reasons,' said José. Eventually everyone seemed to agree that I was allowed to decide if I wanted to get slapped in my own face. Still, he hit me harder than I'd been expecting. It genuinely did knock me backwards for a second. We stared at each other.

Then I raised my hand. 'Look at this rock you just gave me,' I said. 'You just *armed* me. You want to hit me again? You want me to hit you back?'

And we went on staring at each other. Not sure who was going to make the next move in this strange seduction. Not sure what we were even supposed to do, anymore.

'Cut,' called José eventually.

The car doors were opened. We climbed out.

'We'll go again in a sec,' he said. 'I have some thoughts.' He looked at me. 'Not bad at all, Harley,' he said. 'Well done.'

Then he moved on.

We took a break. I went to my trailer to cool off. My cheek was stinging from the multiple takes we'd done of the slap. I put an ice pack against it and breathed out. That had been a breakthrough. I'd never experienced one before – I'd never played a role that called for one. But I could feel it, that shift. It was like a drug. It frustrated me that José didn't seem to see it.

There was a knock on my trailer door. 'Come in,' I called. I hoped to see José or one of the producers there to congratulate me, but it was Elias. He stepped heavily into the room, one hand on his pocket and pulled the door closed. I'd never seen him look so sheepish.

'Sorry,' he said, gesturing to the ice pack. He didn't sound sorry.

'It's fine. I said you could.'

He stood awkwardly, as awkward as Elias could ever be.

'What's wrong?' I asked. 'Are you trying to have sex?'

'No, Harley, I'm not trying to have sex.'

'What is it, then? You look weird.' I eyed him, turning the ice pack over. 'Are you angry about something?'

'What would I have to be angry about?'

'You tell me.'

'I suppose we'll be able to speed up this shoot a little bit, now?' he said. 'Felt like you had a good moment there.' He didn't sound pleased. 'Are you happy?' he asked.

'Yeah. I am.'

'José seemed to actually believe you as Rachael. For once.'

I couldn't read his tone. I waited for him to sit down, and eventually he did, in a chair some distance from me.

'I don't really have a point,' he said.

'Okay?'

'I'm just . . . a little pissed, I guess.'

'About what?'

He breathed out. 'You take this whole thing for granted. You don't try to listen to José, you don't try to improve. You hold every scene up because you're so reluctant to apply notes. And then you have one good moment and – I mean, I can see it – you're walking on air, suddenly. I'm worried we've taken one step forward and two steps back. Now you think you can do it, so you won't try.'

'Is this because you think I was better in the scene than you?'

He half stood up. I flinched. He composed himself and settled back into the chair. He had the energy of an exhausted father as he did it, which caught me off guard, because I wasn't used to thinking of him as older than me. I often forgot about the two decades between us. I wondered if the half-stand had been because his instinct was to hit me. 'God, you're annoying,' he said. 'Harley, you will never be better than me, in any scene. Okay? You're just not that good an actress.'

267

'You sound defensive.'

'Sometimes you make me want to hit you for real,' he said.

'You did hit me for real.'

'I mean, not in a scene.'

'It was still real. Now I know why you went so hard.' He sat there, looking murderous. 'Should I be scared of you?' I asked.

'Of course not,' he said. 'Don't be ridiculous.'

'You seem like you hate me.'

'I do,' he said, 'a little. It's probably good for the film that I do.' He stood up. 'You can come over to mine later,' he said. And then he left, without waiting for an answer.

From outside the trailer came the sound of him running into someone. I heard a familiar voice go, 'Oh, sorry, shit,' and pressed a cushion against my face. The committee to rain on my parade had apparently been busy.

There were two short knocks on the door, businesslike. 'Come in,' I said, against my instincts. Ahn put her head around the door. Her hair was pulled back so severely that it looked like her face had been ironed, or maybe she'd started getting Botox.

'Hi, Harley,' she said.

She was holding her phone, the screen alight – presumably she had something to show me. I gestured for her to approach and hand it over. She pulled up a chair as I scanned the article in front of me. It was an archive piece from 1993, an account of that argument between Greg and Rachael with input from the driver who had apparently heard Rachael shout after the car.

> She said, 'I'm pregnant,' clear as day. I asked Mr Foster
> whether he wanted me to turn the car around so that the
> two of them could talk, but he said that I'd misheard her.
> You couldn't mishear that, though.

'It's rubbish,' I said, handing the phone back to her. 'We know that now. She can't have children.'

'Well, yes,' said Ahn. 'That's what she told us.'

'You think she's lying?'

Ahn rolled her eyes. 'You don't need to say it like it's blasphemous, Harley. She might have told a half-truth. I believe her when she says that she and Greg couldn't conceive. But does that mean she was *never* pregnant?' She shrugged. 'It's probably rubbish, like you said. But it's interesting how these rumours have persisted.'

'We can't do anything about it now.'

'It just feels,' said Ahn, 'like that scene had something *missing* from it. You know?'

'Maybe you should have written it better.'

'Oh, stop it,' she said. 'Don't think I've not noticed that you haven't exactly been excelling at your craft on this shoot.'

That shut us both up for a second. She dropped her eyes to her lap and pressed her lips together.

'You want to rewrite the scene?' I asked.

'I don't know,' she said. 'But I think it would be worth us going to Rachael one more time. Double-checking there's no truth to it. Asking where she thinks the rumour came from. Maybe she shouted something different after the car and the driver misheard her.'

'Do you really think she wouldn't have told us?'

'I don't know,' said Ahn. 'We can't really know, either of us.'

I brushed off the dig and considered what she was saying. 'I do think it needs something more,' I said. 'This whole thing. Some big reveal. Some secret no one else knows. I mean, what she went through trying to have a kid is obviously very sad, but it isn't so much a *moment*, you know?'

Ahn crossed one trousered leg over the other in her chair and frowned at me, as best she could with the skin on her face so taught. 'I'm not talking about that. I'm just talking about faithful storytelling.'

'Right. When aren't you?'

'So you'll do it? You'll talk to her?'

'She won't like it,' I said.

'Probably not. But if anyone can get away with pushing her on this stuff, you can. Just tell her you want your performance to be as authentic as possible.'

'I do want it to be as authentic as possible.'

'Exactly,' said Ahn. 'So you won't even have to lie.'

That night, I went for dinner at Rachael's place in Hidden Hills. She'd made dumplings and spicy rice. She smirked at me whenever I reached for the water. The sprinkler was on to the left of us, spraying the lawn by her pool, the sky a moody blue behind it and getting moodier by the second. She asked me how work had been that day, and I started to tell her about my breakthrough and Elias' strange reaction to it. I hadn't yet told her that I'd been having sex with Elias, but when I was halfway through the story, she looked at me, and said, 'You two are sleeping together?' Like it was an established fact.

'Yes,' I said.

She winced. 'Bad idea, Harley.'

'It's been working pretty well.'

'Don't sleep with your co-workers,' she said. 'It's not a difficult rule to follow.'

I didn't point out the hypocrisy of this. 'Please, I wasn't overcome by lust or anything. It was a practical decision. But I'm starting to feel like he doesn't like me.'

'Hm,' said Rachael.

'What?'

She shrugged. 'From what I know of Elias Jones, he's a fairly self-made man. Maybe it irritates him, feeling like you've had this handed to you.'

'Do you think that's what everyone thinks? That I've just had this handed to me?'

'Some people,' said Rachael, 'I'm sure.'

'But, I mean, I didn't. I've worked for this.'

It was almost dark now, and her porch lights were on. She looked pale under them, faintly luminous. The lines around her mouth and eyes were hidden. As I spoke to her, as she moved her head, listening, it felt like talking to a reflection of myself. A vision on the other side of the veil, staring back at me out of my own eyes. Circles of white in the centre of them. There were insects buzzing around the lamps that lined her pool. She was drinking Chardonnay. She'd offered me some but I'd said no, I was driving. I'd hired myself a car, sick of having to call one every time I wanted to go somewhere.

'People are always going to say what they're going to say,' said Rachael.

'But they're allowed to say anything about people like me,' I said. Her hand moved through the dim light to the stem of her glass. It glinted as she tipped it. 'I mean, I grew up with money, right? I grew up with parents and relatives and friends who happened to work in the industry I happened to want to go into. So, I couldn't possibly have any problems. I couldn't possibly have dreams and desires and disappointments and frustrations and failures of my own.'

'Hm.'

'Oh, please. Just say what you want.'

'I'm sure you've considered that those frustrations and failures might be more severe if you hadn't been born into the position you have been.'

'Of course. But they also might not be. I mean, you weren't born into my position. And you've had much more success than me.'

'Hm,' she said again.

'Well? Isn't that true?'

'I suppose it is.'

I sat back, triumphant. She pushed her plate away from her. There was a low buzz coming from the insects around her pool lights. 'Are you going to stay with him?' she asked.

'I'm not even really with him.'

'Fine, but are you going to keep sleeping with him?'

'I don't know,' I said. 'Whatever's best for the part.'

It was getting chilly. She went inside to get us blankets to put over our knees. Whilst she was up, she dimmed the patio lights so that we were sat in half-darkness, the pool rippling blue and glossy in front of us. I hugged my knees to my chest. I didn't hear her come back out, only felt the blanket on my skin as she draped it over me from behind, wordlessly.

'Thank you,' I said.

She sat back down, without acknowledging me. It was like she had covered up a piece of furniture. She was so rigid in the way she showed affection that sometimes it didn't feel like affection at all, but a chore she'd assigned herself.

'The scene wasn't right anyway,' I said.

'No?'

'No. Ahn thinks it feels inauthentic.' I waited for her to make the connection, so that I wouldn't have to say it. She took her time responding, turning her wine glass in her hands. I had that same feeling I always had when I pushed her on something – that she might click her fingers, and she and the house would vanish, and I would never find either of them ever again.

'This is the argument in the car?'

'Yes. After the proposal.' I wished I could see her face. It was obscured now, the light insufficient. I could only see the outline of her, the lit pool rippling in the reflection of her wine glass. 'It's just such a famous moment,' I said, 'and there's so much speculation around it. I guess it would be good to get some . . .'

'Some?'

'Clarity.'

'Clarity,' she repeated.

'Yes.'

'Clarity,' she said again. 'Meaning?'

'You know. What was said. Whether there were any . . . last words.'

She took a sip of her wine and resurfaced nodding. 'Harley,' she said slowly. 'I've told you that I can't have children.'

'You've said that you and Greg couldn't—'

'You're still curious about this *baby* business. That I'm supposed to have yelled after the car that there was a *baby*. That I've been hiding some secret *baby* from everyone all these years.'

'Have you?' I asked.

I don't know what made me brave enough to ask. She was very still and I could tell that she was looking at me. She sighed.

'God,' she said. 'You people really want all of me, don't you?'

I wasn't sure how to respond to that. It felt too risky to say, *Yes, that's what being famous is.* She didn't fill the silence. 'People love you,' I said eventually. 'They want as much of you as possible, I guess. They want to feel like they fully know you.'

'Do you? Want to feel like you fully know me?'

She had her blanket wrapped around her, tightly under her chin. In the half-light, her silhouette was one of a thin old woman or a very large infant. The only part of her that was visible was her hand holding the wine glass, ringless, her nails plain and clipped. Like it was just anyone's hand.

'I do,' I said. 'I think you're fascinating.'

273

'Hm,' she said.

This wasn't going well, I realised. I would need to say something to provoke her. Dig under the surface a little, prise up the fingernail, see if there were any secrets worth hearing.

'I was thinking,' I said, 'about reaching out to Anna Bianca.'

Her hand extended out to place the wine glass on the table. Her face was still mostly hidden, but I could see enough of it as she moved to know that she didn't like that idea.

'Why?' she asked, in a way that meant, *Why the fuck?*

'I just think she would be an interesting perspective. This whole project is about lifting the curtain, right? Giving everyone an *insight?* I'm just wondering, are we giving them enough *insight?*'

'We're giving them my whole marriage,' said Rachael. 'We're giving them the worst years of my life.'

'Yes. I suppose it's just important that we're showing the worst of the worst, right?' I was aware that didn't sound good. 'You know what I mean. Anna might be able to offer some interesting insight into the wider context of your relationship with Greg.'

She didn't say anything to that. She sat there, looking at me, considering. Then she held the wine bottle out to me. I shook my head.

'You're finished?' she asked, in a way that let me know she wanted me to leave.

I left disheartened, worried that I had damaged our relationship forever. I'd always sensed she didn't respond well to being pushed, and here was the proof. I spent a few hours in my room eating lentil crisps and feeling sorry for myself. Ahn called, buoyant with expectation. I told her it had been a fucking disaster.

'I really thought you'd be able to get it out of her,' she said.

'Yeah, thanks.'

'Maybe there really isn't anything.'

I wanted to throttle her. It was the thoughtful way she said it, like she hadn't risked my entire relationship with Rachael on a hunch.

'There is,' I said. 'There has to be. I'll find it.'

I didn't tell Ahn what I did next. I knew she wouldn't approve.

I logged into my dad's email, something that I'd been doing since school in order to intercept any communication from my teachers. I couldn't find any saved contacts, but when I opened a new email tab and started typing it in, there he was.

Greg Foster. *gregf8@gmail.com*

How strange, to see a man like Greg Foster reduced to his Gmail address.

> From: harley.r0th@outlook.com
> To: gregf8@gmail.com
>
> Hi Greg,

Hi Greg? It felt wrong. There really wasn't any other way to begin though. I wasn't going to call him Sir.

> From: harley.r0th@outlook.com
> To: gregf8@gmail.com
>
> Hi Greg,
>
> I hope this email finds you well. This is an unorthodox request. I'm one of the creative team behind the upcoming Rachael Carmichael film with Cagnoni –

Technically true, I thought.

> – and I'd love to invite you to interview.

There was no way he was going to reply to that. I would have to provoke him, somehow. Let him know we needed something from him that Rachael wouldn't provide. Pretend we were giving him an opportunity to level the playing field.

> With Rachael sharing so many never-before-heard
> details about your relationship in this project, we
> wanted to give you the opportunity to do the same.
> Please get back in touch with your availability.
>
> Kind regards,
> The Cagnoni team

Professional. Intriguing too. Surely the man I understood Greg Foster to be wouldn't be able to resist.

But four days passed, and I didn't hear from either of them. Things were fraught on set. José accused me several times of being distracted, and Elias pulled me aside just to look at me very seriously and go, 'Harley.' When I asked him what his point was, he just shook his head and turned away from me, and then he sighed, heavily. I wasn't sure what to make of it but I knew that it pissed me off.

Then, that night, Ahn rang me.

'What on earth did you say to Rachael?' she asked.

Shit, I thought. Surely she hadn't found out about my email. 'Why? What's happened?'

'She just called me. She called *me*. Said she had some things to share.'

A prickling in my back. My heart thumped so hard I felt briefly nauseous. 'So there was a baby?' I asked.

'No, she still insists there wasn't.'

'And you think she's lying?'

'I don't think so, no,' said Ahn. 'Actually, I'm inclined to believe her at this point.'

'Then what?'

'She says he paid her off,' said Ahn. 'Offered her a few million to keep quiet about how awful he'd been to her in their marriage.'

'How much is a few?'

'Does it matter?' Such an Ahn thing to say. 'She gave it to her mother and Elisabeth. She told me that she felt like it was a way to disentangle herself from financially supporting them, with some-one else's money. At the time it felt like a win. Now she wishes she hadn't taken it. She's ashamed, I think.'

My mind wasn't quite keeping up. It wasn't just the revelation that my family had inherited Greg's hush money. I swam to the source of the confusion. 'Why's she only telling us this now?'

'She said you made her realise that she needed to be fully trans-parent in order for this project to succeed.'

'That doesn't sound like something she'd say. That sounds like something *you'd* say.'

'She's worried he'll try to sue or something. She wants us to be prepared.'

I picked at my cuticle. She sighed at my silence.

'You think we're both lying?'

'No,' I said reluctantly. 'No. I just don't understand why she wouldn't have told me.'

'Well, Harley,' said Ahn, her tone clipped, 'have you ever con-sidered that maybe she doesn't tell you everything?'

We spoke to José and Elias. The new scene went in, right at the end of the film. In reality, Rachael had received this offer through lawyers, but we thought it would make a good opportunity for a final confrontation between Rachael and Greg, one where we see just how intimidating he could really be towards her. 'Up for it?' José asked Elias.

277

Elias looked at me. 'Sure,' he said, but he looked afraid.

It was becoming hard to say whether I liked sleeping with Elias. At the beginning it had felt exciting and productive, a little dangerous sometimes – now it really did feel like hate sex. Which was fine – it worked. Our chemistry on set was undeniable. We worked together like people who were having sex. I was sure everyone knew. And I could feel that our scenes as Rachael and Greg were getting better, more complex, more interesting, the more we really let ourselves at each other. But there were times when I was with him – bent over his kitchen counter, on my back on top of his footstool, on my knees on his bathroom floor – that it really felt like he didn't care about me at all. That worried me. He could hate me, but he had to care. Sometimes he pulled my hair or smacked me in a way that didn't feel passionate so much as detached. Sometimes it felt like he didn't even see me at all.

I told him as much one night, when we lay panting on his kitchen floor.

'I'm sorry,' he said. I hadn't been expecting the apology. I thought he'd vehemently deny it and become more malicious.

'I'm right, then?'

'You get under my skin,' he said. 'The more we do of this, the more I wonder how necessary it all was. I don't like that you talked me into it. I feel dirty.'

I couldn't suppress a chuckle. He heard me.

'Make fun of me if you want,' he said. 'It makes it hard to respect you. That's something you should worry about. You always want your co-stars to respect you.'

'It's something *you* should worry about. You should examine why you can't respect the woman you're fucking.'

'I have examined it,' he said. 'It's because you're not respectable.'

I thought about that conversation a lot, after it happened. I wondered if he was right. I had never tried particularly hard to be respectable.

The next week, we filmed the scene where Greg kicked Rachael in the ribs. I didn't trust Elias to pull his punches by that point, so I was grateful that we were working with a fight choreographer, who supervised us, made sure we were doing the movements safely. I lay on the floor as Elias pretended to kick me and curled around myself, trying to protect my ribs. When we finished rehearsing, he was sweating, like the effort of not actually kicking me was enormous.

We shot the scene all in one take, which meant we had to go through it over and over, like a play. Always ending with me on the floor, curled up, crying. Not sobbing, no histrionics, but a cold, detached kind of crying, empty eyes staring into the camera. It would be harrowing, José said, if we could nail it.

'That's great,' he said, after our fourth take. We went through notes. We were getting on quite well together by that point, José and I. 'Elias,' he said, 'even more. I want to see that monster jump out.'

There was a glint in Elias' eye that made me genuinely frightened.

At the end of our fifth take, as I was curled up on the floor, he actually kicked me. It wasn't as hard as he'd been pretending to, but it was enough to make me lose my breath for a minute. I cried out and broke into coughs. Elias stepped back quickly.

'Cut,' called José. First-aiders ran over immediately, to feel my ribs, to help me sit up. Someone ran to get me some water. Water is treated like a magic elixir on a film set; a cure for all ills. José hurried over and bent down to hand the cup to me himself, encouraging me to drink.

'Shit,' said Elias, still stood a little way off.

As soon as the shock had worn off and I had my breath back, I turned towards him. 'What the fuck was that?' I screamed, half in a whisper. The first-aiders put firm hands on me, forced me to sit still.

'It was an accident,' he said. 'Sorry, Harley.'

'That was not an accident!'

'I obviously didn't do it on purpose,' he said, so affronted that you'd think he was the one who'd been kicked.

'I think it was accidental,' said José diplomatically. He was crouched by my side. 'A very unfortunate accident, though. Let's take some time. Harley, go rest, and we'll reconvene later and see if we're alright to carry on.'

I was helped back to my trailer, even though I was fine, apart from a bit of smarting on my left side. I shot Elias a glare as I went. He turned away, but as I was led off by two first-aiders, I could hear him following a little distance behind.

In my trailer, established with plenty of water and some energy bars, I heard him talking to someone outside. 'I just want to chat with her. I feel really bad.' He was using his broad, cheerful, Hollywood voice – the one he'd used when we met. I hadn't heard it in ages. He opened the door and dodged the cushion that I threw at his head. 'Damn, Harley,' he said, like it had been a brick.

'Go away.'

He closed the door and came inside. 'I really do feel bad.'

'Where the fuck did that come from?'

'It honestly wasn't intentional.'

'Bullshit,' I said.

'Alright, but it was more Greg than me. It was like this red mist—'

'Oh, *please*.'

He sat down. He looked genuinely quite perturbed. The sulkiness had suddenly been replaced by a perverse self-pity. I didn't have the energy to deal with either.

'I'm worried about what this relationship is turning me into,' he said.

'We aren't in a relationship, Elias.'

'Whatever it is. We got in too deep. We cultivated this horrible, toxic *thing* between us—'

'It's good for the film.'

He gestured to my ribs. 'Evidently not, if this is happening.'

'Your violence is very much in your control, Elias.'

'It didn't feel like it,' he said, face drawn.

It chilled me a little, the way he looked. He'd been so jovial and charming when I'd first met him, carrying California sunshine in his pockets. He'd seemed surprisingly boyish for his age. Now he was disturbingly old. 'Elias,' I said, 'do you hate me? Or does Greg hate Rachael? Which is it?'

'I don't know,' he said. 'The second one. I think. I don't know.'

'Because you told me once that their relationship isn't hateful, not really. That it's full of a strange kind of love.'

'I think that's true too,' he said. 'But he hates that he loves her.'

'Why?'

'Because he doesn't want to,' he said. 'Because it's ruining his life.'

He passed a hand over his face, and I saw that he was going to cry. I sat very still, horrified. 'Do you have feelings for me?'

'I think we know that I do, one way or another. But I'm not sure what they are.' His voice was horribly unsure. 'I feel used.'

I couldn't help myself. I laughed. He turned hurt eyes on me.

'This is just the film,' I said. 'Jesus, Elias, this is just Greg and Rachael. They're messing with our heads. They're so fucked up that they're fucking us up.'

'Maybe,' he said. 'Maybe you're right.'

Rachael took a negative pregnancy test whilst shooting *East of Eden* in the Salinas Valley, she'd told us. We would be shooting on location there for a bit, next month, but for the scene in the hotel room we were using a set on the lot. Elias wasn't on camera – he was shooting his end of the phone call separately – but he'd volunteered to come and read his lines off-screen for me, as a gesture of good-will, I thought. We hadn't slept together since the kick and I had a strange feeling of missing him, even though I saw him most days. I wouldn't say that our sex had been particularly good, towards the end, but it had still been a connection that was now gone.

I sat on the end of the hotel bed with the phone to my ear. We had our fight. He told me that he'd slept with another woman. He'd told me it was my fault, for leaving him behind in the city and flying off to shoot a film he'd told me not to do. I tried to stay icy, but my voice cracked, and I had to hang up the phone. We did that quite a few times. I was receptive to José's notes, but he still didn't go easy on me. Eventually he thought we probably had it, and we moved on.

I had Rachael's realisation that it had been three months. Wordlessly, I did the mental maths. My eyes widened. I called the concierge, with trembling fingers. 'Hi. Do you think— do you think you could get me a pregnancy test?' We did that a few times as well. José wanted me to get the delivery just right – professional, faux breezy, with this fear creeping through. We moved into the bathroom.

I sat on the edge of the bath, staring at the test. Eventually, I reached out and turned it over. My hands were shaking so much that it slipped out of them and I scrabbled around under the bath for it. When I found it, I passed a hand over my face in relief. *Negative.*

'And you're feeling something interesting there,' said José. 'You're relieved, but you're also disappointed. The audience don't know about your fertility struggles yet, so this is really a premonition of a pain to come. We want to feel that.'

I heard Elias laugh. José turned to him.

'Sorry,' he said, 'it's just, I'm thinking about how many conspiracy theorists are going to expect it to be positive.'

A number of crew members laughed, including José. 'Well, let's set the record straight,' he said. 'Make sure the crazies know what's real.'

'What's even supposed to have happened to the baby?' asked one of the crew members.

'Oh,' said José, 'most people think she gave it away. Some that she got rid of it.' He looked at me and grinned, abruptly. 'God, you know what I just thought?' he asked. 'How on earth has no one ever brought *Harley* into that theory? Given the resemblance?'

'What?' I laughed. More chuckles from the crew around me. I could feel that they were all examining my face.

'I'm just saying. If Rachael did have a secret child wandering around in the world, you'd be an obvious candidate, no? How on earth has no one thought that before?'

'Because no one knew who she was,' said Elias. I glared at him.

'I should do family thrillers after this,' said José. More laughter from the crew. 'Alright, everyone, let's get back into position.' He put a hand on my shoulder. 'You alright, Harley?'

'I'm fine,' I said.

'Okay, good. Let's get you back against the bath. Let's get that close-up. Action!'

I stared at the test. I didn't even remember to act. I just stared and stared.

'Cut,' said José. I looked blankly over at him. 'Harley,' he said from his chair, 'where's the relief? You're staring at it like it's positive.'

'Sorry,' I said.

'No worries. Let's go again.'

It was no good. I'd lost all control over my face. José's words were rattling around in my mind and I couldn't make them settle. Rachael was so weirdly defensive about the baby rumours. She couldn't stand to talk about them – especially not with me. And she hadn't wanted me to tell my family about the film, but she'd never wanted to explain why not. She couldn't articulate what had gone wrong between her and her sister. Neither could Mum.

What if the test had been positive? Thinking it was over with Greg, not wanting to interrupt her career to raise a child, not convinced she was meant to be a mother, she might have handed the baby over to her family in London. Her sister would have raised it as her own. What she'd done with the hush money made perfect sense, in that case – she hadn't given it to her family, but to her child. It was paternity support that Greg probably hadn't even known he was giving. Perhaps Rachael did her best to forget, but she never quite got over the decision. In time, she might have come to resent her sister for it. She might have retreated into herself. She might have started doing weird, violent films to cope. She might have turned her back on the world.

Until one day, someone rang her gate. A girl with her exact face.

Rachael Carmichael had been pregnant when she'd peed on the stick in Salinas Valley. She'd been pregnant when she'd yelled after Greg's car in LA. And she'd had the baby.

She'd had me.

Chapter Twelve

RACHAEL

15 November 1993

Greg never asked me for the ring back. I spent a week getting my things organised, packing up, and then I flew back to London to shoot the sixth – and final – season of *The Avenue*. Landing back in London in November never gets less depressing, and it's a strange atmosphere on the set of *The Avenue*. Everyone is jovial, none of us too sorry to be moving on to other things, but we have moments of strange collective sadness. Brenda has cried more than once already. I'll admit, the table read for the episode where Jill reveals that she's engaged did make me tear up. I do think that twenty is a little too young to get engaged, but then I'm twenty-four and I was engaged for all of five minutes, so I suppose I can't judge. I will miss Jill. She was too good, at times, and she didn't take enough risks, but she's always been a safe place in which to hide the rest of myself away. It's easy enough to be her, and it'll be sad enough to be without her.

It's also strange because I can feel that everyone around me thinks I'm too famous to be there. They don't say it like that, of course – no one wants to be seen as a star humper – but they compliment me on my loyalty and talk brightly about 'All the amazing things you're doing!' and they thank me for coming home. For finishing this story with them.

'Of course,' I say. 'Always. This is my family. I was never going to miss this.'

I don't tell the truth, which is that I would have missed this in a heartbeat, if I hadn't so badly needed somewhere to run home to.

The first week was tense, because I was debating whether or not to tell them about the baby. I knew that in a few months Jill wouldn't look so girl-next-door anymore, and if the team needed to write a pregnancy into the plot then notice was essential. But there was still a part of me that didn't quite believe I was pregnant. I had surprisingly few symptoms. I wasn't throwing up or feeling fatigued or having cravings, or any of the other things that films tell you should be happening. I hated the smell of the air freshener my cleaner used and my sleep was slightly worse. That was about it.

So the baby remained in this kind of limbo state – not really a baby at all, more an idea, more a pending decision, patiently bobbing in amniotic fluid.

Of course, Greg's driver turned out to be a sack of shit, and now some story about me loudly announcing my pregnancy on the street outside my house is circulating in the tabloids. Gemma, my publicist, refuted it quickly. ('This is a nasty, pernicious rumour with no truth to it whatsoever.') She asked me if it was true, and I told her it wasn't, but I think she knew I was lying.

No one on set asked me about it, although I could tell that they wanted to. Then, one day, in-between takes, Brenda tapped my shoulder. She was looking at me, all motherly, in that manner that sometimes I love and sometimes I dread, and I was convinced she knew. I was so certain she was going to open her mouth and say, *Rachael, you're pregnant, aren't you?* And then, either, *You're going to be a wonderful mother* or *You can't possibly keep it.* And I would know what to do.

She didn't say any of the above. She said, 'Honey, you have a visitor.'

There was a blonde woman hanging around the edge of the soundstage. It took me a minute to recognise her – she was skinnier, and her cheeks were fuller. But she was still the Anna Bianca I remembered from *Here's Hoping,* with her blowout and her white stilettos. She caught my eye and raised an awkward hand. I raised one back, bewildered.

'Everything okay?' asked Brenda.

'She's here for me?'

'I think so.'

'How did she get on set?'

'She's a friend of Mike's.' One of our producers. 'It's a small industry,' said Brenda, which is the kind of phrase you hear a variation of over and over in this business.

We did another take. Anna waited patiently until it was announced that we were finished for the day, and then she touched my arm as I was making my way off set.

'Hi,' she said.

I hadn't been in the same room as her since we shot *Here's Hoping* together. Arms folded across her chest, she nodded towards the door.

'Can we talk?' she asked. 'I've got a car outside. I thought maybe we could go back to your flat.'

For a brief second I wondered if Anna Bianca was planning to kill me. She was antsy, lips pressed tightly together, chest rising and falling under her folded arms. She shifted.

'What are you doing in London?' I asked.

'I'm here to see you.'

'What's happened? Has something happened to Greg?'

'I think you would have heard it in the news sooner than you heard it from me if it had.' She indicated the exit with her head again. 'Come on,' she said. She didn't want to say *please* but I still heard it.

In the car, I said, 'So?' But she shook her head, eyes on the driver. Her expression seemed to suggest that she thought I would have been more clued in by now. And that was when I realised, far too late, what this was really about. She'd heard the rumours. She'd come to ask if it was true.

We were silent for the length of the car ride. I shot quick looks at her whenever I felt I could, but if she did the same then I didn't catch her. She was focused on London, the blurring greys and browns and blues of it, the density and scale. She'd grown up in Pennsylvania, I remembered, in some small town I'd never heard of. She'd been an LA girl since she was sixteen – and she really couldn't have looked more like it. But she seemed rural just then, wide-eyed, staring out at the big city.

We pulled up outside my flat. I got out first and went inside, and then Anna followed suit. We were careful not to be on the street at the same time so that any lurking photographers wouldn't get the shot they wanted. This wasn't something we even felt the need to discuss – we were both old hands, by now.

Inside, I took her coat and hung it in the hall for her. She said, 'Thank you.'

'You're welcome.' We had never spoken to each other like this.

'Nice place,' she said.

'I've had it a while.'

'It's cute.'

Gone were her barbs. Her bite was muzzled. She turned towards me, in stilettos on my carpet, and said, 'Rachael, is it true?'

Her eyes asked me not to play dumb, so I didn't. I just nodded.

'Oh god,' she said. She sat down on my sofa. She was in sweat-pants and a sports jersey. It was too big on her. Maybe it was his. 'I thought so,' she said. 'I thought that's why he'd rushed into this . . .' She waved a hand. 'Proposal,' she said. Actually, it was more like she spat it.

I stood in the entrance to the kitchen, hands behind my back. 'He doesn't know.'

She stared at me for a moment. 'He doesn't know?'

'No.'

'Are you going to tell him?'

'I don't know.'

'Are you going to keep it?'

She was a mother twice over, I remembered. Greg and Anna's kids existed in a separate world in my head. I didn't like thinking about them any more than I liked thinking about her. But here she was in front of me, and she had two children back home. I won-dered if she'd really known nothing before the proposal. I didn't have to ask what that had been like for her, having the news broken like that. I could see it in her gaunt face and fidgeting hands.

'Are you here to ask me not to?' I asked.

She recoiled. 'Rachael, I would never ask that of anyone. Even you.'

'But you don't want me to.'

'I just needed to know.' She looked down at her lap. She hadn't taken her shoes off, and the height of her stilettos meant that her thighs sloped upwards where she sat. Two white needles pierced my rug. 'The thing is,' she started. Her voice cracked. My spine prickled. 'The thing is, you guys aren't together anymore. Are you?'

I shook my head.

'So all I really have to tell my kids is that Daddy and Mommy are going to take some time apart. But if you have a baby with him . . .' She waved a hand. 'Okay, so now what do I say? They've

289

got this other sibling suddenly, a baby that Mommy didn't have. And you and that baby are in our lives forever now. It's all fucked up and complicated, and the world is going to be looking on and talking about it . . .' Her hand was in her hair now. 'God, Rachael, you have his *baby*, and we're a story forever.'

'I suppose,' I said.

'And . . .' She paused again, stretched the hem of the jersey over the knees of her sweatpants. 'It's humiliating. He went and got another girl pregnant. I didn't even know.'

'The world won't know that you didn't know.'

'But my family will,' she said. 'My friends. Colleagues. They'll all know. Everyone will talk.'

'People are talking anyway.'

'It'll be worse,' she said. 'You know it will, Rachael. It'll be so much worse.'

'So,' I said. 'You are asking.'

She looked at me for a second. Then she reached into her bag. I watched her take out a chequebook and a pen, detached for a second, until she started to write and I realised what she was doing. 'Don't,' I said ineffectually.

She held the slip of paper out to me. 'I can make it more,' she said.

'Anna, I make more money than you.'

'I know,' she said. 'I know. I just didn't know what else to do.'

She started to cry. *Shit.* I stood awkwardly in the centre of my living room as Anna Bianca sat on my sofa and sobbed on to the cheque in her hands. For a few seconds, I just let her cry. Eventually she looked up at me, cheeks wet, pale lines in her foundation, and said, 'Do you want to keep it?'

I hesitated. Then I shook my head. Her shoulders sagged.

'Oh, thank god,' she said.

I still hadn't articulated any kind of decision. But I couldn't bring myself to tell her that. It was the way she was sitting on my sofa, not hating me. I mean, she did hate me. She does. I know that logically. But also, she doesn't, at all. She's just sad. She just hurts.

I don't want to have a baby just to hurt somebody.

25 November 1993

The recovery was fast. I told work I had to have routine surgery and they were very understanding. I told Brenda the truth. It disappointed her – she doesn't really believe in abortion – but she was still sweet to me about it. When I appeared back on set, she gave me a pat on the shoulder and said, 'There's our soldier.' It was the most appropriate thing she could have said. I felt out of my body, cut up and empty. I still do, a little, but it's better. You adjust to everything, I'm finding. You find a shelf for it all inside you. You march on.

Small things have helped. An afternoon tea with Amy George where we ate tiny sandwiches and laughed about *Unbeliever* and something terrible she made recently. A Norwegian thriller about a cannibalistic stalker that reminds me things could always be worse. And family. Imagine that. Not words I ever thought I'd write.

Last week, I received a call from a number I didn't recognise. I was in the middle of painting my nails when the phone rang, so I picked it up with the dry hand, flapping the wet one. 'Hi,' came an unfamiliar voice, when I picked it up. 'Is that Rachael?'

The voice was young, with a similar accent to mine, only higher and a little more uncertain. It was decidedly familiar to me but I couldn't work out why.

'Who's calling?' I asked.

'Mum gave me your number. I hope you don't mind. She doesn't know I'm calling.'

'Elisabeth?'

'Yeah,' she said.

I hadn't exchanged many words with Elisabeth beyond 'Happy birthday' in three years. I still sent the cheques home every month, but that was it. She knew me as the name on the slip of paper that paid for her life. Once a year, Mum would put her on the phone at Christmas and say, 'Talk to your sister.'

'How's Hollywood?' she would ask me, over the sound of tearing wrapping paper.

'Sunny,' I'd say.

She'd sigh, and say, 'God, you're so *lucky*.'

I'd thought that I had ceased to be real to her a long time ago. Something must have happened. 'Is everything okay?' I asked her, still flapping my wet nails.

'Everything's fine. Mum's fine, we're both fine. I'm just—'

'What?'

A pause. Then— 'I'm *bored*,' she said, polite phone voice forgotten.

I laughed, more in amazement than anything else. Truth be told, I'd started to think of myself as an only child. And here was this sister, suddenly, seventeen with a voice of her own, calling me because she was bored. 'Mum is driving me insane with the swimming stuff,' she said.

'I thought you were on to modelling?'

'Oh,' she said, 'I went back.'

'When?'

'Three years ago.'

'Really? Why?'

A pause. I remembered snapping at her across the dinner table in that fancy LA restaurant. *God knows she won't make it in modelling.* 'It just wasn't for me,' she said. 'But swimming's not either. I'd missed a lot by then and I'll never be able to get that time back.

Mum's still convinced I'm going to the Commonwealth Games, of course.'

I laughed again. 'Of course.' When had Elisabeth started being funny?

'I just need a break,' she said. 'And I know this is weird, me calling you out of the blue like this, but I've thought about doing it so many times.' A pause. I wasn't quite sure what to say. 'I saw your film,' she said.

'Which one?'

'The big one. The one in Iceland.'

'What did you think?'

'It was messed *up*,' she said.

So, less than a month into being back in London, about to commence shooting the final season, Elisabeth tumbled off a bus with a suitcase and a head full of spiral blonde curls and waved at me with gloved hands. She was only supposed to be staying a week, in her half-term break, but she looked as if she'd packed for a month.

'I just wasn't sure what kind of stuff I should be wearing,' she panted as we lugged the suitcase up the stairs together. 'I mean, I didn't know if we'd be going to parties, or going out—'

'Going out? You're seventeen.'

'Yeah, well, I figured you could sort that.'

'You figured I could age you?'

'Fake ID, Rachael, obviously.' She stood outside the door of my flat. 'You're still in this place? Surely you could afford somewhere nicer by now?'

'I'm moving soon,' I said. I hadn't had the time to think about upgrading in ages but I'd finally bought myself a nice place in South Kensington, with much better security, which is something I worry about a lot. I unlocked the door and we dragged her suitcase into the spare bedroom.

'There.' She set the suitcase down, and then she looked at me. 'Do we hug now?'

'Probably,' I said, so we did. It felt like a dream to be standing there with her – not in that it was something I'd always dreamt about, but in the sense that I'd acquired a sister out of nowhere, in the strange way you can in the logic of dreams. She sat down on the bed. I sat down beside her. 'So? What do you want to do whilst you're here?'

'Oh,' she said, 'everything. I want to see a show – we can do that, right?'

'Sure. I know the girl playing Christine in *Phantom of the Opera* – I'll see if she can get us in.'

'In a box?'

'Never great views, from a box. You're better near the front of the stalls, I've always found.'

She shook her head, curls bouncing. 'You just have the most amazing life.'

I smiled. 'Sometimes.'

'Right.' She bit her lip. I'd been right – she really was growing up pretty. She had this quality that made her seem full of sun and elastic. 'I saw the thing with Greg,' she said. 'The pictures of him proposing, at the airport.'

'Yeah, I think everyone has.'

'Mum said she left you a message?'

'She did. I should have called her back.' I was never going to, though. When the whole world wanted answers, it didn't feel as if she was the one person who deserved them. But Elisabeth was looking at me like she actually cared.

'Are you really engaged?'

Greg's publicist and mine had coordinated and put out a joint statement, claiming that the whole thing had been a poorly thought-out stunt to drum up publicity for our next project together. Some bought it. Most didn't.

'No,' I said. 'He just wasn't right for me, in the end.'

'God,' she said, rolling her eyes. 'I know *all* about that. I just broke things off with my boyfriend, Tommy. He's nice enough but there wasn't really a spark. You know?'

That she was there at all was dizzying – thinking about her dating was slightly too much. I stood up. 'I'll let you get unpacked,' I said. 'I was thinking we could grab some dinner, and then I've got a cast party this evening with all the folks from *The Avenue.*'

She gripped the duvet, and her eyes were enormous. I felt freshly guilty for saying that she wouldn't make it in modelling – she really was beautiful. She had that doll-faced, silent film thing going for her, sort of a modern-day Lillian Gish. 'Are you saying I can come to a real TV party?'

I hadn't been saying that, actually. I'd been about to say that she could stay home and watch a film and I'd leave her money for a takeaway. But the whole of her had lit up, and I thought that maybe it would be nice to have company. What I knew of her so far, this older version of her, I liked. She was a little sheltered, but that could be fixed. I imagined guiding her around the room, saying, *This is my little sister,* watching her stutter her introductions to all the people she'd seen on TV. Brenda would just melt over her. And she needed me.

'Sure,' I said. 'It'll be casual, so don't worry too much about an outfit, but you can always borrow something if you like.'

She didn't even unzip her suitcase. She went straight over to my wardrobe and started to rifle through. 'Is this all designer?'

'Some of it. I don't buy high-end items that often, but they get gifted to me. Some of them I seem to just pick up.' An endless mystery, how I accumulate all the stuff I do. 'Anything you like?'

She gave a little gasp and brought out the black skirt that I'd worn to the bar with Greg. I hadn't touched it since, even though I loved it – it seemed to belong to that night and that night only. Elisabeth held it up against her skinny frame. 'Beautiful,' she breathed. She saw my face. 'Sorry. Is it too expensive?'

'No, it's fine. Go try it on.'

She practically skipped back to her room. Had I been that young at seventeen?

The skirt looked good on her. I could tell that she was feeling young and beautiful at dinner, smiling at the waiter as he refilled her water, sipping daintily at her espresso martini. She still had that little mirror in her purse; she still brought it out to check her reflection. She caught me smiling at her and closed it, with a click. 'What?'

'Nothing. This is nice. I'm glad you called.'

'Me too,' she said.

At the party, she was charming. She didn't stammer or shake at all, but was sweetly deferential to every cast member she met, telling them how much she liked them on the show, but never overdoing it with her praise. Even the twins, Lili and Lola, were impressed by her, and they're the most famous ten-year-old girls in the country and therefore impressed by virtually nothing. Brenda fell on her like she was a long-lost daughter.

'Oh, you are just *beautiful*,' she kept saying. We were in the basement bar where we'd had our first wrap party, celebrating the start of the final season – everyone was feeling very nostalgic, and Brenda was especially sentimental. She turned to me on her bar-stool as we waited for our drinks and said, 'Is she acting?'

'No,' I said, surprised. 'No, she's never even mentioned it.'

'I just figured maybe that's why you'd brought her, to start introducing her to your world. She'd certainly have a leg up, if she decided it's what she wanted to do.'

'She just wanted to catch up,' I said. 'She's a competitive swimmer, actually.'

'Really? That explains why she's so toned, then.' Brenda put a hand on mine. She's started getting some of the lines in her face smoothed out, but I wish she wouldn't. Her face is so beautiful where it creases. I love seeing the depth of her care for me written in it. 'I think it's good that you're reconnecting with your family.'

'Just her,' I said, as our drinks were slid over the bar to us. 'Not my mother.'

'Well, no, I didn't expect so. But this is a great start.' She looked past me and grimaced. 'She's talking to Jerry.'

I turned. Elisabeth was perched on a barstool on the other side of me, chatting happily away to a boy with slicked-back hair, Leo DiCaprio style. 'Hey,' I said, 'Jerry.' He caught my eye. 'You forgot to do up your shirt,' I said. It was unbuttoned to the middle of his chest. He scowled at me.

Elisabeth laced her fingers through mine. 'Listen,' she said. 'Jerry knows this *great* place.' I realised she was tipsy. 'He said maybe we could go for a drink and a dance.'

I looked at Jerry, who had shrunk away from me a little. He plays the cad, but around me he'll always revert to his grumpy teenage self. 'You know she's seventeen?'

'Oh please,' he said. Fair enough. He'd been getting into those *great* places since he was fourteen.

'I think you should come back with me,' I said to Elisabeth. She blinked her big eyes at me and smiled. The strap of her top had slid off her shoulder.

'Rachael,' she said coaxingly. 'I just want to go and explore London. I've only got a week here. And Jerry knows all the best places.'

'Yes, all the best places to get chlamydia.'

She put a hand over her mouth and giggled. 'You're funny,' she said. 'I won't be too late, okay?' She turned away. I put a hand on her arm and she looked down at it. 'Don't be another Mum,' she said.

I took my hand back. I watched her leave with him, weaving through crowds of people. I was aware of Brenda standing behind me, watching too. I turned back to her, helplessly. She shook her head.

'She'll be fine,' she said. 'You're not her parent. You can't stop her.'

'She's just a kid.'

'And it's just Jerry. He talks big but he's a soft little thing, really.'

I wasn't so sure.

My suspicions were confirmed when she fell through the door of the flat early that morning, in the same clothes, make-up smeared under her eyes. 'Thank *god*,' she groaned. 'I was sure I didn't have the address right.'

I'd been sat on the sofa, drinking my coffee, thinking about what I would do if she didn't come home. She took one look at my face and saw that I was angry. She flew to my side.

'I'm sorry,' she said, sitting down and putting her arm around my shoulders. 'God, we only just got to know each other again and here I am, running off and worrying you.'

'I wasn't worried. But that wouldn't have been a fun phone call with Mum, if I'd lost you.'

'It was silly. I was just overexcited. But Jerry was really nice to me. And we were safe.'

'Okay, good.' She sat, looking at me, as if she was waiting for me to figure something out. I played her words back again. 'Safe as in . . . ?'

She put her hand to her mouth. She giggled.

Aside from losing her virginity to Jerry, she was an angel for the rest of the trip. I was amazed that a member of my family was able to be so agreeable so much of the time. We went out for dinners together, and wandered the museums, and she even came with me to set one day. I'd thought she would get fed up after a while and wander off to wait in my trailer, but she sat on her little folding visitor's chair the entire time, watching eagerly.

'Are you not bored?' I asked her during a break, and she shook her head so that her curls flew.

'I *love* it,' she said.

I could tell then that she'd been bitten by the bug. It wasn't a total surprise when she walked into the living room on her last day and announced, with cool composure, that she'd prepared a monologue.

'Oh?' I said, putting down the script I was reading. We were still going back and forth on that Henry James project, but I'd decided I was probably going to pass – the script had gone through a rewrite where they'd added a backstory for the governess that included lots of sex, and I didn't want to make taking my clothes off on camera too much of a habit.

'I wondered if maybe,' she asked, a little jumpy, 'I could do it for you? I did it for Jerry, and he said he thought it was very good.' I didn't point out the obvious, which was that Jerry would have said absolutely anything necessary to get in her pants. 'Would that be okay?' she asked.

I gave her the go-ahead. She moved the coffee table back a little to make space for herself on the rug, as if to indicate there would be choreography involved with this monologue, and then cleared her throat. She started talking, and I realised, to my immediate horror, that she'd memorised my monologue from *Women Who Laugh at God*.

It was awful. She'd transformed it into a thing of melodrama, losing all of Abi's cruelty and monstrosity in favour of pantomime

299

villain eyebrow arches and a seductive sway to her hips. I could see why Jerry had been a fan. When she finished, she looked at me expectantly.

'What do you think?' she asked. 'I've been practising my Carmichael gaze.' She giggled. There wasn't any apprehension in it. She was so sure that she'd been good.

I didn't want to be mean. Bad acting makes me mean, sometimes, but it wasn't her fault that she didn't have talent. She did have beauty, and it's a fair assumption to make that the two might go hand in hand. 'It's great that you're interested in acting,' I said carefully. 'I would maybe start with something different, though. Try something light. Have you ever read *The Importance of Being Earnest*? You should try Cecily. She would suit you.'

'I don't want to do theatre stuff,' she said impatiently. 'I want to do films.'

'I know, but everyone has to start somewhere. You have to learn, you know? Study, practise.'

'You didn't. You just started when you were eighteen.'

'I'd been working on acting for about five years before that.' *And I had talent,* I thought, but I didn't say it. I'd been worried about crushing her, but she didn't look squashed down at all, just haughty and offended. 'Look, it's better that I'm honest with you. This probably isn't your thing. Stick to swimming.'

'You don't think I'm good?' she asked, changing course. Her lip wobbled. She might have succeeded in making me feel guilty, if not for the fact that she still couldn't act.

'Wouldn't you rather know?'

She went cold. Her small mouth puckered. She shrugged a bony shoulder at me and turned away. 'Alright, Rachael. Thanks. I'm going to go pack.'

'Hang on.' She turned back. 'You did ask me for an opinion. You can't be angry with me.'

'I'm not.'

'Even if you do go into acting, even if you get really good at it, lots of people are still going to tell you that they think you're bad, all the time. It's just something you have to get used to.'

She perked up. 'Are you going to help me, then?'

'I mean, you'd be better off working with an actual acting coach.'

'No, not like that. I mean, I'll do that, but . . .' She trailed off. I waited for her to make her point. 'You know people,' she finished.

So that was what this was about. 'No,' I said. 'Sorry. I won't help you like that.'

'Why not?'

'Because that's not how this works.'

'Of course it is,' she said. 'That's how everyone gets jobs. It's all who you know.'

'Is that what Jerry told you? It isn't how I got jobs. Or pretty much any of the actors I respect.' She looked like a moody child. 'Look,' I said, 'I've always sent you guys money. And I'll keep doing that until you're able to make your own. But I'm not going to give you a leg up over other people and start recommending you to a bunch of casting directors, because I don't think that's right. Not unless you're actually the best fit for a part.'

Her face lit up again. The delicate corners of her mouth lifted. 'So if you do think I'm a good fit for something, you would?'

'Yes. Then I would. But that's very unlikely to happen.'

She bent down and kissed me on the cheek. We didn't talk about acting again after that and when she left the next day it seemed as if we were still on good terms. I walked her to her Tube stop, and she turned around at the top of the steps and waved to me. Her suitcase was even heavier now – she'd had a rummage amongst my old things. Someone offered to help her carry it. I could hear her thanking them all the way down the stairs.

31 January 1994

Happy new year! I've never wished you a happy new year before, have I? Seems like a strange time to start, because I've spent most of the day crying. We wrapped *The Avenue* on Monday and I didn't cry then, even though everyone else did, even the men. I did get a bit misty when Brenda put her arms around me and said, 'God, I'm going to miss this face.' And reached up to give my chin a small squeeze.

But I didn't cry. And then the next day, *Unbeliever* came out – my manager Eloise agreed that we could claim scheduling conflicts and let me miss the premiere, even though the studio weren't thrilled – and everyone saw it for exactly what it was.

It's hard to imagine what motivations director Greg Foster might have had for making the film, beyond a sexual fascination with his leading lady, wrote one reviewer – snidely, but also fairly. I'd imagined that when the film did come out, my performance might at least be praised – *Rachael Carmichael is the film's only saving grace,* or something along those lines. Instead, I was lumped in with the rest of the mess. *Greg Foster and Rachael Carmichael give lukewarm, unconvincing performances.* What else had they expected me to do with such a lukewarm, unconvincing script? It hadn't been in my power to rewrite the lines. The best I got was this in the *Guardian*: *Rachael Carmichael, as Helen, does her best.*

I called Robb, furious. 'You are going to get some bad write-ups now and then,' he said reasonably. 'That's true for everyone.'

I wanted to say, *Yes, I know that's true for everyone, but why does it have to be true for me?*

He suggested that maybe we look at a romantic comedy. 'A quality one,' he said. 'Make the world fall back in love with you.'

Was he saying they had fallen out? I told him, no, I wanted to do important films or nothing from now on. I just had to wait for *East of Eden* to come out and then everyone would remember how good I was.

'Sure,' he said. 'That one's going to be massive. But it's also at least a year away. We have to think about what's just around the corner. You know?'

'What's just around the corner, then?'

'Well,' he said, 'a hit! Hopefully.' And he gave this awkward, forced laugh that made me feel terrible about myself.

Anyway, neither of the two things separately made me cry. But today I sat and thought about them together – no more *The Avenue,* being terrible in *Unbeliever* – and the tears came like someone had turned on a tap.

8 March 1994

Elisabeth turned eighteen yesterday. She opened presents with Mum at home in the morning, and then hopped on the coach to Victoria so that the two of us could go out. I bought her a new dress as a present, even though technically I'd already paid for all of her other presents.

She was very well-behaved on our night out, tipsy but not messy, not pouting even when I refused to take her to Naomi Campbell's house party (if you want to keep your social standing, you don't bring your kid sister to Naomi Campbell's house). Unfortunately, she also let slip that she and Jerry have been in contact ever since they hooked up in November. He kept that to himself pretty well during our final season, the little creep.

This morning she slunk off to see him. 'Don't worry so much,' she said, giving me a hug goodbye over the back of the armchair.

'I'm not worried. I'm disgusted. He's disgusting.'

She only laughed. It was as light and unconcerned as the tinkle of a bell.

20 April 1994

In September, I'm booked to shoot a psychological thriller in Ireland called *Seeing Other People,* in which I play a young wife who sees her husband cheat on her but is convinced that she is having hallucinations. Christian Bale, who is also not Irish, plays my husband. I'm not particularly good at the accent yet but I've been assured that I'll be working with a great coach. Until then, nothing.

It's strange to be so untethered. This is one of the few true pauses in my life so far, a space between projects. I don't have to be in Ireland for ages, and we've not found anything else worth filling these months with, so here I am, just being. I go to the shops. I walk around the park. I make myself dinner. I'm thinking of getting a dog. I never will, but I'm thinking about it, and that's something.

People call me, out of the blue, and pierce the silence. Elisabeth, sometimes. Mum, but I don't pick up the phone to her. Amy George, and we chat. My manager, but only ever with something minor and trivial – a phone interview, which I take lying down on my floor with the cord stretched over me, or a red carpet, which I say no to. I wonder if Anna will call me and ask how I am. What a strange thing to wonder. She doesn't, of course. I think of calling her. Saying, 'I'll take the money, actually. Why not?'

'Are you depressed?' asked Amy, on the phone. This is one of the things that I plan to think about, when I've finished thinking about the dog.

28 April 1994

Tonight I rented *Children of the Corn.* I wanted to remember being in that living room with Mais, back in that flat we all lived in when I was eighteen, trying to see how far through the film we could get before she realised and turned it off. We made it past the big massacre at the beginning because I told her that the rest of the film was most likely a police drama. We actually got about an hour in, but as soon as she saw Vicky up on that cross she said, 'No, Rachael, absolutely not!' and turned it off. I've still never watched past that moment, Vicky pointing diagonally, only halfway to the sky. Now I watched them push her upright and thought, *Huh*.

Then the phone rang. My first thought was that it was Mais calling to tell me to turn the film off again. *Imagine*. I'd love to hear from Mais. I assume by now she and Mickey have had either three children or an outrageous divorce, but either way I'd like to know. I picked up the phone.

'Rach? I hope this is still your number.' I almost dropped the receiver. How can a voice, even when uncertain, hold so much warmth? It staggered me a little. 'Are you there?'

'I am,' I said. 'Adam?'

'Hey. Sorry that this is so out of the blue. Someone told me that you wrapped your final season.'

'We did,' I said. 'Nearly a month ago.' Who could that someone have been? My chest squeezed, imagining him talking to someone about me.

'Ah. My intel is late, then.' A pause. 'Well, I just wanted to say congrats. I was thinking about you, and that show, and . . . I just wanted to say it. Congrats.'

'Thanks,' I managed. I was cold all over. Talking to him was like speaking to someone long gone, impossibly. I might as well have been at a seance. He cleared his throat, and I was worried he might be about to end the conversation there. 'How's Holly?' I asked.

Don't ever say that witch's name to me again, is what I hoped he might say. What he actually said was, 'She's good, thanks. The press tour has been a bit rough on both of us, I think, but we're hanging in there.'

'It's true about you two, then?'

'Yes,' he said, 'it's true.'

'What a PR win. I'm surprised the studio isn't singing about it.'

'Well,' he said, 'we both like keeping that stuff private, where we can.' *Yes*, I wanted to shout, *so does everyone!* 'But everyone's going to find out pretty soon,' he said.

Oh god. I was going to be sick. 'Why's that?'

'We're engaged.'

Black, sweet hatred for both of them, the force of which surprised me. I swallowed back bile, clutched my stomach with one hand, and croaked, 'Oh! Congratulations!' into the phone.

'Yeah, we're excited. The wedding will probably be next year.'

'That's amazing, Adam. Really.' I shouldn't have added the 'really'. It made it obvious that I was lying.

'You should come,' he said, and then he hesitated. 'Well, I mean, I would have to check with Holly. Given our—'

'History,' I finished.

'Right.'

'I'll try to be there,' I said. 'As long as Holly's okay with it.'

'I appreciate that, Rach.' Another pause. 'Can I ask you something?' He was using his softer, careful voice, the one he used to use whenever we talked about my family. I thought for a second that was where he was going, but he surprised me. 'Are you with Greg Foster?'

'No,' I said. The pity in his silence made me backtrack, embarrassingly. 'Well, we've had a break, but we're getting back together.' *Jesus.* It was such an obvious lie that it made me wince.

'Right,' he said doubtfully. 'Only, the last time I saw you, you said—' He broke off. 'I guess things change, though, don't they?'

'They do,' I said. 'They did.'

'Well, I'm happy for you both.'

'You too. With Holly.'

'I should go,' he said. 'I hope it wasn't weird, me calling.'

I wrapped both hands around the receiver and started to cry. 'Not weird at all.'

'Are you okay? You sound funny.'

'I'm just watching a really sad film.'

'What film?'

I suddenly couldn't think of any sad films, so I just said, *Children of the Corn.*

A pause, and then he burst out laughing. 'God, Rach, you haven't changed a bit.'

I have, I thought, as we hung up. *I have changed. If only you knew how much.*

31 April 1994

It has been a thousand years since three nights ago, on the phone with Adam.

The next morning I woke up on the sofa, the TV screen buzzing at me black and white, empty Raffaello packets around me. I'd smoked, which I hate doing until I get really sad and then it's my favourite thing in the world. I have an ashtray that Greg gave me – it's from Verona and it has a beautiful carving of the statue of Juliet on it. At the time I thought it was a superbly romantic gift, but now I looked at it and thought it was so like Greg, to go all the way to Italy and bring me back an ashtray. I'd flicked cigarette ash all over Juliet's tits.

The phone rang, and I picked it up, wanting to hear, *Hey, Rach, talking to you last night made me realise that I'm making the biggest mistake of my life.* I lay back down on the sofa, cradling the receiver to my ear.

'Rachael?' came a voice, with the same Californian accent. Not Adam's. I sat up and brushed a Raffaello packet off my chest, like he could see me. I didn't say anything. 'You're there, aren't you?' he asked. 'It's done, baby.' He never called me that. 'It's all done. We're officially divorced. I'm a single man. How's that for romantic?'

This was too much to take in all at once. I set the phone down on the coffee table.

'Rachael?' I could hear faintly. 'Can you hear me?'

The divorce had happened. The elusive, evasive, mythological thing that was the divorce was done. What did that change? Everything, to judge by Greg's tone. I picked up the phone again.

'Are you there, baby?' There it was again.

'I'm here,' I whispered. 'How?'

'How? Good lawyers, a prenup. Got it all done and dusted in six months. Judge said it was the quickest he'd ever sent through. I told him that's how crazy I was about the girl I had waiting for me. God knew I couldn't wait another second for her.' Unexpectedly spiritual, from a man who'd never shown the slightest bit of interest in god in the time I'd known him. 'You'll come, won't you? You'll come out here? Can you get on a plane tonight?' He sighed at my silence. 'I'm so sorry,' he said. 'For everything. The whole way it went down – it wasn't right, any of it. I'll apologise a million times over – I'll fall to my knees until they shatter, if you just get on a plane and fly to me. I love you. I love you. Come home, please.'

'London is home.'

'It isn't. It can't be. Our home is the two of us, together.'

My heart was dancing about, strangely. It was clear, listening to him talk, that in his eyes we belonged with each other, and to each other, and everything else could be solved.

'Yes,' I said, because I wanted to join him in that place. 'You're right.' I didn't know if I believed it. But god, I wanted to. To hear someone talk about loving me with so much confidence, to declare with so much authority that it was all going to be okay, was a release I hadn't known I needed. I wondered if he had any idea yet about the pregnancy, if he'd bought into the rumours. Anna wouldn't have told him. I wouldn't either, I decided. No good could come of it. This would be a fresh start for us. No talk of endings.

'Do you still have the ring?' he asked.

'I do. It's in my suitcase.'

'I thought you might have sold it. Or thrown it out.'

'Throw out a diamond? I never would. Selling it's an idea.' He chuckled.

'I thought I should have chucked it at your head,' I said.

That got a proper laugh. 'I'm glad you didn't,' he said.

'Me too.'

'I know it was all wrong, how I asked you. But I still want to marry you. I want it more than anything. Do you still want to marry me?'

'Yes,' I said softly. I really did.

'Then, baby, get your ass on a plane.'

I flew out that night. I landed in the morning. He greeted me at the airport, no roses this time but arms spread wide, and I ignored the cameras and flew into them. Being held to his chest felt right, and safe, and like how belonging is meant to feel.

In the car, in his white shirt with his sunglasses hanging off the collar, he said, 'Home?'

'Absolutely.'

'Or . . .' He grinned. 'Vegas?'

'What?'

'A little white chapel? We could go right now.'

'We can't do that.'

'Why not?'

'I just landed. We haven't spoken in months. And that's . . . It's a six-hour drive.'

'Rachael,' he said. 'We are parked at an airport. We can go back inside and get on a plane.'

'But—' I stared at him. 'Don't you feel like we need to . . . ?'

'What?'

'Talk?'

'We can talk on the plane,' he said. He took both my hands. 'Rachael, I've waited too long for this. These six months have been torture. A quick flight, a quick service at a little white chapel, and then you and me are a family, forever. That's all I want. Let's get on a plane. Let's get married.'

I looked at him, holding my hands, and it was the happiest I'd ever seen him. I'd never known him to glow like that. He looked twenty years younger. I laughed. He clutched my hands tighter. I laughed louder.

'Okay,' I said.

So that's what we did.

He's in the kitchen making dinner. He's bought a new place in the Hollywood Hills, and the entire front of the house is glass, but it's so tucked away up in the hills that it doesn't feel as if there's any danger of anyone looking in. Besides, he says, the whole thing is fenced like Fort Knox. We couldn't be safer. We couldn't be more private.

We have a pool and a garden, and a chair that hangs from the ceiling and overlooks them both. There's a screening room in the basement, and a space that Greg told me I was welcome to turn into a studio. (I looked at him curiously. 'Don't you paint?' he asked. I shook my head. For some reason, we both found this very funny.) At the bottom of the garden, there's a tennis court. He says he's going to teach me how to play.

Right now, I'm sat in the living room with the huge glass front half open, an orange breeze on my face as I write. He's making burritos, he says. Good, wholesome, celebratory food. I can hear him cursing as he burns himself. My husband. I sit, a married woman, a wife with a glass of white wine beside her, in my marital home, writing in my diary – one childish habit that I can never seem to shake for good.

I feel so very, very happy.

Chapter Thirteen

HARLEY

There were fish in Elias' swimming pool. Small, bright ones, in fiery colours – they wriggled through the water in all directions, glowing like embers. I sat on the side of the pool with my knees tucked up, toes curling over the edge of it, watching them. After a few minutes I saw that they weren't real. They were shiny and solid, tails flicking neatly from side to side, propelling stiff bodies across the length of the pool. Carefully, I unfolded one leg into the water and then the other. I bent down and took hold of one of the shiny fish. It was smooth and hard. I held it in my hands, down in my lap, and watched the tail jerk from side to side.

'Like them?'

Elias had appeared over me, holding a drink in either hand. Gin and tonic, a slice of cucumber on each rim. I stared up at him, and then back down at the fish.

'What are they?'

'A gift from a friend,' he said. 'I bring them out for parties. Little robot fish.'

'Robot fish?' Its tail was like a tiny repetitive slap on my palm.

'They're pretty simple. You charge them up and they swim around for hours. They look cute, don't they?'

'Do they have names?'

He laughed. He sat down beside me and handed me the drink. 'No, Harley,' he said. 'They don't have names.'

Behind us, hundreds of people were spilling out of Elias' huge open-plan living room and kitchen. The glass doors were flung wide to accommodate them. People danced beside them, eyes on their own reflections. Lines were being done off the kitchen island and the pool table – every surface we'd had sex on, actually. Someone was doing karaoke in a room downstairs, with the door open, so that the sound carried all the way out to the pool. They were quite good, whoever it was, belting their way through 'You Oughta Know' by Alanis Morissette. Two of our supporting actresses were making out in the jacuzzi to our left. Ahead of us, Hollywood glowed.

'Have you ever been in love, Harley?' asked Elias.

I took a sip of the drink. 'You've asked me that before.'

'I miss my wife,' he said.

I looked at him closely. At his spacey, tired face. 'What are you on?'

'Nothing,' he said. 'Just alcohol. I just miss her.'

'Huh.'

'What are *you* on?'

'Ket.'

'You're so British,' he said.

It was a beautiful sky. This high above the city, you could see so many stars. They shone down into the swimming pool and the fish darted between their reflections, like they were on an obstacle course. I reached down into the water and picked up another fish. 'A friend,' I said, to the fish in my palm.

'How high are you?' asked Elias.

'Not sure.' I held the fish out to him. He shook his head, so I closed my palm over it.

'We made a good film,' he said, 'I think.'

'You made a good party.'

He laughed. 'Thanks, Harley.'

I opened my fist and released the fish into the water. It swam off without missing a beat. Sturdy little robot fish.

'Are you going to drink that?' asked Elias. 'I made it for you.' He was looking at my gin and tonic. I took a sip, to make him happy. 'It's an apology drink,' he said.

'For what?'

'I don't think I was particularly nice to you, on this shoot. Or away from it. I'm sorry I kicked you. I'm sorry I never let us use the bed.'

'Why?'

'Why am I sorry?'

'We made a good film,' I said, 'didn't we?'

He nodded.

'So,' I said, 'there's nothing to be sorry for.'

He looked a little offended by that. Maybe he'd been thinking I would return the apology. He still carried himself like someone who'd been hurt but was choosing to rise above, like I'd done some damage to him by drawing out a good performance. After a second, he cleared his throat.

'I guess I underestimated how much you actually cared about this project. How much you actually cared about telling her story. You come across as – I mean, when people first meet you, you seem kind of . . .'

'What?'

'Spoilt,' he said, 'I guess.'

Someone ran past us and cannonballed into the pool with a loud shriek. In the resulting splash, I saw a swarm of little red and orange fish, floating through the air in slow motion, beating their tails from side to side.

We'd been cold with each other, in Iceland. We didn't sleep together, whilst we were there, and we hardly interacted out of character. I think he'd been scared to come near me. The project had pulled something out of him that he'd found startling, and his solution was to give me a wide berth. I don't think his performance in Iceland was quite as good as it had been in LA, but no one seemed to notice it except me – José seemed happy with what we shot.

It had been a lonely time generally, in that small Icelandic town, broken up only by Julia's visit. We took a trip to find that waterfall she'd seen online and sat behind it for a while, separated from everything else by a sheet of sound and moving light.

'Doesn't this make you want to do nothing except travel the world and see extraordinary places?' she'd asked dreamily.

'Yes,' I'd said, 'but some of us have to work.'

When we'd got back to sunny LA, Elias seemed to warm with the weather, and had been relatively polite to me for our final days of shooting. This was still the first time we'd had a full conversation since the kick.

He shuffled closer to me along the side of the pool. 'Do you want to make a go of it?' he asked.

'Acting? Of course.'

He shook his head. 'No, Harley. I meant us.'

I looked at him, so very serious with low brows in the low light, and laughed. He was hurt. I kept laughing. The person who had jumped into the swimming pool swam past us, and I saw that it was a man, and that he wasn't wearing any clothes. His buttocks rippled.

'You said you miss your wife,' I said.

'I did.'

314

'Is that true?'

'Yes,' he said, 'but I thought you were the kind of girl who wouldn't mind that so much.'

I laughed harder.

When the party was over and it was eight the next morning, I slid into the water and went swimming amongst the robot fish in bright yellow-white sun. Most of them were dead, bodies bobbing dolefully on the surface of the pool, but some swam on. They were very slow now and I outstripped them easily. I held one and let it die in my palm, tail moving left to right, left to right, and then nothing.

'I'll miss you,' said Elias, from the side of the pool.

'I'll see you at the premiere,' I said.

'Sure, but that's forever away.'

I floated on my back. 'I thought you hated me,' I said.

'Oh, Harley,' he said. 'It's never as simple as that. Hasn't this film taught you anything?'

We decided to stay in touch. It seemed a mad decision even as we made it, but I suppose it was the way he looked at me, floating amongst the dead fish in his pool, like I was someone he understood. It was worth seeing what we were, separate from Greg and Rachael. Us being together wouldn't be a bad thing for either of us or for the film. Besides, Julia had dated a rich older guy for a while and still wouldn't shut up about it, so I was hoping this would level the playing field.

I flew commercial back home, since Carlton either couldn't or wouldn't convince his dad to send the jet back for me. Rachael wasn't around for a final dinner before I went home – she was busy on *Traversers* – but she said we would organise a tennis game when she arrived back in Kent. I was relieved by this suggestion. I thought that if I saw her in person I wouldn't be able to hold myself back from running to her and asking the question.

The conviction that I was the child of Rachael Carmichael and Greg Foster was only growing stronger. I looked like her, but when I scrolled through photos of him on social media, I fancied that I had aspects of him as well – I was taller than her, for one, and Greg was tall. I had not just her talent but his practical business sense. It was me who had pulled her and Elisabeth apart, me that had driven a wedge between the two sisters, both feeling I was theirs more than the other's. And hadn't I felt drawn to this story from the start? Hadn't I known it was mine to tell?

Rachael didn't want it to be known. I had to respect that. But for how long? When did I reveal to her that I'd pieced it together?

When I landed in London, I took a taxi straight from the airport to Carlton's dad's house. I texted Julia. *Meet at Carlton's in 30?* My phone showed me that she was already inside when I pulled up.

I left Carlton's dad's second assistant Kim to lug my suitcases into the hall and headed straight down to the game room to find the two of them waiting for me in armchairs. They jumped up to hug me but I batted them off.

'Listen. You have to listen. I have to tell someone.'

'God, you're so intense,' said Carlton. 'Could you maybe once not walk into a room with the energy of someone in an HBO drama?'

'Shut up and listen.'

'*You* shut up. I've got news too. Julia and I are starting a podcast.'

They were so pleased with themselves, legs tucked up in their chairs, passing a bowl of crisps between them. Julia wiped a salty hand on her Fiorucci hoodie. I looked at them, exasperated. 'What?'

'Carlton's dad's friend is looking for a couple of young people to host a music podcast,' said Julia. 'He's put us forward.'

'Sounds ethical. Neither of you know shit about music.'

'I mean, everyone knows a *bit* about music. We listen to music.'

'And we can't all come up the honest way and sweet-talk our famous aunts into handing over their life rights,' said Carlton.

'Would you both listen?' I took a breath. 'I'm not a Carmichael-Roth. I'm a Carmichael-Foster.'

'You smell like plane,' said Carlton. 'Have you even showered? Did you come straight from the airport?'

'Guys, *listen*. I'm Rachael and Greg's daughter.'

They both looked at me, uncomprehending.

'Rachael told you this?' asked Julia.

'No. I just know. I'm telling you, *listen*.'

We sat, and I laid the whole matter out for them. Julia's eyes grew round and bright, but Carlton crossed one leg over the other and slouched back, looking at me like I'd just told him I wanted to go out for dinner in Croydon.

'Wow,' breathed Julia, when I was done.

'Please,' said Carlton.

'How can you not see it?' I gestured to my own face. '*Hello.*'

'You've got movie sickness. You think you're your character even after the whole thing's done. Which is beyond method acting, *which* is already disgusting enough in itself. Get real, Harley.'

'It's true. I'm going to talk to Rachael about it.'

'Even if it is,' he said, 'which it isn't, by the way, she'd never admit it. You don't have anything resembling evidence. She made this whole thing of telling you this particular story in this particular way and *then* getting you to pass it on to the rest of the world.' He shrugged. 'That's not something you do if you're making space for any alternative narratives.'

'You're a dick,' I said. 'Julia believes me, don't you?'

'Yes, of course,' she said, but she looked doubtful now.

I stood up. 'God, thanks for the trust, guys.'

'You're breaking up this little parliament, are you?'

'I just got off a flight, Carlton. I've got to go home and sleep.'

317

'Good to have you back,' called Carlton as I stomped up the stairs. 'We've had a great few months, by the way.'

Fuck Carlton, I thought. I was getting a little sick of his holier-than-thou attitude. Like I was the asshole for caring about more than nice dinners and hooking up with Imperial undergrads.

I took his dad's car service back to Notting Hill and the driver helped me to lug all my things back into my flat. I looked around at it all and thought, *Why unpack?* I'd be back in LA in no time. Already Warren had a string of auditions and Zoom calls set up for me. The press release about me playing Rachael Carmichael was going to drop in a matter of months, and then the demand would only increase. And maybe one day, if my star rose high enough, other people would start asking the same questions that I had, and land on the same conclusions. Then Rachael would have to come clean with the truth.

Warren really had filled up my schedule with auditions. I'd expected to be reading for leads in big projects now but it was still mostly the same shit, just more of it. Fluffy best-friend roles and guest-star spots in sitcoms. Nothing took. I thought even introducing myself as Harley Carmichael would do *something*, but no. They still just didn't seem to want me.

'Not going well?' asked Dad, after I took yet another disappointing phone call at dinner with my parents. 'You know, that script is still floating around. The one that you'd be perfect for.' I speared a potato and smiled, politely. 'There's rewrites happening and logistical hoops to jump through,' he said, 'all the usual faff, but when it gets off the ground, it could be yours if you want it.'

'I don't need it,' I said.

'Okay,' he said. He picked up his fork. 'But just so you know, it's there.'

◆ ◆ ◆

Winter came to London, deceptively gently at first, and then it hit like a blunt weapon. Elias came to visit and took Julia, Carlton and I out to a club in London so exclusive that it didn't even have a name (or maybe we were just too drunk to remember it). He picked up the tab. I could feel Julia's envy hissing at me over the table every time he squeezed my hand or kissed my cheek. He asked if I wanted to introduce him to my parents and I said, 'No, thanks,' so we didn't do that. He stayed in my Notting Hill flat, which I'm sure seemed tiny and scruffy to him, though he didn't say anything.

We didn't have sex. 'I think the sex we had in LA was quite damaging,' said Elias. 'Quite toxic. I'm in the process of re-evaluating my relationship with sex and I've decided to stay celibate whilst I'm figuring out what that means.'

'Whatever,' I said.

Having him there was fine, but I wasn't distraught when he left.

We spent Christmas skiing in France. I headed back to London in time for the press release to drop on New Year's Day and threw shots back with Carlton and Julia when it got picked up by *People*. I still hadn't booked another job, but I thought, *This is it. We've done it. This is where it all changes.*

Then, 2nd of January, Warren rang, and sang into my ear: 'Pilot season!'

I was hungover. I was confused. I snapped, 'What the fuck do you mean?'

A beat as he composed himself. 'Harley, there's some great scripts coming in that I'm going to try to get the jump on.'

'*Pilots?* I'm not doing pilots anymore. I'm going to be in films.'

'We want your face everywhere,' he said. 'We've got to try loads of different avenues to the top, babe.'

But I'd made up my mind. I was sitting pilot season out. 'Just put me up for films,' I said. 'That's what I want to do. Just that. We have to be strategic here.'

'Harley—' he started, and I knew he wanted to say, *You're not booking anything.* But he couldn't. 'Alright,' he said. 'We can try that.'

We kept trying that. I still didn't book anything.

◆ ◆ ◆

About six months after production wrapped, José called. 'We have a very, very early cut,' he said.

'Already?'

'It's rough, but it's there. I wondered if you and Elias wanted to come over and view it? See what you think? You guys are my collaborators on this. I want your opinion.'

Elias flew back to London two days before. We lay in my bed (clothed – he was still on his celibacy kick) and speculated how we might feel about watching ourselves. 'I think I'll find it weird,' I said, 'watching myself take my clothes off.'

He laughed. 'God, Harley, you're so sex-orientated.' This was a new catchphrase of his. He'd started bringing it out whenever he felt we were exiting PG-13 territory. Around him, my conversation had to be as clean as that of a children's TV host. 'I think it'll be hard to watch me kick you,' he said.

He was very soppy with me now. He treated me like some precious little ingénue. He seemed to forget how he had spoken to me when we first met, calling me a nepo baby as we bobbed around in his pool, and how, by the end of the shoot, he had truly hated me. He looked back on the time he had kicked me and blamed himself, nursing his guilt in what I thought was a very self-indulgent way, but I was sure that in the moment he had blamed me for it. He had thought that I had made myself impossible not to hurt.

I had already decided that when the film was out and had done well, I would break up with him. We barely had a relationship as it was – he could call me sex-orientated all he liked, but really, what kind of a relationship didn't involve sex? And it scared me, the way he could switch up like this, one minute despising me, the next charmed by me. One minute the sad ex-husband who missed his wife, the next curling around me in bed, lecturing me about how obsessed I was with my own sexuality.

He went to shower. Through the bathroom door, I called, 'Julia and Carlton want to go out.'

'Oh,' he said, 'Not tonight. It's like hanging out with kids, you know? I need some recovery time.'

Dick, I thought. I would dump him at the end of the last red carpet.

We took a cab to José's place in Richmond. Elias had a particular company in London that he had to use. He said that I would understand the importance of safety, when I was where he was. I was already sick of him after two days, so I just gave a little 'hm' in response. He looked out the window as we drove through Richmond and said that this was somewhere he could see himself settling down.

I panicked. I did not want Elias in London. 'You are settled. You're settled in LA.'

'Right, but I mean for the second half of my life.'

'Aren't you already in that?'

He took a deep breath in through his nose and then laughed. It sounded forced.

José greeted us at the door of his ivy-covered townhouse. Behind him, in the corridor, stood Ahn. As usual, she was in business-casual – grey trousers and a thick black turtleneck, hair pulled back into a bun. She smiled at me. It was weirdly good to see her.

'How are you?' she asked as we made our way downstairs to José's screening room, Elias and José ahead of us.

'Oh,' I said, 'frustrated and out of work again.' Once upon a time I would never have dreamt of being this open with Ahn, but she grimaced sympathetically. 'You?'

'You know how it is,' she said diplomatically. She had just signed on to adapt a bestselling romance for MGM. I definitely didn't know how that was. 'You haven't seen it yet?' she asked.

'No. You?'

She shook her head. 'No. I'm a little scared.'

'Me too,' I said.

We walked into José's dim, purple-lit screening room. Before we separated to take our seats, her hand found mine, and she gave it a squeeze.

I had to sign about three different documents and do a lot of pleading, but eventually José agreed to let me bring Rachael the rough cut of *Carmichael & Foster*. I went round to her house in the evening. The days were shorter now and it was too dark for tennis, so we sat around in her living room: me, her and Raph. He wasn't always there. When I noticed his absence I would ask after him, and Rachael would say, 'Oh, he's visiting friends,' like it had been his decision.

That night he was on his green cushion, at the foot of her armchair. I brought the disc in its plastic folder out of my bag. José, paranoid as he was about leaks, had made me bring Rachael the film on DVD of all things, with the solemn promise that I took it home with me afterwards. 'No one has a DVD player anymore,' I complained to him, but I knew that Rachael did. She still had a whole library of DVDs at the bottom of her bookcase. I'd asked her about it before, and she said, 'Well, they can't get deleted, can they? I know I own them.' Sometimes I forgot how old she was, until she said things like that.

'What are you playing me?' she asked as I slid it into the DVD player.

I turned around to grin at her over my shoulder. 'Guess.'

It was always satisfying, being able to actually catch her off guard. 'It's ready?'

'Not entirely. But I wanted you to see the first cut.'

She drew breath, settling herself in her chair. Raph stared up at her like he could sense her perturbance. I picked up the remote and looked at her, for permission. She nodded. I took my seat on the sofa. There were no logos yet and very little music, so the film began with just my face, very large, very still, no introduction.

'I don't know what to do anymore,' I said, as Rachael, into the phone.

The real me sat on the sofa with my legs crossed. The real Rachael sat in her chair, a cushion in her lap, hands picking at a thread. We both stared at this creation on the screen, this thing that was both of us and neither of us. Our unorthodox child.

It was a wonderful film. I'd cried my eyes out when I'd watched it at José's house. Elias and I *were* Greg and Rachael. Whatever we'd done – whatever Elias had felt our relationship had infected him with – it had been worth it and beyond. We were magnificent together. He was imposing, strong, manipulative, often terrifying, sometimes pitiful. I was changeable, flighty, cowed, often frozen, sometimes deadly. It was a stirring portrayal of abuse. All his violence towards her laid out inarguably. All his crimes stark and clear. I watched her in the corner of my eye to see what she thought.

She didn't speak. About fifteen minutes in, at the audition scene, she watched him stalk me with the camera and leant closer. I said, 'It must be strange to watch yourself like this—'

'Don't talk,' she said.

My jaw snapped shut.

She didn't speak for the entirety of the film. I barely even saw her face change. Only in the scene with the pregnancy test did she lean even closer, her hands clasped under her chin. Raph stood up on his cushion, tail on end. She watched herself – me, Rachael Carmichael – stare at the test in her hands and breathe out, close her eyes.

She looked over at me and nodded. 'Good,' she said.

The camera was still tight on my face, dark hair falling loose over my bare shoulders.

'Don't you think it's strange?' I asked her, barely above a whisper. 'How much I look like you?'

'Harley,' she said, at the same volume. 'I'm trying to watch the film.'

I turned back to the screen, an ache in my ribs. But after a minute I heard her say, 'Uncanny. It seems almost impossible.'

I didn't dare look at her after that.

Greg and Rachael had a final fight, the one that ended in her taking the money. Elias' face was terrifying, full of real hatred. It made me cold all over. He pushed me up against a wall and there was a moment where even I wasn't sure if he was going to hit me or kiss me. When he finally left, my Rachael curled up on the carpet. She was both distraught to lose him and relieved that it was finally over.

No credits. Just the end of it. It stopped on my tear-stricken face, cheek pressed against the carpet. I switched the screen off and waited for her to speak.

'It's perfect,' she said.

Astonished, I felt my eyes fill up with tears. 'Really?' I croaked. 'You love it?'

'It's everything I hoped it would be.' She reached forward to touch my knee. Her eyes were bright. 'Harley,' she said. 'We did it.'

◆ ◆ ◆

324

Four more months until the trailer. I saw Rachael maybe once in that time – she was suddenly inundated with meetings and other commitments. It seemed that interest around the project was giving her a small revival. Warren called with the news I'd been waiting for.

'You got it!'

'It' was a supporting role in a comedy, alongside an Australian comedian who was supposedly very up and coming. I would be playing the friend whose wedding the whole zany series of events took place at. I thought the script was fun, if not particularly intellectual, but it wasn't anything on *Carmichael & Foster*. I expressed this to Warren.

'Harley,' he said, 'this is a great opportunity for you. There are going to be a lot of eyes on this one. And it shows range, after *Carmichael & Foster*. You're good at comedy. We want to show people that.'

'Sure,' I said. 'No, it's great news.' I walked from my living room into the kitchen, considering. 'But do I want to do comedy?' I asked. 'Don't we want me to do big, serious, award-winning films?'

'Sure,' said Warren. 'Eventually. But we're not there yet. I think you need to understand that. And comedies win awards.'

I put the kettle on. 'I just don't know,' I said.

'Are you serious?' He was getting frustrated now, which I had never heard from him. 'Harley, I'm going to level with you here – we're taking what we can get right now. That's how this industry works. And not only is this what we can get – it's a good role, in what's going to be a good project, with a decent amount of eyes on it. You *can't* turn this down.'

I prickled. 'I can't?'

'I will seriously doubt whether this is a good business relationship if you do.'

'Oh, please.'

'I'm serious.'

'If you drop me before *Carmichael & Foster* then you're an idiot.'

'That film is not a guaranteed career-maker, Harley,' said Warren. 'No film is.'

'It's about as close as it gets.'

'If you were playing the first female James Bond, *that* would be about as close as it gets. This is a very good shot, but it's still just a shot. As is everything. And we've got a role here which is also a good shot. I think you would be truly stupid to turn this one down.'

'You're being pretty rude, Warren,' I said, over the noise of the kettle.

'Take the job, Harley.'

'I don't want to,' I said. 'It isn't the kind of thing I'm interested in. And I don't like how you're speaking to me.'

There was a pause. 'Okay,' he said. 'Let's talk about this tomorrow when we've both cooled off.' He hung up.

But when he called me back the next day, expecting to find me contrite and ready to dive head first into comedy, I was still adamant. I wasn't going to scrabble at the bottom of the barrel for supporting roles. I was on the fast track here – it didn't make sense to take any deviations.

Warren didn't drop me. I could hear in his voice that he wanted to. But I was the niece of Rachael Carmichael and I was about to play her in a movie. It was like I said. He wasn't an idiot.

He wasn't going to drop me until it made sense. Which, as it happened, was three months later.

When the trailer came out, the publicity machine started. The first week, Elias was doing so many interviews that he never had time to call anymore, which didn't bother me too much. He'd slipped up in his celibacy and banged a model, and now all he

326

wanted to do was get on the phone and cry about what an awful person he was, seemingly unable to understand that I could not have cared less who he stuck his dick in. I did a few phone interviews and I'd been offered a quick couch moment on *Sun's Up,* but I wasn't quite as in demand.

'Just wait,' Julia told me. 'When the film comes out, everyone will want you.'

I was sick of waiting. I marked the premiere date on my calendar and every night I would cross off another day. *Two months now, until I'm released from this prison of anonymity. Until everyone knows my name.*

It was a Wednesday when it happened. An awful day, sometime in June, sticky and heavy. I'd sweated all through the night and woke up with the bedsheet clinging to my back. My phone was ringing. It was Elias. I checked the time. Five in the morning. Elias Jones was not a person I could handle talking to at five in the morning.

I had to get up half an hour later and dress for my *Sun's Up* TV spot. There had been many moments over the last year or so that I'd thought would be *the* life-changing one, and all they'd amounted to was a string of disappointments. But it stirred in me again as I looked into the mirror – that feeling that, *This is it. This is the hour of my rebirth.* It was unkillable.

In the back of the car, on the way to the ITV studios, Elias called again. He'd set his own contact photo in my phone. It was him shirtless, his back to the camera, surveying the view from his garden in LA. I rolled my eyes at Elias' back muscles and turned my phone off. I was really starting to wonder if I would even be able to make it to the end of the promotional period before I broke up with him. All the small annoyances hardly seemed worth it if we weren't having sex.

When I arrived at the studio and signed in, the girl behind the desk gave me a curious look.

'Harley . . . Carmichael?' she repeated, with emphasis on my surname.

'Rachael's niece,' I said.

She blinked. 'Right, sure.' She reached into her pocket for her phone. 'Just hold on,' she said.

'I'm on this morning,' I said. 'It should be there.'

'Just give me a second.'

'Harley?' Warren had pushed through the double doors into the lobby, his phone in his hand. He hurried over to me. 'My god,' he said. 'I rang you, just now. Why's your phone off?'

'What's going on?'

He glared at the girl behind the desk, who cowered away behind her fringe. 'It's been shambles. It's all absolutely shameful, how it's been handled.'

'How what's been handled?'

A skinny boy, hardly older than a teenager, rushed past me. He leant over the desk to talk to the girl at her computer, waistband of his underwear poking out from the waistband of his jeans. He was whispering, but not so quietly that I didn't catch a few words. '*He's going on first thing, I think . . .*'

'He?' I repeated. They both turned to look at me in alarm. '*He?*'

'Harley,' soothed Warren.

Elias. That's why he had been ringing all morning. He wanted to be the one to break it to me, all consolatory and smug. 'That *dick*!'

'Harley—'

I ignored the protests behind me and pushed through the double doors, storming down the corridor.

'Excuse me, miss,' said a security guard, behind me. 'Can I see your pass?'

'I'm Harley Carmichael,' I yelled back at him, not slowing down.

'Who?' I heard.

I tried doors. Several led me to empty dressing rooms – one opened into a long corridor with a dormant 'ON AIR' sign at the end. I sped up, practically running now, security coming after me. I could hear consternation behind me. I pushed through the double doors and stopped short. Some crew members turned to look at me, but most stayed focused on their equipment. Way ahead of me, on the set, the two hosts were shaking hands with someone. I put both hands against the back wall and tried to blend in with the crew as I moved further along, craning my neck to get a glimpse of Elias' smug, weasel face.

But it wasn't Elias at all. Settling himself on the *Sun's Up* sofa, hands smoothing down his grey suit jacket, was Greg Foster. It was startling to see him in the flesh. I'd got so used to thinking of him as having Elias' face, but this was a man in his sixties, face taut and just a little too altered not to look uncanny. He still moved like a man used to commanding a set, though. When he reached out for a glass of water, it was like the room leant with him.

I was at the back of the room, out of sight, and the two of us had never met. Still, I had the strangest feeling that he might recognise me.

He said something to one of the hosts, a woman in a blue trouser suit. Mum had done a shampoo advert with her once. Her co-host applied lip balm and smacked his lips together. She gave him a slightly disgusted look. Greg took a sip of his water, placing the glass back on the table. Somewhere near me came a voice. 'Three, two . . .'

I breathed out. They couldn't come in and pull me out of the room whilst the light was on. That gave me a window to work out what the hell was happening here. Greg had obviously been stuck on to the bill last minute. Had they pulled me, or were they being sneaky, trying to get both perspectives on the project? That could only ever be a good thing, I reasoned. When it came to films, all press was good press. Greg talking about our film was great press, even if he panned the whole idea. Let him condemn himself. When the project dropped, no one would be on his side.

'You may by now have seen the trailer for *Carmichael & Foster*,' said the woman in the trouser suit to camera. 'The film promises to be an open and raw examination of the relationship between actress Rachael Carmichael and Greg Foster, with the role of Rachael set to be played by her niece, Harley Carmichael.' I suppressed a squeak of excitement. 'However, it has been suggested that the film takes some pretty huge liberties with the truth, and Greg Foster is keen to set the record straight.'

She turned towards Greg, who gave a tight smile, the kind you use to show that you're polite even under duress.

'How are you doing?' she asked him, her voice low and serious.

'Not too bad,' said Greg. 'It's been a taxing few hours, I won't lie.'

'So, you've actually seen the film?'

'Yes – I did manage to get hold of a copy.'

That couldn't be true. There was no way José would have sent a copy to Greg Foster. Perhaps an overenthusiastic employee in Marketing had gone rogue? It didn't alarm me, but it was perplexing.

'And what were your thoughts?'

'It horrified me,' said Greg.

Out of sight at the back of the studio, I rolled my eyes.

'I mean, it would be one thing if this film was just telling Rachael's story. But it's doing much more than that – it's added whole events that just never happened and it all seems designed to paint me in the worst possible light.'

'We now know that the film intended to portray a physically abusive relationship between Rachael and yourself. I'm assuming you contest that?'

'Vehemently,' said Greg. 'Listen, the two of us could really argue, when we set our minds to it. But I never laid a hand on her. I mean, at one point in this – *film*—' He wrinkled his nose when he said the word, like what we'd made wasn't even worthy of it. 'They have her lying on the ground whilst I kick her in the ribs over and over.'

'Wow,' said the male host solemnly.

The woman shook her head.

'Not only did that categorically not happen,' said Greg, 'but Rachael's sister Elisabeth was living in the house with us for much of our marriage, right up until Rachael left, and would be able to attest that she never saw me lay a finger on Rachael.'

Mum had lived with Rachael?

The doors opened. Warren. Heads turned in his direction, people made frantic gestures, but he waved a hand. He beckoned to me. 'Come on,' he mouthed.

I shook my head.

'Come *on*.' He still made no sound, but he exaggerated the words.

'It gets worse,' said Greg. 'The film alleges that Rachael accepted several million from me under the condition she would never speak out about our relationship.' His expression was one of incredulity, so confident in his bemusement that the hosts mirrored it. 'I mean, that's an incredibly dangerous thing to put out there. And wholly untrue. The film suggests she handed the money off to her sister, Elisabeth, and I'm willing to bet that Elisabeth will deny those claims as well. The Carmichael sisters are both self-made women – to imply that either of them gained their wealth from some shady pay-off isn't just insulting to me, but to them.'

He was laying it on ridiculously thick, and it was so obvious to me that he was lying. The manner of the hosts amazed me. They nodded and grimaced and made sympathetic sounds, as if they had some kind of victim on their couch. Still, his repeated mentions of my mum confused me. What kind of relationship had he and her had that he was this confident she'd back him up? Maybe he had something on her, I thought.

'And how does Rachael Carmichael feel about all this? Have you spoken?'

'We've spoken,' he said.

Had they? That would have been an outrageously dangerous lie if not. This was beginning to feel like a nightmare.

'It turns out she's not actually involved with the project at all. The screenwriter did some interviews with her in the early stages, but they've totally run with their own narrative and twisted her entire story around. She's also furious.'

I breathed out. That confirmed, at least, that the man was lying. Whatever lawsuit he thought he had, he was talking out of his arse. Greg Foster and Rachael Carmichael had not been in contact.

'Is she willing to help you fight this?' asked the host.

'Of course,' said Greg. He leant back, crossed one leg over the other. And then he smiled. 'Who do you think gave me the film?'

My breath caught.

I'd left the film in her DVD player.

The hosts turned back to the camera, began to transition into an ad break. Greg went on smiling, arms spread over the back of the sofa. He was a man who'd always had everything. He still did. This was a small legal nuisance in his life. A minor irritation. This summer, his book would come out, and it would be a bestseller. He would make more money off this story and he would get richer and more famous. And where would I be? What would I become?

332

They went to an ad break. Security were on me immediately, but Warren reached me first and fought his way through. 'It's okay,' he said. He handed one of them his card. The burly security guy looked down at it, baffled. 'We're leaving,' he said. 'She's coming with me.' He leant down and whispered, 'I've told them you're not doing your slot.'

He escorted me out and down the corridor, his arm around my shoulders. I was shaking. 'It's going to be fine, Harley,' he kept saying. The girl on the desk gaped at us as we moved past. I flipped her off. 'Just keep it together until we get in the car,' said Warren. 'I've got one outside for us.'

In the car, he did my seat belt for me like I was a child. 'What the fuck?' I spluttered, as he reached across me. 'What the *fuck?* Can he just lie like that?'

'He's not lying,' said Warren.

'Of course he is.'

'Harley.' He was typing on his phone, giving me half his attention, but his tone was urgent. 'I need you to understand what's going on, and I need you to digest it very quickly, before you turn your phone back on and everyone and their mother is asking you about this. Okay?'

I nodded.

'I don't think he's lying,' he said.

'He has to be. What's Rachael saying?'

'We don't know yet. No one can get hold of her. Everyone's focused on trying to put out this fire.' He pressed his hands together. The car pulled off. 'Now, the studio could argue artistic licence, do a sudden pivot in the marketing and call it all a fictionalisation, but it's unlikely they'd win that one, at least without incurring costs too significant to make it all worth it. Greg's team have already got a cease and desist on Sidonius Cagnoni's desk. And Rachael's refusing to cooperate, which again makes their job harder.'

I was nodding along, but none of his sentences meant anything. He gave me a pitying look. 'Do you understand what I'm telling you?'

'But, my mum – I mean, she won't back Greg up.'

He hesitated, and the way he was looking at me was unbearable. So much pity, and just a little rancour. Like I was some ugly, bleeding thing on the side of a motorway. 'She's going out with a statement,' he said. 'It's— Well, she has.'

I stared back at him, and the feeling came over me suddenly that he must be incurably stupid, to believe that all of the things he was saying were really happening. 'She wouldn't do that.'

'Do you want to read it?'

I took his phone. It wasn't really a statement, just an Instagram story. A photo of her TV screen, taken in our living room. Text over the top that read: *Shocking lies! I never took any lump sum from my sister and witnessed nothing untoward in their house. Hoping @gregfoster and Rachael can set the narrative straight. Truth wins!* This was followed by two emojis: an angry face, and a dove.

'He's lying to everyone,' I said, handing the phone back. 'Mum's just got caught up in it.'

'Harley, the man isn't lying. My best guess is that Rachael tried to frame him and then got cold feet. She realised who she was up against.'

'But that doesn't make any sense. She— We added the bit about the money in last minute. For *authenticity*.'

He took hold of my shoulders. 'I don't have the answers,' he said. 'I don't know what the fuck is going on. But you need to understand something. The project's dead.'

What a strange thing for him to say, I thought.

'The film's not coming out. I don't think it ever is.'

'It has to,' I said. I almost smiled. It was almost funny.

'It can't.'

'It *has* to, Warren! Shit, this is everything. This is two years of my life, and I'm *great* in it, and everyone is going to watch it— And— And—' I'd run out of words. I wasn't sure why I was trying to bargain with him. 'And—' I bleated.

'Harley,' said Warren. 'Listen, Rachael clearly had her own agenda here. It backfired, and we were all just collateral damage. I'm so sorry. But you can come back from this. It'll be okay.'

He was a mask of faux sympathy, businesslike and practised. It was the same face he'd shown me time and time again, after every bad audition, every disappointing meeting, every failed pilot. He was good at it. But even he was getting tired.

'Do you really believe that?' I asked him.

He said nothing. He gave me a small grimace.

I nodded. I was almost grateful for it. It was the most honest anyone had been with me in months.

Chapter Fourteen

RACHAEL

16 June 1995

The worst part is when they point to the ultrasound and say, 'You see this area, here? This is where the problem is.' And then they explain.

Today Greg cut in and said, 'We know, thanks. We've heard it before. Nothing to be done?'

'Nothing,' said the doctor.

Greg turned in his chair and looked at me. Sort of like, *See?*

I wasn't ever sure I wanted kids. And then they told me I couldn't have them and I raged against the accusation. I wanted to say, *What do you mean I can't get pregnant? I've been pregnant.* We walked out of our first appointment, and I turned to Greg, and I said, 'I want to see another doctor.' And he squeezed my hand and said that we would. That was back when he still found everything I did and said endearing.

I whispered it to a doctor once, when Greg was in the bathroom. 'I've actually been pregnant before.'

'Oh,' he said, 'you have? Well, it's never an impossibility. But your odds are very small. Statistically, that pregnancy was likely an anomaly. And there's nothing to say that it would have gone to term.'

Greg came back in the room before I'd had a chance to beg for the doctor's discretion, but he must have sensed it, because he didn't bring my first and only pregnancy up again. Maybe he didn't believe me.

The part that irritates me is that Greg was the one who wanted kids – *more* kids, I should say, because he already has two. He was the one who talked me into trying and said that we should both get checked out. I wasn't even fussed at the start. Now he's forgotten that. He acts like this is all one big indulgence, and that he and the doctors we see are going out of their way for my benefit alone. I suppose it's better this way. If he was the one pushing for this, hoping, then I'd feel even guiltier for doing what I did.

'What do you think?' he asked in the car. 'Last one? Time to give up the ghost?'

'God,' I said.

'What?'

'Could you be more insensitive?'

He pursed his lips. 'If it helps,' he said, 'I never thought you were supposed to be a mother anyway.'

'Then why on *earth* would you want to have kids with me?'

'I'm just saying,' he said. 'Maybe it's all worked out as it should.'

'Yeah,' I said. 'Maybe.'

I've got good at swallowing my anger. Back when neither of us did it, we would just argue for hours. We learnt early on that neither of us gets tired and neither of us is ever inclined to back down, so we can both scream at each other all night long if that's how we're feeling. He's never laid a hand on me, but sometimes I can feel him wanting to, and equally I want to launch myself across the room and scratch the flesh from his face. But fights like that are boring and get far too convoluted, and these days it's better just to say something short and hold all the anger in my stomach. Not that it's easy to do. Sometimes I throw up because I hate him so much.

It isn't like that all the time, of course. Half the time it's wonderful. I suppose I thought that a married version of us would be very different from anything we were before, but we're exactly the same. Half the time we're still director and actor, screaming at each other, always at odds, him trying to govern and me unwilling to let myself be governed. And the other half we're man and mistress. Overly effusive, overly physical, like we don't know when we'll next hold each other. How do you piece together a marriage out of all that? I don't have the answer, but god knows I've been giving it a go.

I take a granola bar out of my purse and unwrap it. Greg watches me, eyes flickering between me and the road. I take a bite and he winces.

'What?' I asked, through the granola. 'I haven't eaten all day.'

'You're getting it all over my car.'

'*My* car. I had this car long before you. I'll have it long after.'

'Very long after, at this rate.'

'Charming.'

'Sorry,' he said, his voice softening. He reached over to rub my leg. 'Strange day. You should eat. You're getting too skinny.'

The tabloids agree. One of them ran a side-by-side comparison of me and a Halloween skeleton.

'Hey,' he said, squeezing my thigh. 'You should finish reading *Lulubelle,* when we get home.'

'I finished it last night,' I said.

He removed his hand. 'You don't like it.'

I wasn't sure what to say. I should have said, 'Spot on,' because he was. *Lulubelle* is his newest screenplay, the first one he's written since *Unbeliever,* and if it's possible I hate it even more. I hated it

338

when he first pitched it: a woman possessed by the spirit of a creepy twelve-year-old girl whose husband has to soothe the vicious spirit in her in order to get his wife back. Ultimately, it would be two and a half hours of me doing a creepy little girl voice and Greg infantilising me and giving me 'fuck me' eyes. I could do without it.

'It made me uncomfortable,' I said.

'It's supposed to.'

'Well, job done, I guess.'

'You always say you want to do stuff that pushes the boundaries,' said Greg.

'Right, but not towards paedophilia.'

He looked affronted. 'How can you say that? I'm a father myself.'

'The whole thing is creepy, and not in the right sort of way. It's not the sort of project I'm interested in.'

'Well, what sort of project are you interested in, Rachael? Because you haven't shot a film in well over a year.'

I wanted to point out that I'd been working since I was sixteen so maybe a year off was not the end of the world, and that I would have shot that film in Ireland with Christian Bale if Greg hadn't convinced me to pull out of it so that we could 'enjoy our time as newlyweds'. But I've thrown that one at him before, and he always reminds me that I'm a strong adult woman, capable of making my own choices. Funny how when a man says that to you it's never a compliment.

'I want to work with you again,' he said.

'Then bring me a good script.'

'This is a great script. Maybe you just need to read it again.'

'I don't need to read it again,' I snapped. 'It's shit.'

He went very still at the wheel, and I knew that I'd done it, and neither of us were getting any sleep that night. Fighting takes hours for us. It used to transition into make-up sex, but it doesn't anymore. We haven't had sex in three weeks. I've been counting, and vaguely wondering if that means he's getting it somewhere else. Anna would love that. 'Once a cheater, always a cheater,' she told *Page Six*, when our honeymoon pictures came out. 'I wish Rachael luck.' These comments from her don't bother me like they used to.

We were yelling by the time the car pulled in through the gate. I opened the door and stormed into the house, leaving Greg to tuck the car away in the garage. He likes to cover it with a sheet, to protect it from god knows what. I made myself an Old Fashioned at the sitting-room bar and waited for him to find me. He was already calling out to me when he strode back through the house.

'You're so goddamn entitled. Your agent's going to drop you any day now, and then where will you be?'

'Sitting pretty on all the money I've made, thanks.'

'What do you have, Rachael? A cute little savings account? It'll run out faster than you think.' He laughed. 'Sorry, I forgot. You bagged yourself a rich husband.'

'I bagged nothing. *You* bagged yourself a twenty-something you thought you could keep on all your sets in case you needed something to stick your dick into.'

'Are you drinking?'

I raised the glass to him.

'Fuck me,' he said. 'You are poisonous.' His new insult of choice. It's all over *Lulubelle*. 'No wonder your body can't grow anything. You're fucking rotten.'

'At least I can tell a good movie from a shit one,' I said.

And on we went. He likes to throw insults at me, call me names, try to elicit some kind of emotional response from me. When he can't, it confirms all the worst things he thinks about me. I like to pretend that none of it hurts. The colder and sharper I get, the harder he works to undo me, until he's near tears and I'm frozen and twisted.

Then, sometime before the sun comes up, he gets on his knees. He starts to take his words back. I slowly thaw. We don't fall into each other's arms anymore, though – we stand on opposite sides of the room and agree, at a certain point, without either of us explicitly saying so, that it's over. Then he asks, 'Will you come to bed?' Sometimes I go. Sometimes I stay and make myself another drink.

'Will you come to bed?' he asked tonight.

'No,' I said. 'I'm going to stay up a little while.'

For over a year this book has been hidden in our pantry, behind all the gin, because Greg never reaches for the gin. I've often thought about getting it down since I stashed it there. I thought about it tonight, and then I called Elisabeth instead.

'What's happened?' she asked in matronly tones. I laughed. She's used to my calls. I like to call my sister and tell her about our fights and hear her gasp at all our worst lines. She never tells me I should leave him, like I'm worried other people might. She seems to understand that's something I don't need to hear. I told her about this evening's round of pleasantries. 'He's right about one thing,' she said. 'You should do another film.'

'Nothing's right for me.'

'I'll write something for you,' she said. 'Or better yet, get Greg to write something good and put us both in it.'

I like talking to Elisabeth because she makes everything sound so simple. At nineteen she's remarkably unblemished and robustly optimistic. I used to think that growing up on my money would make her spoilt and unbearable, but instead she's cheerful and outgoing and very sure of herself. I like knowing that I had a hand in that.

I hung up with Elisabeth, and then I did go into the pantry and take out this book after all. It's a big notebook, thick with a red leather cover, and it's well over halfway full now. There are entries in here from before I'd even done *The Avenue*. Even with my sporadic diary-keeping habits, at some point I'll have to get a new one, and that will probably feel like beginning a new life. How strange that is to think about. This life I live right now feels never-ending.

2 July 1995

I hate him more than I know what to do with. This awful life of ours – how can I possibly be expected to live it? I tried to sleep with him the other night and he actually pushed me away. He's been auditioning girls for *Lulubelle* and I can't stop thinking about him circling some young and pretty thing with his camera. Sometimes the actresses want meetings first and then he's out late and comes home smelling like cigarettes and drink and other appalling stereotypes. I've not smelt another woman's perfume on him yet, to be fair, but it's possible that's what the cigarettes are for. They all still want to work with him, even after *Unbeliever*. It astonishes me. Meanwhile, the films I'm getting offered aren't anywhere close to the work I did on *East of Eden* and *Women Who Laugh at God,* and I'm growing tired of throwing terrible screenplay after terrible screenplay into the fire.

'You need to take something at some point,' says Robb, but I tell him I will when it's right.

The few times I have been excited about something, it's been very strange. I've gone for a meeting and they've loved me, and I've been so sure it's mine. Then a few days later, they call Robb and tell him they've decided to go with someone else.

I explained this to Robb and he said, 'Yes, that's normal. You've had a string of extraordinary good luck, Rachael. It can often feel like they really want you until they don't.' He sounded irritated.

But I don't think it's as simple as my luck turning. This meeting tonight all but confirmed it. I was having a drink with Sarah Griffin at The Peninsular, in a quiet corner of the bar, Sarah ordering rounds of some honey cocktail that she currently swears by. I hadn't seen her since she directed me in *Here's Hoping* and it caught me off guard again, when I saw her, just how tall and statuesque she was. When she hugged me, I felt like a child in her arms.

'Congratulations,' she said. 'I won't be offended that I didn't receive an invite to the wedding.'

'No one did.'

'Well, then I won't even have to lie.' She smiled at me. 'You look well,' she said. 'You've been doing enormously impressive things.'

'Not recently.'

'Please. I've seen all those nominations for *East of Eden*.'

'Yes,' I said, 'but I shot that years ago. It hardly feels like my work anymore. I worry that I'm forgetting how to act.'

'I wouldn't worry about that,' she said. 'It doesn't seem to me that you *could* forget because you never really learnt. You're one of those lucky few who just has it in their bones. Talent like that doesn't leave you.'

'It's still a craft.'

'It is. But, listen, I'd love to work with you again.'

I hoped she couldn't hear my heart pounding. 'You would?'

'Absolutely. You're a dream to direct.' She was doing her own take on *Northanger Abbey,* not as dark as her other stuff. 'I want to show how girls are really still the same,' she said. 'How we still get swept up and let our imaginations carry us off, for better or worse. It's Austen's youngest novel and I want to make something that feels young and funny and sweet.'

'So, no men being beheaded in this one?'

She laughed. 'Unfortunately all the men will survive. Still, I like the idea of doing something different. And it would be a change of pace for you as well, if you were to be my Catherine Morland. A wannabe gothic heroine played by a true gothic heroine. I think it could be really interesting.'

Her Motorola went off and she flipped it open.

'Sorry,' she said. 'I'll just step outside.'

I waited at our table, sipping my honey cocktail. She went to stand on the pavement, just about visible through the window. It surprised me for a minute, that when she said 'outside' she really meant outside, where anyone could see or hear. But people don't know Sarah's face like they know her name. She doesn't have to be vigilant.

When she returned, her manner was changed. She was flushed, and strangely sheepish, something I had never known Sarah to be.

'Rachael, I hate to do this,' she said. 'I have to run.'

'Oh.' I pushed my glass away from me. 'I hope everything's okay?'

'Everything's fine. Just a prior commitment I forgot about.' It was such an obvious lie that for a second I just stared at her, waiting for her to correct it. She didn't. She held out a hand and I stood up to shake it.

'So,' I said, 'we'll pick this up sometime soon?'

'Sure.' She waved a hand. 'Listen, this is all very preliminary stuff. No guarantee that this project is actually going ahead.'

'Of course.' She went to pull her hand away, but I hung on. She looked at me, startled. 'Tell me the truth,' I said. 'Was that Greg on the phone?'

She met my eyes. She didn't have to say anything. She released my hand.

'We'll talk soon,' she said. We both knew this was a lie too.

So now I know. Now I'm sat in my little sitting room, the one corner of the house all my own, hating him. I don't call Elisabeth when I hate him this much. I call Adam.

He always picks up. He always pretends to be confused. 'Hi, Rachael. Is everything okay?' Sometimes he picks up and says, 'I can't talk right now, sorry,' and that's how I know he's with Holly.

The first time I called him was on my honeymoon, after Greg mentioned that he saw me cutting back on acting in a couple of years. I said I didn't see that at all, and he said, 'Well, you'll want to be a homemaker, I imagine. That instinct kicks in after a bit, in all women.'

Seething, I went back to the hotel room and dialled Adam's number, the one he'd rung me from the year before to congratulate me on the end of *The Avenue*. I'd kept it in my address book, just in case I ever needed it.

He picked up and said, 'Hello?'

'It's me,' I said. 'I got married.'

'Me too,' he said.

There was a pause, and then both of us started to laugh.

He and Holly had tied the knot about two months after Greg and I, in a small 'family only' ceremony, because they hadn't wanted the press to find out. There had been rumours, of course, but I hadn't thought any of it was really true. They were going to make the announcement the following month, to coincide with the news that the next *Dragonborn* film would be the last. A happy ending for Greg and Holly and a happy ending for their characters. It was kind of genius. I told him that. He bristled a little.

'I mean, that's not why we did it.'

'Of course not.' A pause. 'But you thought it through, right?'

He laughed. 'You're so cynical. God, I can't believe how long it's been since I last saw you.'

'I can't believe it either,' I said, staring up into the bare white of the hotel ceiling.

He's used to my calls by now. I'm always the one ringing him, but neither of us mind the dynamic. I think he likes knowing that his marriage is far more peaceful than mine, and I like knowing that he'll always pick up the phone to me when I need him to.

'Do you ever think you should just leave him?' he asks me now, at the end of my rant.

'I'll hang up if you say things like that.'

'Why?'

I shake my head, although of course he can't see.

'Why?' he repeats.

'Because I love him.'

'Well,' he says. 'That's not always a good enough reason to stay.'

Sometimes I hear his voice like that, low and very serious through the phone, and I wish that I could go back in time and burn those Polaroids up before he ever found them.

'No,' I say. 'I suppose it isn't.'

15 July 1995

Last week, Elisabeth called. 'I'm *so bored*,' she said. 'I'm wasting away.'

'You're nineteen. You have no cause to be bored. You could go anywhere.'

'Anywhere like . . . LA?'

I laughed. 'You can always come visit if you want to. We don't need to play any games about it.'

She instantly brightened. 'Really? Greg wouldn't mind?'

'Greg likes you.' He met her once before, when she came to stay in her Easter break, and they got along surprisingly well. She was behaving pretty coquettishly, which she does well, and she can be very funny when she wants to be.

'Your sister's a hoot,' he told me. 'Is your mom the same?'

I told him that she wasn't, and, anyway, he was never going to meet her. The only relationship we had by that point was a financial one. Happy with Greg I might be, but resentful of the loss of Adam I will always remain. It's a very female gift, to be able to hold these two truths at one time and love and hate so wholly in synchronicity.

I waited in the car for Elisabeth at the airport and my driver went in to collect her. When they came out, he was pushing about four or five suitcases on a trolley. I jumped out of the car. 'What on earth is going on?'

She threw her arms around me. 'Don't be mad.'

'When you came for Easter you brought a carryall and nothing else.'

'I thought maybe I could stay a little longer this time.'

I watched the driver loading the suitcases into the back of the car, grunting. 'How did you even get this all on the plane?'

'It cost a bit,' she said. 'But people were generally very helpful.'

'How long is a little longer?'

'That's yet to be decided,' said Elisabeth. She grinned. 'Your face! Would it be so bad having me hang around for a while?'

'Does Mum know?'

'Of course she does. Don't stress so much.' She opened the car door for me with a solemn gallantry that did make me smile, even though I was still thrown. 'You'll love having me,' she said. 'You'll barely even notice I'm here. And I can weigh in on all your arguments with Greg.'

'That's something you will definitely not be doing.'

'I bet you guys won't even argue with me here,' she said, clipping herself into her seat. 'You'll be too delighted.'

Greg was delighted. He thought it was a riot when he saw all Elisabeth's massive suitcases being dragged from the boot of the car and he bent double in the doorway with laughter. She threw her arms around him in much the same way she had me, which irked me a little. Shouldn't she have a little more loyalty than that, after all the things she'd heard? I'd half expected her to hate him.

We've set her up in the room with the balcony over the pool, the other side of the house from us. She stood on the balcony and stared out over the hills, silenced for once. 'I still can never believe that this is your life,' she said eventually.

'She's a cute kid,' said Greg later that evening, putting his coat on for yet another late-night meeting. 'Is she interested in acting?'

'She was once,' I said. 'It was just a phase, though.'

'I don't know,' he said. 'Why else would she be here?'

I stared at him. 'For me.'

He chuckled, like that was a hilarious thing for me to say.

I called Mum, just to check that she knew. We communicate more often than we did these days, now that we have a shared interest in Elisabeth, but these communications are formal and perfunctory. We talk when there is admin to be done, and other than that we leave each other be. It probably breaks her heart a little. It used to break mine. Sometimes it still does, but mostly I am able to ignore it. Women like me don't need their mothers.

'I know,' she said. 'I told her it was a great idea. She said she would call you in advance and check it was all okay.'

'Right,' I said. Unsurprised.

9 August 1995

He's finally written me something. In typical Greg fashion, he's being unnecessarily elusive about it, probably because he knows it's good. I had to go digging around in his desk myself to find it. He hadn't left it in any of the locked drawers but sitting at the top of a pile of papers in the top right of his desk. He hasn't spoken about *Lulubelle* in a while and I wonder if maybe he's finally given up on it and decided to pursue this one instead. It's untitled right now – or maybe that's actually what he's calling it – but wonderful. This young ingénue joins a modern brothel in 1960s London and forms a twisted mother-daughter bond with her madam. I had imagined he would be pursuing me in his scripts forever, but he isn't even in it. He's finally giving me a green light and an open road. Now I understand why he's been trying to keep me away from other projects.

I snuck back into his office to return it, and Elisabeth caught me on my way out. 'You've got a mischievous look about you,' she said.

'I'm just happy.'

'Why?'

'Why not?'

She laughed. 'Alright, weirdo.' She was on the hall phone, the receiver pressed to her ear.

'Who are you talking to?' I asked.

'Jerry,' she said.

I pulled a face.

She mouthed, *Be nice.* She turned away to wrap up the conversation, one hand in her curly hair, giggling quietly. When she ended the call, she looked a little sad.

'Do you miss him?' I asked.

'Yes,' she said, 'and he misses me. But he gets it.'

I'm not really sure what it is that Jerry gets. I've asked her what she wants out of her time here. I've even broached the acting thing. She just laughs and says, 'I'm figuring it out,' and drifts around the place like a cheerful little sprite. Greg says to give her time. He says girls that age need to discover themselves.

I waited up for him this evening. But when he did slide into bed beside me and asked, 'Why are you still awake?' I didn't bring up the script. I'll let him play this game however he wants, so long as I get a great part at the end of it.

16 August 1995

He still hasn't said anything. He's still out a lot, which, if it isn't related to *Lulubelle* anymore, makes me nervous. Elisabeth has met a group of aspiring models about her own age and has started going for dinners and drinks with them. I reminded her that you need to be twenty-one to drink in this country but she reminded me that

349

no one actually cares to ID you when you're young and blonde and leggy. For a while I wondered where she was getting the money for all of this socialising, but it turns out that Greg has given her an Amex. When she revealed this, I wasn't quite sure whether to be pissed off at him or not. But he genuinely does seem to care about her. That and the script are the two things I hold on to when he slides into bed beside me at three in the morning with cigarette ash under his fingernails and a whisper like crunching rocks.

When I'm alone here, I call Adam. We talk about Holly, who is re-landscaping their garden whilst they wait to start work on the final *Dragonborn,* and about Greg, who has suddenly got very into cigars. We laugh about both of these things, but no one ever says, *All four of us should get together for dinner sometime!* because we know it isn't like that.

'Does Holly know we talk?' I asked him once.

He paused, and we both realised that I had crossed a line there, by trying to turn these conversations into something that existed within the world of secrets and boundaries. He doesn't have to tell Holly when he brushes his teeth. He doesn't have to tell Holly when he takes himself for a hike to clear his head. Ergo, he doesn't have to tell her when he, equally innocuously, picks up the phone to talk to me.

4 October 1995

Hello, Diary. Strange to think of you like that, when you look so different. I don't really like you in blue, but I did promise I would do this. And Gill was so earnest when she gave me this notebook.

Gill is my therapist, and she has very short spiky grey hair and an attitude like everything she says is a proverb, which almost makes you believe that she's right. She likes that I keep a diary.

Usually everything I say is met with, 'Do you think that's a constructive thing to say?' or 'And how can we healthily navigate these feelings, do you think?' When I mentioned the diary, she got all happy and said, 'Rachael, that's very constructive. Very healthy. I'm pleased.' I nearly cried. No one has said that they're pleased with me in a long, long time.

Still basking in the 'pleased', I did mumble that it had been a while since I last updated the diary.

'How long?' she asked, eyes narrowing.

I confessed that I hadn't written anything since mid-August, before everything happened.

'I see,' she said. 'And why do you think that is?'

'Well,' I said, and then it was like my lungs folded in on themselves, because I realised why I hadn't written in my diary. I didn't have it anymore. It was still sitting behind the gin in Greg's pantry, where I'd left it. He might have found it by now. It was unlikely – he never drank gin – but he would surely uncover it eventually. And then what?

'Is everything okay?' asked Gill.

'I lost it,' I said. 'That's all. I just realised.'

'You should get a new one,' she said, but she seemed to know that I wouldn't because at the start of our next session she handed me this blue clothbound book with a soft smile, and said, 'Here. Your new diary.'

I put my hand on the book, to take it, but she didn't let go.

'Write it all down,' she said. 'If that's the coping mechanism you're used to, then it isn't one you should abandon now.'

I wanted to tell her that I wasn't sure I would call it a coping mechanism, but she let go of the book, and you were mine. I just nodded.

Let me take you back to the 23rd of August.

INT. GREG'S BIG HOUSE – EVENING

WE OPEN on a sparsely decorated sitting room with one large window along one side. The centrepiece of the room is an obnoxiously large decanter on a gold tray, which itself is perched on top of a cherrywood coffee table. The owner of the house's wife has often told him how hideous this decanter is and that it should, if anything, be tucked away at the top of a bookshelf, but he insists on displaying in the centre of the room for reasons known only to himself. RACHAEL sits in one of two armchairs, holding her phone to her ear. She is talking to ADAM.

> RACHAEL
> *(charmingly)*
> It sounds as if Holly has a real vision for that rock garden.

> ADAM
> *(winningly)*
> Slightly too much of a vision, I'd say.

> RACHAEL laughs.

> ADAM
> How are things with you?

> RACHAEL
> Oh, you know. The same.

> ADAM
> Are you——

> RACHAEL
> He has a script. He hasn't given it to me yet, but he's got one. I saw it in his desk drawer.

> ADAM
> A good script?

RACHAEL

Great, from what I read.

ADAM

A good part for you?

RACHAEL

A great one.

ADAM

Well, you deserve good parts. I saw *East of Eden*
the other week. Shit, Rach, you were exceptional. You'll sweep awards season, just wait.

RACHAEL

You always get my hopes too high.

ADAM

How am I getting them too high? It's a sure
thing.

RACHAEL

If it was up to you, I'd win everything.

ADAM

If it was up to me——

RACHAEL

I know.

'If you know,' he said softly, 'then why do you stay?'

I flicked the lamp on beside me. There were corners of the
room I still couldn't see. Outside, LA shone. I turned my back to it.

'No one will ever understand it quite like the two of us,' I said.

'That's true of any love,' he said. 'It's not a reason to keep going.
Not if it hurts you.'

I saw, suddenly, that Greg was standing there. I hadn't heard
him come in. He was in the doorway, with his hands in his pockets,
very still.

'I have to go,' I said into the phone, and closed it.

353

We looked at each other for a second. He didn't ask me who I'd been speaking to. He said, 'I thought you'd be in bed.'

Behind him, a creak. A giggle.

I looked at his very tall, very rigid form, the way he was holding himself, as if trying to appear natural, and then I jumped up from the chair and darted around him. His hand shot out to stop me but I was too fast. I ran out into the hallway for a look at this girl who he'd brought back with him, thinking that I would be asleep. Had he really got so cocky? Had he really got so *sloppy?* I was embarrassed more than anything else.

But it was just Elisabeth. She was holding her heels, creeping across the floor, suppressing her laughter. She was in one of my dresses, white mid-length satin, with a halter neck. She met my eyes and bit her lip, but it was with a smile.

'Why are you doing that?' I asked.

She put a finger to her lips. She wasn't just tipsy – she was drunk out of her head. From behind her finger – pink glittery nail pressed into the soft brown of her lipliner – she giggled.

'Elisabeth,' said Greg, from behind me. 'It's alright. Go to bed.'

He didn't sound surprised to see her. There was something so strange in the way they were both behaving. 'Were you—' I couldn't get the words out. They both hung in front of me, like bad omens. 'Were you two together tonight?'

Silence from both of them. The hall was still dark, no lights switched on and the windows black and full of nothing, but for me the world went white, in that moment. I felt myself swivel and launch my entire body at Greg, nails out, spitting and hissing like a cat. He grabbed both my wrists as I fought with him.

'*She's nineteen – my fucking sister – you goddamn monster—*'

'Rachael,' said Elisabeth, behind me. She sounded scared.

'It wasn't like that,' said Greg. He was controlled in front of Elisabeth, but he held my wrists tight enough to break them. 'Calm down. She's just a kid, Rachael. I'd never do that.'

Even in the blinding whiteness of it all, I believed him. I let myself relax against him. Still, there was something. 'Did you take her out and get her drunk?'

He sighed. 'It wasn't just me. Frank and Graeme kept getting rounds—'

'This was an industry thing?' I looked back at Elisabeth, who was gently swaying. 'You said you weren't interested in acting anymore.'

'I said I was figuring things out,' she said.

'So, what? She's going to be your *Lulubelle?*

'*Lulubelle*'s over,' he said, surprised. 'I thought I'd told you. You were right – it wasn't good.'

'I know I was.'

'I was just feeling stagnant. Everything was so stale. But then Lis arrived—'

'Since when is she Lis?'

'Don't be jealous,' said Elisabeth coaxingly.

In the shadow of the corridor, standing close to the staircase, she looked unlike herself. It was like something else entirely had come over her.

'I wrote something new,' said Greg.

'I know – I read it.'

'It's good. And I'm trying to find a lead.'

I saw the shape Elisabeth cast against the staircase, the black shadow of her on the grey of everything else. Blonde curls dulled and spiralling over the shoulders of her shadow-self. She was slender, tall in that young way that reminds you of a running deer, or a filly. She couldn't act. I knew in my soul that she couldn't. But she made your head turn. And she had the kind of self-assurance that made you want to remain in her sphere.

'She's got a certain something, I think,' said Greg. 'Must run in the family. And she's got that young ingénue thing going, you know? She's got that naive, girlish quality. We thought we should give her a meeting.'

'She's not an actress,' I said.

'She says she'd like to start. Why not give the kid a shot?'

'That isn't a shot. That's begging. That's leveraging. That's dancing through the doors of rooms other people work their whole lives to get into and holding your hand out for a role.'

The drink delayed her understanding, but I saw her face twist in anger.

'And what's it called when you take dirty Polaroids to get a part?' she asked.

I lost my breath.

She had angled herself against the staircase so that her shoulders were resting against it, arms folded across her chest. The lower half of her body jutted out into the hall. I could see her hipbones through the white material of her dress. She cast a lazy shadow, a leaning, skeletal thing with chin upturned, as if already bored of this conversation. Her face was blank. She met my gaze and raised her eyebrows in challenge. Then she smirked, like the whole thing was funny.

'You told her about that?' asked Greg.

'No,' I said, 'I didn't. Elisabeth, how do you know that? Did Mum tell you?'

She shook her head. A cloud of blonde curls haloed around her. I knew how she knew.

'It was you,' I said. 'Mum didn't put those pictures on my pillow. She didn't break me and Adam up. It was you.'

'I was just looking for some cash,' she said.

She'd gone rooting through my room, looking for more of my money. She'd found the pictures. She'd put them on Adam's pillow. For what? So I'd come home?

Exactly that, I realised. Only it hadn't been a sentimental act. She hadn't felt my absence in any kind of sisterly way. She'd had exactly the same motivations I'd assigned to Mum. She'd been fourteen. Old enough to put two and two together. She'd put the pictures on my pillow so that I'd come home and do the next season of *The Avenue*. So that I'd take the money.

Because she wanted to go to private school.

'You awful little leech,' I said.

'I just missed you,' she said, voice high and girly. We both knew she was lying.

She hadn't been coming to London for me. She hadn't moved out to LA because she was bored and she missed me. She wanted what I had. She wanted my connections and my opportunities. And now she was in my house, trying to curry favour with my husband, being young and girlish and bright, wanting to slip a pink glittery nail underneath my skin and slice it off, all in one piece like peeling an orange, and wear it like a coat.

'You're going back to England,' I said.

'Like hell I am,' she said. 'You can't make me.'

'I can kick you out of this house.'

'For fuck's sake, Rachael,' snarled Greg, 'calm down. We're not turning her out.'

'She's my sister.'

'It's my house,' he said.

'Jesus, Greg. She's nineteen. That's a little young even for you.'

'I told you, it's not like that.'

I got very close to him. I put a finger in his face. 'I don't believe you. You piece of shit. You are fucking scum. I want a divorce.'

'You don't have a lawyer,' he said.

357

I still find it funny, actually, to think about. The things I was saying to him, the way I was jabbing my finger in his face, and that's where his mind went. *She doesn't have a lawyer.* Smug and reassured. *She can't get a divorce without a lawyer. So, all good.*

'I can hire a lawyer, you fucking *moron*.'

Elisabeth laughed. I turned on her.

'And you. Stay in LA if you want. Nothing you build will mean anything. Everything you have ever driven your nails into, every taste you have ever had on your fingers, every soft thing you have touched, *everything*, has been built on my back. Do you understand that? And if I shift beneath it, I can bring it down.'

She was quiet, one hand holding the banisters, displaying a smooth white underarm. I knew she didn't believe me.

I called Mum to explain how things would work going forward. I'd set her up with enough money for her retirement, but I'd worked it out carefully with my accountants. She would be provided for – because not to do that would feel like killing her, because I knew that she was dependent on my money to the point where she genuinely might starve without it – but not a penny was to go to Elisabeth. She cried. Even though I now knew it wasn't her that brought me back to London, away from Adam, I was stony against the sound of it. I'd already closed my heart to her. To open it again was too hard. And I suppose it still had been her fault, in a way. Elisabeth had got it all from somewhere. She hadn't been born greedy. It had been a learnt behaviour, something the two of them had practised over and over as they looked around the house I paid for and said to each other, *Wouldn't it be nice if we had another thing to put in this place?*

'What will your sister do?' Mum kept sobbing on the phone. 'What will she do?'

'I think she has a pretty good idea,' I said.

Elisabeth called me once after I moved out. I was back in my house in Hidden Hills – it had stood vacant since the wedding, and we'd often talked about letting it out. Thank god we never did. She told me she was sorry. I asked her what for.

'The thing with the pictures,' she said. 'I never should have done it.'

'That's all?'

'Isn't that all you're mad at me about?'

'Never mind,' I said.

'You're upset that you had to provide for the family for so long,' she said. 'But that wasn't my fault. I was a kid. Blame Mum, if anything.'

'I do. But you're not a kid anymore.'

'I'm nineteen. I'm still figuring things out. Most nineteen-year-olds are.'

'I wasn't.'

'No, you were trying to go into acting. And that's all I'm doing. I mean, Jesus, Rachael, did you never think that maybe we just want the same thing? That we just have the same talent? We are related, much as you like to pretend otherwise.'

'Then put in the work,' I said. 'Go back to London, find yourself an agent, and live off your own money.'

'It was never going to work the same for me,' she said. 'I walk into that room with your surname, and it's different. Don't you get that? Positive or negative, they've made a judgement already.'

'But there's still a way to do it with integrity,' I said.

'You don't think I have integrity?'

'I don't think you have a gram of it.'

'And I don't think you have a gram of compassion,' she said.

'Greg isn't helping you out of the goodness of his heart, you know. He'll want something from you eventually.'

'Maybe,' she said. 'Or maybe you just gave everything to him pretty readily. Maybe I'm not like you.' Then she hung up.

That's about it. Therapist Gill will have to be happy with that.

The last thing, which I won't tell her about, is this. I called Adam, and I told him that I was getting a divorce. Our lives had seemed to be mirrors of each other's for a while now, both of us in these strange situations that we talked about in whispers down the phone. There was a part of me that thought I would say, *I'm getting a divorce!* and he would say, *Wow, me too!* And we would laugh.

'Oh, Rach,' he said. 'I'm sorry. I'm proud of you, though. It sounds like it's for the best.' There was so much pity in his voice. I imagined Holly in the garden, up on a ladder, pruning the wisteria. She would lean backwards a little to look at him through the kitchen window, as he stood with the phone pressed to his ear, and they would wave at each other. 'I'm always here if you need to talk.'

'No, you're not,' I said. 'Sometimes you're with your wife.'

There was a pause.

'I really hope things get better for you,' he said, and I wanted to drive a knife through one of his eyes.

(Probably best not to share that with Gill, either.)

17 November 1995

Re-read that entry from last month. It appals me. I sound glib and nonchalant, like I'm taking it all on the chin. Like I'm one of those people who talk about studying at the school of hard knocks. That obnoxious little screenplay halfway through. I'm losing my mind. I look at those words and think, *Who wrote them? It wasn't me.* There aren't even any past entries to turn to anymore and remind myself that I used to be sane. Maybe that's for the best. I'm not sure I ever was.

How is it possible to be this alone? Every time I think I understand the feeling, it grows another head. The fact of my alone-ness surrounds me, especially in the dark. It leers at me from every corner of the room, with different faces on. I can't be more than one woman and feel more than the loneliness of one person. But I feel the daughter's loneliness, and the sister's, and the ex-girlfriend's, and the divorced wife's. I am alone so many times over. I am just myself in a hundred empty rooms.

I took a role. I thought maybe it would help. The script is awful, but they aren't sending me the good things anymore. Robb hates me and my manager is tired of arguing with me. So I'll do *Soccer Mom* in March to shut them up and to remind people that my face is still my face, and my talent is still my talent, and they shouldn't forget about me forever.

I miss the ghost of me bound up in that red leather book. Maybe, years from now when Greg finds it, he will read it and for the first time, he will actually feel bad for me.

23 March 1996

Soccer Mom is the worst thing I've made since *Kiss It Better*, even worse than doing *Unbeliever* with Greg. Still, the feeling of being back on a set again is a glorious one. In some respects I don't even mind that what we're making is awful. I called Robb and told him to send me out for anything, anything at all. He said they were struggling to find directors who were willing to work with me. He didn't say it, but the implication was clear: none of them wanted to jeopardise their relationships with Greg.

I should go out, he says, go to parties, go to events, go to cast mixers. Network, make new connections, try to undo the damage that Greg has done. I don't. I can't find the energy. I spend a lot of time thinking about what would have happened if Adam and

I hadn't broken up, if I'd quit *The Avenue* and thrown myself into films like I'd wanted to at the time. Even if I'd still made *Women Who Laugh at God,* I would have had Adam there to make it all easier. Or I would have fallen for Greg anyway, and it all would have been so much worse. You can never really know, can you? But knowing that I can never really know doesn't make it easier. And it doesn't make me hate them less, Greg and Elisabeth. She's still living in his house. I know because my lawyer told me. She has the big bedroom now, with the walk-in wardrobe.

'He says he thinks of her like a little sister,' said my lawyer.

I wonder if this is true. I wonder how Elisabeth thinks of him. I would wager that their relationship is a little beyond filial.

15 April 1996

I took a meeting today with Norwegian director Alfhild Fossli. She's easily my favourite person I've spoken to in the last six months. She wants to make a film about family trauma where I play a daughter who eats her mother alive piece by piece.

I said, 'Alfhild, I can't think of a single part I'd like to play more than that one.'

18 June 1996

Two months today since I last spoke to Adam on the phone. Our last call ended with him saying, 'Rachael, I don't understand why we do this anymore.' Implying that this was one thing when we were both married, but that it's another thing when I, soon to be no longer married, call him over and over.

I said, 'I don't understand either.'

So we don't do it anymore.

26 June 1996

I see pictures of myself from during the marriage and I am stick-thin. My bones jut out in strange and awful ways. My face is gaunt and without the colour and the shape that allow me to use it to full effect. I have been working with a nutritionist, at Therapist Gill's suggestion, and I am finally starting to feel healthy again. Today I stepped on the scale, and my weight is back to where it was before Greg and I ever met. I used to fear gaining weight. Now it feels like a return to myself.

Of course, the tabloids don't see it as a regaining, just a gain. Their latest pet name for me is 'Rachael Carb-michael'. I'm sure someone in the office got a bonus when they came up with that one.

19 July 1996

I went to the afterparty for the Beverly Hills premiere of *Phenomenon* tonight, partly because my team still think I'm not making enough effort to be seen, and partly because Amy George called to ask if I was going to be there. I haven't seen her in over a year. I thought she might be mad at me, but she just put her arms about me when I got inside, and said, 'I know this isn't the place. But I've been worried about you.'

'I'm sorry,' I said.

'Don't be sorry.' She was just as beautiful as ever. Tabloids call her the British Lucy Liu, even though the two of them don't really look anything alike. Amy is round-faced, full-cheeked, with large brown eyes and a small jaw that gives her a look of perpetual sweetness. It isn't deceptive – she has always been an incredibly sweet person. It's why she's one of the only people in this industry I truly consider a friend.

We were offered champagne. The taste of it was nostalgic. When you don't go out, you don't drink champagne. It had been a while since I'd drunk anything so celebratory.

'I miss drinking with you,' she said. 'I miss the three of us running around London causing havoc.'

I smiled into my glass. 'I miss it too.'

'Do you ever talk to Adam?'

I shook my head. I would have elaborated, but really, what was there to say?

She was talking about the detective show she'd just booked when her eyes saw something over my shoulder and she put a hand on my arm, as if to ensure that I stayed focused on her and no one else.

'Is it him?' I asked.

Guiltily, she nodded. 'And I'm the one that convinced you to be here.'

'Please. I don't care about seeing him.' I cared about people seeing me seeing him, though. I kept my eyes fixed on Amy. She still looked shifty. 'Is he with someone?' I asked.

'She's very young. Way too young. Incredibly blonde.'

I turned like a shot. She was there, hanging on to his arm, pretty and curly-haired in a lilac dress with a matching satin scarf which she wore over her shoulders. He was introducing her to people and she was shaking their hands. She greeted some of them like she knew them. A young TV starlet tapped her shoulder, and she turned and flung her arms around the girl's neck, both their voices raised and full of youth and energy. Greg watched, with an empty smile.

'I'm sorry, Rach,' said Amy.

'That's my sister.'

She nearly choked on her champagne. '*What?*'

'My younger sister. She's living with him.'

'He's been taking that girl around with him everywhere,' said Amy, dabbing self-consciously at her nose, where a little of the champagne had shot out. 'God, Rach, I didn't think— I mean, the two of you don't look anything alike.'

'He's been taking her everywhere?'

'Carts her all over. Introduces her to everyone. They've avoided getting photographed as of yet, but everyone in the business has seen them.'

'Is she going to be in his film?'

'The new one? No, I don't think so.'

He'd realised that Elisabeth couldn't act, then. So he was just doing this to hurt me. And Elisabeth – she knew all the worst things he'd said to me. He'd probably said worse about me behind my back to her, by now. She was probably delighted to be able to tell people she was my sister. She knew what a humiliation that would be for me. I pressed my glass into Amy's hand and moved, almost without meaning to, in their direction.

Greg saw me before I got close. He put a hand on the small of Elisabeth's back. She looked up and went a little white, and then the colour rushed back into her cheeks with defiant force, and she called, 'Rachael!' She moved forward to hug me. I let her, but I was rigid in her arms. 'My sister,' she said, turning back to the group they'd been talking to. As if they all didn't know exactly who I was.

'Tell me once and for all,' I said. 'Are you two fucking?'

The people around us each murmured something incomprehensible and moved away in different directions. A few of the more shameless hovered close to listen.

'For god's sake,' muttered Greg, but Elisabeth laughed.

'Jesus,' she said. 'No.'

'I told you,' said Greg, 'she's a kid.'

I wasn't sure if I believed them. I still don't know. Actually, I'm not sure I even care. They've still hitched themselves to each other, and it's still unforgiveable from them both. Greg is a monster, but I don't think he knows it. Elisabeth is worse, because she knows. She let me confide in her over the phone. She saw how Greg treated me in our own home. I don't share Greg's opinion that Elisabeth is a kid. I wasn't a kid at nineteen, and she doesn't get to be one either.

And I don't believe whatever it is inside her that needs everything to dance to her tune will lessen with age.

'Rachael,' said Elisabeth, 'listen. I understand that you don't like me. I think that's a shame. But we're both going to be in this town for a while. We might as well try to be civil with each other when we do have run-ins like this, hm?'

It was the little 'hm,' that did it for me. Like she had twenty years on me. Or like she was the new, endlessly arrogant young girlfriend talking down to the washed-up wife.

'Greg doesn't think you're talented,' I said. 'He just hates me enough to lie to you.' I looked over at him. He was trying to smile like nothing was wrong. 'You'll never know anything like me again,' I told him.

As I walked away, I heard him murmur to her, 'Lord, I hope not.' And I heard her giggle.

It will never feel satisfying. It will never feel clean. It will never be that moment ten minutes from the end of the movie where I get the final words in, leaving him no time to reply before the credits roll. She will never be stuck forever screaming in frustration, trying to squeeze champagne out of her dress. We will all go on living lives, and we will all diverge and come together and skid off-road now and then. Sometimes I know this, and I'm able to live with the endless lack of an ending. Sometimes I sit and think up bad luck for them both until my skin is tinged green. Sometimes I want them both to be cursed forever. I want it so bad I taste metal in my mouth, and my hands feel as if they could tear apart muscle.

27 October 1996

Well, she's done it. They both have. They've got her cast in a medical drama, the kind almost guaranteed to run for seven hundred seasons and keep her in the money for the entirety of her twenties.

It's almost like a magic trick. I want to applaud them both for pulling it off.

I'll watch it, probably. I'll have to know the worst.

I'm doing that film with Alfhild Fossli, the one where I eat my mother. Robb couldn't talk me out of it and in the end he dropped me. 'I'm sorry it's come to this,' he said. I said he was a fool, that he had money to make off me yet. 'It's not just about the money, Rachael,' he said, and I get that, because if it was then I wouldn't be making films like this one. There's an Italian newcomer who's doing something very interesting about a woman with a corpse fetish, and I think I'd like to throw my hat in the ring for that one next, if I can find representation that I'm happy with in time.

I want to make horrible films, the kind that people can't tear their eyes away from. I want everyone to see the things I do onscreen and feel disturbed, and a little disappointed in me. If I'm going to be alone, I'll be alone in esteem as well. I'll be the only one who likes the things I do.

30 March 1999

I've just found this book. I can't believe I forgot about it. It had fallen down the back of my bedframe. I took the whole thing apart today to find a lost earring, and there was this book instead, just tucked away, waiting. I haven't read anything apart from the last entry – I'm not sure I'm ready to go back in time, but I had to see where I'd left off. How strange it is to see me talk about those films and be so spot on. I'm making one in Germany right now that is truly disgusting. Sometimes halfway through the scenes I want to stop and be sick, but that's how I know that it's good stuff.

My co-star Betta asked me the other day if I would ever do a romantic comedy again. 'I loved you in *Kiss It Better,*' she said in her gentle accent. 'You made me fall in love.'

I had gore down the front of me, standing over a model of a mutilated body. I tilted my head, grinned. 'You aren't in love anymore?'

How funny, also, to see me talk about Elisabeth's show. How spot on I was there too. As far as I know – which isn't a lot, as I'm far too fringe these days to get much of the good industry gossip – Greg and her stopped appearing together pretty soon after the *Phenomenon* party. I can't imagine that she would have taken her claws out of him willingly, so I suppose he must have got bored.

She's a very interesting person, Elisabeth. She got what she wanted, and then she gave it up, after only three seasons, and went and had a baby with Jerry. They're married now, living back in London. She's got a skincare line. Imagine her, an entrepreneur. I wonder who she's got doing all the work for her.

She's reached out a few times over the years. I've never responded. Sometimes her messages are frustrated, sometimes coaxing. Sometimes she pretends to cry. None of it moves me.

Actually, this is interesting. She had a commercial on TV the other day. Elisabeth holding up products, gliding creams over her skin. Jerry walks onscreen, and she holds her arm out to him. 'What do you think?' she asks. He strokes it. 'As soft as a baby's,' he says.

And then this baby crawls into frame, and they both laugh. They look down at the baby. The baby looks up at them and smiles.

I thought, *Cute baby.* Because she was. Very chubby and dark-haired and dimpled. A bit old to still be crawling, perhaps, but cute. Then I realised whose baby it was. It was theirs. Elisabeth's and Jerry's. Their daughter. Still crawling, and on a primetime TV commercial.

Imagine who that kid is going to grow up to be. It doesn't bear thinking about.

Chapter Fifteen

HARLEY

Rachael was my most irrepressible ghost. The others would appear in the mirror with me sometimes or walk ahead of me through train stations. The Hooker leered at me out of a Soho alleyway, and the Nurse stepped back to let me on the Elizabeth line first. The Schoolgirl giggled at me on the bus. The Lover caught my eye and smiled, sympathetically. I would see them in laughing strangers and plucky teenagers on TV. They would drift in and out of my mind as I fell asleep. At the time it had felt like torture, but I realised now that there had been no violence in those hauntings. They had been with me constantly, sometimes maddeningly so, but they hadn't been trying to hurt me.

Rachael wanted to hurt me. I could feel it in the way she jumped right out of my face as I sat doing my make-up and leered at me, hands scrabbling at the glass on the other side of the mirror, trying to get through. I had her voice in my head as I went around London, pleading with Greg not to hurt her, thinking, *God, I miss my baby*. But it all took on a mocking note now. Had that really been who I had thought she was? She asked me the question, over and over. How could I have got her so wrong? How could I have fallen so pathetically under her spell?

I called her. I sent texts. After a while I stopped trying to get answers and just invited her for a tennis match, or a lunch. She didn't reply to any of them. I drove down to her house in Kent once, and rang the gate, but she didn't come. I wasn't sure how, but I could feel that she wasn't there. She'd run off somewhere. Maybe she was scared to show her face. Maybe she was just bored, and off looking for some new chaos.

Greg put out a damning statement following his appearance on *Sun's Up*. The studio responded with one of their own – the project was dead, they said, and they were incredibly sorry for any distress caused to Mr Foster. Clearly, they mused disapprovingly, someone involved with this project had had libellous intentions.

After three days, Rachael put out a statement of her own, from wherever she was in the world.

It is with horror that I learnt of the slanderous depiction of my and Greg's separation in Carmichael & Foster. *I would like to be very clear about the fact that, whilst I did give some interviews ahead of the writing of this screenplay, I was in no way involved with the making of this film and, had I had any sign-off, I would have certainly made corrections. It is obvious that significant liberties were taken with the truth. I hope one day to have the opportunity to tell this story honestly.*

Ahn went to ground. I tried to call her a few times. The only time I got through, she snapped, 'How could you not have known she was lying?'

'I didn't really know her at all,' I said.

The realisation was more than devastating. I knew nothing about the real Rachael Carmichael. Maybe I never would.

I had to private my social media accounts. People had twigged that I had been more than just a cast member by now, thanks to insinuations made by Ahn to cover her own back (a nice lack of loyalty there). My comments were flooded with insults and death threats. In the end, it was easier to go quietly. Like Warren did. He dropped me in an email.

I'd been ignoring my parents' calls. Eventually, Mum texted the family group chat to tell me that if I didn't reply to them they would cut me off. Dad laugh-reacted the message, which undermined her point a little, but I still wasn't looking to get evicted.

What do you want? I texted.

She told me to be there for dinner that evening.

Dad opened the door. 'There she is,' he said.

I wanted to cry. I gave him a weak smile.

'Your mother's very upset with you.'

'Are you upset with me?'

'I'm just upset,' he said. 'You should have brought it to us. We both could have told you she wasn't to be trusted.' He was in a Balenciaga t-shirt, sunglasses hanging off the neck. I reached out and took them off. Trust my father not to worry about stretching the neck of a Balenciaga. 'I've known her a long time, Harley,' he said. 'She's not a good person.'

I didn't know how to tell him that Rachael would have said the exact same thing about the two of them, and that, when it came down to it, her trust meant more to me than theirs did.

Mum was in the kitchen, staring at her *Grub's up!* picture. She didn't turn her head as I walked in the room. I went to stand beside her, the two of us leaning against the kitchen counter, watching the housewife in the picture stand perfectly still and beam, arms gripping the giant turkey like it was about to fly away from her.

'Not cooking tonight?' I asked her.

'Poppy's making a mushroom lasagne in the downstairs kitchen,' she said.

'Very nice.' I privately wondered whether it would be anywhere near as good as Rachael's. 'Your lips look bigger,' I said.

'It's not filler. Chloé bought me this new oil. There's snake venom in it, or something.'

She really was ridiculous, I thought. And entirely my mother, in every biological sense.

'What did she tell you about me?' she asked.

'Very little,' I said.

She nodded, as if she didn't believe me.

'She just said she didn't want you to know.'

'Well, of course she didn't. She knows I would have put a stop to it.'

She pursued swollen, snake-bitten lips. I felt a little disgusted. 'You screwed me over too, you know,' I said. 'With that Instagram story. You didn't have to do that. You could have said nothing, rather than making the whole thing worse.'

She placed her phone down hard on the countertop and turned to me, hand on her hip, a little frantic in the eyes. 'Do you know why she hates me?' she asked.

'You always said it was because she was jealous of us.'

'That's true. She is. But she also hates *me,* specifically. She thinks I'm a freeloader.' She laughed at that, staring at me, like she was expecting me to join in. Her hair was looking dry, I thought. 'Like she's given me a penny in the last thirty years. Like I haven't built everything I have entirely by myself.'

'You did grow up on her money, didn't you?'

'Yes,' she said, 'but that was our mother's choice, not mine. As soon as I was old enough, I wanted to make something happen for myself. And I did. I networked, I auditioned, I got into the rooms I needed to get into. *I* did that, not Rachael. As much as she wants to take credit for everything that I am.'

'So why doesn't she see it that way?'

'Because women like Rachael can't accept that someone else's hard work might look different from theirs. That's why.' She closed her eyes for a second. 'And she tried to tell the world that she took a payout on my behalf,' she said. 'That I am what I am because she handed me millions of Greg Foster's money. I couldn't let that stand. I have things to protect too, Harley. You're not the only one always turning your face to the world.' She studied me, waiting for backtalk. 'I'm furious with you,' she said.

'For not telling you?'

'For not trusting me. I mean, Jesus, Harley, I'm not that bad a mother.'

'I've never said you were.' I actually think she's an okay mother. She's not winning any awards – she's a proponent of brutal honesty and she never taught me how to do my laundry, and it's no secret that she'd ten times rather be partying on some millionaire's yacht than at her child's piano concert – but she did do alright. She was supportive, and generous, and she passed down a fantastic skincare routine.

But she also released a statement supporting Greg. I'd read her official one. In it, she testified to the fact that she lived with Greg and Rachael for a while, when she first came to Hollywood, and she never saw any poor behaviour from him. That Greg Foster had been a good friend to her for many years. And sure, she didn't write it. She probably hadn't given it more than a cursory glance. But she'd still posted it. She'd still put her name to it. She'd still aligned herself with Greg, over Rachael. Even after everything, I wasn't sure if that was something I was ready to do.

'I would have given you good advice,' said Mum. 'I don't know what you're trying to prove by always cutting your father and I out of your career. We're the ones who've been through it all before.'

'I just want to make it on my own.'

She was quiet for a second. She fiddled with her dry ends. 'Well,' she said, 'after all we've done for you so that you never have to do that, I think that's quite an ungrateful thing to want.'

373

We didn't talk about it much over dinner. Dad mentioned Greg's *Sun's Up* appearance, but only to comment on how overly Botoxed his face had been. As Poppy started collecting up the plates, he said, 'Harley, you know that script I mentioned to you a while back? Any further thoughts?'

I felt tired. I said, 'Yeah, Dad. Maybe.'

On my way out the door, Mum handed me something.

'For her,' she said. 'When you see her.'

It was a white envelope with the word '*Rachael*' written across it in Mum's neat black handwriting.

'I don't think I'll ever see her again,' I said.

'Oh,' said Mum, 'I think you will. She'll want a chance to gloat.'

A week later, lying on my living-room floor in my pyjamas, eating Mini Cheddars on my back for breakfast, I decided it was time to take drastic action. I called Elias.

'She lives,' he said.

'Sorry.' I made my voice tremble. 'It's been a difficult time.'

'Yeah, for me too. I wasted two years on this project of yours.'

'It wasn't *my* project.'

'Could have fooled me,' he said. 'You certainly wanted everyone to think so.'

'Come back to London,' I said. 'We can go out.'

'I don't think that's a good idea.'

'You must be bored of this celibacy thing by now. Let's have some fun.'

'It was never fun with you,' he said.

'Look,' I said, rolling over and sitting up. A Mini Cheddar fell off my chest. 'I got screwed over here too. Way worse than you. I don't have a Hollywood mansion to hunker down in, okay? I can't just skip off and do a quirky action film with Daniel Radcliffe. I am stuck in this shit now.'

'And you'll have to get yourself out of it,' said Elias.

'That's not fair. What about all those times I've been there for you?'

'Harley,' he said, 'I don't think you've ever really been there for anyone except yourself.'

I hung up. I resumed my position on the floor. When I lay back down, I heard the Mini Cheddar break under me. I slid my hand up underneath my shoulder blade to gather the pieces, and then I ate them.

A few centimetres away, my phone rang again, an insistent buzz that sent vibrations through the wooden floor. I flipped on to my stomach and scrabbled for it, my fingernails finding crumbs in the grooves between the wooden floorboards. It wasn't Elias. Julia's smiling face filled the screen. I picked up.

'Hello?'

'God, you sound awful,' she said. 'Listen, do you remember Gina Brambilla?'

'Who?' I mumbled, cheek pressed against the floor.

'We went to school with her? Dark hair, hated you, got her nose done in year eleven but swore she hadn't even though it suddenly looked like a ski jump?'

'That was all of them.'

'No, she was the one who lost a Prada pump on our year nine activities weekend and was hopping around screaming that someone had stolen it.'

'Had they?'

'Yes, Harley, us. We hung it halfway up a tree. Your memory is shocking.'

'Oh, her. I remember her.'

'Well,' said Julia, 'she's in Greece.'

'Okay,' I said.

'Mykonos. This really exclusive resort. She's dating this billionaire about twice her age. You'd know all about that.'

'Elias isn't a billionaire. And we're not dating.'

'She's been posting like crazy about it. Pretty tacky of her, I think.'

'Julia,' I said, 'why the fuck do I care that Gina Brambilla is in Mykonos?'

'Because look what she just posted on her private Instagram story.'

I opened the message she sent me. Gina Brambilla relaxing by a pool in a tiny white bikini, a lurid blue sea visible on the horizon. One leg was crossed over the other, and she had a hand over her eyes, head turned sideways and up, as if gazing towards her vapid future.

'She's for sure had her tits done,' I said.

'Look in the background, moron.'

And then I saw her. Sat under a white cabana, in a long blue dress, her hair up. She had sunglasses on, and she was only just in frame, but I knew it was her.

'Gina's posted it like she hasn't even realised who's in the background,' said Julia. 'Like it wasn't completely deliberate. Tacky.'

'Where is this place?'

'I told you, Mykonos. I can find you the name of it if you give me a second. I think my dad's been before.'

'I'm going to go,' I said. I pushed the tub of Mini Cheddars away from me. 'Fuck it. I'm going to go find her. I'm going to *make* her talk to me.'

There was an excited intake of breath from Julia on the other end of the phone. 'What will you say?'

'I don't know. I have no idea. I might hit her.'

'Damn,' said Julia. 'Make sure someone films it.'

'I just need to see her, face to face. I need to look her in the eyes.'

'Carlton's dad has the plane in Mexico,' said Julia.

'I'll fly business. I don't give a shit. I just need to get there.'

'Shower first,' she commanded. 'I can practically smell you through the phone.'

Julia sent me the name of the place. I packed in a frenzy, paying little to no attention what I threw into the suitcase – mismatched socks, an armful of skirts, a lipstick without a lid. There may have been a sweater in there. I bought the first flight out that I could get.

When she saw me crossing over the pool deck towards her, she did me the courtesy of looking surprised. It was sunset, and the handful of other guests were at the restaurant or drinking up on the terrace bar. Rachael was having a private drink at the poolside. They'd set her up with a big white pool bed on a wooden frame, white curtains surrounding it. She was sitting to the side of it at a small table, on a chair with white cushions. In her hands was a large notebook of red leather, which she had been writing in with great focus.

She closed it when I approached her, placing the pen on top. Her surprise only lasted for a moment. The wind on the terrace was very gentle, and lit from behind as she was, one or two stray hairs shone gold as they danced in it. However long she'd been there, she'd barely tanned. She was still pale enough that the colour ran dramatically to her cheeks, as it had once been known to do. She'd become so practised at keeping her countenance with me that it was strange to watch her lose control of her face like this.

'I told the staff that I wanted to be alone,' she said.

'I told them that I was your niece.'

'They believed you?'

'Well,' I said, 'I think everyone knows, by now. And the family resemblance is pretty undeniable.'

She smiled. 'I can't argue with that.'

She was drinking champagne. Her glass had a strawberry on the rim, and on the plate beside her were three chocolate truffles. I watched her reach over for one, holding it between slender fingers, her nails red. There was no air of guilt about her, no sheepishness. It built a pressure behind my eyes.

'Celebrating?' I asked.

She looked past me and raised a hand. A man appeared at the top of the deck, nodded briefly, and disappeared. 'They're bringing you a chair,' she said.

She put the chocolate in her mouth and chewed. We waited. The breeze that had been playing with the ends of her hair rustled through my skirt, salty and musical. Still chewing, she raised her eyebrows at me. I looked away. I wondered if she could see how angry I was. If she found it funny. If she even cared.

A chair was brought. The girl who brought it couldn't have been much older than eighteen or nineteen. Behind her, a boy of similar age held a silver tray with another champagne glass and an open bottle on ice. He set both down before us. Rachael nodded her thanks. The boy and girl preserved professional silence, but I saw the look they exchanged as they turned away from us. They would tell this story for years.

When they were too far away from us to hear, she asked, 'How did you find me?'

'I'm friends with the right people,' I said.

'I should have found myself a cottage in Salisbury. Somewhere far out of your orbit.'

'I couldn't picture you in Salisbury.'

'We used to go on weekend trips there, growing up.'

'Mum never told me that,' I said.

'She probably doesn't remember,' said Rachael. 'I don't think Elisabeth can even envision a time when her life wasn't charmed.'

But I knew that Mum did remember a time before Rachael's money. I could see that she did, every time she got excited over some new purchase or some fancy hotel room. People like me, people raised with money, can spot the people who weren't.

I watched Rachael sip her champagne. There was an air of victory about her. She must have wanted to be found. 'Why did you come?' she asked.

'You knew I would.'

'No, I didn't. I actually didn't think you'd be able to face me at all. I thought you'd be too humiliated.'

'I am humiliated.'

'Oh,' she said.

'Not that you'd care.'

'I think there are worse things in the world to suffer through than a little humiliation,' she said. 'That's all.'

She took another sip, and then pulled the glass away from her face, considered the remaining amount, and drained the last of it. The whole performance was so self-indulgent that I thought I actually might hit her.

'Why do you hate me so much?' I asked her.

'I don't hate you.'

'I gave you two years of my life. My career is basically over now before it even began. You don't do that to someone that you don't hate.'

'Oh, please,' she said. 'Over? Everyone knows who you are now.'

'I'm blacklisted. Sidonius Cagnoni was the best connection I had in this industry and he's not touching anything I'm involved with ever again.'

'So what? Cagnoni isn't the only producer in Hollywood.' She refilled her glass. 'This is the problem with people like you and your mother,' she said. 'You have a completely different definition of what it means to really work for something.'

'I have been working. I've—'

'Yes,' she said, 'I know, nothing has been handed to you, has it? The shows you were in weren't a success just because you were in them. They all got cancelled after the pilot. You don't walk into auditions and get parts just because people know your parents. That isn't how it works.' She paused, waiting for my response.

'I know that,' I said tersely.

'That isn't how it works for anyone. Only you take it personally.'

'I don't deserve to be punished for who my parents are. I've never asked for handouts.'

'You don't have to ask,' said Rachael. 'You know you'll get them.'

'And that's my fault?'

'I did wonder,' she said, 'for a while, if you were different. I was interested, when you showed up at my gate. Of course, you showed your hand pretty quickly, when you brought up the film. But with Greg's memoir . . .' She shrugged. 'I thought, if you were going to use me, I might as well use you back. To put it indelicately.'

'So why didn't you? Why did you send Greg that film?'

She smiled at me sourly. 'Because you are just like your mother.'

The sparkling expanse of sea was turning slowly pink. Rachael stood up, her glass still in her hand and walked over to the pool edge to look at it. The beach below was private, and entirely empty. Even in a place like this, Rachael Carmichael was distinct from the Gina Brambillas and the rest of the wealthy clientele. It had been decades since her star had climbed to its highest, and here she was, still powerful enough to command a corner of the world to be quiet for her.

'I gave you my whole life to use,' she said. 'It still wasn't enough. You wanted a shocking secret. I gave you one. It just happened to be fake.'

She was still facing away from me. I got up from my seat and went to stand next to her, holding the delicate stem of my champagne glass.

'I've never had a baby,' she said, 'by the way.'

I didn't really believe that I was her child anymore. I had told myself I no longer wished to be associated with her at all. Still, it was strangely disappointing to hear it confirmed.

'I thought you'd be satisfied when I told you that I couldn't have children,' she said. 'That was hard for me to share, Harley, truly. It's not something that I've ever spoken about. But I thought, alright, they'll need something. Everyone will want *something*. And I tried to make it interesting for you – calling you late at night, lighting the candles, preparing my monologue. Giving you all the drama you wanted. I thought that would satisfy you.'

'That's a bit fucked up,' I said.

'Is it? It was self-protection. And it was honest. I just added some theatre.'

'All those things you told us Greg did to you? They were all honest? Because Greg Foster had a lot of issues with our film.'

She nodded down at her glass. 'Greg Foster made me feel like the smallest person in the world. But you can't really get it across on film. I suppose I told you the very worst version of everything. What he did to me was hard to define. It never quite seemed like enough to put any kind of damning label on it. When you know someone's out there writing the worst version of you, you want to do the same to them. You just want to be believed.'

'You didn't know he was writing bad things about you,' I said. 'What if you'd read his book and you came across well?'

She was quiet for a minute. 'You've never met him,' she said eventually.

'What could he say?'

'It's not what he could say,' she said. 'It's what *I* said.' Her hand felt for the bracelet on her wrist, twisting. 'I left a diary,' she said, 'in his pantry, when I walked out.'

'What? Why?'

'It obviously wasn't deliberate.' She shrugged a pale shoulder. 'I left so many things behind at that house. I took off with what I could fit in a suitcase that night. I never quite had the courage to go back for it. But I knew he had it. There are— There are things in my past, Harley, that I would prefer to remain mine. I knew, when he suddenly decided to write a book, that he'd found my diary, and that he knew those things. I thought maybe, if we put this film out, at least I could tell a different version of the story.'

'If you wanted that, why ruin it? Why throw it all out?'

'I didn't,' she said. '*You* did. What on earth possessed you that made you think it was a good idea to email him?'

I'd nearly forgotten about the email. By that point, I assumed he'd never received it. The question sent an awful feeling over me, a dread like I'd never felt.

'He recognised your name, of course,' she said. 'He contacted me. It wasn't easy – I've made that very difficult for him, over the years – but through various people, he got to me. He wanted to know what I'd told you.' She took another sip of her drink. 'Of course, it's all different in his head. He considers most of my diary a hysterical reimagining. Still, having read it, it wasn't a version of himself he wanted to see on film. So he threatened me. Vowed to print extracts of my diary unless I got the whole thing shut down.'

'Why would that have mattered? If he doesn't come off well in it?'

'Like I said. There are things in there that I'd prefer to stay secret.'

I stared at her. She smiled, strangely, in her uniquely unsettling way.

'But you didn't get it shut down,' I said. 'You let it go to post-production. You let the fucking trailer come out.'

'Well,' she said, 'yes. That was my idea, actually.'

'Yours?'

'I didn't want the project to tank because I'd pulled it, with my name attached. This is still a story I want to tell, one day. I convinced him to be patient. I told him that if I gave you something concrete he could dispute – that pay-off I got Ahn to add in – then when the film was in post-production and we got the first rough cut, he could even be the one to blow the whistle. Lots of publicity for his book. He liked that idea, of course.'

'So . . .' I said.

She waited.

'So . . .'

'So,' she said, when I didn't continue, 'we traded. The film, for my diary back.'

I glanced behind me at the red leatherbound volume on the table, and for a second, everything in me told me to pick it up and run. To carry the real story of Rachael Carmichael far away, where she would never find me, and pore over it until I understood exactly who she was.

'I'm not stupid enough to think that he hasn't copied pages,' she said. 'But I have it now. I can tell my story in my own words.'

'And if you do that, and he reveals this . . . secret?'

She smiled again. 'I'm sure I'll figure something out. I always do.'

She was monstrous, I thought, but beautiful with it. There was something so comfortingly terrifying about her. You knew she'd slice you down the centre if it was what she thought she had to do, and if it was, then you wanted her to. Because you knew her like this. Because you loved her like this. Teen dream, scream queen, and everything in-between.

'You still could have warned me,' I said. 'Before you blew up my life.'

'I know.'

'Why didn't you?'

She turned her head towards me, dark hair blowing backwards. 'I don't know if you'll understand.'

'I still want to know.'

'When you came to me,' she said, 'to my house in the Hills, in the middle of the shoot, wanting more, wanting *salacious,* wanting some huge acting moment for yourself, *hoping* I'd been through some greater misfortune that might translate into a better role for you—'

'I wasn't,' I said, but it was as if she hadn't heard me. She shook her head. The light reflected from her earrings fell over her arms in thin gold waves.

'And then you contacted *him.* For information about *me.* Whatever you thought your intentions were, you'd be lying if you said they weren't entirely self-serving. And I know that.'

She seemed so sure of it that I didn't protest, as much as I wanted to.

'I do have secrets,' she said. 'Everyone does. They aren't salacious or exciting. They're just mine. I want some of them to stay that way. But you wanted everything. Just like your mother.' The dread mounted. I didn't want to know that was who she saw when she looked at me. 'Everything Elisabeth has is built off everything I earnt. She befriended me to get ahead, and when that didn't work, she befriended the man who made my life hell. And along you came, a mini her, ready to profit off everything I went through

384

again—' She pursed her lips. 'I was going to let you do it. But I don't want your family's fingerprints on my story anymore. I'd rather just tell it myself.'

I watched her in her cold, frozen anger. Her face, despite the flush in the cheeks, was like marble. She was alluring in a way that made you afraid of how close you wanted to get. Rachael Carmichael. You made yourself forget that you knew she would hurt you. You wanted to be near her all the same. In that moment, just for a second, I forgot my resentment. I felt fanatical.

'It's never enough for you people,' she said. 'It never will be. Because you brand yourself as *ambitious*. You say that you have a *relentless* drive for success. And if someone hands you everything, then you need more. Because you need to have something to strive for, because being content means coming to terms with the fact that you live off family money and family fame. That's a hard thing to come to terms with, for people like you.' She took a sip. 'In a way, I empathise.'

'Except you didn't just screw over people like me,' I said. 'You screwed over a bunch of people who worked on that film. Ahn Lu in particular.'

'Don't act like you care a cent for Ahn Lu,' said Rachael. Her voice softened. 'She's a talented girl,' she said. 'Hard-working too. I do feel bad that this might have marred her. But I'll take care of her. I'll make sure her career doesn't suffer because of me.'

What had Ahn done, more than me, to deserve this consideration? 'She wanted the baby story in there too,' I said. 'She told me that I should ask you about it.'

'Don't be bitter, Harley,' said Rachael. 'You'll still die with more money than she's ever seen in her life.'

'It's not about the money.'

She smirked. 'It's always about the money.'

Someone on the other side of the pool was folding away sun lounger cushions, very quietly, with a bent head. I watched them for a while, to see if I could catch them sneaking a look in our direction. They stayed religiously focused, looking anywhere but at our corner. Arms full of sun lounger cushions, they disappeared inside.

'How did your parents take it?' asked Rachael.

'They weren't happy,' I said.

'That's understandable. I suppose your mum thinks I'm the devil now.'

'She gave me something for you,' I said.

I reached into my bag and handed her the letter. I waited whilst she read it, watching the patterns of sun on slowly moving water. It was only a page, although I didn't get a good look at any of what Mum had written. After a while, I heard Rachael laugh softly. She folded the letter back into the envelope and tucked it into her pocket.

Shoulder to shoulder, we stared out over the sea.

'Beautiful, isn't it?' she asked. 'I come to places like this, and I wonder why any of it matters.'

I rolled my eyes.

'What?' she asked.

'If none of it mattered, you'd never get to be in any places like this.' I took a gulp of champagne. 'People make it and then they act like they've descended into some realm beyond material things, when we all know they've gone to the lengths they've gone to because they want all the material things they can get. At least I'm honest. At least I say what I want and why I want it.'

She scoffed, quietly, and I hated her for it.

'And it's not just about the money, before you say anything. It's about the craft, and the highs and lows of it, and the way it feels to be there, in front of a camera, doing good work. I know you understand that.'

'But you can do that at any level,' she said. 'You can do that in a student film. Why does it have to be A-list or nothing?' In response to my hesitation: 'Because that's what you were raised on. Why accept less?'

'You were ambitious.'

'Yes,' she said, 'ambitious. Not expectant.'

'You'll never make it anywhere without faith in yourself. Everyone who makes it says that they always knew they would.'

'Harley,' said Rachael, 'these days, half the people who make it have a head start.'

Behind us came the quiet sounds of service. When I looked back, the girl in the uniform was already walking quickly away, head bowed, and there were fresh chocolates and strawberries on Rachael's small plate.

She walked back over to the table. 'Do you want to sit?' she asked.

'I'm enjoying the view,' I said, so she brought the plate to me and we selected a chocolate each.

'I came here once in the nineties,' she said. 'It was after Greg and I had split up and I was doing lots of horror. I loved those films but they could be taxing. They got under your skin. I thought, I'll do a solo trip, why not?' She rolled the chocolate between her fingers. 'There's something about this place that makes you feel clean again.'

I wasn't brave enough to ask if that meant that she hadn't felt clean, after everything that had happened. Instead, I said, 'Don't you feel sad that the world won't see what we worked on? You did say you loved it.'

'If we're being frank—'

'We are.'

'I'm glad the film wasn't made,' she said. 'I was so focused on making sure the world saw him for what he was that I made him pantomime. He was over the top. Elias played this spitting, roaring, leering monster. That wasn't Greg, exactly. It was all more insidious than that.'

'Do you feel guilty?' I suppose that's what I'd really wanted to ask her all along.

'That's an interesting question,' she said. 'You are very interesting to me.'

I didn't ask why. I waited for her to continue.

'When you turned up at my house that first time, I thought maybe we had things in common,' she said. 'When you first brought Ahn over, I thought you were your mother's daughter all over. You might have looked like me, but all I saw was her. She saw me as a resource before she saw me as a person. I knew that sooner or later you would want something from me.' She looked at me almost admiringly. 'Now I know that you're more complicated,' she said. 'You're smart enough to know that being a leech is a bad thing to be – you're less shameless than she was, but you still don't quite get it. You know, logically, that people don't deserve incredible things just by nature of being born into certain families and certain positions, and yet you feel deep in your soul that you *do* deserve those things. That you're the exception.' She drained her champagne glass. 'This industry is full of little monsters like you, Harley,' she said. 'I'd feel bad for you, if I didn't expect that eventually you'll get exactly what you want.'

That callousness in her shocked me. It was a casual kind of cruelty, as if she didn't even really consider me to be a person who might want the same things as her, who might have the same dreams and callings.

'You think I was just born lucky,' I said.

'Of course. Don't you think so?'

'Well, yes. But it isn't like being born with a winning lottery ticket. It doesn't actually amount to anything if everyone's always going to be against you.'

'But they aren't against you. Everything in this industry is set up for people like you to succeed.'

'But that's the thing,' I said. 'It *isn't*. Because no one really wants us to succeed. Sure, once we're in, we're in. But when we're still trying, it's brutal. We're spoilt little industry babies. We're talentless nepo hires. It's easier for the ones who slip under the radar, who have uncles who are big-time producers, not household names, but I look *exactly like you*. My comments have always been full of people telling me I'm a Rachael Carmichael knock-off. Saying I'll never be as famous as you.'

'Is that the worst thing they can say to you, Harley?' she asked. 'That you'll never be as famous as me?'

I wasn't sure how to respond to that. She raised her empty champagne glass. 'Top up?'

'Please,' I said.

She brought the bottle over.

'Okay,' I said, as she filled up our glasses, 'this is what doesn't sit right with me. I was born lucky, and so no one's ever going to be rooting for me. But you got lucky too. It was just a different kind of luck. You had it hard, and then you worked hard, and then you got lucky. People are just petty about what order the luck comes in, that's all.'

'Hm,' she said.

'I don't know exactly what went down between you and my mum. That's between you guys – you've both made that very clear. And I can do that whole acknowledging my privilege thing if it makes us both feel better. But I am willing to work. I do want to improve and I do want to pay my dues, and I don't want to just get things handed to me. I was trying to make something happen for myself, with this film. And sure, I was also trying to leverage my connections and take advantage of you, to a certain degree. But isn't that what everyone in this industry does?'

'It is,' she acknowledged.

'I don't think I deserved for you to set me up like that just because I was pushy.'

'Maybe you didn't,' she said.

We were quiet for a moment. The sun had all but disappeared behind the water and the sky had broken into colour. There was a thin line of cloud severing the sky. It lit up like fire. Beneath us, the sea was empty.

'I do like you,' she said. 'I didn't want to. But, strangely, I do. I'm fond of you.'

It was almost comforting to know this.

'The film *was* good, in the end,' she said. 'I'm glad it didn't come out. But it was good, all the same.'

'You really did like it?'

'I really did,' she said. 'You're not a once-in-a-generation talent, Harley. I think you know that. But you were good in that film. I enjoyed watching you.'

The feelings I had about this little speech were too confusing to begin to unpack just then. I took another sip of my champagne, and the bubbles went to my nose. I blinked, hard.

'This was just something I had to do,' said Rachael.

I still didn't understand, not really. But all the anger that I'd thought I'd had towards her had left me suddenly. Rachael Carmichael's real history would remain a mystery to me. But the woman who stood beside me was gnarled and twisted by pain of some description. There was no ignoring it. It made her a difficult person to hate.

'Where are you staying?' she asked.

I pointed a little way along the coast. 'I've found a place in that direction. I fly back in the morning.'

'What's the name?'

'The Andronikos.'

She didn't respond. I walked over to the table and set my glass down. When I looked back towards her, she was standing with her back to the sea, regarding me with something like approval.

'You've been a good sport,' she said.

When I checked out of the Andronikos the next morning, I found that, somehow, she had picked up my tab.

I lived slowly for a while, back in London. I didn't try to chase down new representation or rehabilitate my image. I stayed off social media. I took walks round Royal Crescent Gardens. Julia and I had a board games night. She found it incredibly tedious, but I loved how simple and domestic it felt. Perhaps this was what it was like to live in your twenties without huge self-destructive ambitions.

Meanwhile, Rachael came out of hiding. She did a talk show, which she hadn't done for over a decade, and played up the betrayal of it all, the shock when she realised the liberties that had been taken with her life story. She took a guest spot on a popular sit-com and was *funny*, for the first time in years. Social media was flooded with people either talking about how shocked they were to see her do comedy, or how old they felt because 'all these kids so surprised that Rachael Carmichael is funny have clearly never seen *The Avenue*'.

About two months after I'd tracked her down to Mykonos, she called me. 'How are you doing?' she asked.

I was astonished that she cared, and a little on guard. 'Not bad.'

'I have some news,' she said. 'I'm producing a film.'

'Congratulations.'

'Thanks. It's a horror-comedy about complicated families.' She laughed. 'We all thought it would be kind of fun if you played my niece.'

I was so astonished it took me a minute to collect myself. 'We?' I managed.

'I wasn't all for it, at first, but the studio think it would kill. Sidonius wasn't particularly keen either but he's been persuaded.'

'You're doing it with Cagnoni?'

'We are.'

'Sidonius hates me. He can't want me in one of his films.'

'He understands the appeal of it.'

'You hate me.'

'I already told you. I don't hate you.'

I was wary, sensing a trap.

'There's no catch here,' said Rachael, like she'd read my mind. 'This would be right for the film. My fingerprints are all over this one, so if I let you fall on your face again then I'd be falling right alongside you.'

I imagined what it would be like to work with her, for real this time. The two of us on set together. Acting opposite each other. My heart ached.

'Thank you,' I said. 'Really. But no.'

A pause. 'No?' she asked.

'I want everyone to respect me.' I swallowed. 'I— Look, I want you to respect me. One day, maybe, if I've earned it. If I'm going to do this, I want to do it right. And this . . . I don't know. It sounds like a great project. But it wouldn't be right.'

'Hm,' said Rachael.

'I'm sorry.'

'Don't apologise.' Her voice was softer. 'Those are good reasons for saying no. Good luck with it all, Harley.'

'You too.'

The line went dead. I sat with my phone in my hands and fought the sudden, very powerful urge to call back and tell her that I'd changed my mind. It rested on me for a second, and then

392

it lifted. And I was someone else. I was someone entirely of my own making.

Carlton thought I was crazy. We had a reconciliatory drink in his dad's basement, because he could tell I hadn't been happy with him lately.

'I'm sorry I haven't been supportive,' he'd said on the phone, when he'd invited me over.

But he'd been right, infuriatingly. Who did it help to dress up nepotism as anything other than what it was? Either I leant into it, like Carlton did, and fuck what everybody else thought, or I carved my own path.

'The first one,' said Carlton. 'Obviously.'

I liked the second.

I opened my emails for the first time in weeks. Dozens of offers of representation from potential managers, and even a few agents in there. *I'd love to get coffee and talk about where we could take your career.* The whole *Carmichael & Foster* debacle might have thrown me on to a slightly different path, but it hadn't buried me. More people now knew my name than ever. I'd underestimated the power of that. There were thousands and thousands of nameless unknowns in London who would have killed for a scandal like mine.

I took meetings. Some of them struck me as sleazy and opportunistic, but a few seemed genuinely interested in helping me rise. The agent I went with was young, new, and very ambitious. She came from a working-class family in Newcastle and prided herself on being able to spot a good opportunity, she said.

'I think you're a fascinating challenge,' she told me, and I liked the idea of being somebody's fascinating challenge.

In one of our earliest conversations, Rachael had reflected back on the early years of her career, and she'd described her younger self as 'scrappy'. That word pulsed in the back of my mind as I took these steps. I wanted to earn whatever I got. I wanted to feel like

I'd fought for it, tooth and nail, so that I never had to be embarrassed when I finally got to lay my hands on it. I told my new agent to send me out for anything and everything. I'd do community theatre, if it came to it. I was more than willing to pay my dues.

The money mattered. Despite what I might have said to Rachael, it did. I didn't want to be forty and still living off my parents. But the respect mattered more. I wanted people – Rachael Carmichael included – to look at me, and think, *She did it all on her own. She's one of us.* I didn't want to be anyone's easy target ever again.

'I've hardly seen you,' complained Julia on the phone.

'I've been busy,' I said. 'It's been a whirlwind. I love it, though. I've never felt more productive.' I had a self-tape to do that afternoon, and I was fiddling with the lights I'd bought for myself. The camera was already set up on a tripod – I'd watched four different YouTube videos on how to use it, and I finally felt ready. Gone were the days in which I just hired a videographer for the hour.

'And I'm happy for you,' she said, 'if you're feeling fulfilled, but we miss you, Carlton and me. I know you've had a lot going on lately—'

'Putting it mildly,' I said, biting off a piece of electrical tape.

'Let's go out tonight. My dad has a table at the River Café he isn't using. What do you say? I could murder their Dover sole.'

'Alright,' I said. 'You're paying, though.'

'Starving for your art already, are you?'

'Shut up. Send me a picture of your outfit before you leave and don't pretend like you forgot just because you love the element of surprise.'

'I do love the element of surprise,' she said. And she giggled.

I arrived at dinner late, like I always am, expertly. Carlton and Julia already had a table at the back window. She was in yellow, which is a colour that Julia always looks wonderful in, and

Carlton was wearing a waistcoat, which is a tragic thing to write but not completely unexpected. He looked up from his menu as I approached and gave a gasp like he was seeing a ghost. 'Can it really be you?' he said, placing a hand on my cheek.

I shook him off. 'You guys are so dramatic. Why has no one ordered me a wine yet?'

'We thought you probably drank cognac now. Isn't that what *artistes* drink?'

'Jesus, I'm sorry for taking my job seriously.'

'Oh, we're just teasing you,' said Julia, squeezing my arm. 'We're proud!' She was positively glowing with it. I touched her hand with mine. 'Our self-made girl. Rachael Carmichael isn't going to know what hit her when you show up at the *Vanity Fair* party with her next year.'

'Oh, please. It'll take a lot longer than that. Besides, if she isn't fazed seeing me pop up at her exclusive Grecian resort then she's probably not going to be caught off guard on a red carpet.'

I'd told them all about Mykonos the day after I'd arrived back, of course, but they still weren't tired of talking about it. 'God, she's iconic,' said Carlton. 'She absolutely knew you'd track her down, and there she was, waiting for you with champagne.'

'I don't think it was planned,' I said.

'How can you know with that woman? You literally never can. She's completely brilliant.'

Julia slapped his shoulder. 'She very much tried to ruin Harley's life.'

'Please. The only people who could ruin Harley's life are HM Revenue and Customs if they ever decided to investigate some of the things her dad claims are tax write-offs.' He raised a finger. 'Or has this new leaf got you thinking you'd like some independent income? Your own capital, in case Mr Roth goes down?'

'Are you asking her if she's going to get a waitressing gig?' laughed Julia.

'I could,' I said. 'Rachael did it. I'd like to feel self-sufficient.' They were exchanging smug looks with each other across the table. I tossed my hair over my shoulder. 'I wouldn't expect either of you to understand anything about that,' I said, pointing at Carlton. 'You'll be a cheerful sponge forever, and I think the last job Julia had was year two line leader.'

Carlton grinned and raised his glass to that, but Julia smiled to herself. 'Actually,' she said.

'Actually what?' I asked, but she had seen our waiter approaching and was waiting for him, a polite smile on her face. Carlton took an excruciating amount of time choosing what he wanted to eat and what wine he wanted to pair it with. The whole while, Julia sat there, smiling. I watched her with an inexplicable sense of unease.

She waited until the waiter had turned his back on us before she resumed. 'Actually,' she said. 'It's the strangest thing. I have an audition tomorrow.'

We both stared at her.

'An audition for what?' I asked.

'This thing my grandfather's working on.'

'A film?'

'That is what he does,' she laughed.

'But Jules,' said Carlton, 'you're not an actress.'

She straightened her fork and folded her hands primly into her lap. Her nails were long and pearly white. 'Not yet,' she said.

I was trying very hard not to realise that I knew of at least one project that Sidonius Cagnoni was working on. But she was probably talking about some bit part in some other thing – one line in an action film, a gift from Sidonius to his favourite granddaughter.

But an audition? Julia would never have to audition for any-thing like that.

'How's this come about?' I asked. I did my best to speak casually.

'I told Granddad that I was interested in acting,' she said, also very casual.

'First we've heard of it,' said Carlton.

'Harley just makes it all sound so fun. And it's always been something I've wanted to try, but it's scary, isn't it, taking the plunge?' She looked to me for encouragement. I said nothing. 'Anyway, I went for it. Called Grandad, and he said he had some-thing that I could audition for, but not to expect any special treat-ment. Which, of course, I wouldn't want anyway.'

She looked at me again, a broad smile on her face.

'This is the funny part,' she said. 'If I got it, guess who'd be playing my aunt?'

I cleared my throat. She stared at me, a little defensive. I saw that she'd had a lash lift.

'Julia,' I said. 'You know they offered me that part.'

'I know. But you didn't want it, that's what you said.'

'Why didn't you tell me you were auditioning?'

'Oh,' she said, 'you've been so busy. And it's come about quite suddenly. And I wanted to tell you in person. I mean, I figured you'd be excited for me. You know, since this wasn't even something you wanted in the first place.'

'But I did want it,' I said. 'I mean, I didn't turn it down because I didn't want it. But you have to have *principles*.'

'I do have principles,' said Julia petulantly.

'Your grandfather's just handing this to you. Wouldn't you rather do something for yourself?'

She laid a hand on mine. One of her pearly white nails gently sliced my index finger. 'I think it's great, what you're doing, Harley,' she said. 'Really, I do. But it just isn't me. I mean, it's not what I want to do. This isn't a super-serious thing for me. You know? It's just for fun, right now. It's just to see what happens.' She took a sip of her wine. Carlton smirked into his. 'Anyway,' she said cheerfully, 'I probably won't get it.'

'You alright, Harley?' asked Carlton. 'You look funny.'

'Migraine,' I said. 'It's been coming on all day. I'm going to get some air.'

Fuck Julia, I thought, as I stalked out of the restaurant. Fuck her entire charmed existence. Able to just call up her grandfather and little-girl-voice her way into an audition that people would kill their own mothers to get. A waiter with a tray of drinks side-stepped me, tray hastily raised over my head. I glared at him.

Why hadn't I just taken that part? I'd thought I was doing the right thing, stepping aside, opening it up for someone deserving. I'd thought it might have been someone's big break. But I hadn't been opening any doors for people like that. Opening doors for people like that was impossible, because girls like Julia would always muscle in first. Spoilt princesses who didn't really give a shit about acting, didn't give two figs about the craft of it. They had never worked to get under the skin of a character or offered up their bodies and souls to a perfect performance. They would get on set and expect it to come easily to them, just like everything else always did. Those other girls, the ones who grew up with parents who worked in offices and took them on holiday to Blackpool, would never even get a look in.

This restaurant was full of Julias, laughing tinkly laughs, wearing tinkly bracelets, lifting tinkly champagne flutes to twinkly teeth. This whole neighbourhood was. They walked up and down the street in front of me, in long leather trench coats or casually bank-breaking puffer jackets. In distant high-rises, they stood in living rooms decorated by their father's assistants, staring down out of floor-to-ceiling windows, surveying a city they all but owned. Right then, in that moment, I felt Rachael's rage enter me with all the force of a possession. I hated them more than she ever had.

But, unlike she had been, I wasn't powerless against them.

There would always be a Julia lurking around every corner. There would always be five, or ten, or twenty of them up for any role that captured my heart. Principles weren't any good in a fight like this. If I wanted to get ahead, I would have to use everything in my arsenal. I'd be stupid to do anything else.

I took out my phone and called my dad. He picked up from the golf course. 'Harley,' he said, 'I'm in the sand.'

'Sorry to hear that, Dad.'

'Everything alright, chicken? Or is this just a social call?'

'It's a business one.'

'Ah,' he said. 'My favourite kind. What do you have for me?'

'Actually,' I said. 'I was hoping you had something for me. You haven't finished casting for that script yet, have you? The one you thought I was right for?'

'Harley,' he said, 'I don't care if we're two days out from production starting – if you want that part, then we haven't finished casting.'

'Good. Let's talk.'

Through the restaurant window, there she was. My Rachael. Not the real one, of course, but the ghost I had created. The version of her that would never exist. Her red lip was drawn on imperfectly. Her eyes were heavy with suppressed secrets. She was picking at her fish, nose wrinkled. When she looked up at me, her expression was one of bratty disappointment.

Epilogue

RACHAEL

Dear Ahn,

Before anything else, I would like to apologise. I did think long and hard before turning you into collateral damage – and when I write those words, I don't know if reading them will make you feel better or worse. But I thought you deserved to know that you were a consideration, if ultimately not a large enough one to stop me. If that reads as an insult, I apologise. It isn't intended as one.

I have also thought long and hard about how to make things right with you. I believe you are a truly gifted writer, and I don't say that lightly. You deserve to be recognised for your work, and you deserve to be compensated. If the first doesn't happen, I at least hope to be able to provide the second.

This is a diary that I kept off and on between the years of 1988 and 2000. Enclosed is a second volume, in which I wrote a handful of entries after misplacing this original book, which has since been returned to me. It is a record that I wrote without agenda, with the sole intent of getting my thoughts down on paper, and as such is as clear a picture of the truth of my life as a person is ever likely to get. I'm sure you know that my ex-husband is soon to release what I'm sure will be a completely unbiased piece of literary excellence. I've thought long and hard about how I want to tell this story, and I think this is the best way. I'm not a writer, and I don't know how best to organise these thoughts, but I'm hoping you will. If you're interested, I'm willing to pay the most generous ghostwriter fee in the history of publishing (I say that with no frame of reference for a generous ghostwriter fee, so take it with a pinch of salt. But my intentions are true.) It may be best to treat these writings as a leak, rather than a bequeathment – I'm aware that the statement I put out in Greg's defence may have put me in a difficult position, and god forbid anyone should have cause to call me conniving. Regardless, this is something we can work out with our respective legal teams at a later date. I want this story to stand apart from the circus we've both been caught up in. I suppose it remains to be seen how possible that is.

I know that money won't make up for everything that happened. But I'm hoping it will be a start.

There's only one thing in here I'd rather keep to myself, and that's my pregnancy. I'd rather not include it, or the visit that Anna made to me. I think we both deserve that secret.

You should know that precisely one other person has read this book in its entirety. I wanted to be sure that Adam Feldman wouldn't mind it being made public, and he doesn't. He also said that he very much enjoyed reading it, even if some parts were a little painful/scary. When he returned it to me at my property in Kent, he said, 'Rach, if I wasn't scared of you before, I certainly am now. And I was definitely scared of you before.' And then he hugged me, very tightly, for quite some time.

For narrative purposes, you might be interested to know that Adam and I became friends again around the time of his divorce, about ten years ago now. We first ran into each other at the drinks reception for the first *Traversers* film. I spotted him across the room, but he didn't see me until I was close to him, and then he said, 'Rach!' with a big grin, and it was only then that I realised I'd walked straight over to him.

He had a blue suit on – not navy, but a light powdery blue, with a purple pocket square and the first thing I said was, 'What are you wearing?' Again, completely without thinking. Luckily, he laughed.

'I know,' he said. 'New stylist.'

'Fire them.'

'You look great too,' he said. 'Asshole.'

Neither of us talked to anyone else that night. I heard all about his divorce from Holly – very amicable, as all parts of their relationship had been – and how grateful he was that they'd never had kids. He'd wanted them, he said, but they'd just never got around to it.

'Did you want children?' he asked.

'No,' I said. 'Well, sometimes. For a while. But it was all for the best, in the end.'

He asked after Greg. I told him the truth, which was that the two of us hadn't spoken in years, but that I still despised him.

'Not so amicable, then,' he said.

'Could you see me in an amicable divorce? I couldn't.'

When we'd exhausted all the serious talk, we started trying to land olives in the glasses of the people around us. We were caught after Adam made a particularly impressive shot from clean across the room into Tina Fey's martini. After that, giggling like kids, we got in a car together and went back to my house in the Hills. We talked until it was something like 7 a.m. and I had to leave for the airport. He sat on my floor as I packed my suitcase and said, 'Do you really have to go?'

'I do,' I said. 'I have to get home.'

'This is two decades we're catching up on here, Rach. Twenty years that we've been out of each other's lives.' We looked at each other over the top of the suitcase, the look of two people who know that they're having the exact same thought. He said, 'It doesn't feel it.'

I said, 'No.'

When he started doing *Cold Cases* in London the next year, he bought a place about twenty minutes down the road from mine. He liked the neighbourhood, he said.

'Sure,' I said. 'Stalker.'

He spread his hands with a helpless grin.

One evening, about a month after he moved in, he turned up at my gate. Through the intercom I heard, 'Rach, it's Adam. I've done something really stupid.' Followed by this smug little bark.

'Was that you?' I asked.

'No, it obviously wasn't.'

He stood on the doorstep with this tiny little mop of a thing by his foot. I stared down at it, and then up at him.

'I have a dog now,' he said.

'I can see that.'

'Do you want the dog?' he asked.

I said, 'No, I don't want the dog.'

He'd been driving and had come across it. No collar, no microchip. He'd taken it to the vet and the thing was healthy, although it didn't look it. He wasn't sure what to do. 'Because I can't take it to a rescue centre,' he said. 'Look at it. Nobody will want it. But what do I do with a dog?'

Without really knowing why, I said, 'I'll help.'

So, for almost a decade now, Adam and I have owned a dog together. We drive him between our two houses, and we chat. We take the dog for walks. We have dinner together. We play tennis. He's very good, but I've improved a lot since playing against him. When he's on a busy shooting schedule with *Cold Cases,* or I'm in LA for *Traversers,* the other one takes the dog. But often we're there with Raph together. Adam has a room now, at my place. I have one at his. Moving in together has never been discussed, because it isn't like that, really. I'm too used to thinking of myself as an independent organism, and he and I are very different people, these days. If we tried to do anything traditional – move in, celebrate anniversaries, put words to whatever it is that we are – then I don't think it would hold up. It's good like this. There were times in my life when I couldn't imagine having anything quite so good. I don't need it to be more than what it is.

Sometimes I look at him, golden under English country sunsets, Malibu kid in wellies and a big coat, and I see him just as he was. That nervous boy, who wasn't sure how to talk to me. Who wanted to hold my hand through the movie.

Ahn, I hope that when you receive this package, you take it in the spirit in which it is meant. And if you want to burn the book, ritualistically or otherwise, that's fine too. But I would only ask, if I'm allowed to ask any favours, that you read it first. I'm probably biased, of course. But I think it's a good story.

And it's a funny thing, because it hurt an awful lot when I was living it all. Those performances I gave took something out of me. Those sets weren't easy to be on when I was young and in pain. But when I flip through this book, there are so many moments in there that are now so much bigger than myself. There are so many things I did that will last forever. There's a strange privilege in reading all the things I scribbled down during those young, painful years, those years that held me open even when I wanted to close up and cower, and thinking, *At least I did something. At least I had something to say.*

ACKNOWLEDGEMENTS

First and foremost, Ella, I hope you can forgive me for not dedi-cating every single book to you for the rest of time and that you'll be satisfied with the first huge thank you instead, for keeping me company on writing trips whenever you visit, cheering me on and generally being you. Also thank you to Joe, who is turning into someone I am endlessly proud to know, and to my amazing parents. I am so lucky to have you all in my corner.

Thank you to my wonderful agent, Silvia Molteni, who is up to lend her expertise to whatever lands in her inbox with no warning, for everything. Thank you to Victoria Oundjian and Celine Kelly for being so excited about this idea from the start and working so hard to shape it into its final form. A huge thank you also to Kasim Mohammed and Victoria Haslam for getting it over the finish line. Thank you to Melissa, Sadie and everyone else at Lake Union who had a hand in editing, polishing and publishing Born For This.

My friends and family who tolerate me disappearing off the face of the earth for weeks at a time and are always there to lift me up regardless – thank you, and I love you all so very much. And finally, thank you to Paul – for being this book's first reader, for cooking for me every night, for helping me through the hard bits, and for everything else. I love you.

ABOUT THE AUTHOR

Photo © 2023 Caitlin Devlin

Caitlin Devlin studied English and Creative Writing at Warwick University before graduating to work in music and theatre journalism. As a teenager, she started writing novels as Christmas presents for her younger sister and brother. Her work has been recognised by competitions such as the IGGY & Litro Young Writers' Prize, the Flash 500 short story competition and the Exeter Writers short story competition. She is also a performed playwright. Her debut adult novel, The Real Deal, was published by Lake Union in 2024.

Follow Caitlin on TikTok at @catmdevlin.

Follow the Author on Amazon

If you enjoyed this book, follow Caitlin Devlin on Amazon to be notified when the author releases a new book!

To do this, please follow these instructions:

Desktop:

1) Search for the author's name on Amazon or in the Amazon App.
2) Click on the author's name to arrive on their Amazon page.
3) Click the 'Follow' button.

Mobile and Tablet:

1) Search for the author's name on Amazon or in the Amazon App.
2) Click on one of the author's books.
3) Click on the author's name to arrive on their Amazon page.
4) Click the 'Follow' button.

Kindle eReader and Kindle App:

If you enjoyed this book on a Kindle eReader or in the Kindle App, you will find the author 'Follow' button after the last page.